DARK MORNING

William H. Lovejoy

Pinnacle Books
Kensington Publishing Corp.

http://www.pinnaclebooks.com

PINNACLE BOOKS are published by

Kensington Publishing Corp.
850 Third Avenue
New York, NY 10022

First Printing: March, 1998
10 9 8 7 6 5 4 3 2 1

Printed in the United States of America

A tilt of the glass to friends:
Tom and Connie Henry
Bruce and Cherie Snyder
May your days be long and prosperous,
And your dreams fulfilled.

THE PEOPLE

Palestine Medical Assistance Team, World Health Organization (WHO)
Jack Blanchard - Team Administrator, America
Melanie Masters - Chief Physician, America
Lars Svenson - Physician, Sweden
Dean Wilcox - Physician, Canada
Lon Chao - Physician, Thailand
Ben Gordon - Anesthesiologist
Dana Harper - Anesthesiologist
Cale Perkins - Nurse, America
Deidre Joliet - Nurse, France
Emma Wachter - Nurse, Germany
Maria Godinez - Nurse, Costa Rica
Polly Brooks - Nurse, Britain
Robert Timnath - EMT, America
Tina Ambrosia - EMT, Spain
Sam Delray - Assistant Team Administrator, Australia
Dickie Armbruster - Administrator, Britain
Jillian Weiss - Team Translator/Pharmacist, Israel Ashkenazim
Roberto Irsay - Team Translator/Computer programmer, Argentina
Steve Mackey - Sanitation Engineer, America
Del Cameron - Cook

Government of Israel
Jacob Talman - Operative, Shin Bet, Major, Comet
Deborah Hausmann - Venus, agent in Jericho (Leila Salameh)

Levi Avidar - General, commanding Shin Bet
Isaac Stein - Colonel, Shin Bet
Moshe Perlmutter - Operative, Shin Bet, Major
Beit Horon - Ultraconservative and influential Jewish leader

Palestinian Authority
Amin Rahman - Deputy Chief, Palestinian Police Force
Adnan Boshogi - Jericho Security Force

Sword of God
Ibrahim Kadar - Leader
Abu el-Ziam - Second Leader
Khalid Badr - Freedom Fighter
Omar Heusseni - Freedom Fighter
Oma Kassim - Freedom Fighter
Nuri Hakkar - Freedom Fighter
Ibn Sapir - Former Leader

TUESDAY, JULY 13

Do unto others . . .

One

"Damn it!" Masters yelled as she bounced clear of the seat. Jack Blanchard looked over at her and grinned.

"Slow down!"

"Pull that belt a little tighter," he advised.

"Go to hell," she said in that firm, no-nonsense way she had.

"We're practically there," Blanchard told her, leaving open for her interpretation whether he meant hell or Kiryat Arba.

The former was a definite possibility.

The temperature was in the high nineties but the dry air made the July sun's glare merciless. It bounced off the white hood of the truck and was barely absorbed by the tinted windshield. The fiberglass top was white for its reflective quality, but still the heat soaked through and permeated the interior. The sliding plastic side windows were barely cracked open because of the dust, and so the heat was effectively trapped inside. Sweat ran freely off Blanchard's face, and he was aware of the damp patches on Melanie Masters's safari jacket.

Sometimes he dreamed about rain. They hadn't seen rain in eleven weeks, and then it was a squall that lasted less than five minutes. Every day was bright.

When the Hummer hit a level stretch of ground, he shifted up a gear, then lifted his aviator sunglasses and wiped the sweat from his eyes with the back of his hand. They stung a bit with the salty bite of perspiration.

Masters tightened her seat belt.

"You're going to kill us both, Colonel."

"Not on purpose, Mel. Hey, you're the one who said it was life or death."

She just pursed her lips. She only called him "Colonel" when she was really, *really* ticked at him. Normally, she was only really ticked off. Her mood hadn't been improved by the radio call from the medical clinic in Hebron. She had been truly serious when she told him that a life hung in the balance and minutes counted. In the time they had worked together, her concern for life had rubbed off on Blanchard.

So he assumed she didn't mean what she said about his driving and kept his speed on the ragged edge of control.

The Humvee tilted forward and rushed down a wadi that crossed the rutted track he was trying to identify as a road. He didn't use the brakes, but he did take his foot off the accelerator pedal. The loss in speed wasn't noticeable.

Glancing in the rearview mirror, he saw the second Humvee following close in his dust. It, too, was finished in white with the logo of the World Health Organization (WHO) on its doors, but aft of the driver's seat, it was fitted out as a mobile operating room. He felt sorry for the four people inside. They not only had to cope with the oppressive heat, but also with the thick cloud of beige, finely powdered dirt he was throwing up. The truck was entirely coated in a film of surplus Judeo-Galilean Highlands landscape.

There was a lot of surplus around them. The barren terrain was supposedly suitable for grazing, but Blanchard had noted that even the most primitive of goats or sheep had forsaken the area. The sporadic clumps of dried grass weren't worth waging a land war over. Personal opinion, he knew.

He downshifted as the far side of the wide wadi came up, and the truck growled aggressively as it climbed the steep side. At the top, the front wheels cleared the edge, grabbing air for a moment, then banged down. And he was racing again, holding the forty-five miles an hour that he'd been striving for.

"Goddamnit!"

"I haven't topped fifty. It's not like it's Indianapolis or Monte Carlo, Mel."

"You act as if it was."

He tried diverting her attention from his speedometer. "So, what'd they say was wrong with this guy?"

"They don't know, have never seen anything like it. That's why we're going."

"But he's dying?"

"That's what they said."

On the left, he saw hills rise from the desert horizon, tinged with a pale green that indicated a tree or two. They seemed particularly inviting, but he ignored the invitation and got his attention back on the ruts in time to see the right-hand rut disappear. It had washed away into a steep ditch running along on the right. Since it only rained an inch a year in this region, he figured it had taken a few decades to accomplish the washout. Maybe it was the wind.

Hauling the steering wheel to the left, he managed to get his left wheels up on the rise to his left and bypass the mini-gulch. The action seemed to put the Humvee on its right side.

Melanie Masters looked out her side window, gasped, and slapped both hands on the grab bar mounted to the dash panel.

Then he was back in the ruts and level again.

For a change, she didn't complain.

To be honest, she only criticized his work infrequently. Because he was damned good at what he did. Melanie Masters wasn't disenchanted with his day-to-day operations; she was unhappy with the decisioning process, and that was mainly because she didn't like Blanchard, his history, or his philosophies. That was okay with Blanchard. He didn't think she wanted a full and frank discussion of her own shortcomings. He could probably work up a list.

He checked the mirror.

Dickie Armbruster, the competent Brit behind the steering wheel of the second vehicle, performed the same daredevil feat of bypassing the washout. Armbruster had it easier; if he was getting complaints from his passengers, he could always blame Blanchard.

On the distant horizon, more hills appeared. Here, they called them mountains, but Blanchard, who had been raised in Wyoming, knew what real mountains looked like.

He eased the wheel to the left, departing the rudimentary road.

"What are you doing?" Masters demanded. She was a proponent of advanced, long-range planning, unless it was she who had changed her mind.

"Shortcut."

Since they were no longer following a road, but streaking across relatively level terrain, Armbruster pulled out to the right, flying along like a wingman's jet fighter in formation, to get out of the dust raised by Blanchard's vehicle.

The desert floor appeared to be more even—the chuckholes disguised, the shifty sand a bit firmer—the farther they went; and ten minutes later, Blanchard saw the black ribbon of the paved road crossing his line of travel. He was approaching it at an oblique angle, and he gauged the traffic the closer he got.

There was one bus, headed toward Hebron, followed by two automobiles. Aimed the other way, toward Jerusalem, was a convoy of four trucks. He accelerated to fifty to beat the bus and turned a little farther to the left, to allow the trucks some clearance.

Soon he was running in parallel to the two-lane asphalt highway, which was about four feet above him, the embankment sloping away from the road at about thirty degrees.

The trucks went by the other way, drivers and passengers staring incredulously at the two military vehicles racing the other way alongside the highway.

"Hold on!"

Masters reached for the grab bar.

Blanchard swung the wheel slightly to the right, and the Hummer whipped up the slope, leaning precariously to the left, crossed the verge, and settled on the pavement a quarter mile ahead of the bus. Armbruster made the transition, too, and fell in behind him.

The big tires with the aggressive tread whined on the hot

asphalt. The road didn't improve the heat, but it did give some relief from the dust. He cracked open the plastic window on his left to its full extension and let some of the dry heat blow through. Masters did the same with the right window.

"You're just real proud of yourself, aren't you?"

"We're getting the job done, Doctor."

Jack Blanchard used her proper title when he got tired of her being really ticked off.

She knew that, too. "Always the damned Marine. Be prepared."

"That's the Boy Scouts. Ex-gyrenes always respond to *Semper Fi.*"

"Same thing. Just as childish," she said.

She'd never been there, and Blanchard was damned sure she wouldn't understand the attitudes even if she had been there. He wasn't going to even attempt an explanation.

Ten klicks later, he backed off the pedal as they approached Kiryat Arba, a disputed Jewish settlement on the outskirts of Hebron.

"You know where we're going?" he asked.

"I have a fair idea."

Masters had taken the radio call from the clinic, along with the directions.

He slowed to a conservative twenty miles an hour as they entered the village. Speed had to give way to safety once in a while, especially since little kids ran alongside the trucks, curious and even gleeful, not in the least afraid of the huge tires rolling past tiny bare feet. Blanchard often wondered what they had to be gleeful about. It would take a hell of a dose of ideology, or religious conviction, to put up with living in a place like Kiryat Arba. He had his own convictions—displayed in a couple of wars—but they didn't include relocating permanently to a kibbutz or moshav, a collective or cooperative community in the middle of a literal nowhere.

There were trees, but the spindly olive and fruit trees wouldn't be called a forest in Wyoming. They did pass a couple groves where someone was trying to create an agricultural base of olives and their by-products. The houses appeared to have grown right out of the desert land in color and composition.

Lots of concrete and concrete block. Thick walls to ward off the heat, small windows, recessed doorways. Little shops where suspicious eyes peered out from the gloom within as the white Humvees rumbled past.

"There," she said. "The market. Turn left, then seven houses down on the right."

He spotted the produce market on the corner and turned into a dirt-encrusted street. Counted houses and stopped at the seventh, easing up to a skeletal privet hedge that wouldn't provide privacy for a mongrel dog. There was no curb, no sidewalk. Armbruster parked about ten feet behind him, and everyone began to spill out of the vehicles.

Blanchard noticed right away that they didn't gather a crowd. Standing beside the truck, he turned and looked around.

The crowd was there; about forty people strong, it was just staying way back, three, four hundred feet away.

"These people are scared, Mel." He was over being irked by her really ticked-off condition.

"Yes, it looks that way," she said, opening the rear door and reaching inside to get her medical bag.

Armbruster walked up to him. Like most of the rest of them, he was dressed in jeans and a lightweight khaki safari jacket. It wasn't a uniform, particularly, but the loose-fitting jacket helped reflect the heat when they were working in the desert. Most of the team also wore baseball caps, some with the WHO logo, some adorned with the names of favorite professional athletic teams. Armbruster wore the WHO; Blanchard supported the Denver Broncos.

"You want us right away, Jack?" he growled.

"Just Jillian, right now."

Jillian Weiss was standing right behind him, and she nodded. She was transplanted from Chicago, now an Israeli citizen grouped with Ashkenazim—Jews who came to Israel from Europe and North America. The Sephardim had their roots in the Middle East and the Mediterranean. One of the three translators, she spoke English, Hebrew, Yiddish, and Arabic as if she'd been born to all four languages.

Through the open doors of the Humvee, Masters gave him a baleful stare. As the chief physician for the team, she often thought she was the boss—one of the roots of their mini-debates. And she frequently, though not vocally, demonstrated her displeasure when others turned to Blanchard for leadership.

Masters wasn't alone in her views, of course. The doctors and nurses generally were in her corner.

"Let's go," Blanchard said and walked around the front of the Hummer to a gap in the privet hedge. He passed through it, then stepped aside to let Weiss and Masters precede him.

The translator crossed the barren yard and a struggling vegetable garden in order to knock on the front door.

It was tentatively opened by a short, elderly, and weatherworn woman in a thin print dress. The expression on her face was one of high anxiety.

A barrage of Hebrew was exchanged, then they were quickly ushered inside.

It was substantially cooler inside the dimly lit structure. The main room featured a highly polished round walnut table with four chairs, a long Danish-modern sofa with collapsed cushions, and about ten tons of bric-a-brac. Framed cross-stitch proverbs in Hebrew hung on the walls.

The woman led them rapidly back along a short hallway and into a tiny corner bedroom, her slippered feet shuffling along the linoleum with unrestrained urgency. Inside the room, there was one tall dresser, a chair, a single bed, and more proverbs hanging on the whitewashed walls.

One young man lay on the single sheet of the bed.

Oh, Jesus! Blanchard almost said aloud.

TWO

Though it was a tiny, beleaguered, and import-driven nation, Israel could boast a high standard of living. Ninety percent of its citizens were literate, having been educated by a system of state-supported public and religious schools. Both Jewish schools, conducted in Hebrew, and Arab/Druse schools were funded by the government.

Health care was also among the highest offered around the Mediterranean, though the best of that was provided in the urban areas. That was understandable since ninety percent of the population lived in urban centers.

The health-care crisis was in the West Bank region.

The West Bank, which had been occupied by the Israelis after the Six-Day War in June 1967, was bordered on the east by the Jordan River and the northern half of the Dead Sea. Almost 2,200 square miles encompassed much of the Judeo-Galilean Highlands, running from the river and the shores of the Dead Sea westward for thirty miles and from the southern Negev Desert for eighty miles north, to the city of Jenin.

With the return of the area to Palestinian control—the Palestinian Authority—had come the flight of many young medical professionals from the hinterland to the cities of Israel, leaving a health-care vacuum the slim cadre of Palestinian and a few remaining Israeli doctors had found difficult to fill. Outbreaks of dysentery, several cases of cholera, a resurgence of typhus, and a lack of basic preventative medicine had prompted the World Health Organization to dispatch an emergency medical team to the country to provide temporary assistance.

Blanchard's unit—the Palestine Medical Assistance Team, or PMAT—had been in-country for nearly six months, and he had witnessed a great deal of neglect, suffering, and disease in that time. During his active-duty years, he had seen similar conditions in various parts of the civilized and less civilized world.

But nothing like this.

The light penetrating the curtained window washed the room in a haze that should have taken some of the shock out of the scene, but didn't. Not by a long shot.

The young man, with long jet-black hair and a smooth, unlined face, was no older than twenty-one or twenty-two. He was unconscious, and he was also Arabic, a fact that jacked up Blanchard's respect for the Jewish homeowner by several notches. It might be one of the reasons why her neighbors were being so standoffish.

But probably not, if any of them had seen the patient.

He was dressed in a pair of ragged gray undershorts. If he had had a sheet on, it was gone now. The weight of any kind of covering might have been painful.

His legs, torso, and arms were almost totally a hot-pink color, as if he'd been doused in a bath of scalding water. In large areas, the skin was roughened, a rash that had been scratched at unceasingly. A peppering of white blisters were rampant on the insides of his legs and along one forearm. Several large pustules—a couple inches in diameter—were visible on his abdomen and lower legs. A couple had burst, oozing pus, fluid, and blood. Several sections of skin on the abdomen and lower legs had been peeled away, revealing thc pink inner layers of muscle.

His face might be twenty years old; his body was ready for the grave.

Jillian Weiss's face suggested she was trying desperately to stifle a gag reaction. Blanchard could understand it; his own stomach was ready to rebel.

Masters popped open her bag, found latex gloves, and started to pull them on.

"How long has he been here?"

Weiss struggled with herself, looking away from the bed to the woman, then translated.

The old woman chattered a response. Blanchard only recognized the word *"shiva."*

"For seven days, Dr. Masters. She could not wake him this morning, and that's when she called the clinic."

Masters moved around the bed, studying the man. She probed at his eyes, lifting the lids. "No one has seen him? From the clinic?"

After the translation, and a long reply, Weiss said, "They would not come here. They wanted him brought to Hebron, but she could not do it. She does not have a car. This morning, after the village administrator complained, they finally sent someone. She doesn't know whether he was a doctor, and he was here for only ten minutes."

"Has he eaten?"

A short burst of Hebrew.

"Some soup, a little juice. Nothing else."

"Any urination?"

Chatter.

"Very little."

"Renal failure," Masters said to herself as she rubbed the flesh of his upper arm. The flesh appeared to move with her finger, and kept moving. "Nikolsky's sign."

Blanchard couldn't fathom what the hell she was talking about, but in six months, he had discovered that she knew what she was doing. Masters was one of the most competent people he'd ever met, and in his forty-six years, he'd met a lot of very able people. Her shortcomings were not in her medical capability.

"All right," she said. "Let's get him out of here."

Blanchard went to the front door and waved Armbruster and the two nurses, Cale Perkins and Deidre Joliet, inside.

"Bring the gurney," he called.

Once in the bedroom with the gurney, Perkins and Armbruster donned gloves and transferred the patient from the bed with more delicacy than Blanchard would have expected from either of the big men.

"Deidre," Masters said, "raise the roof. We're going to operate immediately."

"Of course, Doctor." The French nurse hurried out.

"Right in the street?" Blanchard asked.

"Right in the street," Masters answered.

"For what?" Blanchard asked. He couldn't imagine a procedure for skin rash.

Masters didn't have time for foolish questions. She turned to Armbruster. "Dickie, would you gather up the bedclothes, take them outside, and burn them? Then spray this room with disinfectant?"

"Righto!"

"Jillian, ask the woman if she knows who he is, and if he has any family."

The results of that inquiry were no and unknown.

Blanchard grabbed one end of the gurney and began backing out of the room with it. Perkins, a Kentuckian with a telltale accent, worked the other end. They had to lift a bit going over the threshold of the front door and down the single outside step. Blanchard tried to move as if every jolt would be fatal.

Out in the street the crowd was still hanging around, still staying away, still as silent a group as Blanchard had ever seen.

At the second Humvee, Joliet had activated the hydraulic pumps, which raised the canvas roof in back of the driver's compartment about four feet. That provided standing room inside for anyone less than six feet four inches tall. There was plenty of room for Masters, who had to stretch to reach five five. A little less for Perkins, whose lanky frame topped six feet by three inches.

Blanchard and Perkins rolled the gurney onto the lowered lift at the back of the Hummer, and Perkins hit the raise button on the panel fixed to the rear fender. The lift rose to the level of the deck inside. Deidre Joliet unzipped the nylon curtain down the center and held it wide open, and Blanchard turned the stretcher so that they could shove it inside.

The man on the gurney hadn't moved, groaned, or otherwise indicated he was alive. Blanchard could see a minute movement of his chest.

Once inside the stifling heat of the interior, Perkins locked the wheels of the gurney. Joliet was already pouring basins full of disinfectant and was beginning to wash.

Around the gurney was about eighteen inches of walking space. Two seats behind the driving compartment, which was now walled off with curtain, and built-in cabinetry took up the rest of the space. The flexible nylon-and-plastic sidewalls were white, allowing translucent light in, but there were also small plastic windows on the sides. A large operating light hung from the center of the top.

Perkins lifted the tops of some cabinets, and electronic instruments rose into place out of their cushioned compartments. Blanchard didn't understand half of it, and didn't want to. He stepped outside and back onto the lift, bent over to the controls, and lowered it halfway so that it acted as a step up to the deck level.

"Jack," Perkins said, "could you crank up the power unit, get some air in here?"

"Betcha."

He went around to the left side, just ahead of the rear wheel, grabbed a recessed handle, and jerked it open. The hatch lifted on hydraulic arms, and he left it propped open. Squatting, he reached inside the hatch, found the controls, turned the power switch to the on position, and hit the ignition button.

The small diesel motor under the floor coughed twice, hiccuped once, and then settled into a steady, undertoned roar. The generator provided enough juice to keep the operating lights bright and the electronics functioning. It also ran the pump for the onboard thirty-gallon water tank. Once it had settled into a steady buzz, he shoved a lever and activated the air-conditioning.

He stood up to find Masters behind him.

And below him. She stood about nine inches shorter than he.

"Deidre," she called, "start a ten percent glucose."

"Right away."

"Take this, would you?" she said to Blanchard

He helped her out of her safari jacket, leaving her in jeans, a damp T-shirt, and a coating of his imagination. She shoved her arms into a green smock and turned.

He tied the ties.

"Thank you," she said.

Every once in a while, she was civil.

He handed her up to the step, and she slipped inside the curtain. Cale Perkins zipped it shut. At least there was no wind today. In some places they had a hell of a time keeping the interior free of dust and somewhat sterile.

He stepped back, watching the white sidewall blossom as someone turned on the overhead operating light.

Walking over to the other Humvee, which was Blanchard's command vehicle and was well equipped with specialized electronics of its own, which he understood better than heart and blood-pressure monitors, he opened the door, tossed Master's jacket into the rear, and sat sideways on the driver's seat.

Armbruster came back.

"Can you spare some gas, Jack?"

"Sure." He got up and went to the back to open the tailgate. Inside, snapped into a holder on the left side, was a five-gallon jerry can. On the other side was a stack of electronic components. A satellite dish, which could be moved to a stanchion on the right rear fender, was clipped to the floor. Stacks of towels, sheets, some olive-drab army blankets, MREs— meals ready to eat—and cardboard boxes haphazardly filled the rest of the space.

He unfastened the jerry-can clip and pulled the can free. Armbruster got a plastic bottle of spray disinfectant from one of the boxes.

"The mattress was soaked, so I'm burning it, too. The lady doesn't like it."

"Can't say as I blame her, Dickie. I'll see if I can make it up somehow."

Blanchard rummaged around in the cardboard boxes. Most of the vehicles carried a supply of plastic-cased first-aid kits. They were fairly comprehensive and made good gifts—the team passed them around liberally. He grabbed two of them, along with a couple of multiwashed but clean sheets.

Walking back to the house, he encountered Weiss and the old woman standing in front of the door. The conversation seemed animated, and he assumed that Weiss was trying to explain why they were burning her belongings.

He dug in his pocket and found a hundred bucks' worth of shekels. He held his empty right hand out to the woman, and after she stared at it for a moment, she placed her hand in his own. He shook it solemnly.

"Thank you for your assistance."

Jillian Weiss translated. *"Toda."*

He turned her hands over with his own and placed the sheets, first-aid kits, and money in them.

She grabbed it all with both arms.

Smiled at him and spoke. *"Toda."*

"She thanks you, Jack."

He smiled back and said, *"Erev tov."* Good evening, he hoped.

Then he and Weiss went back down the walk.

"They're operating?" she asked.

"That's my best guess."

"What can they do?"

"I can't even guess at that, Jillian."

He opened all four doors on the Hummer, to let what little breeze there was pass through. Jillian crawled in the backseat, found the five-gallon pot of iced lemonade, and filled six paper cups. Blanchard took three of them over to the other Humvee, announced his mission, and passed them through the curtain to Perkins. When he came back, Armbruster was behind the wheel, so he took the passenger seat.

The crowd of people was still hanging around. On the other side of the house, a black pall of smoke rose into the clear sky.

A few kids ventured close, but when Blanchard gave them a smile and walked forward to talk with them, the small band went running off, giggling and laughing.

Counterpoint to whatever was taking place in the operating room. The op-unit, as the team members called it.

The three of them made small talk for a while. Dickie Armbruster crawled in the back with Weiss, and the two of them started a game of gin rummy with the well-used cards Armbruster always carried.

Blanchard lifted the microphone from its hook and called Mercy Base.

Mercy Base was always wherever the greatest concentration of his unit was located, currently at a small village, two miles from the Dead Sea, inhabited by nearly nomadic sheepherders.

"Hey, Jack, you got me," Sam Delray said.

Delray was his second in command, an Australian without much of an accent. He had fought hard to lose it so he could be a Hollywood actor, but that hadn't worked out, so he got a law degree. That hadn't worked too well, either, so he'd gone to work for the United Nations. That worked better.

"Nothing's blown up, I hope."

"Ah, hell, no. No excitement at all in this burg. How about yourself?"

Blanchard brought him up-to-date.

"Nothing contagious?"

"I don't think so. Melanie hasn't enlightened me just yet. I don't know how long this is going to take, but we may be back late."

"I won't wait supper on you, then."

"You wouldn't have, anyway."

He replaced the mike and leaned back in the seat, resting his head on the top of it. A nap wouldn't come around because Jillian exclaimed so loudly every time she won a hand. She seemed to be winning a lot of them. He suspected Armbruster of playing the game that way.

Around five-thirty, with the sun starting a dive toward the horizon, but without a whit of alleviation in the temperature, or much of a decrease in the size of the mob hanging around, he heard footsteps. He stretched and got out. Pulled his glasses off and wiped the perspiration from his face with a towel he pulled from the door pocket. One thing this outfit had was plenty of towels, all of them about half the size required for effectiveness. He reached inside for another one.

Masters looked like a wreck. Browned stains of blood spattered her green surgical smock. It was a lot more blood than he might have expected, and he supposed she had put a large dent in the inventory of blood. He'd have to reorder. Her surgical mask was tugged down around her neck, and a bitter frown pulled her lips down. She stripped away a paper hair net as she walked toward him. Her chestnut-brown hair tumbled free, but it was damp and matted. The air-conditioning unit for the operating room helped beat down the heat, but not a great deal.

"Dickie, let's have a shot of that lemonade. Punch it with a little vodka."

Armbruster handed him the cup as Masters reached him. He passed it on to her and she took a long sip. Then he gave her the extra towel. She dabbed at the perspiration on her face and throat.

"How we doing?" he asked.

"Not good. I want to wait a couple hours before we start back. Make sure he's stable enough to travel."

It was only fifteen miles, but Blanchard didn't argue with her. On the medical questions, he never argued. Well, infrequently.

He stepped out of the way, and she flopped on the seat. Armbruster and Weiss folded their cards.

"I amputated both of his legs. Above the knees."

"Jesus."

"He'll probably lose his right arm, too."

Twenty-one, twenty-two years old. Blanchard felt sick.

"Dickie, you want to mix me one of those concoctions?"

"Sure thing, Jack."

He watched Masters's eyes. They were distant, the hazel color turned muddy.

"What is it?" Weiss finally asked.

"Toxic epidermal necrolysis."

"Help me, Mel," he said.

"A bacterial flesh-eating disease."

Blanchard felt his own flesh crawl, and thought about a long and hot shower.

"If I remember right, the mortality rate is high. Around thirty percent."

He thought this kid might be better off dead, but he didn't

voice the opinion since it was one Masters would vehemently argue against.

Armbruster handed him a cup, then made two more drinks as Perkins and Joliet appeared.

"Not contagious, is it?" he asked, remembering Delray's question.

"Not in the least," the doctor said.

"How do you know?" he asked, looking toward the other Humvee and suspicious of Masters trying to downplay the risks.

She gave him one of her looks that would have withered other men on the spot. "It's in the literature."

That was a relief.

Jacob Talman was thirty-seven years old and hardened by his time in the Israeli Defense Forces (IDF). His dark hair was retreating early, leaving a prominent widow's peak as the rear guard. Heavy brows shaded deep-set eyes that viewed most of his world with suspicion. He was a major, and though he appeared quite fit and military in a uniform, he had worn his but three times in the last two years for ceremonial occasions— all funerals. They were not just any old funerals, either. All had been friends and colleagues, and Talman was not happy with the attrition rate.

Born in the port city of Haifa and a graduate of Tel Aviv University, Major Jacob Talman had intended to pursue a career in civil engineering. His three-years mandatory service in the army, however, had changed his mind and solidified his views of his world. An ardent patriot and an avid supporter of the philosophy of preemptive strike, he had been personally opposed in 1982 to the withdrawal of Israeli forces from the Sinai and fully in favor of the invasion of Lebanon and the siege of West Beirut in the same year. He had been a lieutenant commanding an infantry unit in Lebanon before he was detached to Shin Bet to be schooled in intelligence operations. With that education had come an even greater awareness of the fragile hold Israel maintained on her independence.

He had resolved to assist in the struggle with all of the tenacity within him.

As a company grade officer, and therefore a long long way from the halls where policy was made, Talman had been unable to voice his displeasure over a number of developments in a way that might have counted. The partial withdrawal from Lebanon in 1985, leaving a security-zone force in place, had been premature in his opinion. The Palestinian uprising in the occupation regions of the West Bank and the Gaza Strip in 1987 should have been met with a great deal more force. And high on his list of governmental debacles was the decision to show restraint toward the bombardment of Israel by Scud missiles unleashed by Saddam Hussein in 1991. He knew the Cabinet had made its decision in light of more global issues than Talman had in mind, but he cared little about the delicacy of foreign relations—meaning three or four billion in financial aid—with the United States. Not when lethal weaponry was impacting his homeland.

If one military decision overshadowed his disgust with his own strategists, it was that of the United Nations forces in the Persian Gulf war. They should have driven the full distance to Baghdad, razing the city to the ground if required, in order to eradicate the insane Chairman of the Revolutionary Command Council. That hundred-day war would forever haunt the Middle East because it had not been stretched another ten days.

While he was in favor of the peace accords and developing self-rule as a way of promoting Israel's continued sovereignty, Talman was also convinced that the secession of territory to the Palestinian Authority was not workable. He had met very few Arabs he could trust to carry through on a promise, mainly because for every trustworthy man among them, there were ten others who would do their best to screw it up. Plus, his three friends had not died of old age; they had been helped along by zealots who thought that plastic explosive and nine-millimeter rounds were the only means for achieving objectives.

Most of his firmly held beliefs tended to interfere with his present assignment. Talman had been working under cover in the Jerusalem district for three years, before and after the accord with Yassir Arafat's Palestine Liberation Organization (PLO). Talman was doing his best to maintain an even keel in rough seas, seeking ways to maintain the peace, but he was frequently called into the office of his superior, Colonel Isaac Stein, to be reminded of his duty.

He assumed that was why he was now waiting in the outer room of General Levi Avidar's temporary office. A meeting with Avidar was one step above his monthly trysts with his commanding officer. Talman figured he was in deep trouble, but had no clue as to the source. No doubt, one of his informants had complained to a policeman because he had not received enough baksheesh, and word had somehow gotten back to Shin Bet.

If he was to be dressed down for some unknown transgression, however, he would just as soon have it come from Levi Avidar, a man he respected.

Atarot Airport, to the north of Jerusalem, was the chosen site for these meetings, since there was an obvious mix of civilian and military people. Shin Bet maintained a small suite of three offices in a building adjacent to the terminal for miscellaneous purposes, and he supposed this was a miscellaneous meeting. Talman arrived in his typical civilian attire of chino pants, running shoes, sport shirt, and loose-fitting sport jacket. The colors were not all complementary, he had been told often, but he was not a fashion plate.

When he was called in, he found the general in a business suit rather than a uniform, typical of these meetings. Many people knew who the general was, and what he did, of course, but it was illegal under Israeli law for anyone to identify him, particularly members of the media. He was of moderate height, and his features were blunt, but his closely styled gray hair and steely eyes distinguished him.

Avidar did not comment on Talman's wardrobe, and his unnamed aide—also in mufti—went to stand in a corner of the room.

"Please sit down, Jacob."

"Yes, sir."

There was a desk and accompanying chair in this anteroom, along with a sofa and two easy chairs. Avidar was in one of the soft chairs, so Talman sat in the middle of the couch. He sat on the front edge of the cushion, his back straight, as close to attention as he could maintain.

Avidar was not fond of small talk. He went right to the point. "The Palestinian Authority is in dire straits."

"Sir."

"You are aware of their problems, of course?"

Talman knew the Palestinian Authority was struggling to make its government work in the self-rule regions, but unemployment, the lack of services, the degradation of the education systems, and the deterioration of infrastructure like roads, bridges, and sanitary systems threatened to bring about the Authority's downfall. Personally, he also thought that ineptitude and corruption were rampant within the Authority, and that wouldn't help their cause, either.

"I am, General."

What was taking place was just what Talman might have predicted. However, he was also surprised that Avidar raised the issue in such a solemn and all-encompassing way. Only infrequently was he provided a larger picture; the normal course of events was to give him an assignment to procure a certain type or aspect of information. How his little acquisition might fit into the larger scheme of things was for others to decide.

"The Authority," Avidar continued, "has appealed to the World Bank and to the superpowers for financial assistance to overcome these deficiencies. They are asking for twenty billion dollars American."

Talk about a welfare state. These people wanted to set up their own government, and then have someone else pay for it. Worse, the other nations would do it, strictly with the objective of preserving a shifty peace.

"That is over a five-year period, of course."

Oh. Well, that makes a difference.

"The Knesset and the Cabinet have judged that it is in our best interests if the Authority is successful in its quest."

They would think that way.

"I have been charged with helping them get it, and you will be my agent."

"Pardon me, General?"

"Our task is to prevent any extraordinary event—a rebellion, a bombing, a protest of undesirable proportions—that would bring about world attention and reflect badly on the Authority.

If we can maintain the peace for approximately forty-five days, it is likely that the Palestinians will gain their financial backing. That works to our advantage. With a full treasury, the Authority can relieve some of the tensions present in the Gaza Strip, Jericho, and other West Bank areas they will control.''

Talman was not certain what he was hearing. "In essence, General, we are working *for* the Palestinians?''

"I prefer to think that we our working toward our own goals, Jacob.''

"My God! How am I to police a million Palestinians? Do I run around asking if they have lust in their hearts, murder in their minds?''

"You will have help. I am assigning twelve persons to the task force you will command. You will base yourself in Jerusalem, under your present cover, and deploy your agents in Jericho and throughout the West Bank.''

"The Gaza Strip?''

"Will be under the scrutiny of another task force, commanded by Major Perlmutter.'' Avidar signaled his aide, who withdrew an envelope from his inside jacket pocket, walked across the room, and handed it to Talman.

The general leaned forward, placing his elbows on his knees, and commanded Talman's attention with those intense gray eyes. "I place my faith in you, Jacob. You have an exemplary record, if we discount a few stains here and there. We will designate them as youthful indiscretions. What is important to me, you have never disobeyed an order. In fact, you have always excelled, going far beyond the expected call of duty in order to fulfill your goals. I expect no less of you in this instance.''

"I hope your expectations are not too great, General.''

"They are not. In the envelope is money. Use it as necessary. Also included are the names . . . the code names . . . of the agents who will work with you. They will be contacting you at your office.''

Talman operated a travel bureau as his cover.

"Please destroy the list of code names before you leave. Are there questions?''

About five thousand.

"I am to stop protests? With the force assigned to me?"

"A single murder or two will obviously go unnoticed, Jacob, unless it is the murder of a prominent politician. I should not worry about those. If you uncover a plan that would incur media attention, do what you can to derail it. We do not expect anything major to occur in the next six weeks. Indeed, the Palestinian Authority will also be working hard to deflect any disruption in their plans, and they say they have secured a truce of sorts with Hamas. If, however, you uncover a plot of immense proportions, which you have no hope of preventing, you will call me directly. We will assign it to a specialized unit of the IDF."

Avidar stood up, and the meeting was over.

Talman remained in the room until he had memorized the names on the list, then burned it in an ashtray. The money, in American dollars, Israeli shekels, French francs, and Italian lira, amounted to about $50,000. He stuffed it in his pockets.

The amount of his discretionary funds alone was an indication of the importance the Cabinet was placing on this operation. He had never before been given more than $5,000.

It was dark when he returned to his car in the parking lot. It was a three-year-old Toyota Camry with more than its share of bruises. He unlocked it, got in, and started the engine and air-conditioning.

Talman understood the rationales being put forth by Avidar. Still, it rankled miserably to think that he was working in the interests of Palestinians whose basic objective in life was to see Israel burned to the ground. He thought that regaining the West Bank and the Gaza Strip served only as a stepping-stone to their goals, and he couldn't help but think he was to assist in his—and his country's—own downfall.

Shifting the car into gear, Talman spent the next forty minutes fighting heavy traffic between the city and the airport on the way back to his travel bureau on Hativat Hatzanhanim. There was a space in the back of the building for parking the car, and he lived in one of three small apartments on the second floor above the agency.

As expected, someone had parked an old Renault in his space. Someday he was going to drop a grenade in one of the offending cars. He drove down the alley and parked next to a stack of trash barrels. Then he got out and walked back to the rear door of the office. He let himself in with a key and looked over the three-room space. His two assistants had left for the day, sweeping the floor, dusting the furniture, and installing the plastic covers over the computer terminals before they left.

One of Talman's secret joys was that his cover of travel agent was actually making money, enough to support his assistants and the costs of his salary. If the agency did not belong to Shin Bet, he would have been a successful entrepreneur.

He went out the side door, not onto the street, but into a small foyer and climbed the wooden stairs to the second floor. In his two-room apartment, he showered away the heat of the day and dressed in fresh clothing. In the small closet of the bedroom, he stooped to lift the carpet, then dialed the combination and opened the safe set in the floor. He deposited most of his discretionary fund, keeping one thousand shekels back for immediate use.

It was a seven-block walk into the Muslim Quarter to one of his favorite restaurants located on Flowers Gate, and he reached it by nine thirty. He ate there once a week and was well known to the proprietor, who seated him at his normal table near the kitchen doorway at the back wall. From this vantage point, Talman was able to keep an eye on those who came and went.

After the disappointing meeting with Avidar, he was not hungry, and he ordered only coffee and felafel, a deep-fried patty of ground chickpeas. His waiter, a man he knew well as Ya'akov Arif, delivered his coffee, and he sipped it while waiting for his meal.

It was placed in front of him a few minutes later, and he took his time eating.

Working out from under the plate the small piece of paper.

He chewed silently, watching the passersby through the front windows, taking momentary glances at the note, which was written in small fine handwriting: ''The Sword of God has a new leader.''

Well, yes. Interesting.

The Sword of God was a spin-off of Iziddin al-Qassam,

which was the military arm of the Islamic Resistance Movement known as Hamas. The Sword, composed of a half-dozen fanatics who didn't think Iziddin al-Qassam was militant enough, had been around for a year. A couple of incidents were attributed to them, but they were so minor, and so badly screwed up— a car bomb that didn't go off for lack of a detonator—that Talman gave them high marks for zealotry and failing marks for effectiveness

But a new leader?

When Arif came by to replenish his coffee, standing so as to block the view of other patrons, Talman mouthed the word "Who?"

Arif responded with a slight shrug of the shoulders and moved on.

This probably meant that Arif knew only that the current leader of the group, Sapir, was out of favor or, more likely, dead.

It was, of course, valuable information and worth following up. A new, more charismatic chieftain, one who had some common-sense familiarity with high explosives, could possibly turn that small band of misfits into the killers they viewed themselves as being.

When he was finished eating, Talman left a three-hundred-shekel tip.

As it turned out, they spent the night in Kiryat Arba.

When she decided that her patient was still *in extremis,* and likely to remain so, Melanie Masters decided to give him the benefit of several more hours of rest. She informed the group that they'd have to wait until morning to return to Mercy Base.

No one complained.

Dickie Armbruster broke out MREs and passed them around. Perkins and Joliet flipped coins to determine their watch rotations. Jillian Weiss walked down to the intersection to see if she could buy some fresh fruit, but the market had closed. In Israel, many markets closed by noon. And if the shops were Jewish, they were closed all of Friday afternoon and Saturday. Muslim shops and services closed down on Fridays. The Christians picked Sundays. Buses and railways didn't run on Friday afternoons and Saturdays. Finding something open around the weekend was akin to taking one's chances in Atlantic City.

Blanchard got on the radio and told Sam Delray of Masters's decision, sounding, she thought, a bit more derisive than was necessary: "Dr. Masters is keeping us here tonight, Sam."

He could have said something like, "Circumstances are holding us up," but no, he wanted to firmly establish the *responsibility* for their delay. Just like a military mind, she thought, wanting to note for the record the pertinent responsibilities for later hearings on the matter. A Mylai mentality.

Perkins and Joliet took their packaged meals back to the op-unit Humvee, where they would take turns trying to sleep in the front seats while one of them monitored the patient. She told Cale she wanted to be called immediately if there were any changes in his condition.

Masters took a long walk around the village, both to stretch her muscles and to shed some of the stress she felt. Many smiled at her from their doorways as she passed, and many would know via the grapevine that she was a doctor, but no one approached her to talk. In most of the settlements, people swarmed over her, more than willing to share their symptoms with her, begging for relief from headaches, diarrhea, in-grown nails, or exotic diseases they *thought* were afflicting them.

Not here. She suspected an innate fear resulting from her contact with the Arab boy deterred them.

By the time she got back, as the sun was disappearing, Blanchard was involved in a game of poker with Weiss and Armbruster, the three of them cramped into the backseat. Weiss sat cross-legged on the floor.

Pulling the tailgate open, Masters spread some of the extra sheets out in the back and then crawled in on top of them. It was still hot, but soon the desert air would turn chilly.

She couldn't get to sleep. The distress of the young Arab man bothered her terribly. Masters hated seeing children in pain, and though he was no longer a boy, her patient faced a dismal future. Masters had often wanted to have children, but suspected she'd have been a terrible mother, one full of cautions about everyday, normal living.

The diesel generator in the op-unit maintained a steady buzz, which became routine, but no less irritating. The three card players, obviously aware that she was trying to sleep, kept their voices low, but that was irritating, too. She could hear them, but could not quite grasp the content of their dialogue. Someone had tuned in a Tel Aviv radio station that was playing American country music. She couldn't quite hear the lyrics, either, because of the murmur of voices.

A few flies had located her, and one particular fly took great satisfaction in walking the back of her bare arm, where she couldn't quite aim at him when she swatted. She sat up and pulled her jacket on.

Instead of counting sheep, Masters counted the number of irritants in her life, and she was . . . startled when the world instantly turned black.

And then realized she had fallen asleep.

What woke her?

The radio was still playing. "My Special Angel." An oldie.

No conversation. The card players had given it up.

The generator still buzzed.

She sat up and looked around.

Except for a dim illumination through the canvas wall of the other Humvee, the town was utterly dark. There were no streetlights in Kiryat Arba. No moon, either. She looked upward. The stars were out in impressive force, very vivid in the clear desert air.

"Sorry if I woke you," Blanchard said. From somewhere.

She could barely see her hands, and she couldn't see him.

But he saw her. Eyes like a cat.

She slid forward and dropped her legs over the edge of the tailgate. Then she saw his outline, barely defined by the light of the stars, standing a couple feet away, next to the rear fender of the truck.

Had he been staring in at her? Was that what awakened her?

"What time is it?"

"Quarter after three."

"Why aren't you asleep?"

"My time of night," he said.

He was like that. Sometimes, it seemed to her, he was a man

on the verge of paranoia. Others had commented on it, too, seen him walking around at night, like a specter maintaining a vigilance over a haunted mesa.

"Are we under attack?" she asked facetiously.

"Not yet." His low voice contained the conviction that they soon would be.

"I've got to check on—"

"It's okay. Deidre just took over the shift."

She didn't want to sit here in the middle of the black night, chatting with Jack Blanchard. And she was wide awake, now.

"Could you get me a satellite channel, Colonel?"

"Sure thing. Hop off there."

She slid to the ground before he could help her, and he reached inside to retrieve the antenna. In the dark he worked with assurance, and a few minutes later, had the eighteen-inch round antenna mounted and aligned, using the digital readouts on the equipment to do so. He unclipped a telephone handset from one of the electronics boxes and handed it to her.

"There you go."

Blanchard didn't need prompting. He wandered away down the street, leaving her in privacy.

It was after seven in Chicago, a good time to call, she thought.

On the lit keypad, she tapped out the number for the apartment. She could imagine the view from the huge windows of the living room, twenty-six stories above Lake Michigan. The lake would be slate gray, the morning sun bright. Freighters would be under way, a few sails dotting the lake. Some diehard sailors liked to get a couple hours in before work.

The phone rang.

And rang.

And rang.

The answering machine didn't even come on.

Three

Dickie Armbruster had only three-quarters of his stomach left, which explained his erratic eating habits. He didn't eat full meals, but he ate six or seven times a day, and he could frequently be found with his big paw wrapped around a candy bar or cookie. His metabolism absorbed the calories without complaint, however; he was whip thin and rawhide tough.

At forty-four, he was two years younger than Blanchard, but from his appearance, one would think they'd been harder years. With the sleeves of his jacket rolled back, his forearms revealed tight musculature covered by thick black hair. His hands seemed oversized for his body, pocked with scars and an enlarged knuckle on his right forefinger. They gripped the steering wheel with fierce authority.

His head, too, was out of proportion—larger than one would expect. He performed his own barbering with an electric razor that left a uniform quarter-inch growth of jet-black stubble over his pate. His face was lined deeply with about sixty years of street-level wisdom. Under brows as craggy as granite, deep-set dark eyes peered at the world with a trace of caution. The rugged demeanor was offset by a mouth that was mostly trapped in a smile, as if he found the world full of small and amusing ironies. In yet another counterpoint, the smiling mouth issued a voice with the relative resonance of gravel sliding out of a dump truck.

Dickie Armbruster had retired as a sergeant major from the Special Air Services (SAS). He'd been wounded once in the Falklands, and though his personnel file didn't say so, Blanchard figured he'd suffered the stomach wound in Ulster. Armbruster never talked about any of it, and Blanchard had never pressed him on it. There was no need for him to know, and there was an unspoken bond between them, only seven months old—from when they'd first met—but comfortable and stronger every day. People with military experience often felt that way about one another after breaking the ties that bound them to one service or another.

As they rolled along at the pace of racing snails, Blanchard found himself automatically scanning the wadis and out-croppings for animate objects. He was aware that Armbruster was doing the same thing. For all its advanced state of civilization, Israel and the West Bank were not entirely nonhostile areas. One stayed alert to the possibility of ambush. They'd had only one confrontation with a small group of Arabic demonstrators a couple of months before, and though it was mostly shouting and arm waving, Blanchard hadn't relished the public attention. He wanted to keep his group as low profile as possible.

"Bloody hell!" Armbruster swore as he was forced to downshift yet again.

He was driving the command vehicle. Melanie Masters, apparently worried about the combination of her patient and either Blanchard's or Armbruster's skill behind the wheel, was driving the other Hummer herself.

About a hundred feet in front of them.

And at less than twenty miles an hour.

She didn't raise much of a dust storm, but what there was of it seeped through the side windows and layered Armbruster and Blanchard.

"I don't believe I'd say anything out loud about women drivers, Dickie."

"Ah, hell. I know she's worried about the bugger, but this is bloody ridiculous."

Neither of these Humvees was outfitted as an ambulance, and the mobile operating vehicle ahead was required to have its roof lowered while moving. Even with the gurney collapsed to its lowest height, there wasn't much headroom in the back, and Perkins and Joliet were probably suffering cramps as they tended the Arab.

When Blanchard had taken on this assignment, he'd been half surprised at the logistical materiel necessary to support six doctors—two of them anesthesiologists, twelve nurses, and twelve emergency medical technicians (EMTs). It was almost worse than a military combat unit. He commanded twenty-five nonmedical personnel, four deuce-and-a-half trucks—that carried most of their gear and towed water and fuel trailers—and nine Humvees. Some of the Hummers towed trailers when they were in convoy, also. Besides his command truck, the other Humvees comprised two mobile operating rooms, four ambulances, and two general-purpose vehicles. Whenever he saw all of them together, he found himself composing a parody of Ogden Nash: *What a wonderful truck is the Humvee; its shape can be whatever you want to see. . . .*

Finally they emerged from an eroded wash, and the village loomed before them.

Well, "loomed" wasn't the right word. The place was a hectic collection of about forty huts, shacks, and hovels located on the Wadi Ghar. It was unnamed and looked like it probably wouldn't be here six months from now, if a good storm came along. One strong wind would move the tin, plastic, and card-board structures to a dozen simultaneous destinations.

In addition to a couple hundred Arab men, women, and children, an amazing number of goats, sheep, and dogs bolstered the population and were allowed to roam just about wherever they wanted. On top of that, several hundred more people, reacting to rumors of free medical attention, had appeared on the desert horizons and calmly joined the long lines at the clinic.

On the southern edge of the settlement, the PMAT's tents were erected: the large pair of operating rooms they called a hospital, the smaller clinic, the two wards, the three twenty-man sleeping tents, the double tent of the mess hall, and the single administration tent. A hundred yards farther to the south were the canvas panels that provided privacy for the open-to-the-sky latrine, and to the east, the portable showers had been set up. One of the water trailers was parked next to the showers, one was backed up to the mess tent, and another serviced the hospital.

Blanchard had a particular interest in the showers. Even the five-gallon daily dribble he allowed each member of the unit assumed the welcome image of a cascading Rocky Mountain waterfall when it had been denied for thirty hours. Added to the water deprivation was the itch he'd been feeling since first viewing the Arab kid.

He didn't get to it right away, however.

Armbruster parked next to the administration tent, which was also serving as a garage at the moment. The snout of a Hummer was shoved up to the back of the rolled-up rear wall, the hood raised as one of the mechanics tinkered inside. On the other side of the Humvee was parked one of the smaller trailers, this one containing the base communications gear. Antennas sprouted from its roof, and cables snaked from it to the tent. One of the generators was snorting out by the latrine. Its black power cables were strewn over the dry earth in some semblance of logical spaghetti.

Masters swung the op-unit around by the entrance to the hospital, and one of the doctors—Chao—and two nurses scurried out to help retrieve the patient. Over at the clinic, a long line of women and children were waiting their turns to see a paramedic. They squatted in the dust and heat as if they were unaware of either.

"You need me for anything, Jack?"

"Not at the moment, Dickie. This afternoon, though, why don't you grab someone who needs a little break, and the two of you scout out a new site for us?"

"How far do you want to go?"

"Make it about ten klicks north. Somewhere close to Mar Saba. The medicos see that area as our next hot spot."

"Will do."

One of the determinations the medical team had made early on was that the patients wouldn't come to them if they had to travel very far. So, Blanchard had moved Mercy Base every two to three weeks, hopscotching up and down the West Bank. First they had addressed the pockets of intense health problems, then settled into a routine of approaching people who hadn't seen a medical professional in years, if at all. Moving was a chore, but one they were getting better at accomplishing.

Adding to the chore was the fact that when they were set up, they tended to accumulate patients in the ward tents. When they moved, the patients were reluctant to go along, so he usually ended up leaving a tent behind, tended by hurriedly trained indigenous personnel. He had four tents out in the desert now, left in the wake of their travels, and one of the doctors made a weekly circuit to assess the medical progress of the patients.

He slid out of the truck and went into the administration tent, shoving aside the netting. It was a standard-sized twenty-man tent of white canvas, and the sides were rolled up to allow any errant breeze to pass through the wall of fine mesh, supposedly designed to keep insects at bay. There were no errant breezes, and a three-foot fan on a tall pole stand at the back of the tent did its best to substitute. What it was doing, though, was helping to disperse the gas fumes from the running engine of the Humvee evenly throughout the tent.

Blanchard yelled, "Paulo! Shut off either the damned engine or the fan!"

Paulo grinned at him, stepped away from the grille of the truck, and shut off the fan.

The groaning engine, which was misfiring badly, continued to create a racket that echoed inside the tent.

Two people were working on this end of the tent, on the right side. Dr. Lars Svenson, a Swede, was on a phone. He waved a hand airily at Blanchard, who nodded back. Well, maybe he wasn't working. These people made lots of long-distance phone calls to family back home. Svenson yelled into the phone, to outshout the Hummer, without apparent irritation. He was pretty easygoing.

Emma Wachter, a nurse from Hamburg, was engrossed in one of the diagnostic programs on a computer. She didn't even look up.

Shaking his head to clear it of the fumes, Blanchard crossed to the left side and sat down at the desk. Which wasn't really a desk. All of the furnishings were foldable to enhance their transportability, and so the admin tent was a collection of canvas director chairs and folding tables. The doctors got a table desk, and the administrators got a table desk. More tables along the sidewalls held computers and wooden boxes containing patient files or unit records. Though patient records were computerized, the medical people felt better having hard copies available. And there was some justification for their paranoia about electronic data.

There were four computers—supposedly designed for rugged use. One was for Blanchard, and three for the medical staff. They were usually draped in plastic to ward off the dust, but the frequency with which they were down, undergoing repair by Roberto Irsay, the resident computer expert, was high. Blanchard's arguments about the likelihood of all four machines being inoperative at the same time went unheard, so he was faced with transporting an increasingly high mountain of paper every time they moved. In six months of operation, the doctors and paramedics had seen over forty thousand patients, and each patient generated, at minimum, one sheet of paper.

Each patient also forced the creation of an electronic file, and at some point in the future, those names were to be shared with the Palestinian Authority as that body attempted to assemble a more reliable census of its population.

The floor was of folding plywood panels to facilitate moves, but the sand and dirt tracked in, and the surface was often gritty and slippery.

At the back, Paulo started singing something in Italian, attempting to drown out the engine howl with his own roar. Svenson continued yelling into his receiver.

Blanchard started through the papers on his desk. They were held down against that errant wind—when it came by—or the output of the oscillating fan with a varied assortment of weights (bolts, a broken hemostat, a coffee can full of lemon drops, a couple lug nuts). Locating the duty roster, he scanned it.

Del Cameron, the head cook, had taken a truck to Atarot

Airport to pick up a load of supplies. He also had a 1,500-gallon water trailer with him to be refilled.

Six people were on twenty-four-hour rest—a doctor, a nurse, two EMTs, and two support personnel. They had scheduled a Humvee for a jaunt to Jerusalem. Shopping trip.

Blanchard did his best to give everyone a free day every six days. The work was a morale-killer as it was, and the opportunity to look forward to a break helped a little.

From where he sat at the table, he could survey his domain through the netting pretty well, and he was aware that he was missing another Humvee. The other operating-room unit.

Sam Delray came in the back way, skirting the maintenance operation Paulo was conducting.

"You missed breakfast, too," he called out in his basso voice.

The voice didn't really fit the man. Delray was a skinny six feet of Aussie. His face was sun reddened, and his blond hair was thin, combed straight back. It wasn't an imposing image for a trial lawyer (perhaps the reason he had abandoned that course) but his eyes were a sincere green. They were backed up by his integrity.

He scooted one of the canvas chairs over to sit across from Blanchard. Loose sand on the floor grated under his boots.

The Humvee's engine suddenly surged into a strain-free song, and Paulo shut it down. The silence was deafening.

"You see the patient?" Blanchard asked.

"Not yet."

"When you do, you'll know why we're late. Where's the other op-unit?"

"Wilcox took Ambrosia and Timnath and the unit."

Dean Wilcox was a physician; Ambrosia and Timnath were paramedics.

"Dean was supposed to be taking his off-day today. I assume this wasn't a joyride?"

"Car wreck."

"You've got to be kidding."

"Not in the least, old man."

"Two thousand square miles of desert, and two cars actually run into each other?"

"I don't know how they did it, Jack. But then, we've got to keep in mind that, not only are automobiles scarce out here, so are insurance, driver's licenses, qualified drivers, and common sense. A pickup truck squashed a Fiat, Wilcox told me when he called in. They're setting some broken bones and stitching some cuts. Dean says there may be a ruptured spleen involved."

"We're not only making house calls; now, we're making calls to accident sites."

"It was about the same difference," Delray said. "We've got the clinic full, both wards are over capacity—what with the quarantine tent, and there's an appendectomy under way in the number one OR."

"What's the status on the quarantine?"

"Still active. Seventeen cases of cholera we don't mess with."

"Damn," Blanchard replied with a sigh. "This is all preventable, Sam."

"Yeah, it's sad as hell."

Blanchard thumbed through a stack of paper until he found a manifest.

Svenson was still yelling, though the engine had been silenced. Wachter got up and went to the back of the tent to turn the fan back on.

Looking down the list of supplies, Blanchard found what he expected. "We've got three more tents in the shipment Cameron's picking up. You think we should set up another ward?"

"Probably, yes."

"We might have to revamp the duty roster to get some coverage on it."

"I'll do that if it's necessary. You explain to Melanie why she loses some people on the day shift."

"This is one I think she'll understand."

"Maybe," Delray said, lowering his voice. "These doctors have trouble when it comes to numbers. In private practice, they watch every penny. With public money, the sky's the limit."

Blanchard conceded the point. He was having a hell of a time trying to work within the budget that had been allocated to the unit by the director general of WHO. Unexpected expenses cropped up with dismaying regularity.

The hot zephyr from the fan rustled across his back and fluttered some of the paper, then disappeared as the fan rotated back the other way.

Masters suddenly appeared at the front of the tent, whisked the net entrance aside, and clomped on in.

"Hi, Mel," Delray said.

"Sam," she replied, but her mind was somewhere else. She crossed the floor to one of the tables and sat down in a chair in front of a computer. Found the switch and turned it on.

Delray looked at him, an eyebrow raised high.

"Preoccupied," Blanchard said.

"Well, give me the duty roster and I'll see who I can shift—"

"Damn it!" Masters yelped. "Why won't this goddamned machine work?"

Blanchard started to get out of his chair, but Lars Svenson hung up his phone and went to her aid.

"Let me have a look, Melanie."

He was bending over her shoulder, manipulating the mouse, when a bloodcurdling scream ripped through the encampment.

Blanchard spun around, searching for the source.

And saw one of the ward tents collapse.

The agreement on Palestinian Self-Rule in Jericho and the Gaza Strip, as the official document was entitled, was the primary instrument arising out of the peace process agreed to in Madrid in October 1991. The twenty-three articles of the agreement covered everything from the establishment of the twenty-four-member body of the Palestinian Authority to the creation of a 9,000-member Palestinian police force. The autonomous areas remained under the umbrella of Israeli control in such arenas as foreign relations and external security, but the Authority was provided legislative powers relative to basic law and regulations as long as new law did not conflict with broader Israeli tenets. In one exception to the foreign-relations caveat, the Authority was granted the power to enter into negotiations and contracts with international states and organizations for economic assistance and cultural, scientific, and educational development.

One of the key deficiencies of the accord, to Ibrahim Kadar's mind, was the provision that, while Israel was required to withdraw its military forces from the autonomous regions, turning over control to the Palestinian Police, they were allowed to maintain a police presence at Jewish settlements within the autonomous territories. Others felt as he did. Haidar Abdel-Shafi, who had once served as the chief Palestinian negotiator in the peace talks, had circulated a petition signed by prominent Palestinians that opposed the continuing construction of Jewish settlements in the occupied territories. The newspaper *Al-Thawra* in Syria had condemned the agreement as a partial solution. The Front for the Liberation of Palestine—a PLO faction—still flatly opposed the agreements signed by Yassir Arafat. There were many splinter groups of the Palestinian Liberation Organization who felt that their concerns had not been addressed by Arafat's supposedly mainstream organization, al Fatah. Who was Arafat to sign off on their futures?

As yet another example of the second-class status of Palestinian citizens, while the Authority could issue passports, the Israelis still controlled the borders, determining who could come and who could go. There was a safe passage provision for Palestinians traveling between the Gaza Strip on the Mediterranean coast and the inland Jericho area, and three routes were designated for settlers to reach Israel from Jericho, but the roads were still controlled by the Israelis.

And the Israeli police and military retained the authority to pursue Israeli criminals into Palestinian lands. They often abused this right, Kadar knew, using the "hot pursuit" rule to detain Palestinian nationals.

And worse, in his mind, was what the agreement did not state. Certainly, the autonomous region was to expand throughout the West Bank with time, but what of Jerusalem? The holiest of cities belonged in the Palestinian camp, but nothing had been agreed to in that regard. Arafat continued to rage about his right to govern Jerusalem, but it was as if he accomplished his rages in private, and nothing substantial had resulted. If for no other reason than that the Jerusalem question was unsettled, the accord should not have been signed.

The fact that it was signed had no bearing for Kadar. He was not bound by the signatures of others, only by the guide of the Koran. He took that lead from those in Hamas and Iziddin al-Qassam who had been his mentors for much of his youth.

His youth had been far from a happy one. Born in an unnamed camp in southern Lebanon, he had grown up in a succession of unnamed camps, watching his father train resistance fighters. Beyond the constant hunger, one of the roots of his unhappiness lay in the fact that he was only allowed to watch the training; he could not participate. Whether as a result of some undefined vision or as a condition of Ibrahim's deformed left foot, his father had decreed that Ibrahim was to be a diplomat rather than a soldier. His father described for others in animated discourse how Ibrahim would lead his people to the land of their origin with his wit and his words. So fiery and passionate were the speeches that even Ibrahim believed him.

To learn the words, he was sent to Beirut and schooled in the Hebrew and English languages. His tutor in English was a Shiite Muslim who spoke English with a broad British inflection that was almost colonial, and who, as a matter of opportunity, also took it upon himself to make certain that his young charge gained a firm faith in—rather than an understanding of—the tenets of the Koran.

Kadar's schooling lasted until he was fifteen, when it became apparent that his father was not to return from some secretive mission upon which he had been sent. A lieutenant in Iziddin al-Qassam explained that fact of life to him, and Kadar immediately forgot the words and demanded the action. He would be trained as a soldier; they owed it to him.

Despite his slight size and the limp associated with his deformed foot, he was allowed to initiate his paramilitary training. If the leadership had hoped that he would fail, their desires were soon dashed. What Kadar lacked in physical attributes were more than compensated for in tenacity, endurance, and ferocity.

And fifteen years later, he was a respected leader in the movement to return Palestine to Palestinians.

And just as ferocious as he had ever been.

And just as determined to make his principles reverberate across the land.

So it was, that he stood in the main terminal of the airport in Damascus and studied the faces of those debarking from the Baghdad flight.

The man he was seeking was near the end of the queue departing the aircraft, and as soon as he was clear of the line and had caught Kadar's eye, Kadar turned and walked down the concourse to a grouping of plastic couches. He settled onto one, and a few minutes later was joined by the man he had first met in Beirut ten years before. He dropped his canvas bag on the floor and sat with a heavy thud. He had gained much weight since Kadar had last seen him.

"Ibrahim Kadar."

"Majib Khabanni, my brother. It is good of you to come all this way."

"It is for a short time. I return on the next flight, and I have but fifteen minutes."

"We are all hurried. It is the nature of war."

"So it is. How will you travel?"

"Overland, I think. It will be safer."

Khabanni gave him an appraising glance. "Safety should be your main concern, brother. More accidents will not be appreciated or condoned. This is the last."

Kadar did not like the condescension or the implied threat in his friend's tone, but chose to ignore it. In fact, he was required to ignore any criticism of his performance since he had no other sources.

"There will be no accidents. The plan is in place."

"Good." He was interrupted by an announcement made in Arabic and then English on the public-address system. "That is my flight."

Khabanni stood up, and Kadar sprang to his feet.

"Go with God," he said.

"As you will," the Iraqi said. They embraced, then Khabanni turned and walked back down the concourse.

Kadar watched him go for a minute, then looked down at the floor.

The canvas bag was still there, and he bent to retrieve it, then turned and left the terminal, limping slightly. The special shoes he had had made for himself while he was in Damascus helped a great deal.

He found his automobile in the parking lot, a well-used Land Rover painted gray and streaked with rust, and unlocked the door. Once he was inside, he untied the web strap of the pack and pulled the flap back.

Inside was a wadded roll of soiled clothing and a six-pack of Coca-Cola.

It was just what he had expected.

Blanchard was the first to reach the downed tent, followed closely by Masters.

The cacophony of yells and curses issuing in Arabic from beneath the collapsed canvas was louder than the ailing Humvee's engine had been in the admin tent.

The tent poles had tilted sideways, but still kept the heavy canvas from settling completely on the patients confined to cots inside.

Stepping carefully over a tent peg and its slack restraining rope, Blanchard hurried around the front of the tent to the other side. Here he found that two of the corner tie-downs had been sliced, allowing the tent to topple. The quarter-inch nylon ropes were parted with surgical precision.

He looked up to find out why.

Between the deflated tent and the adjoining ward was about eight feet of space, an alley interlaced with more of the tent guy ropes. Halfway down it, a figure was sprawled on the bare earth. Dressed in a white lab coat splashed in crimson, the woman was writhing about, moaning loudly. Standing above her was an Arabic man of indeterminate age. He was wearing gray linen pants and leather sandals.

He was also brandishing a scalpel.

His eyes looked half crazed to Blanchard. His teeth were bared in a near snarl. Backing slowly away from the woman on the ground, his head swiveled left and right. Looking for something. Enemies?

Faces from the ward tent on the left peered through the netting.

The Arab scurried backward, backed into a tent rope, and nearly tripped.

Melanie Masters reached Blanchard, screamed, and dashed past him for the downed nurse.

He stretched for her, got an arm around her waist, and hauled her off the ground, pulling her back against his chest.

"Let go of me!"

"Just hold up, Mel. We'll get to her."

"Damn you! She's hurt!"

"I know. Easy, now, or you'll join her."

"Blanchard!"

"A couple minutes, Mel. Hang on."

At the far end of the alley, Cale Perkins appeared and started toward the man with the blade.

Blanchard held up his left hand palm out, and Perkins stopped.

The rogue spun around, saw Perkins, and stumbled to a stop. His head was snapping back and forth, his eyes daring both Perkins and Blanchard. In his dark face the prominent whites of his eyes enhanced the impression of his madness.

Blanchard turned to put Masters down behind him, then stepped around a rope and walked forward.

One foot at a time.

He gained seven or eight feet before the Arab yelled something unintelligible and darted back toward Blanchard, his feet dancing, the scalpel waving back and forth. The sun flashed off the surgical steel in bright, hot glints.

Blanchard stopped.

Felt Masters's hand on his back as she bumped into him.

The Arab hesitated.

Perkins advanced a couple steps, murmuring. Ten feet away from the Arab.

Blanchard saw in his peripheral vision a black-stubbled head appear under the edge of the collapsed canvas on the right.

He kept his eyes glued to the Arab so as not to give away Armbruster's position. Using his left hand, he gestured, trying to get the man to understand that he was supposed to drop the blade.

The Arab's eyes followed his gesturing hand.

Dickie Armbruster moved slowly, trying to ease himself out from under the heavy canvas, up behind the Arab.

Blanchard took another step forward, moving within six feet of the Arab and next to the woman on the ground. Maria Godinez. She was a nurse from Costa Rica.

Keeping his eyes on the Arab, locking stares with him, he squatted to touch her shoulder. There was an ugly gash down her upper arm. Blood oozed from it.

"Hold on, Maria."

Masters reached around him and clamped her hands on the wound. The blood seeped between her fingers.

Blanchard stood up and stepped over Godinez.

Perkins was now aware of Armbruster. He said something in Kentuckian, and the Arab spun around toward him, leaped toward him.

Blanchard jumped a rope.

The Arab rotated and lashed out with the scalpel. Blanchard went sideways, sucking his stomach in as the blade flashed past.

Dickie Armbruster grabbed the man's ankles with both of his big hands and jerked upward.

The son of a bitch went down on his face, screaming.

And Blanchard landed with both of his knees on the man's left shoulder trying to pin down the arm. It continued to flail about, the hand still gripping the scalpel. He reached out, aiming to capture the wrist. Armbruster scrambled out from under the canvas, holding the man's legs down. Perkins hit the ground on the other side, grabbing the man's right arm.

Blanchard got a firm grasp on the wrist, twisting it until he dropped the blade.

"Jesus Christ!" Masters yelled from behind him. "Don't kill him!"

Masters and Dr. Chao closed the gash on Godinez's arm with fifty-four stitches after Chao repaired several arteries and veins. Godinez complained of numbness in her hand, and Masters was afraid there might be nerve damage. They wouldn't know for a while, not until the local wore off and some knitting took place.

Godinez was trying to be brave, but it was difficult when it was your own skin that was laid open.

"You vill be just perfect, very soon again," Chao told her. A native of Bangkok, Chao had learned his English from a German while in medical school, and he vee'd his "double-ewes." He was slight, barely larger than Masters, with a smooth face and thick black hair that tumbled low on his forehead. He was a meticulous man and doctor, and his devotion to perfection was evident in the fine knots he tied in his stitches.

Godinez was in her forties, thin and angular, with perfect skin, and she was a very capable nurse. There were tear tracks in the dust on her face.

"I left San Jose because it was dangerous," she said, trying to smile.

"What happened, Maria?" Masters asked.

"I . . . we were in the clinic, the front exam room? I think the man is syphilitic. I told him he would have to undress—that is to say, Roberto told him."

In addition to his computer technician role, Roberto Irsay was one of the interpreters.

"And then he just went berserk. He took the scalpel from the tray and threw the tray. He kicked Roberto and grabbed my arm. I think he wanted a truck; he was dragging me toward one when I tried to get away. That was when he . . ."

"I know," Masters said. "The best part is you get a couple weeks of rest. Unless you want to go home?"

"Oh, no! There is so much . . ."

"We'll see. For now, you rest."

Masters patted her on the shoulder, then pushed the curtain aside and stepped out of the room. The clinic, a standard tent, was subdivided into five areas by curtains, and she went down the narrow corridor, dodging the tent poles, to the entry space. Two paramedics were greeting the line of people, doing initial screenings. Outside, under the flap raised as a sunshade, two others were taking names and medical histories. In most cases the histories were extremely short or nonexistent. Some of these poor people had never seen a doctor before.

Edging past the line, she went outside and saw that Dickie Armbruster had five people repairing the downed ward tent. Several nurses were inside, calming the patients. She walked over and caught Armbruster's eye.

"How's she doing?" Armbruster asked as he helped others tugging on a tent rope. Another man was tying new rope to the grommet in the canvas.

"She'll be okay, Dickie. A few stitches, and there'll be a scar."

"That's too damned bloody bad. Oughta kill the bastard."

"Where is he?"

"I handcuffed him to a Humvee bumper."

"I should take a look—"

"You stay away from him, Doctor. My orders." Armbruster gave her a stern look.

"But, he—"

"I've got more handcuffs. I need to use a set on you?"

She let her shoulders slump. "No."

"We got hold of the Palestinian coppers. They're coming out to get him. If he's sick or something, they can deal with it. Let him be, Doctor."

She walked on toward the admin tent and went inside. Only the fan was operating; no one else was there. She took advantage of the privacy to dial her home number in Chicago. This time, the answering machine was on.

"This is Greg. If it's personal, leave a message. Otherwise, call my office."

At the beep she said, "Greg, it's Melanie. Call me as soon as you get a chance. It doesn't matter what time."

She replaced the phone and looked at the computer, which was still on. She didn't feel like researching toxic epidermal necrolysis at the moment, so she shut it off. Paulo had moved the truck out of the back of the tent, and the netting was still raised, so she went out the back and crossed toward her tent. She saw Blanchard and Delray talking to the driver of a truck— Del Cameron—that had just pulled in on the other side of the hospital. They were disconnecting a water trailer from the rear hitch.

The twelve women of the PMAT shared one tent, and when she entered, she found only Jillian Weiss present. She was flopped on her stomach on the steel-framed cot writing a letter. Underneath the cot a small radio played Israeli music.

She looked up, "How's Maria?"

Masters related the progress report and then went to the end corner of the tent to her space. Since there were only twelve of them, they each were allotted a fair-sized area, but there wasn't much to put in it. Her bed, with its mosquito netting and frame, her footlocker, her upright locker, and a camp stool didn't take up much room. Privacy was an ideal; there were no dividing curtains. The outside walls were down because women came off shifts, or went on them, all through the day and were constantly in and out to change clothes. A large fan at each end of the tent kept the warm air circulating, but the place still smelled of trapped heat. The air was heavy.

The men were less modest. They kept the sides of their tents rolled up in the interest of staying cool, and when they changed clothes, they didn't give a damn who watched them. Sam Delray said it certainly wasn't his problem if someone wanted to peep.

She should take a shower. Her skin felt gritty, like the sand on the floor.

But later. Now, she was just tired.

She thumped her hand against the sheet on the mattress. A fine cloud of dust rose around her hand. Not caring, she turned around and sat, then used her toes to lever off her Reeboks without untying them. Picking up the pillow, she held it over the floor and batted it several times to clear it of dust, then settled back on the bed and stared up at the mosquito netting overhead.

The situation with Greg wasn't going to get any better, she thought. He had been adamantly opposed to her taking a leave of absence from her practice, which she shared with four others, and spending a year on the WHO team. The year before, he had been made a full partner in his law firm, Justin, Swearingen, Halcourt, Noxon, Trickle, & Masters, and he was determined to enlarge his social and public personas, and therefore, his business. Greg specialized in corporate affairs and didn't spend much time, if any, in a courtroom. A recent encounter came to mind:

"We've got to do more in our community, Melanie. Give back a little."

"Feeling guilty, are you, Greg? Give your money to charity. Why don't you start with UNESCO."

"You're feeling guilty, I think. You've made your million bucks, and now you think you've got to run off to some Third World country and do all this humanitarian shit to ease your conscience."

"That's bullshit. I know you don't do anything without thinking of personal advantage, but I don't think there's anything wrong with helping others."

"Not a good time, Melanie. I need you with me. Here. And now. You're going to have to put this off for a little while."

"Why? So you can get your picture taken at the fund-raisers with your cute little doctor on your arm? What are you after, Greg? The wild world of politics?"

"Now, Melanie—"

"That's it, isn't it? You've got aspirations. Give it up, Greg. You're a wonderful lawyer, but I don't think you're cut out to be a mayor. Or is it a House seat? Senate?"

"That's nonsense! The firm has simply decided that we need more public exposure. Everyone's going to—"

"Lester Justin at the Fall Ball? He's so old, he'll make his grand entrance on a walker."

"I don't know what your problem is, Melanie, or why you want to get away from me, but I think this whole damned WHO thing is just an excuse—"

"Kindly go to hell, Greg. Would you do that?"

With Greg, all arguments were unwinnable. And if he even perceived that he might have lost, he found little ways to get back at her. He refused to admit that he had political goals, but she could see no other reason for his sudden desire to be seen in the limelight of other luminaries.

To be honest, it wasn't all Greg. She was dissatisfied for some reason, and she sniped at him as much as he did at her. Masters thought she wanted space and time, but she wasn't certain why. She still loved him deeply, but it seemed as if he had always been there, directing her.

So, she had told him she was going, but that she'd fly back every month or six weeks to be with him. Even go to some of his exalted social gatherings.

But she hadn't made it back. There was too much work to be done. And after she had missed the first two planned weekend trips, he had stopped calling her. When she called him, he was distant with her. Yes or no response, usually yes, though he obviously didn't mean it. He had to prove to her that it was his way, or no other.

Or was this humanitarian getaway all an excuse on her part?

The little injustices built up over the years, and she suppressed many of them.

He hadn't wanted children; they interfered with careers.

She had tried to let an accident happen, abandoning her diaphragm, but it didn't. And only by chance (since she was part of the medical community) had she learned that Greg had gotten a vasectomy, forging her name to the spousal waiver. Enraged, she had confronted him with the issue, but he had shrugged it off. What's done is done.

And now, he wasn't talking to her. That could be a result of his stubbornness, or his determination to prove to her that she was unnecessary. It had happened that way in the past. Until he found a need for her.

The back part of her mind wanted to raise an image, that of Greg meeting some charming damsel at one of his soirees, but she kept pushing it back into its place.

Masters was about to sit up, pull on her running shoes, and go try the phone again when she heard feet shuffling outside the tent.

Blanchard's voice: "If anyone's undressed, close your eyes. I'm coming in."

He pushed through the flap, said hello to Weiss, and walked to the back of the tent. He was carrying two glasses of amber liquid that tinkled from the ice cubes.

Using his foot, he pushed her camp stool over by the bed, then sat on it. He handed her one of the glasses.

"Medicinal J&B, Mel."

She sat up. "What time is it?"

"Nearly five. If we had a ship handy, we'd have seen the sun go over the yardarm."

"And you think I need the medicine?"

"You've had a long couple weeks, Mel. Today's events didn't help."

She sat back a little and studied him. Most of the women found him desirable, she knew, from the discussions that took place in the tent. He *was* handsome in a beat-up sort of way. The short haircut—mostly steel gray—didn't help much, but the electric-blue eyes were direct and unwavering. His lips were thin, set in a straight line that he broke often with a smile, but sometimes the smile wasn't carried through with the eyes. The nose had been broken once and set slightly crooked. It was narrow with a slight bump. Deep lines were etched at the corners of his eyes and from the nostrils to the outside limits of his mouth. Right now, there was a stubble of dark whiskers covering his jaw. His shoulders were John Wayne broad, tapering through the torso to narrow hips. He tried to find humor in many situations, using it to ease tempers or soften the impact of some of the dreadful conditions they faced. There was, she thought, a certain degree of arrogance. Too often, he thought he knew what was best for all of them, and she tired rapidly of being told what to do, and when.

She could see why the other women found him attractive. On the other hand, they didn't have a firm understanding of his attitude.

"How'd you get the scar?" she asked.

"This?" He ran the four fingers of his left hand along the puckered white line that traced his left jawbone from below the ear to the side of his chin. "Ka-Bar."

"Ka-Bar?"

"That's a military knife. It was my own, but this go . . . this Viet had taken it off me. He was going to peel my face for me."

Jesus, she thought.

"I wouldn't think you'd allow that," she said, firmly believing it.

"At the time, they had my arms tied behind my back. At

the elbows. But you're right, I wasn't in favor of nonelective surgery. So I took my knife back.''

"How?''

"You really don't want to know, Mel. Anyway, I came in here to tell you two things. One, we're putting up another ward tent.''

"Good. We were getting crowded.''

"Sam's going to shuffle the duty chart if it turns out we need more coverage. Two, you and I are going to Jerusalem tomorrow.''

"Tomorrow? I can't—''

"You don't get a choice, Mel. I've got a couple errands to run, but you're taking the day off. I'll drop you off somewhere, then pick you up later.''

Masters was instantly irate. "You can't just—''

"Yes, I can. I'm responsible for *all* of the personnel. You haven't taken any of your scheduled off-days in the last two months. I—''

"You haven't, either!'' She may have been yelling.

"Doesn't matter. You've been getting a little testy here, and—''

"Testy! I'll testy you, you son of a bitch!''

Masters shot off the bed, standing in front of him. Blanchard remained where he was, looking up at her. A little grin on his damned face.

"You haven't got the faintest damned clue about me or my capabilities! If anyone decides what or when I . . .''

She ran down as he sat there looking at her.

When she stopped talking, he said, "Trust me on this, Mel. I've got a few years of experience watching people. You need a break. Hell, you need a couple weeks, but all I'm forcing on you is one day.''

"What time are you leaving?''

"Seven.''

"I'll wave goodbye to you.''

"No, you won't.'' He stood up, raised his glass in toast, then walked out.

Masters collapsed on the edge of the bed, then saw she was still holding her glass. And hadn't even spilled any of it.

She took a long sip, then noticed Weiss watching her.
"What are you looking at?"
"He's right, Melanie."
"Go to hell."
She downed the rest of the drink.
The arrogant bastard!

Jacob Talman dismissed his two assistants early at five o'clock, telling both of the young women it was a reward for a profitable day. And that was true. Their bookings to date were running about twelve percent ahead of the previous year's.

On occasion Talman considered the possibility of seeking early retirement, then purchasing the agency from Shin Bet. He could make a comfortable living. A comfortable, boring living. He would travel extensively in search of excitement.

Like any Jewish business, the travel bureau was closed on Friday afternoons and Saturdays. The agency did not normally close its doors until six o'clock on other weekdays in the attempt to capture those workers in the city who left their workplaces at four o'clock or five, so he spent some time cleaning and rearranging brochures while he marked time. He had covered two of the three computer terminals, and was sitting at the third when an older woman came in.

As it turned out, she really wanted to go to Rome for a week, and he was tapping away at the computer with his client seated on the far side of the desk when another woman entered. The bell over the door tinkled.

"Hello. I will be right with you."
"There is no hurry," she said and moved to the far wall to study the posters stapled there.
"A rental car?" he asked his Rome-bound client.
"I think not."
"Very well."
He keyed the print key and told her the amount. While she wrote out a check, Talman got up and went to the printer to collect the airline ticket and hotel reservations. There was also a multiple-copy itinerary. He ripped off his copies, tossed them

in the file box, and folded the rest into an envelope that advertised the agency, Golden Horizons.

The woman left, the bell tinkling again, and he turned to the next customer.

"How may I help you?" He spoke in Hebrew.

"You have no one else here?"

"No."

"I am Satin."

"Ah, yes. Satin. Please have a seat. I am to tell you, 'Trump Card.' "

She smiled. She had a pretty smile, very nice teeth. Dark hair cut short that curled around a pixie face. She wore a linen suit of pale yellow with the jacket cut short at her waist. A study in, not beauty, but in prettiness. Very deadly, he assumed.

He had met with three men earlier in the day, and none of them offered the enticement of Satin. Unfortunately, his service believed in compartmentalization. Rarely did he learn the true lives of many with whom he worked.

She sat on the opposite side of the desk, and Talman again took his chair.

"Do you have a code name for me?" he asked.

"Panther," she said. She had a small imperfection in the curvature of her upper lip which he found intriguing.

"From now on, it will be 'Comet,' and you will be 'Venus.' Is that clear?"

She nodded.

He had taken it upon himself to change the identification codes for his operation. There was no telling how many others knew of the code names Avidar had given him. He gave her a telephone number and asked her to repeat it back to him.

"That is the number where I can be reached. It is my separate line in the office, as well as a second line in my apartment. The telephones do not ring, but blink. If I do not answer, you may leave a cryptic message. Should you not be able to reach me, and you have urgent news, use your encrypted radio channel to call the communications section, and they will probably know where to find me."

"I understand."

"Now, you. Your cover?"

"I am known as Leila Salameh, and I own a garden restaurant along the main street in Jericho."

"This is true?" He would not have believed it.

"Of course not. The real Leila disappeared years ago—who knows where? In her place, I have claimed the inheritance of her father, the cafe."

"That is very good," Talman said. "And business?"

"Business is terrible. If it doesn't pick up soon, I shall lose my cover."

She was being subsidized, of course, by Shin Bet, but a business needed traffic so others would not wonder why it stayed in operation.

"We will send tourists your way."

"That would be most helpful." Again, she smiled.

"Now, the housekeeping details aside, let me explain the mission."

He took fifteen minutes to pass on the gist of his charge from Levi Avidar. The woman did not give much away, but a slight alteration in the set of her mouth led him to the conclusion that she found the assignment just as distasteful as he did.

"Are there any questions?"

"This, ah . . . no."

"Come . . . Leila. Let us not have misgivings or doubts."

She no longer smiled. "It is as if we work for the Palestinians."

"My very comment! I was assured by highest authority that the goals merely happen to coincide for a few months."

She slumped back in her chair, her eyes tracking his own, looking for reassurance, no doubt. Talman felt compelled to keep his eyes on her own for that reason, when he really would have liked to explore the thrust of her breasts.

"To have doubts," she said, "is not very professional . . . I am sorry."

"These are confusing times, and we must do the best that we can to cope with them. Have you heard of any threatened actions?"

"No. But there is one thing."

He raised an eyebrow.

"Do you know of Ibrahim Kadar?"

"A misbegotten son of Iziddin al-Qassam. I think he was once a Palestinian freedom fighter based in Lebanon. I know of him." He mentally reviewed a file of the man. It was not an attractive one. "And there is something else. Was it a falling-out with Iziddin al-Qassam? I think yes."

"In the last several weeks, he has been seen frequently in Jericho. I have seen him twice, one time in my cafe."

"This is interesting, Leila. I wonder what has caused him to surface?"

"As I understand it, he is wanted for questioning in the bus attack in Haifa two years ago."

"That is correct, he was. The attack was attributed to Iziddin al-Qassam, however, and the search for Kadar was abandoned since he was no longer with them. My thought was that he had left the country, rather than be mistakenly arrested along with his former comrades."

Or what else? Something else.

"Or, now that I think of it, he may have become associated with the Sword of God," Talman continued.

She said, "Khalid Badr is a member of that group . . . a lieutenant to Sapir."

"But Sapir is dead. Or out."

"That has not been in any intelligence digest . . . unless I missed it."

"It is recent information, not yet confirmed."

"Badr is in Jericho."

"Then perhaps the Sword of God is there, as well. Let us see what else we learn of Badr and Kadar."

"Of course," she told him. "Is there anything else?"

"Not at the moment. Look, I have to lock up, then we could go to dinner."

Was that a lightning strike in the dark eyes? One of interest, or of fear?

"I think," she said, "the general would not approve."

What do generals know?

"I think you are probably correct," he agreed reluctantly.

"Then, I will pass."

Satin/Venus/Leila rose effortlessly from her chair and passed through the front door.

The bell tinkled.

She disappeared into the crowd streaming along the thoroughfare, and Talman felt the loss.

It was just as well.

In his line of work, those who became his friends frequently became deceased.

And then he had to wear the uniform.

Four

Melanie Masters rose from her bed just before five in the morning. In the dark, she felt her way to her hanging locker, opened the door, and found a terry-cloth robe. She shrugged into it, then bent over and retrieved her shower kit and rubber thongs from the bottom of the locker. Setting the thongs on the floor, she stepped into them and worked her toes around the plastic stem.

The sleepers in the tent created a strange buzz. Little chortles, long sighs, and Deidre Joliet. The French nurse, who could have been an advertisement for wholesome good looks, was a snorer. Deidre swore she didn't snore, but she had eleven roommates who testified that, when on her back, Joliet rattled like a tin can going down an alley. Masters was aware that Joliet now went to sleep on her stomach, but sometimes in the night, she rolled over, and like now, the whispering sound of the others was punctuated with an irregular "uhhhnnn-snort-uh-uh-uh-uh-huh."

Her eyes were accustomed enough to the dark to note, on her way out, that two of the beds were unoccupied. People on duty.

Outside the tent she looked around. The generator was chugging away over by the latrine. There was a light on in the admin tent and the clinic. Blanchard kept someone on the phones every night, and two of the medical staff were posted in the clinic to make routine passes through the wards. Dim lights shone from the three ward tents. Lights were also on in the showers. In the night, she saw a form trudging along the outer perimeter playing the beam of a flashlight one way, then the other. One of Blanchard's guards. He couldn't shake his military upbringing, though he said the patrols were only to keep down thefts.

He was overly conscious of security, she thought. None of the members of the unit were armed, but he insisted on posting a nightly guard with a portable radio.

Avoiding the clumps of weeds that sprouted haphazardly, Masters crossed the field to the primitive showers. Canvas walled and open to the sky, they were divided into male and female sections, and each section was composed of six shower-heads spaced over a plastic tarp on the ground. The earth was graded so that the water flowed over the tarp to the east and into a trench dug outside the wall. On the near side, plywood flooring was used beneath a long counter with three sinks and three mirrors hung on a wooden framework. Flexible garden hoses connected everything.

As she reached the structure, she heard a fitful humming from the men's side. Somebody was trying to get the tune to "Arrivederci, Roma," and missing badly.

She pushed through the flap and entered the floored side, which was lit by three 100-watt bulbs over the mirrors. Jillian Weiss was there, fully lathered beneath one of the showerheads. She had large, full breasts, a waspish waist, and flaring hips that Masters was quick to look away from.

Weiss said, "Good morning, Doctor."

"Morning, Jillian."

"That's Del Cameron singing. He's no Dean Martin."

"I noticed," she said, surprised that someone as young as Weiss even knew Martin's name. It was probably attributable to the English-language radio stations.

Masters placed her kit on the counter, then slipped out of

her robe and pajamas. She rummaged for her shaving cream, razor, and soap.

Masters was not self-conscious about her body. She was in good shape, maybe a trifle thin from the time in the desert and the long hours. She lacked a couple inches and a cup size in comparison to Weiss, but everything was still firmly in place, and not too shabby for a forty-year-old, she thought. She was, of course, her only feedback. Greg had ceased commenting several years ago.

Stepping off onto the plastic tarp, she chose the first shower, then turned and looked at the big clock on the wall. Blanchard had the showers operating at a gallon per minute, fed by an electric pump, and dispensed as a fine spray. Everyone was allotted five minutes of water time each day. She pulled the chain and felt the cool mist descend upon her. It wasn't heated water, and the stream wasn't heavy or fast enough, but it got her wet and she released the chain. She bent over to foam her legs and began to shave them quickly.

"Jillian, I want to apologize for snapping at you last night."

"That's okay. There's been a lot of strain on everyone."

"It's not okay. The next time I get out of line, you tell me to go to hell."

"Deal. You going to Jerusalem today?"

"No. There's too much to be done."

She sensed an immediate disapproval from the young translator, but didn't look up to check on it. Finished with her legs, she set the shaving cream and razor aside and soaped her body.

Heard Weiss rinsing off.

"Oops. I think I went ten seconds over. Jack'll probably fine me or something."

"He's a dictator, but I don't think he'd go that far."

Masters regretted the comment as soon as she said it. She might not agree with everything Blanchard did, but it wasn't her place to make her editorial opinion public.

"He's probably got a video camera hidden, just to check on water consumption," Weiss said as she stepped up on the plywood and began to towel off.

Masters felt a chill run up her spine at the thought, and her hand froze. She checked beneath the counters for a lens. Silly.

Above were only the pipes hanging on a wooden frame, a few stars, the glow of dawn creeping from the east.

She finished soaping, then tugged again on the chain. This was the best part, a full four-and-a-half minutes of cool moisture running down her skin. She used her free hand to rub away the soap residue. She should wash her hair, but she had a rotation system going. Legs one time, hair another.

Weiss left.

Del Cameron was still crooning on the other side of the curtain, now into "Everybody Loves Somebody." She looked hard; the wall was eight feet high, no gaps.

She thought for a minute of saying to hell with Blanchard and running another five minutes of water, but this was an honor system, and when the second hand reached the twelve, she reluctantly released the chain.

Patting herself briskly with the towel, she dried off, then pulled her robe on. It took her ten minutes to cleanse her face, comb out her hair, apply a touch of lipstick. Did her face look gaunt? Her high cheekbones and narrow jaw gave her a lean appearance, but the weight loss seemed to exacerbate it. Her eyes appeared larger.

And why the hell was she even worried about it, out in the middle of the desert? She felt as if she were getting ready for a date. Ridiculous.

Back in the tent she found Emma Wachter and Tina Ambrosia up and digging out their shower kits. They all said good morning, sotto voce, so as not to awaken anyone else. She stopped by Maria Godinez's bed to check on her. Resting the back of her hand softly against Maria's forehead, she thought there might be a little fever.

"Emma, when Maria wakes up, check her temperature, would you?"

The German nodded. "Infection?"

"Maybe. We'll want to see where she is on penicillin shots." Masters already knew she was up-to-date on her tetanus.

"I'll take care of it, Doctor."

She went back to her area to pick out clothes for the day. Normally, just because they were so much easier in an unpredictable workday, she wore jeans and T-shirts. For some reason, today she selected a skirt-and-blouse combination. Pale green, with soft blue stripes running through the blouse. No panty hose, but she pulled on panties and slipped into a bra, then donned the rest. Found rubber-soled leather shoes that were a little smarter than running shoes, but still good for long days on her feet. After making her bed, she gathered all of her soiled clothing and shoved it into the laundry sack. She carried it outside and dropped it in front of the tent. Today, someone would make the laundry run to Jerusalem.

Breakfast was served from six until seven-thirty, and she saw people already gathering at the mess tent. Masters went over, but only for long enough to get herself a mug of coffee. She carried it with her to the second ward tent.

Polly Brooks, a Brit, was on duty, and together they made the rounds. Setting up the other tent had relieved the congestion, and some of the bunks in the most crowded ward had been moved to the new tent.

In this ward there were eighteen residents, all but one of them victims of cholera, now on the road to recovery. In the United States, where it almost never occurs, a single case of cholera, which can cause death within a day, invoked quarantines and reports to state health departments and the Centers for Disease Control. Here, they had run into twenty-one cases, reported them to the Israeli government in Jerusalem and to the Palestinian Authority in Gaza City, then quarantined the patients in a single tent. Despite an immediate program of rehydration with lactated Ringer's solution coupled with tetracycline in the attempt to build blood volume and increase body fluids, they had lost four patients. But after six days of quarantine, the seventeen survivors were doing well.

Two of them were children, both girls, one six years old and the other five. Though she didn't have an interpreter with her, she took a few extra minutes with both of them, as she always did. They looked so morose, so ill, but they tried hard to please her, taking turns with the crayons. Masters colored the hair of a little girl in the book yellow, then handed it to the first girl. She colored the dress blue and passed it on. They did this for several minutes, then Masters patted each of them on the shoulder and stood up. She knew she could look back in a little while, and they would have given up, too sick to care.

She checked the other charts and made a few recommendations to Brooks. None of the patients spoke English, and those who were awake smiled grimly at her.

In the last bed was her Arab from Kiryat Arba. His condition being what it was, she had elected to place him in the quarantined tent, away from the less serious patients. It didn't seem likely that he would contract cholera at this stage of recuperation for the other patients.

"He hasn't regained consciousness?"

"No, Doctor. The vitals seem to have stabilized some, though his blood pressure is still extremely low."

She pulled back the sheet covering the lower part of his torso, and in the poor light, bent over to examine the surface of his skin. The flaps she had made over the stumps of his legs were healing, though very slowly. The color was pink and almost healthy looking. That was the extent of positive sign. The pustules had been drained, but now appeared to be filling again. Several new ones were forming on the inside of his thighs. There was no marked improvement in any of the abdominal rashes.

"The right arm looks gangrenous," she said.

"Yes. I thought so, too," Brooks agreed.

"With the trauma he's suffered already, I don't want to perform another procedure right away. Let's keep a close watch on it."

She finished her coffee, then went to the next ward, the one that had collapsed yesterday. The cases here ranged from hysterectomies to appendectomies to gall bladders. They had one bypass patient. She was finished by seven-ten, and headed for the hospital to meet with Chao, Svenson, and Wilcox. Dean Wilcox was supposed to have had yesterday off, but had been pressed into service for some car accident.

She was halfway to the hospital when she heard her named called.

She turned to find Blanchard striding toward her. He was wearing khaki-colored slacks, a blue knit sport shirt, and highly polished brown Wellington boots.

"I've been looking for you."

"I'm right here."

"Let's go. I'm all loaded."

"Go? I'm not going anywhere."

"If I have to pick you up and carry you, you're still going with me."

"Back home, they call that kidnapping, Colonel."

"Here, we call it following orders. Doctor."

Those electric-blue eyes bored right into her, just begging for defiance.

"I can't—"

"I've already told Wilcox you're going to be gone. He said, 'good damned deal.' "

"Shit!"

"Right this way."

He tried to take her arm, but she shrugged away from it, and turned to follow him toward the car park next to the admin tent.

"I have to get my purse."

"I'll wait that long."

Ibrahim Kadar could have sent one of his underlings on this mission, but he took it upon himself. He believed in leading by example, and on any operation that involved high risk or great responsibility, he could be found in the forefront.

A simpler truth was that he did not totally trust his subordinates to accomplish a task of greater than normal complexity without fumbling in some manner. Four months ago, before he had assumed leadership, the Lebanese recruited by Ibn Sapir had closed a satchel containing a bundle of dynamite, then pressed the contact button, intending to arm it. He had depressed the wrong button and immediately blown himself up, practically on his own doorstep.

And the young radical, Hakkar. Kadar had entrusted him with the simplest of chores, and the idiot had immediately made an accident of it. Kadar could not be certain, but the accident may have been the result of divine intervention. It was possible, was it not? Many of the things that could not be fully explained in his life, Kadar had taken for messages. He might himself be a messenger.

In any event, Sapir had died, leaving the leadership open, and Kadar had wasted no time assuming the mantle.

Some events were foreordained, so perhaps Hakkar had served a purpose greater than he might have expected to serve on this earth.

Still, while Kadar was recognized widely for his leadership ability, his organization was small as yet, and he had not attracted a membership as skilled as he might have hoped. He was forced to work with a cadre of people who were extremely dedicated, but who were also lacking in basic arts.

A larger and grander organization would arise, he knew, and he continually thanked the one and only God in advance of its evolution. Especially when his brothers learned of his latest exploit, they would clamor at his door for admittance. It thrilled him just to think about it.

When he reached a bluff looking over the Wadi el Harir, he stopped the Land Rover and shut off the engine. From here, he could see into Jordan.

He opened the door, then got out and walked ten paces directly away from the car door. Stooping, he shoved the car key into the earth at the base of a struggling oleander. Smoothing the earth with his palm, he backed away. Someone from Hamas would eventually retrieve the car he had borrowed from them.

He pulled his backpack from the rear, checked the contents, then shrugged it over his thin shoulders. He bent to pick up a rock and used it to scuff up his new shoes, rubbing soil into the leather. It would not benefit him to have someone notice new shoes. Slamming the door shut, he turned to the south and started walking.

It was only a four-kilometer walk to the border, trailing down the wadi, and when he reached it, he found the border crossing manned. A short line of refugees from one cause, or land, or another, was assembled. There were only two vehicles, both trucks, and the people had to wait while inspections of the cargos were accomplished. The Syrian inspectors did not seem to care about the contents; the Jordanian border guards were more circumspect.

Private automobiles were a rarity here and therefore invited increased scrutiny of both the vehicle and the occupants. It was strict enough that Kadar had elected to leave the Land Rover behind and avoid the added attention.

The trucks roared off, and the line of people shuffled forward. When Kadar's turn came, he showed the Palestinian passport issued to him in Jericho. The name on the passport was not his own, though the picture was. The Palestinian Authority had rushed into their new responsibility for issuing passports, and their procedures were substantially flawed. Kadar owned seven passports. The Syrian waved him onward.

Crossing the narrow no-man's-land to the table beside the next gate, he showed his passport to the Jordanian inspector.

"You are coming from . . . ?"

"Damascus. I visited my mother."

"And going to?"

"I will return to Jericho."

"Show me what is in the bag."

Overcoming an urge to issue a long sigh, Kadar slipped the pack from his shoulders, laid it on the table, and unzipped the top. The inspector pawed around inside, finding only toilet articles, clothing, and, of course, Coca-Cola.

"It is the real thing?" he remarked, grinning with rotten teeth.

Like others in the line, Kadar was dressed as though he did not have a shekel in the world, but he did have soft drinks. After waiting a full minute, with no indication by the guard that he should proceed, Kadar said, "Would you like one?"

"There are two of us."

With reluctance, Kadar reached into his pack, and worked two cans from the plastic web that held them together. He handed them to the inspector.

"Be careful. Stay on the roads."

"I will."

He rezipped the pack, pulled it on, and stepped through the gate.

Not until he was a kilometer away, walking along the side of the road leading to Er Rafid, did he allow himself a self-congratulation for having the foresight to purchase a second six-pack of Coca-Cola.

It took him twenty-five minutes to reach the small village of Er Rafid. He continued walking through the village, and on the other side, turned to the east and walked up the slope. Within minutes he spotted the ramshackle hut with the beige Subaru parked beside it. The car was not conspicuous; it appeared as if it would barely run. It was, however, uncommon in Er Rafid.

Walking up to the door, he knocked rapidly.

After a short wait he heard the wooden bolt pulled, and the door opened to reveal a man in his sixties. He was deeply weathered, his face a series of protrusions.

"I have come for the car."

The man stared, as if the sun had affected his vision. "What is your name?"

"Kadar."

"Come inside."

Kadar stepped in to be greeted by an overpowering smell of cooking grease and goat meat. The man went to a wooden box standing on the floor next to the iron stove, rummaged about, and came back with a key.

"The money?"

Nodding, Kadar bent over and pulled up his pant leg. Wrapped around his ankle was a small pouch. It was where he carried his money. And his knife.

He came up with the knife.

The old man looked at it, uncomprehending for a moment. Then his eyes widened, he dropped the key, and tried to step backward.

Kadar followed, stepping on his left foot, and driving the five-inch, honed steel forward and up. It caught the man below the breastbone, slicing easily into flesh.

He twisted.

The man yelped in his sudden pain and threw both of his hands on Kadar's wrist. There was not much strength in his hands, Kadar noted, probably arthritic.

He twisted the knife some more.

It only took a minute, and there was very little blood.

The man's knees collapsed first, and he dropped to them. Kadar bent to follow him down, then had to tug hard to free the knife. The old man rolled sideways, crashing to the dirt floor in a heap.

"You may join our God, old man, a true martyr, and therefore, welcomed into Paradise with open arms."

Kadar squatted to wipe the blade and his hand on the man's shirt and then reinsert it in his ankle scabbard. He picked the key up from the floor and stood up.

Majib Khabanni had issued an order that Kadar was required to respect: He was to leave no evidence of his passage, no one to recognize him. The old man, a longtime adherent to the cause, had become a liability in his dotage.

Avoiding a trail of witnesses was easy enough, and it was cheaper, also.

He went outside and closed the door behind him. It might be days before anyone discovered the body. The old man had no relatives, and no friends in Er Rafid. He had only lived here for one month, at the order of Kadar's assistant, Abu el-Ziam.

Crossing to the Subaru, he unlocked the door, placed his pack inside, then got in. He pushed the key into the ignition slot.

As luck would have it, the car would not start.

Blanchard had driven northeast on dirt ruts until he intersected Highway 60, then fell into heavier traffic as they approached the city, which was only twenty kilometers from where he found pavement. The white Humvee attracted attention even though military-type vehicles were not uncommon on Israeli highways.

If there was one thing he missed, it was the wide open spaces of four-lane highways. Only in a few spots along the coast did Israel offer that luxury.

As usual, they were coated with dust by the time they reached asphalt, and Masters performed a little slap dance with her hands, trying to get it out of her clothes. She was wearing a skirt, an event that had happened only a couple times before, so Blanchard figured she'd intended to make the trip all along.

"This is under duress," she said.

"Riding with the laundry, you mean?"

The backseat and the cargo area were crammed with laundry bags. The smell, as C.W. McCall said in "Convoy," was "gettin' intense up here." They had the front windows cranked as far open as they could get them.

"Riding with you, I mean, Colonel."

"Doctor, I'm not Sir Galahad hauling a fair maiden off to a glass-and-redwood castle. I'm quite aware of that gold ring. But there *is* a dragon out there. It's called fatigue, and you need to get away from it for a while."

Glancing sideways, he saw her take a quick look at her left hand. Then she darted her eyes toward him and caught him looking.

"I think I can judge my limits very well." The old ice voice.

"Maybe. Or maybe you're less than objective. I've been evaluating people in my commands for a long time. We're going with my judgement."

He thought she was going to argue, but she rode silently for five klicks. Then she said, "You're not very compassionate, are you, Colonel?"

"Not like I used to be, no. Say, when I was ten or eleven years old."

"Why is that?"

"I've seen a lot of good people maimed and killed. Some of them were good friends. You learn to back off a little. Maintain some distance."

"Very professional," she chided.

"In my profession."

"Which you've abandoned."

He didn't respond to that.

They were in the southern outskirts of Jerusalem now. The city tried hard to be green and white, but Blanchard tended to see it primarily as ancient blocks of white Jerusalem stone piled one on another, on the very edge of crumbling. That might be expected since the city dated from the Paleolithic period. Layers and layers of civilization. Four hundred thousand people baking in the sun. And the farther they went, he was certain most of them were trying to use the streets, all of them in their new—

to them—automobiles. The ownership of private cars had been increasing steadily in the last few years. The traffic clumped together, starting and stopping amid yelled encouragement from other drivers.

"Why did you go to work for the UN?" she asked.

"They needed some managers, and I'm pretty good at it. Just like you're very good at what you do."

The attempt at a compliment passed right over her.

"Double-dipping?"

He grinned at her. "My salary is a buck a year. Plus I get health insurance. The pension plan isn't so hot."

He could tell she wasn't satisfied with the answer, but he wasn't going to elaborate. His job description didn't include the requirement to let liberal do-gooders investigate his mind. Personally, he viewed his new career as half humanitarian and half therapy. When Glenna died, he'd tried the bottle for a year, but didn't find solace there. He'd spent a year teaching university classes, trying to forget, to heal, and had ended up more or less numb. He had become quickly disenchanted with dealing in abstracts, and the UN seemed to offer a chance to use his skills in a more active way. He had only been with them a few months when this World Health gig came along.

A couple kilometers later, he made a right turn off the highway, now known as Herzog, and drove a few blocks until he reached an intersection with Ychernichovsky. Just around the corner he pulled up to the curb in front of the laundry with which he had contracted. The proprietor behind the counter, an Arab, immediately spotted the truck through the front window and came rushing out with two kids. It took them all of five minutes to unload the packed laundry bags from the truck. Then the kids spent another ten minutes loading the last week's shipment aboard. This was more easily packed. Everything was neatly packaged in white paper, with the owners' names written in black ink on the outside.

When he got back behind the wheel, Blanchard asked, "Where do you want me to drop you off?"

"You're actually going to dump me? What if I want to go with you?"

"You're here for R&R. I've got errands to run."

"I'll stick with you," she said.

"Shopping? Sight-seeing? What's your pleasure, Mel?"

"Jesus," she said with disgust. "Neither. Take me to Hebrew University."

He went on around the block and made his way back to Herzog. When he got a gap in the traffic, he pulled out onto the boulevard and stayed with it until he reached the major traffic circle, then turned north onto Hanassi Ben Zvi. After passing the Monastery of the Cross on his left, he turned left again onto Ruppin.

The street curved to the right, working into an oval back to the north, and on the right, inside the oval, were the major government buildings—the Knesset, the ministries of finance and the interior, the prime minister's office. Up the hill on the left, behind a large stadium, was the campus of Hebrew University. Blanchard drove on around to the northern end and parked in a no-parking zone.

"This all right?"

"This is fine."

"You have enough money?"

"Don't worry about me, Colonel."

She pushed open the door and got out.

"Where do I pick you up? What time?"

"I'll hitch."

"Come on, Melanie."

"Here. Five o'clock."

She went marching off, her back rigid, and melded with the throng of students crossing the campus. Her purse hung from a long strap over her right shoulder, and her right hand clutched it as she walked. From the back, she looked like any student. A more mature flare to her hips under the skirt. A little more anger in the stride.

He halfway wished she wasn't so mad at him all the time.

But, hell, she was married, anyway, right?

Blanchard shifted into low and pulled away from the curb just before the driver of a campus-security car was about to motion him on. He got away with a lot of traffic violations as a result of the WHO logo on the door. He went back the way he came, but crossed Hanassi Ben Zvi onto Ramban. Six blocks later, he headed east on Agron, and from there, it was a simple turn to the left to get him into the middle of Independence Park.

Parking places for Humvees were hard to come by, but he lucked out about halfway through the park and got the Hummer up against the curb. The Mamilla Pool, where he'd been told to meet his contact, was just across the lawn.

Sliding out of the truck, he locked it up. Wouldn't want anyone to steal the laundry. Or about fifty thousand dollars' worth of high-tech comm gear. The command vehicle was equiped with a hard top, though, so it was easier to secure.

He was an hour early. The meeting was set for nine-thirty, but Blanchard didn't fancy driving around town, wasting minutes. Instead, he found a stone bench near the corner of the pool, well entrenched in the shade of a eucalyptus tree. He settled back so he could keep an eye on the truck, crossed his arms, and relaxed. Both combat arenas and Glenna had taught him to take his relaxation where he could. The ability to unfocus his mind and force tension out of his muscles made him less reliant on the time off that he urged on everyone else.

In his hell-raising days, before he had met Glenna, Blanchard had devoted every liberty to drinking every drink, experiencing every pleasure, and fighting every fight. He and a Navy lieutenant off the *Bronson* had once tried to drink Angeles City in the Philippines dry. They hadn't succeeded, but they got into a helluva good fight with five Army chief warrants, and all seven of them ended up at the hospital at Subic Bay with contusions, bruises, and cuts.

Which is where he met Glenna Raymor. She was a Navy nurse who outranked him by a grade—he was a first lieutenant, and she was a Navy lieutenant, equivalent to a Marine captain. Beyond her seniority, she also refused to go out with him.

But Blanchard had always been relentless, some said stubborn, and his persistence led to a date, then a lifetime. If one could cram a lifetime into twenty-one short years. Before she succumbed to the cancer, Glenna had given him loyalty, happiness, a daughter, and a sense of moderation. He had learned to relax at a moment's notice without a bottle in hand. Scratching the one year in which he tried.

Glenda, now twenty-one, was a senior at the University of Colorado, and Blanchard worried about her and her future. It was about all he had to worry about, anymore, and he frequently savored the task.

He had his feet stretched out in front of him, idly watching the passers-by, when he heard footsteps approaching across the grass in back of him. He tensed his muscles a tad and checked his watch: 9:25 A.M.

He sat up straight.

The man came around the end of the bench.

"Mr. Blanchard?"

In the shadow of the tree, it was hard to see his eyes. They were set so deeply, they seemed black.

"Mr. Talman." He stood up and offered his hand.

Talman, who was much shorter than Blanchard, shook it gravely.

"Please, Mr. Blanchard, let us sit."

They did, halfway cocked on the bench so they could see one another. Talman's hand had been hard, revealing a strength that his clothing—a yellow shirt under a pea-green jacket—disguised.

"I appreciate your agreeing to meet me," Talman said.

"Levi said it was important."

That caught him by surprise. His mouth gaped open a little. "You know the general?"

"We once worked together on a joint strategy team. It was a long time ago, and to tell you the truth, I was a bit stunned when he called me personally."

"I see. I want to say something, but I must be delicate . . ."

"Not necessarily, Mr. Talman. I know what Levi does, and I assume you work for him."

Some of the tension went out of the guy's shoulders. He settled back a little farther against the backrest of the bench. "That should cover it, yes."

"So I know vaguely what you do. For the life of me, though, I can't figure how it might involve me."

"I have a particular task at the moment, Mr. Blanchard . . ."

"Jack."

"Jack. And I am Jacob. I am supposed to be looking for

anomalies in certain regions. And when I looked around, I found a very obvious one.''

"The medical-assistance team doesn't fit the regular pattern of life for the West Bank, right?''

"You are very quick, Colonel.''

"Ah. You looked me up.'' The team had been vetted by Israeli security before it arrived in-country, but he assumed Talman had dug a little deeper.

Talman smiled. "It is my job. All of the principals of your medical team were examined. And all, I must say, are above reproach.''

"I'm pretty proud of them, myself.''

Talman looked around, checking the proximity of possible eavesdroppers before saying, "When I asked General Avidar what I should do about you, he suggested this meeting. He never once mentioned that he knew you.''

"He's good at his profession.''

The Shin Bet operative went on to tell him about an apparent Israeli government concern for the Palestinian Authority. They wanted the Palestinians to qualify for some huge loan dependent upon the maintenance of peace in addition to alterations in the way the Authority did business. It was pretty fair criteria, Blanchard thought. He thought that Talman had reservations about it. Whether his reservations related to the Palestinians or to his assignment, Blanchard didn't know.

"So you're playing Marshal Dillon, right?''

"Dillon?''

"Peacekeeper.''

"I try. That raises my interest in your medical team. Do you understand why?''

"I'm afraid I do, Jacob. We would make a nice target. High profile. International incident. Lots of media coverage.''

"It would not be good for the Authority or the Israeli government.''

"Not to mention my doctors and nurses.''

"Exactly. It is my job to worry about you, about tour groups, about foreign students, and the like. I watch where you are and what persons might be interested in you. There are a number of groups that we are attempting to monitor.''

Talman gave him some names—Iziddin al-Qassam, the Front for Palestinian Liberation, the Sword of God, the Islamic Jihad, others.

"Do you have a solution?" Blanchard asked.

"My solution was denied by the general."

"That was to move us out of the country."

"At least for six weeks."

"So, instead, you want to ask me to increase our vigilance."

"It is weak, I know," Talman said. "But you are isolated from our protection, and if you are alert, perhaps anyone intent upon placing a bomb would be deterred."

"You know how many people we see a day? The docs and EMTs are averaging two hundred and fifty. They haven't got time to check every bag or package."

"I know."

"How about if you give me some hardware?"

"I could place a couple of people with your unit."

"Can you spare them?"

"No. But when I asked him, the general said that you were not to be armed."

"I have four people with previous military experience," Blanchard said.

"Yourself, Armbruster, Perkins, and Timnath."

"You have done your homework, haven't you?"

"I considered the possibilities, is all. But General—"

"Damned near every Arab in the country is carrying an automatic weapon, Jacob. Don't get me wrong, though. I don't want Mercy Base to become an armed camp. Hell, my medical people would go ape-shit if they saw an Armalite in the mess tent. I'll tell you that Armbruster and I have been, let's say, sensitive to the possibility of a terrorist attack. We've been keeping our eyes open. Being alert and being prepared are two different things, however, now that you've raised this special issue."

"But General—"

"Levi doesn't need to know."

In fact, Blanchard preferred leaving the military tactics to the military. He knew, though, that some flaming zealots didn't often make the distinction between civilian and military targets. Count the buses that had gone up in flames. That specter had always made him nervous. He knew how to be cautious for himself, but it was difficult to be cautious for fifty people, some of whom didn't know the meaning of the word. Melanie Masters came immediately to mind.

Talman looked around the park, looked down at his hands, looked back up at Blanchard. "I always follow orders, Jack, but I have been known to circumvent the regulations. I am frequently reminded of my lapses by my commanders."

Blanchard grinned at him. "You came prepared to do that, right?"

"After I studied your dossier, I felt a certain level of trust. You would do nothing to embarrass me?"

"Count on it. I don't want it, Jacob, but if some strange truck comes rolling into my camp, I'd feel better if I could respond with more than a dirty look."

"Come with me."

The two of them got up and strolled across the park, heading for the street. They walked on past the Hummer, crossed the street, and stopped beside a dented Toyota. Talman unlocked the trunk and retrieved a canvas duffel bag.

"You did not get this from me."

"I distinctly remember Yassir Arafat handing that to me," Blanchard said, taking the bag. It was heavy.

Talman gave him a business card: Golden Horizons Travel Agency.

"Besides my superiors, only you now know about my cover, Jack. I—"

"It stays with me."

"I would appreciate a telephone call, should you see or hear anything that seems suspicious. Use the second number."

"You can count on that, too. I'd much rather have you guys come riding to the rescue than have me cast as Marshal Dillon."

With his left hand, Blanchard fished one of his own cards from his shirt pocket and handed it to Talman. "We've got both satellite telecommunications and radio. The frequencies we monitor are on the card.''

''Very good, Jack. And one day, you must tell me about this Dillon.''

''I'll do that.''

Talman got in his car, started it, and drove away quickly.

Blanchard went back across the street and down to the Hummer. He opened the tailgate and shoved the bag under the clean laundry.

Masters finds out about this, she'll have my nuts.

He spent the afternoon on some personal errands. Bought himself some new shirts. Found a bottle of J&B Scotch to replenish his personal medicine chest. The Israelis weren't big on liquor—a fact reflected in their low alcohol-related traffic-accident rate, and it took him a while to hunt down the scotch. He found a nice handmade shawl for Glenda, had it wrapped in gift paper, then a cardboard box, and mailed it off to Boulder, Colorado.

Love, Dad.

He felt guilty about the little time he had spent with her in the last four years. She was already off to school when Glenna died, and then expressed shock when he retired from the Corps. ''What are you going to do, Dad?''

Drink. He hadn't been much of a father for the ten months it took to get to be bosom buddies with J&B.

The last year had been better. He'd been teaching at Metropolitan State College on the Auraria campus in Denver, and he and Glenda had gotten together at least monthly. She'd been relieved to know he was doing something respectable and had gotten over his love affair with scotch.

Then, he'd zapped her again by enlisting in the UN. It was still respectable, but the distances were greater.

By five o'clock he was parked in front of Hebrew University, again in the no-parking zone. Masters didn't show.

He guessed she was going to show him who was boss.

After fifteen minutes of waiting, he figured she'd actually hitchhiked home.

After twenty minutes she came sauntering down the walk. Backlit by the lowered sun, her face had a quality he found slightly memorable for some reason, as well as enticing. Sophia Loren. That was the reminder.

He reached across the seat, unlocked the passenger door, and shoved it open for her.

She had a little smile on her face, maybe looked more at ease. There was still a tension in her that he couldn't place, but he thought her day had gone pretty well.

"How you doing?" he asked.

"I'm fine," she said as she swung into the seat and closed the door. "Did you get your secret chores done?"

He pulled out into traffic. "I had a long meeting. I did some personal shopping. I found a present for my daughter and got it shipped off. She's going to be twenty-two next week."

"Oh. I didn't realize you had a daughter, Jack."

Jack? *There* was an easing of tension.

"She'll graduate from the University of Colorado at the end of the summer."

"I'll bet you're proud of her."

"I am."

At Hanassi Ben Zvi, he continued straight.

"You missed the turn."

"We're going to the Sheraton. On King George the Fifth Street."

"Whatever for?"

"Dinner. Comes with the R&R package."

She didn't complain. Maybe it was just hunger.

He had made reservations during the afternoon, and they were shown right into the dining room. The air-conditioning was going to kill his acclimation to the desert.

They were seated at a small table near the windows, and Blanchard ordered two glasses of white zinfandel and *mazza*.

"What's that?"

"Appetizers. A little salad, olives."

"All right. I'm starved." She fingered the linen of the table-cloth. "It's nice to sit down to something that isn't plastic."

The lighting was subdued, and Blanchard noticed that Masters's face seemed to glow a little. Probably all that accumulated heat from the desert. Her hair framed her face nicely. Little glints of honey and gold.

The hors d'oeuvres arrived, and they picked at them as they talked. He couldn't get over how much more comfortable she seemed to be with him.

"What did you do at the university?"

"Can you imagine that I just sat for a couple hours in the library and caught up on my international reading? I can't believe how far behind the news curve I've fallen. Then, I went to the cafeteria for lunch and talked with a bunch of kids all afternoon."

"Glad you enjoyed it."

"I *did* enjoy it." She sipped from her glass. "Thanks for pushing me out of the rut."

"Any time. You want me to order?"

"Please."

He flagged down the waiter and ordered beef kebab and *mahallebi* (a round grain rice with attar of roses, sugar, and nuts) for the two of them.

While they ate, she told him more about the students with whom she had spent the afternoon—their goals and their concerns. He devoted his attention. She seemed to appreciate talking about something unrelated to medical crises. After dinner he ordered cappuccino.

"What's she going to do?"

"She?"

"Your daughter."

"Glenda. Med school. How about that? She's accepted to CU Med, and all I have to do is come up with the bucks."

"You're going to do that on a dollar a year and a Marine pension?"

"I'll manage." He grinned. He had set aside most of the proceeds of Glenna's insurance policy to cover the exorbitant costs of medical school.

"What about your wife? Do you mind my asking?"

"Glenna died three years ago. A little more than that."

"Oh. I'm sorry, Jack."

"Cervical cancer. It wasn't easy."

She understood, of course. "That's a shame."

"I thought so, too." He wanted off the subject. "Your husband, what's he do?"

DARK MORNING   87

Even though he already knew, from her personnel file.
"Lawyer. And a wannabe-mayor or governor or something."
She sounded bitter.
And not ready to talk about it.
"Let's go," she said. "Back to the job."

Five

Ibrahim Kadar did not understand the first thing about automobiles. They were simply transportation, designed to assist him in his endeavors.

He had realized immediately, though, that the Subaru was a tremendous liability parked next to the house with the body in it. With the car there, someone would investigate. Still, he almost left it, walking down the slope to the highway.

And then he became aware that it *was* a slope. It was not much of one, perhaps ten or fifteen degrees. Possibly, it would be enough. He went back to the house, went inside, and searched until he found a canteen of water. He took that out to put in the car. He leaned inside to shift the transmission to neutral, then canted the wheel to the left and began pushing it in reverse. It did not want to move at first, then began rolling backward, turning in a broad circle. He shoved as hard as he could, and as it turned back into the hill again, it slowed and stopped, perpendicular to the grade.

But now it was almost aimed down the slope. He turned the steering wheel to the right, and with the driver's door held open, again began to push. It did not want to budge. He remembered instructors in the training camps who were as stubborn, and he redoubled his effort, felt his shoulders pumping with blood, his knees begging to give way, his face reddening with the strain.

And it moved a few centimeters. Then a few more. As it picked up speed, he reached inside to straighten the steering wheel, and it fell into line with the ruts of the track to the highway. The Subaru did not gather very much momentum. When it was going as fast as he as thought it might, he leaped into the seat, almost falling to the earth.

He pushed the clutch in, slapped the gear into first, then released the clutch.

The wheels grabbed at earth, and the car nearly slid to a stop. He quickly pushed the clutch down again.

He remembered the ignition and turned the key.

Then he let the clutch out.

The car bucked, the engine coughed into life, died, caught again. He pumped the accelerator pedal, trying to keep the engine running.

He clutched again when it sounded as if it would keep going.

Coasting slowly down the hill, he worked the accelerator, but the engine kept misfiring. Two little boys playing in a yard looked up with interest as he went by. He floored the accelerator pedal as he rolled onto the highway, turning right, then let the clutch out slowly. There was a screech of some kind, but it kept running. It took him nearly ten minutes to work it up to fifth gear, and the most he could get out of it was forty-five kilometers per hour.

The old man had sold him junk. He deserved the payment he received.

He wanted to stay on secondary roads, and with the car running the way it did, felt it was just as well. He passed nervously through Irbid, afraid of stalling in the traffic, but managed to work through the narrow streets and head south on Route 23. In the late afternoon, though, there was too much traffic, primarily trucks carrying goods, honking at him because he drove so slowly, and so, when he reached the crest of a hill, he pulled to the side of the road and shut off the engine. Locking the doors, he crawled into the backseat. He used small amounts of water from the canteen to wash his hands, face, and feet before saying his prayers, then went to sleep.

Awakening just after midnight, he had found only one set of taillights disappearing across the desert ahead of him. This time, the car almost started with the ignition switch, but then the battery gave up its ghost again. And once again, he got it running raggedly by coasting down the hill.

Fifteen kilometers later, he made a decision to stay on the road for Ajlun, which would eventually put him on interregional roads with more traffic, instead of taking a fork for the lesser traveled highways. Still, the night took away some of the drivers, so he had assumed he would not be noticed.

Trying to get through Ajlun, however, he saw for the first time that the old man had outsmarted him once again. The gas-gauge needle was on empty. Of course, there were no gasoline stations open.

He could not shut off the engine for fear it would not start again, and he could not find a suitable grade on which to park. He drove through the narrow streets, looking into the shadows and the darkness next to sleeping houses. Unfortunately, the only suitable target was a military vehicle parked outside a barracks.

He parked on a side street and delicately lifted his foot from the pedal. The Subaru idled wretchedly, but at least it continued to run. He set the emergency brake.

Taking his knife from his ankle sheath, Kadar slipped out of the car and ran back toward the barracks as quietly and swiftly as he could on the dirt street. The darkness protected him, but then it always did. He slowed to a walk as he neared the utility vehicle, and he kept his eyes on the windows and doors of the barracks, prepared to bolt if anyone appeared.

There were no movements, no light.

Walking up behind the truck, he found the gas can was secured with only a single webbing strap. He sliced it quickly, lifted the can out, and backed away.

It took five minutes to pour the gas into the Subaru's tank, then he threw the can in the back, engaged the transmission, and found the route out of the town.

Unfortunately, the gas gauge still read empty.

The gauge might be faulty, but he still didn't know how much gas he had.

It was a battle all the way. The engine struggled, vibrating badly. On uphill climbs the car barely made it, slowing to under ten kilometers per hour, cresting the hill, then picking up speed. He reached the main route, 45, which paralleled the Israeli-Jordanian border, at Kureiyima after three o'clock in the morning and turned south. There was more traffic, most of it belonging to commercial trucks, and the old car stood out like a smashed thumb. Two military patrols passed him, one of them going in his own direction, and the soldiers eyed him speculatively as they went by.

Forty kilometers later, just after four in the morning, the car died finally on a level stretch of road. The battery was stronger, having charged itself, but only lasted through five attempts to restart the car. He got out and shoved it off the highway and locked it. Shouldering his pack, he hiked the short distance into the oasis of Shunat Nimrin. He was only seven kilometers from the border, and he immediately set out to the west. Once he was outside of the village, he left the road to say his morning prayers. When he was done, he drank one of his Coca-Colas. It was warm and sweet.

Back on the road more than a dozen eastbound vehicles passed him, but none slowed to offer assistance.

The sun was well over the horizon when he reached the Allenby Bridge over the Jordan River. The checkpoints allowed him to pass without hassle, and then he faced the last nine kilometers to Jericho. His long march made him appreciate his new shoes. He was fatigued, but thought his limp was less noticeable, and certainly, his foot did not hurt as much as it normally did on an extended trek.

The closer he got to the town, the more lush became the vegetation, a trademark of Jericho. It was nearly seven o'clock when he reached the town's border, and the Israeli border guard took one look at his passport and inside the backpack, then motioned him onward.

That insouciant attitude just cost you your life, Mr. Soldier, Kadar thought. The guard might have demanded a Coke, and Kadar might have given him the real one.

He continued walking into the town. Though he knew it dated back to 8000 B.C., Kadar had never given much attention to its history. It was simply an old oasis, with abundant freshwater springs that provided irrigation for bananas, oranges, and dates. Someone had told him that Herod the Great wintered in Jericho, but he knew little of Herod, nor cared. All of Kadar's intellectual intensity was focused upon the future. The past might guide him, but only through the teachings of the Koran.

The population of Jericho was static at seven thousand, comprised mostly of people who tended the fields and orchards or managed the small shops along the main street. Most of them were Arabs, and the town was practically the only one in which Kadar felt as if he belonged. It was the reason he had chosen it as his headquarters, moving the Sword of God from its storefront site in Jerusalem.

It took twenty minutes to reach the house, two blocks from the main street, and he pushed the door open without announcing himself. It was his house, after all.

And it was occupied by five people, including himself. Oma Kassim was making bread at the stove in the small kitchen off the main room. Khalid Badr was stretched out on a ragged old sofa, his eyes closed as he dreamed of a new world. Badr had visions, many of them quite intricate, and all of them mind numbing when one was forced to listen to his interpretations of them.

Abu el-Ziam and Omar Heusseni sat at the round table, drinking thick coffee.

El-Ziam leaped up as Kadar barged in, snatching up a Kalashnikov assault rifle as he did. He let its muzzle sag to the floor when he recognized Kadar.

"Ah! Ibrahim! You are back."

"Without thanks to the rotten automobile. I had to walk forty kilometers."

Kadar exaggerated the distance to emphasize his misfortune.

"That cannot be. The automobile was running perfectly when the old man left."

"Well, it was not running perfectly when I found it."

"I told the old man to remove two of the spark-plug wires, so no one could steal it. You replaced them?"

Kadar would not know a spark-plug wire from an asp, but he said, "Of course."

"I cannot understand it."

"Nor I," Kadar said, approaching the table to place his backpack on it. He unzipped it and removed the six-pack.

"That is it?" Badr asked.

"Yes. That is the downfall of Zionism, and the recovery of Jerusalem."

Blanchard didn't drive far. Just a quarter of a mile south of Mercy Base and down into a wadi. As soon as the camp disappeared from his mirror, he braked to a stop and shut off the engine.

"For a little exercise after breakfast," Dickie Armbruster said, "this is also a trifle disappointing."

"Hop out, guys."

Blanchard got out, went around to the back, and opened the tailgate. He pulled the canvas duffel out and unzipped it as the three men gathered around him. Reaching inside, he pulled out the first weapon. It was wrapped in an oily cloth, and when he peeled that away, he found an Uzi submachine gun. The dark metal gleamed under its thin coating of oil.

"Holy shit!" Armbruster said.

"I don't believe," Cale Perkins said in that slow drawl, "that that thing is part of the Table of Organization and Equipment."

Bob Timnath asked, "That's an Uzi? I've never seen one up close."

Timnath was twenty-six years old and short. His records told Blanchard that he'd been an infantryman stationed for most of his term of enlistment at Fort Hood, Texas, except for a short stint in Kuwait during the Gulf War. He hadn't taken his paramedic training until a couple of years after he'd been discharged.

"That's the baby," Blanchard told him. "You think you could use it?"

"No sweat, Jack."

He handed the first one to Armbruster, who first checked to make certain the chamber was clear. In the bag he found a second Uzi and gave it to Timnath. The third one, he handed to Perkins.

"Now, Cale, I know you were a noncombatant, a corpsman, during your active-duty time. Would you feel uncomfortable hauling that around?"

Perkins looked it over carefully while he considered his answer.

Blanchard noted that Armbruster was also watching the nurse closely.

"I had weapons training, Jack. In basic. M-16. I'm not afraid of it, but hell, I don't know. Maybe it'd help if I knew why we had them."

Without identifying Talman, Blanchard explained his meeting the day before, and the possibility that the WHO unit might be a target of extremists.

"I've watched you and Dickie," Perkins said. "I know you've been nervous."

"I don't think I'll stop being jittery," Armbruster said. "But this might ease the nerves a little. What else have you got?"

Blanchard emptied the bag. There was a fourth Uzi, twenty loaded thirty-two-round magazines of nine-millimeter ammo, and two fragmentation grenades.

"Not much of an arsenal," Armbruster noted.

"Better than nothing, Dickie."

"True. We can't waste rounds on practice, though. Do I read it right when I say Masters doesn't know about this?"

"That's correct. If everything goes well, she'll never learn about it."

"So this's just a kinda stopgap measure?" Perkins asked.

"I don't want to use them, much less see them, unless it's necessary, Cale."

"Under those conditions, I don't have a problem, Jack."

"Good. Dickie, Bob?"

Armbruster and Timnath didn't have problems, either.

"All right, then. What we want to do is spot these around the camp in some handy places where they won't be found, but where the four of us will be able to get at them in an emergency. Ideas?"

"One in the Hummer, here," Armbruster said. "I can fashion some clips out of coat hangers, hang it under the driver's seat."

"The autoclave in the hospital," Perkins suggested. "It rests on a little aluminum cart that has some shelves on it. But underneath the bottom shelf, there's a four-inch-deep space. I can work up a tape arrangement.''

"Good. And I'm going to put one in the personnel file box in the admin tent. Under 'U.' No one but Sam and I ever look in those files.''

"The mess tent?'' Timnath asked. ''The table with the beverage dispensers?''

"I'll take a look at that and get back to you all,'' Blanchard said. ''Not a word of this to anyone, now.''

"You are going to say something to the others about the threat, aren't you?'' Armbruster asked.

"Yeah, Dickie. I'll give a little speech about the need for increased awareness. But it's going to be up to the four of us to go the extra step if we need to do it.''

He thought that both Timnath and Perkins were happy that he'd felt he could rely on them. Armbruster naturally expected it.

"I suspect you've got some experience with the Uzi, Dickie.''

"I have played with them, yes.''

For forty minutes Armbruster gave them an accelerated course in the machine gun: how to disassemble, clean, and reassemble it. Armbruster tried to explain how the gun felt and reacted in operation.

A live practice session wasn't necessary, anyway, because Blanchard figured they'd never have to use them.

Masters was in the admin tent, updating charts, when Tina Ambrosia stepped inside and called to her. Ambrosia belied her name. She was a tall Spaniard, thick set, and blessed with a waterfall of ebony hair.

"The Arab boy, Doctor, he awakens.''

She rose from the director's chair. ''Is he talking, Tina?''

"Yes, but not English. Is not Spanish, either, so must be Arabic.''

"See if you can find Roberto or Jillian, will you?''

"Sí.''

She crossed the space to the ward tent and shoved the netting aside. Polly Brooks was bent over the boy, changing a dressing. Masters looked down on eyes that were wide open and flitting from side to side, perhaps not terrified, but confused. He moved his arms about listlessly, as if testing them for strength.

"Good morning, young man," she said. *"Sabah el-kher."*

He didn't react.

"He's not responding to bedside charm," Brooks said.

"Is he aware of the amputations?"

"Oh, yes. The first thing he tried to do was get up."

Masters empathized with the boy's pain and despair. To go to sleep one day and then to wake another without extremities had to be as traumatizing as it could get. He would have been aware of the epidermal deterioration for days before he slipped into unconsciousness, of course, and his apparent refusal to look at himself now suggested he recalled that condition all too clearly.

Brooks was wearing latex gloves as she worked, and Masters felt in her pocket for one of the half-dozen pairs she carried with her. She pulled them on, thereby attracting the boy's attention. He muttered something. There was no force behind the words, and she assumed the painkillers were having an effect on his speech.

She reached out.

"La!"

"No? I must. *Aiwa."*

His eyes reluctantly followed her as she explored his ravaged torso. There was no improvement that she could see. On the contrary, the deterioration of the epidermis was even more pronounced. More blistering and a spreading of the rash over a much larger area.

"Discharges?" she asked.

"Nothing to speak of. His kidneys are barely functioning, I think."

Taking his right hand, she lifted it and examined the arm. It was badly discolored and bloated to twice its normal size. He tried to tug his arm away from her.

"Not good, is it, Polly?"

"I don't think you can wait any longer."

Roberto Irsay arrived. An Argentinean from Buenos Aires, he was fluent in half a dozen languages, as well as being a top-notch computer programmer. Blanchard had selected support staff who had at least two skills to offer the team. He was shorter than Masters, with a soft Latino face that was smoothly handsome and crowned with a drooping forelock of dark hair. Almost painfully full of good humor, Irsay was the root of every practical joke that had occurred in the last half year.

Irsay went right to the head of the bed and said something in rapid-fire Arabic.

The patient didn't respond.

"We need his name first," Masters told him. "And put some gloves on, please."

She passed him a pair, which he quickly slipped on. Masters required that everyone—from nurses to orderlies to translators—wear gloves.

He chattered on to the patient, who seemed less than impressed that Irsay knew his language. His mind, she was certain, was on other matters.

The patient said something.

Irsay said, *"Ana mish fahmak.* I do not understand."

The patient gave up, though Irsay did not.

Even the small detail of a name took some cajoling on Irsay's part. After a few minutes, he said, "Nuri Hakkar."

"Where is he from?"

A battle of words.

"He will not say, Dr. Masters."

Well, medical and other histories would have to come later.

"Tell him that I must perform more surgery. His arm is gangrenous, and it must be amputated."

Irsay looked down at Hakkar, gulped, then translated.

Hakkar's eyes went to his arm, then to Masters. He shook his head violently, issuing a spate of slurred words.

"La! La!" A few more words tumbled from his gaping mouth.

"What did he say, Roberto?"

"He . . . says that . . . you are to . . . kill him."

"That will not happen. We are trying to protect his life."

Irsay passed that on, then reported, "You cannot do so, he says. Something about the sword of God protecting him."

"I'm the one here and now."

More words.

"You are a woman, Doctor. You are not to touch him."

She had run into it before.

"Polly, will you see if Dr. Svenson is available?"

"Will do."

As soon as Brooks turned away, Hakkar jerked his hand free of Masters's grip, reached across his body, and yanked the IV feed from his left arm. He tried to roll sideways, off the bed. Oxygen and catheter tubes got in his way. A tray of bandages and disinfectant resting on the side of the bed clattered to the plywood floor. A bottle broke, and liquid spread quickly over the plywood floor.

Both Masters and Irsay reached down to restrain him. It wasn't difficult since his strength was all but nonexistent.

Hakkar twisted about, his eyes feverish and flashing. He was trying to yell.

"He keeps saying we must kill him," Irsay told her. "You cannot take his arm."

"We must, Roberto."

"I know. It is just . . . I don't know . . . inhumane."

A few minutes later, Brooks returned with Svenson.

Masters brought him up-to-date.

"Poor damned kid. Ask him if he'd feel better if I performed the surgery."

That didn't help, either. Hakkar's head flew back and forth. His twitching around in the bed had to be painful.

"Let's give him a sedative, Polly, then prep him," Masters said. "Tell Dr. Gordon we'll need him." Ben Gordon was one of the two anesthesiologists with the team.

She and Svenson stepped away from the bed. She was aware of the silent, accusing eyes of the other patients staring at them. Though none of them professed to understand spoken English, she understood that some of them might, and so they talked in hushed tones.

"I'll do it," Svenson said.

"You don't have to, Lars."

"Afterward, he might feel better if he knew it was me."

"All right. Thank you."

As soon as Hakkar had calmed down under the power of the sedative, she went back to the admin tent.

Blanchard and Delray were seated on either side of the administration desk, going over paperwork. Jillian Weiss was at a computer, updating her pharmaceutical inventory. In addition to serving as a translator, Weiss was also a pharmacist.

"How's our boy?" Blanchard asked. "I heard he came around."

"Not good." She brought a chair over and sat with them. "Lars is preparing to amputate his arm."

"Ah, jeez!" Delray said.

"He didn't want a woman operating on him."

Neither of them attempted a humorous comment on that, which, except for the circumstance, she might have expected. Blanchard had, in fact, been fairly mellow since yesterday. After their dinner at the Sheraton, she had almost begun to believe that she might have misjudged him. But then, he'd started making all of those nosey inquiries about Greg.

Still, after her day of doing nothing, she did feel a lessening of stress. It had probably been good for her.

"We know anything more about him?" Delray asked.

"I can put a name on his chart now. Nuri Hakkar. Not much else."

"That's all he gave you?" Blanchard asked.

"He said God would protect him."

"God, huh?"

"Actually, the sword of God. There's a contradiction there."

"He said, 'sword of God'?"

"That's right. Why?"

"There's a militant group called the Sword of God," Blanchard said. "Terrorists."

Christ! Blanchard's always looking for hidden agendas.

"I don't give a damn what his politics are, Colonel. I care about his life."

"I know you do, Mel. Hey, I'm not making any judgments."

"Anyway," Delray said, veering the topic in another direction, "Jack and I need to know when you want to move."

"You've found a site?"

"Dickie did, near the monastery at Mar Saba, where the Jewish and Arab settlements are located. That's where you and Lars saw some need."

Delray acknowledged the medical staff's priorities, and she appreciated it.

"I don't know, Sam. There's still an awful lot to be done here."

"Well, whenever you're ready . . ."

"But, damn it! There was a case of typhus up there. We need . . . I'll tell you what. Let's move half of the PMAT to Mar Saba. We can bring the rest along—"

"No," Blanchard said.

"What!"

"We're not splitting up the team. Sending an op-unit out on its own now and then is one thing. But we can't afford to divide our resources."

"The hell you say! I'm declaring a medical need, Colonel."

"And I'm declaring a security issue that outweighs you."

"Security, shit! You can't do that!"

"The hell I can't."

Furious, Masters turned back to Delray. "Sam—"

"He's right, Melanie."

Oh, fine. Now the two of them were ganging up on her.

"At lunch today, Mel," Blanchard said, "I'm going to pass on a warning I received from military intelligence."

"Military!"

"They seem to think that we're a prime target for terrorist activity. Something to create a highly publicized incident."

"That is utterly, fantastically ridiculous. This team has no political value."

"Political value doesn't seem to be required," Blanchard said.

He was deadly serious, she saw.

But then, so was she. "I'm going to call headquarters in Geneva."

"Go right ahead. I think the director general will side with me."

"We're the Palestine Medical Assistance Team, goddamn

it. Not the Jack Blanchard Memorial Fighting Unit. We're here
to help people.''

"And we will. But as we can get to them.''

Shit. I know damned well Geneva will accept his recommendation. All that can come out of this is my losing face. These
damned self-serving—

"Dr. Masters!''

She looked up to see Joliet at the tent entrance.

"There's a cardiovascular problem in—''

She sprang to her feet. "I'm coming.''

At least there were a few things she could do to relieve
suffering. If Blanchard weren't continually in her way, she
could do more.

And she didn't think she could wait until the end of the
year's tour to write him up in some report. There had to be a
way to get rid of him.

Just after noon Talman left Maidal Bani Fadil, and headed
south on Highway 458. He had been as far north as Jenin in
the morning, where he met with Jupiter. According to Jupiter,
little was happening in the northern section of the West Bank.

In Maidal Bani Fadil, Neptune reported that Ibrahim Kadar
had assumed the captaincy of the Sword of God.

"Where did you hear this?''

"From a long-established source. Arabic, and very reliable.''

"Do you know much about Kadar?''

"You know more. He is a product of the Lebanese camps,
very dedicated.''

"Zealous?''

"Absolutely.''

"How about a location?''

"Unknown.''

"What happened to Sapir?''

"Dead.''

"Killed?''

"Violently? I do not think so, though I have no evidence.
My source just said he died.''

Now, as he approached Highway 1, the major link between

Jerusalem and Amman, Jordan, Talman thought that he should have the analysts dig deeply into Kadar's background. It sounded as if the man intended to become a major player.

He turned left onto the highway, and accelerated to seventy kilometers per hour. He was going to be a little late. Twelve kilometers later, he passed the mosque of Nabi Musa, then the turnoff to the northbound Highway 90 to Jericho. He eased up on the pedal and lost speed and, a kilometer later, turned right onto a regional road that eventually led southward to the Dead Sea.

He drove a few hundred meters, until he saw a car drawn off the road beneath a copse of pine trees. It was a ten-year-old Chevrolet sedan. He did not know what Venus drove, but this appeared suitable to her cover as an Arab restaurant owner, so he drove in beside it.

She sat up behind the wheel as he parked. He looked around, but saw nothing of interest. One old woman walked by on the road, but her attention was devoted to the two goats she led on a tether. He got out, opened the Chevrolet's passenger door, and sat down. He left the door open for ventilation.

"Comet," she said.

"Hello, Leila. You did not have trouble getting away?"

"We are closed today."

Most Muslim restaurants closed on Fridays in Israel. He studied her for a moment. She was wearing a shapeless overblouse that nevertheless defined a shape that he found intriguing. Her eyes stayed with him, filled with curiosity.

"I have been meeting with each agent," he said.

"I thought you might have something special for me."

"As a matter of fact, I do. Ibrahim Kadar returned to Jericho this morning, from the east. He used a passport with a false name, but the guard recognized him."

"I was going to report that to you. I don't know where he came from."

"Perhaps he was in Jordan. I will check. Neptune," he said, not defining who Neptune was, "reports that Kadar is now the leader of the Sword of God."

"Is that true? I had not heard of it."

"It may or may not be true. I am hoping you can learn more."

"I will see. I have not seen Ibn Sapir for some time, so it is possible."

"Sapir headquartered the Sword of God in Jerusalem, but he is reported no longer of this world."

"There is a God," she said.

"Do you know where Kadar lives?"

"It is an old house, perhaps three rooms, about two blocks from my cafe. I have seen a woman there, along with a younger man I think they call Heusseni. There is another, called el-Ziam."

"But not Badr?"

"Not in some time, but I do not continually watch that building."

"Could you possibly get pictures of anyone entering or leaving the house?"

"If it does not interfere with the times I should be in the cafe."

"That would be helpful. Is there anything you need?"

"Talk money. My reserves are very low."

Talman pulled his wallet from his hip pocket, and riffled through the bills. He withdrew about three thousand in shekels and handed them to her. Her fingers touched his own, and felt soft.

"Thank you."

"There is more if you find that you need it. This is very important."

"I have heard no rumors of an impending action, Ja—, ah, Comet."

"Nor have any of our listening posts. I hope that it stays that way."

She shoved the bills under her blouse and into the waistband of her skirt, then put her hands on the wheel. "I suppose we should go."

"Yes." He did not make a move to get out of the car.

"Sometimes," she said, "it gets lonely."

"I know the feeling, Leila."

He did. He had been in undercover assignments for months

when he was unable to converse with anyone with whom he could share a truth rather than a lie.

"Could we talk for a few minutes?"

"Certainly."

For forty minutes they talked of nothing in particular—cultural events taking place in Jerusalem or Tel Aviv, the horrendous rate of inflation, the growing job market in computer-related services. They did not probe each other's backgrounds, and the topics were innocuous, simply a basis for continued conversation. It was always helpful, Talman had learned, to speak of such things with his agents. Too often, their only discourse was that of politics and madness.

Finally, she reached over, took his hand, and squeezed it lightly. "Thank you."

"I am at your service anytime, Leila."

"It helps to know that."

He returned to his Camry and waited until she had backed onto the road, then driven away. Then he started the car and returned to the Old City in Jerusalem. For once, his parking space at the back of the building was clear.

Inside, he checked on the transactions for the day, which were mounting nicely, then went into his private office. It was small, barely three meters on a side, but the desk also was small to keep it in scale. He sat behind it, facing the closed door, and checked through the telephone memos on the blotter. There was nothing of a business nature that demanded his immediate attention.

With a key from his keyring, he unlocked the lower left drawer and pulled it open. The answering machine for the second line was blinking. He listened quickly to the short message, then withdrew the telephone and dialed the number.

It rang four times and a female voice said, "Palestine Medical Assistance Team."

For an encampment somewhere in the desert, the connection was quite clear.

"I am calling for Jack Blanchard."

"Hang on a moment."

Within a couple minutes, he heard, "Blanchard."

"Do you know my voice?"

"Say that again."

"Do you know my voice?"

"I do."

"You left a message?"

"Yeah, I did." His voice was lower, as if there were others present. "We've got a kid in the hospital, maybe twenty-one, twenty-two years old, calls himself Nuri Hakkar. He mentioned something to the translator about the Sword of God. I don't know if it's important, but I thought I'd pass it along."

"It may well be, Jack. I do not know the name, but I will find out about it. What is wrong with him?"

"He's in very bad shape. A disease called toxic epidermal necrolysis."

"You lost me on the first turn."

"Flesh-eating disease. Bacterial, from what I understand."

"I am appalled," Talman said, and meant it. "I have read of it."

"The doctors amputated his legs and his right arm, trying to save him."

"May the Lord bless him. Will he survive?"

"Dr. Masters says there's a high fatality rate, so I don't know."

"Did he tell you anything more about himself?"

"I wasn't there, but I don't think it was much. He's probably suffering badly."

"I can imagine." Talman thought about this call for a moment, appreciating the fact that Blanchard called him as soon as heard about the Sword of God, and decided to share some information. "There is a new development with the Sword of God. They may have a new leader by the name of Ibrahim Kadar."

"A raging fanatic?"

"Of the highest order."

"I hope he's not around here."

"We have a watch on him in Jericho. Should he leave, I will let you know."

"Yeah. Thanks."

He hung up, then spent a few minutes organizing his thoughts for a quick report to Colonel Stein. He remembered he had to ask for a file on Ibrahim Kadar.

He keyed in the number.

The mess hall didn't work out as a fourth site for stashing an Uzi submachine gun, so Blanchard parked it in the bottom of his hanging locker, along with fourteen magazines and the two grenades. Each of the other three Uzis had two thirty-two-round magazines cached with them. He went over to the deuce-and-a-half in which Paulo kept his tool chests, clambered up in the back, found a key-making machine in one of the tool lockers, and made extra keys for the padlock to his locker. During the afternoon, he passed them out to Armbruster, Perkins, and Timnath.

His little speech at lunch didn't work out well, either. Most of those assembled in the mess tent—about eighty percent of the PMAT complement—couldn't possibly imagine themselves as victims of extremist groups. Nobody shot at Florence Nightingale. And in case Blanchard hadn't realized it, the PMAT was *helping* the Palestinians. No one would harm an ally, right? Masters had a self-satisfied little smirk on her face when the others pooh-poohed his fears.

Blanchard thought he'd been making some inroads with Masters, but their morning argument had put everything back in perspective. Her perspective.

After a decent dinner of roast beef, potatoes, and carrots— the cooks did a fine job most of the time, he thought—Blanchard headed for the tent he shared with nineteen roommates. His space was next to the front entrance, with Armbruster quartered across the aisle. Sam Delray bunked next to Blanchard.

He'd learned to travel light over the years, and his footlocker was only half full, his upright locker containing only a few hanging shirts and jeans—and of course, part of the armory. Grabbing his shaving kit, he walked over to the showers and made quick work of a shave and a five-gallon dousing. Then he went back to the tent and stretched out on the cot, dropping the netting around him. The flies and mosquitoes seemed to enjoy the after-dinner period most.

He was asleep instantly, and at eleven o'clock he came fully awake when Delray touched his arm.

Someone near the back of the tent had a radio turned on low; it could barely be heard over the drone of other sleepers. The dozens of radios in camp served as a link to other, and perhaps better, worlds.

Delray said, "Your turn, Jack."

"Got it. Thanks, Sam."

He hadn't told Delray about the weapons, but he had emphasized his concern about security with his second in command. With a duty roster that was already tight, they hadn't wanted to add to the load of anyone else, so they'd decided to cover the night by themselves.

Until Armbruster mentioned his own uneasiness in mid-afternoon and became part of the team.

Blanchard lifted the netting and tied it up, then levered his feet out of the bed. He had laid out his clothing on his footlocker, and he quickly donned jeans, boots, and a dark-brown sport shirt. He topped it off with a navy-blue nylon windbreaker and his Broncos baseball cap. He clipped the three-cell flashlight to his belt. Everyone in camp had a flashlight for nighttime strolls to the latrine. The unit went through batteries like M-60 Gatling Guns went through belts of ammo.

Before he slipped outside, he saw that Armbruster was already in his bunk, preparing for his 3 A.M. shift.

He had had Washington Apt, an electrician and a driver, lay a few more cables in the afternoon, and now they had five floodlamps on the perimeter of the camp. They weren't high powered at 150 watts, but they were aimed outward, illuminating the field surrounding the encampment with a few dim pools of light. There were still areas of darkness, and perhaps they seemed more sinister by contrast. Blanchard could imagine the view from above: a bull's-eye. Fortunately, no one had told him that terrorists had air forces.

Not bothering with his flashlight, he walked out toward the latrine, heard the tinkle of liquid. Mercy Base was not noted for its privacy. He turned north and started along the perimeter, staying inside the arc of lights and skirting parked trucks. When he reached the ten-foot pole of the first floodlight, he stopped to scan outward. Nothing moved. There wasn't even a breath of wind to stir the clumps of grass.

Hearing footfalls behind him, Blanchard turned to see a figure barely definable in the dark trodding along behind a cone of light. Headed back to bed.

He continued his pacing, arriving at the showers. He couldn't hear any activity, but he poked his head into each side anyway. The lights over the mirrors were active.

As he made his way along the northern edge of the camp, past another light, he could see the blocks and rectangles of the village. They were darker than the camp. He paused again, watching for any movement.

Saw it.

A man coming his way.

He recognized Roberto Irsay when he was about ten feet away. Irsay had the normal night duty. Normal meant tending the phones and radio, and taking an occasional walk through the camp. The original objective had been to deter pilferage of the supplies and equipment.

"Hi, Roberto."

"Hello, Jack. You're taking this threat seriously, aren't you?"

"Seen anything unusual?"

"No. Some of the ward patients are restless. Out there, about a hundred meters to the east, there's five or six people camping out. They want to be first in line in the morning."

For the simple reason of not being able to handle the work-load, the clinic operated only from eight in the morning until six at night. Everywhere they had been, Blanchard had seen the people lined up overnight, waiting. It was almost like kids waiting in a ticket line for a rock concert, but not nearly as enjoyable.

"How we doing in the computer department?" Blanchard asked.

"Number Three's down, a hard-disk crash. I'll have it back up and on-line by the end of my watch."

Blanchard wanted to tell him that he'd prefer it if Irsay spent his watch, on watch. Looking outward. But the man put in his regular shifts, and when he drew night duty, he didn't waste time, either. Blanchard frequently found him working on the machines during his off-hours. He was also helping the computer illiterate become proficient, from nurses to mechanics.

"Okay, Roberto. Good."

He went on until he reached the back of the ward tents, checked two ambulances parked behind them, then made a circuit of the wards. He used his flashlight so he wouldn't trip over the guy ropes. In the backwash of the light, he saw a couple of sleepless faces peering at him through the netting. They were pale faces, haggard, ghostly, pained.

He walked the rest of the perimeter, then came back and went through the admin tent. Irsay was back, his head buried in the innards of a computer. The cover and his tools littered the table beside him. Blanchard went over to the mess tent.

Two of the support people, an inventory and supply specialist and a civil hygienist, both of whom also took shifts as orderlies, were drinking coffee and playing gin under a 100 watt bulb. They waved a hello to him. Jillian Weiss was under another hanging light in the corner, reading a novel. Blanchard got a mug of coffee and went to sit down at her table.

"Hi, Jack." She laid the book facedown on the table. He noted that it was Wilbur Smith's *River God*.

"I don't want to interrupt a good book."

"It's all right. I'm biding the time until sleep comes around."

"It's tough, isn't it? We have abnormal cycles around here."

"I don't mind." She fiddled with her wristwatch, then said, "The warning you gave at noon. Where did that come from?"

She was Israeli, and he didn't hesitate. "Shin Bet."

Nodding, she said, "I thought as much."

"Do you think they're alarmists?"

She looked him right in the eye. "Not in the least. I've lived here for four years, Jack. I've seen what these people do."

"I wish some of our other inmates were as realistic as you."

"She's going to be difficult to convince," Weiss said, smiling wryly.

"I'm not talking about a particular person."

"Sure you are."

Blanchard sipped his somewhat tepid coffee. "You're too cute for your own good, Jillian."

She sat up straight and pulled her shoulders back, which did reactive things for her full bosom. "I am, aren't I?"

Weiss was twenty years his junior, and Blanchard had no intention of becoming involved with her.

"But, cute or not, I still like you," he said. "What are you going to be doing next year at this time?"

"You don't want to flirt?"

"Not just now, Jillian. I've got other worries."

She wrinkled her nose at him. "Next year I'll probably be back in the pharmacy in Tel Aviv. Unless something comes up out here. I like helping people."

"You're good at it, too."

"Would you write a recommendation for me? Maybe there'll be another team."

"I'd be happy to do that."

"Thanks." She continued spinning her watch on her wrist, looking down now at what she was doing. "You like her, don't you?"

"Who?"

"Melanie."

"Melanie and I don't see eye to eye, but she's very dedicated and very able."

"She likes you, too."

Blanchard didn't think he should be part of this conversation Particularly since he'd seen little evidence of Weiss's assertions.

"I'd better get back to my rounds."

"You want company?"

"Better if you get back to Wilbur."

He finished his coffee and stood up.

"She's got troubles at home, Jack."

"What?"

"Her husband won't return her calls."

"Jillian, I don't think—"

"Just so you know." She picked up her book and went back to it.

Blanchard slipped back into the darkened compound, stopping outside the tent to let his eyes adjust to the darkness. On the other side of the admin tent, most of the Humvees were parked. He didn't see any movement around them.

He wondered whether Jillian Weiss was taking wild guesses; had an intuitive sense for people; or actually knew what she was talking about.

He checked the clinic. The anesthesiologist Dana Harper and Emma Wachter were on duty, sitting in the lit reception area of the clinic between tours of the wards. He said hello and moved on.

The hospital was the largest tent in the compound, square and tall. It was divided by curtains into four sections: a kind of receiving room; an equipment, storage, and preparation area; and two operating arenas. A light was left on during the night in the first room.

One generator was dedicated to the hospital, powering the electronic equipment and air-conditioning. Because of the need for sterility, the tent walls were always down, sealed as well as they could be at the base. The plywood floor had a plastic sheet spread over it. Rubber soles squeaked on the plastic when people were working.

As he went by the side of the tent, Blanchard heard a squeak.

He stopped in midstride, instantly alert, listening. He could hear the muted voices of the gin players at the mess hall.

Someone in one of the wards coughed.

And two more squeaks.

Putting his toes down first in the attempt to avoid noise, Blanchard advanced toward the front of the tent. The first thing he noticed was that the light wasn't on; it usually cast a glow on the white sidewall.

Since the tent sides were pegged down, the only entrance was at the front, and he slipped around to it.

Still listening.

No more sound from inside.

Reaching out, but not standing directly in front, he slid the flap aside.

No squeaks.

He stepped inside, pulling his flashlight free of his belt.

Holding it out to his side, he snapped it on.

Nothing moved.

Played the light around the reception area. A gurney. Two chairs. A folding table stacked with supplies.

Moving silently, hoping the plywood wouldn't grate, he parted the curtain to the prep room and ran the light around in there. The curtains leading to the operating rooms were closed. Cabinets, a washstand, a portable X-ray machine, the autoclave, a couple of small tables stacked with prepared trays and other supplies.

Heard a click.

From the back of the left operating room, OR One.

Immediately killed his flashlight.

A click?

Like a safety being released? He knew the sound.

Three steps and he was kneeling before the autoclave. The table it was on had rubber wheels, and the lowest metal shelf stood about four inches above the floor. He reached under it, feeling for the Uzi that Perkins had hidden there.

But didn't find a damned thing.

And then the darkness erupted with gunfire.

The cacophony deafened him as rounds bounced off the autoclave and the X-ray machine.

Six

Blanchard couldn't believe it.

He was flat on his stomach on the floor, the *BR-RR-RUP!* of the Uzi ringing in his ears. He'd dropped his flashlight. This was a position he had never expected to be in again. The icy fingers of fear clutched at his stomach, gripped his throat. Despite the fear, as in the old days, he was thinking:

The gunman was firing south, away from the inhabited tents. Got to keep him that way. Nine-millimeter rounds wailing around to the north or east would play murderous havoc in the wards. Trying to go around him through OR Two on the right would draw fire to the east. Straight ahead, then.

The short burst—maybe five rounds, leaving him twenty-seven—had awakened most of the camp. He could hear people calling to each other. Probably on the run to the hospital to check it out. Didn't need that.

Plus, it was his own goddamned gun.

The guy was waiting, listening for movement. Had he hit his target? But he had to be getting impatient, too. He could hear others converging on the tent. Blanchard wanted to shout for everyone to take cover, but he couldn't give away his location.

Moving as rapidly as he dared, Blanchard felt for the rubber wheels of the autoclave cart, found the levers that locked the wheels to keep it from rolling, and released them. With his right hand, he gave it a shove toward the X-ray machine.

He went to his knees.

Grabbed the bottom of the dividing curtain.

The cart slammed into one table or another, boxes and trays clattering to the floor.

The Uzi barked. Short burst, slugs slapping into wood, tearing up the dividing curtain.

And six feet to the right of where they hit, Blanchard threw up his hands and charged under the curtain.

Made three staggering steps, and in the dark, whammed into the heavy operating table.

BR-RR-RUP! The muzzle flash lit the dark, identifying the assailant's position on the other side of the table.

The slugs went into the table and over his head. He scrambled on all fours toward the head of the table, got his legs under him, then heaved upward as hard as he could.

The table was heavy, but it went over with a resounding crash, and he went right behind it, diving over it and toward shadow. He swept his arms to either side as he went, feeling his left forearm slap into metal. The Uzi went flying, and the assailant went down under him. Blanchard's knees caught the side of the operating table and threw him off balance.

The guy gave up easily, though. Probably because Blanchard outweighed him by three times. He struggled for only a moment, with Blanchard lying across his waist, pinning him to the floor. In the dark it took a few seconds to locate a wrist and circle it with his fingers. That wasn't hard, either. The wrist was frail and not much larger than a Butterfinger bar. It felt just about as brittle, too. He was suddenly careful, afraid he might break something he shouldn't break.

"Who's in there!"

That was Armbruster.

Blanchard called out, "Dickie, it's me! Come in, but come by yourself. OR One."

A few seconds later, he heard the curtain rustle, and Armbruster's flashlight beam blazed into the room.

"Christ, Jack! You all right?"

"Get a light, would you?"

Armbruster turned on an overhead bulb, and Blanchard pushed himself off the floor, dragging his captive with him by the wrist. He saw that the former sergeant major had picked up an Uzi of his own on his way to the hospital.

"They come in all sizes, don't they?" Armbruster asked.

The kid looked to be ten or eleven, but he might have been a couple years older. He was so emaciated, it was difficult to tell. A huge mop of uncut black hair draped low over his eyes. His clothes were rags held together with bits of wire and twine.

He stared at Blanchard with pure hate in his eyes, tugging impatiently at Blanchard's grip on his left arm.

"Big enough to prime an Uzi and get the safety off, Dickie. Doesn't look to me like he's overwhelmed with remorse, either."

Armbruster walked around behind the kid and picked up the weapon and ejected the magazine. He ran the bolt to eject the round in the chamber.

"This is our own, Jack?"

"Yeah."

"Bloody hell! A man can't be sure of a hiding place anymore."

"What's in the bag?" Blanchard pointed to a dirty cotton bag on the floor.

Armbruster picked it up, opened the top, and peered in. He laid both Uzis on a cabinet and used one hand to paw through the bag.

"Bandages, hypodermics and needles, pills and drugs of some kind, portable radio, surgical instruments. The kid wanted to start his own hospital."

"Or sell one. I can't believe the little SOB shot at me."

"It's that good home training, Jack. What are we going to do with the bugger?"

"Turn him loose, I suppose. We don't want to get into a discussion of arms limitations with the doctors, I think."

Blanchard and Armbruster talked to each other as if the kid couldn't understand English. Maybe he did, but Blanchard didn't care.

"What in the *hell* are you doing to that boy!"

Melanie Masters came through the curtain flap, hazel eyes blazing like Doc Holliday's six-guns. Her chestnut hair was tousled, gleams of cinnamon shining under the single light. She had pulled on jeans and a blouse, and not much else. The blouse was buttoned, but in the wrong buttonholes. Everything was delightfully lopsided. Blanchard wondered how she managed to look sexy in all the wrong situations.

Dickie Armbruster moved to stand in front of the cabinet, hiding the weapons from her sight with his body. No fool, Dickie.

Blanchard said, "I'm not doing anything to him, Mel. He came by to steal a few things, take some shots at me."

"Your sarcasm is not appreciated. Let go of him, Colonel."

"Melanie—"

"Now!"

Blanchard released the little wrist.

The boy stood there for a moment, rubbing his arm, looking around at all the big people. Pretty confused, probably.

"Come with me," Masters told him, "and we'll check you out."

She beckoned him forward with her hand.

He didn't understand English. But he understood that his chances of freedom were getting slimmer by the minute.

He bolted toward the curtain opening. Blanchard reached for him but missed.

The kid, with both arms stretched out in front of him, slammed them into Masters's stomach.

She went backward, tripped, and landed on her butt on the floor. The kid leaped over her, flashed through the curtain, and was gone. Stunned yells from outside suggested he had surprised those gathered around the tent and gotten through that blockade, as well.

Blanchard thought it was probably better this way. No wannabe terrorist explaining to horrified doctors that he had obtained his weapon right in their sacred temple. He went over to help Masters up, but she ignored him, rolled over, and accomplished it by herself.

Armbruster said, "I don't think he wanted to be checked out. Quite likely, he's scared of doctors."

Masters gave him a withering look, then stomped out. "Pick up that table."

Blanchard and Armbruster righted the table and centered it under the big lamps hanging from the tent framework. There were four holes in the right edge of the plastic surface.

Blanchard grinned at the Brit.

"I *know* I'm scared of them," Armbruster said.

The Gaza Strip was home to 650,000 people, and the better half of them lived in refugee camps which were the epitome of squalor and poverty. They had done so for years, devoting their energies less to improving the conditions of their environment than to condemning the Israeli occupiers who had surrounded them and stayed since the Six-Day War. Jacob Talman thought that, if the population had directed their efforts into their hands and minds rather than into hate, the standard of living in the Strip would be considerably higher today.

It was a tolerable area, with perhaps twenty percent of the land infertile. There was a large region of permanent crops in the form of grapes, dates, and other fruits. Grain and vegetable farming were supported well by irrigation, and the industrial sector centered on textiles, food processing, and light manufacturing—woodworking and furniture, primarily. Tourism was a healthy source of income at one time, but the hatreds, which had boiled over into armed attacks against transportation and Jewish settlements, had driven away any tourist with common sense. The Arabs would do their damnedest to foul any source of revenue whatsoever, he thought. Those momentary flashes of hot blood that resulted in violent acts always wiped their minds clear of any reflection on the consequences.

Forty kilometers long and up to ten kilometers wide, the coastal enclave had become an Arabic heartland controlled by Egypt after the war of 1948–49 when Arabs from Palestine fled into it. The Strip was momentarily in Israeli hands after the Suez War, but was again returned to Egypt in 1957. From 1967 until the peace accord and the granting of self-rule, Israel had occupied the region under a military administration. With the governance of the Palestinian Authority, Talman thought that most of the Arabic camps had fallen into even greater ennui. No one did anything except complain. Except perhaps, shoot. Since the beginning of the accord, some 200 Israelis had been killed by Palestinians.

If he were forced to be objective, which was occasionally the case, Talman would have to admit that nearly 350 Palestinians had been slain by the Israeli side in the same length of time. Neither side had adequate excuses to offer in most cases, he supposed.

He knew, also, that the prime irritant could be traced to the Jewish settlements, fifteen of them here in the Gaza Strip, with a population of 5,000 people. In the West Bank 36,000 Jews populated some 130 settlements. Talman was of the opinion that a person should be allowed to farm, or to ply his trade, wherever he wished, and if the Palestinians were not themselves to develop thriving and productive communities in inhospitable lands, why not the Jews?

If he could not agree with some of the military strategies of his government, at least Talman could agree with the Knesset's hard-line stance in regard to the settlements. He saw no reason to remove people from the places of their livelihood simply for political reasons. And yet, he knew it was going to be a source of friction within the accords for many years to come.

He drove the Camry slowly into Gaza City, the heart of the Palestinian Authority's blossoming bureaucracy. He drove slowly because the streets were in such poor repair. Palestinian potholes were the enemies of Jewish suspensions.

The fifty percent unemployment rate was as evident as the torn-up streets. In storefronts and open-air cafes along the street, the men were gathered to drink tea and play cards. As he passed, they looked up and stared at him, their eyes following his passage with undisguised hostility.

He could do nothing about that. With self-rule had come new security restrictions to keep the radical suicide bombers out of Israel proper, and many Palestinians had lost their jobs in other parts of Israel. There were no jobs to replace them in the self-rule regions.

He continued down the street, looking for the office building where the meeting was to take place. The stink was palpable. Huge piles of rotting garbage were stacked along the streets. The sewage systems were backed up and inoperable. He knew that power outages were frequent and that the telephone system worked erratically.

Talman was forced to brake to a stop when a Jeep shot out of a side street without regard for a stop sign, without a blaring of the horn. It was loaded with soldiers aiming Kalashnikov assault rifles at the sky. Directly behind it came a black Mercedes, then another Jeep packed with bodyguards. The vehicles were bearing Palestinian license plates, yet another symbol, like postage stamps, of a real country. The registration plates and the stamps were the minor efforts to generate income for the fledgling government, though Talman doubted there were many in the Strip who could afford automobiles, much less license plates for them. Some would struggle for the money to purchase a stamp.

He could not see through the darkened windows of the armored limousine, but knew it would probably contain Arafat. The man insisted upon being called *rais,* the Arabic for president, and he conducted his affairs in ceremonies worthy of a head of state, even though the power was supposed to be in the hands of the twenty-four members of the Authority.

Unlike most presidents, Arafat clung steadfastly to his uniforms, and kept his fingers active in all parts of his bureaucracy. He led all-night meetings, punctuated with fiery sermons about the "holy war" for Jerusalem, and overruled the Authority on most matters. Only the president was capable of making decisions or handling money. One anonymous Palestinian quoted Arafat in a December 1994 cabinet meeting as telling his subordinates, "Don't believe it when you are called ministers. . . . I am the minister of everything, and nothing can be done without my approval."

The hiring of employees was accomplished by the president, who spent a great deal of time writing letters to ministers telling them who to employ. Most government jobs went to loyalists, or their relatives, of the Fatah movement, Arafat's mainline organization within the Palestine Liberation Organization. If there were not enough jobs in one agency, additional agencies were created, duplicating efforts. Talman knew, for example, that there were eight security agencies, all of them bloated with inept employees.

There were over 40,000 members of the new government. He had heard that as many as 17,000 policemen had been hired, twice as many as approved by the accords. Then again, it was easier to create a policeman than, say, a garbage collector. A policeman did not have to have skills, only carry a weapon. And who wanted to be a garbage collector, or had to be, when a cousin was a minister?

And they wondered where the money went and begged the world for more, Talman thought bitterly. They wanted the salary checks and the perks; they just did not want to pay for them. It should be handed to them, preferably on sterling platters.

He stepped on the gas and released the clutch as the short caravan finished blocking the road.

He hoped Levi Avidar knew what he was doing, sending him here to this meeting. His cover was in definite jeopardy.

There were four Palestinian policemen outside the white-washed, two-story office building, apparently with nothing better to do, but their presence did not make him feel any better about parking his Toyota. He locked it.

Inside the thick walls of the building, it was much cooler, and another policeman led him to the back where a large room had been furnished with a boat-shaped table and a dozen chairs. Two large ceiling fans moved the air about.

Colonel Isaac Stein, his immediate commander, was there. A short man with an intellectual high forehead, and a fringe of short white hair circling a bald pate, Stein was a stickler for organization and regulation. To his credit, he could overlook both if the results were worthwhile. His relaxation of the rules did not happen often.

"Good morning, sir."

"Jacob. It is good to see you."

Talman was not surprised to see Moshe Perlmutter in attendance. Like himself, Perlmutter was a major and an operative. Prematurely gray, Perlmutter's hair was still curly and thick. He had bright green eyes amplified by thick lenses in dark frames. He recalled Avidar telling him that Perlmutter had been assigned the equivalent chore for the Gaza Strip that Talman had been tasked with for the West Bank.

Perlmutter offered an exaggerated wink.

That was the extent of the good guys.

There were nine Palestinians present, and while he had never met them before, Talman knew who five of them were from Shin Bet dossiers. Two of them, he also knew, had served prison time for criminal offenses. The ranking man was Amin Rahman, Deputy Chief of the Palestinian Police Force. Adnan Boshogi was a district commander, resident in Jericho.

Stein introduced his agents to Rahman, who introduced the others.

Rahman urged them to take seats around the big table, and one of the policeman was detailed to serve them all coffee.

There was polite chatter for fifteen minutes.

These meetings were always awkward, Talman thought. Everyone was aware of the obvious, but no one would state it for fear of offending someone else. He could figure that a couple of Rahman's aides were also on Islamic Jihad or Hamas payrolls and would report back in detail.

"Our governments have instructed us to meet," Rahman said, getting to the point, "to share with each other whatever intelligence we have gathered."

"In relationship to the specific goal of restraining protest and terrorism," Stein clarified for everyone. He would not allow a free-for-all grab at Israeli intelligence.

"Of course," Rahman agreed.

"Why don't you go first," Stein said.

Rahman smiled. "Certainly. Our commanders for security in the Gaza Strip, Jericho, and the West Bank"—he nodded toward the three men on his immediate left—"have assured me that the extremist groups have apparently conceded the necessity of acquiring financial aid. All of them are cooperating in maintaining the peace."

That would be quite a concession, Talman thought. The major players, like Islamic Jihad and the Islamic Resistance Movement, had always disapproved of the peace settlement. Their only goal was complete autonomy for Palestine *in place of* the Israeli nation. Peaceful coexistence was not a factor for consideration. If what Rahman said was true, then the Authority had made significant inroads with the extremists. Of course, all one had to do was show them the stinking garbage, the potholes, the idle workers, and the tremendous payroll of the government to convince them of the need for money.

Financial resources had been in short supply from the beginning. In 1994, 825 million dollars in foreign aid had been promised, but only 240 million had been delivered, ostensibly as a reaction of foreign governments to the way Arafat organized and mismanaged his empire. In 1995, 1.1 billion dollars had been promised, but again, the total disbursement had fallen far short. Nineteen ninety-six was not any better. The Palestinian Authority was getting deeper and deeper into the red, and it had been forced to promise reforms in the structure and management of the government in order to secure additional pledges of assistance.

Shin Bet intelligence sources reported some reform taking place. Excess personnel were being furloughed, but that could be simply a result of lack of money with which to pay them. Outside management consultants were conducting studies in various ministries, and supposedly, their recommendations would also have an impact on the amount and timing of additional foreign aid from the superpowers.

"I am impressed," Isaac Stein said. "Have these groups also volunteered to turn in their weapons? To insure the peace?"

Rahman, whom Talman always thought of as oily—possibly because he was so handsome, lost his smile. "That is an issue not on the bargaining table, Colonel. Not at this time. We are quite happy to have achieved the progress so far demonstrated."

Part of the weapons problem could be attributed to Arafat, also. He refused to allow the extremists positions in the government, and yet he needed as much of their support as he could amass. To placate them, he allowed them to maintain a weapons inventory that would be envied by many legal nations. To demand their weapons would be to instigate civil war within a supposed administration not yet five years old

To the Authority's credit, Arafat had established a Higher Court for State Security in February 1995, and it was taking a much firmer stance with terrorists charged with crimes. Before the court existed, the Palestinians often would capture extremists suspected of bombings or other incidents, hold them for a few weeks, then release them, claiming a lack of evidence. The process supposedly placated Hamas and the Islamic Jihad. Since then, some terrorists had actually been *convicted* of crimes and were spending a few years in Palestinian prisons. The sentences were never harsh enough, Talman thought, but it was a start in the right direction.

"There have been no incidents, at all?" Talman asked.

"None," Rahman said, his smile back in place. He was a striking man, tall for an Arab, with a strong, straight nose, a wide smile full of white teeth, and very direct, very dark eyes. Today, he wore a business suit of European cut, with a blood-red tie over a white shirt.

Moshe Perlmutter said, "What of the shooting the night before last?"

"Shooting? Where?"

"At Abasan."

That was in the southern end of the Strip.

Rahman looked to his assistant, who leaned forward to confer quietly.

Straightening up, Rahman said, "A family matter. A feud between brothers."

"How many dead?" Perlmutter asked. Talman assumed that Perlmutter knew the answer.

Another conference. Rahman was not getting the intelligence he needed from his assistants prior to his needing it.

"Four. All were Palestinians, and therefore, not of concern to Israel."

"A large family," Perlmutter said. "I am amazed it did not make the media."

"We do not wish to encourage the media when it is unnecessary."

"At this point," Stern said, "that is prudent."

"What can you tell us of Ibrahim Kadar?" Talman asked.

"Kadar? I do not know the name."

"Once of Iziddin al-Qassam," Talman said.

Again, he conducted a conference with the aide who directed

security in the city of Jericho. Adnan Boshogi was a hawk-nosed, bleary-eyed, chinless individual who disguised his lack of jawline with a beard, which was so thin it was unnecessary.

"Kadar," Rahman said finally, "is a minor functionary in Iziddin al-Qassam. He is reported to be hot-headed, but ineffective."

Talman glanced at Stein, who gave him a slight nod.

"I have information, Deputy Chief, that Kadar now leads the Sword of God."

"This is not true. Sapir—"

"Is dead."

Rahman gave Boshogi a look that should have either frozen or superheated the man on the spot. To Stein, Rahman said, "We will investigate that matter."

"Perhaps," Talman told him, "you will learn where Kadar spent the last week?"

"He has been in Jericho," Commander Boshogi said, ignoring some previous agreement that Rahman would make all of the statements. "We have long known of his location."

"From Saturday, July tenth, until Friday, the sixteenth of July, Kadar was absent from Jericho. He crossed the border on Friday morning, returning to Jericho."

Amin Rahman was going to have to have a long talk with his security experts, Talman thought. Either fire them up, or fire them, period.

This was the kind of thing he hated. Having to work for, or with, the Palestinian Authority was bad enough, but having to do the work for such an inept organization was worse. Now, Boshogi, having been shown up for his lack of knowledge, would likely spend his time trying to uncover the Shin Bet operatives in his region rather than attending to the more important mission at hand. The obvious had not been stated, but everyone in the room was acutely aware of it.

Stein sensed the same thing. He said, "What is paramount here, Chief Rahman, is that we make certain that we keep a careful watch on any potential embers that might be fanned into flames. Let us not be sidetracked by inconsequential issues. Keeping an eye on Kadar for the next six weeks is as important for you as it is for us."

Rahman studied Stein for a moment, then said, "Exactly. We shall do that."

Talman did not think they could handle it.

Masters sat at the back of the mess tent with Blanchard and Lon Chao. Ahead of them, seated at the picnic-style tables, but all facing the front of the tent, were about fifteen Arab elders, administrators, and anyone else from the village that they could induce to attend the lecture.

The lectures lasted fifty minutes, no more, since it was extremely difficult to maintain attention spans on the subject for much longer.

At the front of the tent, with his flip charts on a pair of easels, was Steve Mackey, a sanitation engineer originally from Cleveland. He was a personable young man who spoke passable Arabic and who had been appalled at the conditions he encountered after first arriving in the region.

Because it didn't do much good to treat disease without doing something about the causes of it, the PMAT had a subteam of four sanitation and hygienics specialists with it. Mackey and his colleagues lectured, demonstrated, and helped villagers to revamp their living arrangements in the hope of preventing the recurrence of disease. Some of the Arabic towns in the West Bank were centuries old, and despite the excellent sanitation designs of their founders, alterations in the ensuing centuries had tainted the systems. In fact, it was the newer settlements, some only a decade old, that needed the most help. For every place they had been, Mackey had developed general engineering recommendations for the Palestinian Authority to follow whenever they found the money to bring in heavy equipment and make changes. In the meantime, Mackey's group tried to do the best they could as an interim measure.

Since its inception on April 7, 1948, the World Health Organization had been dedicated to eradicating major diseases throughout the world. The mission included protecting the health of mothers and children, promoting mental health, and improving sanitation and water supply—Mackay's charge. The permanent services included information dissemination; setting standards for drugs, vaccines and biological substances; promoting medical research; and exchanging information. These services were provided to over 140 nations.

The daily workload was overseen by the director general of the World Health Assembly, who developed the programs and budgets and governed through six regional organizations. The PMAT, since it was a somewhat unique field unit, reported directly to the headquarters in Geneva while providing reports to the regional office in Alexandria, Egypt. Only infrequently had WHO organized a field team for such direct intervention as Masters was making in the West Bank. The normal course of events was to train locals for the necessary tasks.

Greg Masters had never been able to understand how much of an honor it had been for Melanie to be selected for this team, nor how much of a need there was for it. His idea of an honor for her, she had decided, was for her to be seated at his side at the head table of a University of Chicago foundation banquet.

Sometimes, thinking about him, she absolutely ached to have him near. He was the only man she had ever loved, and she couldn't imagine being married to anyone else. He was so handsome, so charming. The catch of the decade, her girlfriends had told her when his parents announced their engagement.

Perfectly at ease and smoothly articulate with bankers, politicians, and corporate CEOs, Greg had worked for the Reagan and Bush campaigns and raised thousands of dollars for them. She also knew, though, that he had difficulty adapting to any environment different from that in which he had been sternly reared by Gregory Simpson Masters, Senior. He would be completely ill at ease in Israel, she thought. He didn't like being around the sick and the lame. On the street he found other interesting sights to look at if someone confined to a wheelchair passed by. At a hospital fund-raiser she had cajoled him into attending, he had blustered his way through the evening. No, Greg would not do well at all in the West Bank.

He didn't understand sewage and water problems, for one thing.

People of the desert understood water, of course, and Mackey played on that theme as he talked—splitting his discourse into both Arabic and English for the benefit of three visitors from South Africa. The single small well in the village had to last forever, as it were, and its protection had to be the first priority of every villager, from six to eighty. The low volume output of that well, in fact, was the reason that Blanchard trucked the PMAT's water in from Jerusalem. He had also sweet-talked the Israelis into providing a ten-thousand-gallon tanker of water for the village, replaced every third day, until the village well recovered.

The problem here was that the villagers understood less about how to deal with human waste. If it couldn't be used for fertilizer, then it just had to be discarded, and in this village they hadn't understood geography and geology very well, either. The communal latrine had, over the course of several years, contaminated the well, and now she had seventeen people in the ward, having lost four, trying to rehydrate them with salts, glucose, and water. Every one of them had been in such severe stages of cholera (tachycardia, cyanosis, low arterial pH, hypotension) that they were eliminating nearly four gallons of fluids per day, when the team found them. Another thirty people had been treated for the beginning signs of the disease.

Mackey's team had immediately resited the latrine, then brought in backhoes borrowed from the Israeli Defense Forces and excavated a huge trench along one side of the well. Filling the trench with concrete, they had successfully isolated the well from the source of contamination, and the daily tests of the water were showing steady improvement. Mackey's lectures and training were intent upon keeping it that way.

Masters glanced sideways at Blanchard. He was here because he had recruited the villagers for the lecture and was setting an example for them, as well as serving as host to the South Africans, but she could tell he was bored to death. He'd heard it all before. Lon Chao was here because it was his day off, and he hadn't wanted to go into Jerusalem. Chao was something of an academic. He went to lectures, seminars, and symposiums for the sheer joy of learning something new.

Blanchard was on the verge of nodding off, she thought, and figured now was as good a time as any to prove to him that she didn't allow details to slide.

Leaning toward him, Masters whispered, "What did you do with the gun?"

That snapped him out of his reverie.

"Gun?"

"That the kid took into the hospital."

"Got rid of it. You don't want guns around, do you?"

"Of course not!" she snapped. "But I do want a replacement for the autoclave, and I want it right away."

"And the X-ray," Blanchard added. "I've already ordered replacements, but it's going to take a couple days and a reshuffling of the budget. Let's slip outside, Mel."

He stood up, got his leg outside the bench seat, and stepped away from the table. Masters watched him, then slid her legs over the bench, and followed.

The flap at the front of the tent had been raised on poles to provide a sunshade, but it was still hot. Behind her she could hear Mackey approaching the climax of his talk. He had a few jokes, which went over mildly well.

Blanchard leaned against one of the poles and locked his eyes on her own. Whenever he did that, she felt violated. Like he was dressing-down some private.

"You did notice how easy it was for someone to shoot up this camp?"

"He was scared."

"For God's sake, Mel! The little bastard could have killed someone."

She was fully aware that Blanchard had been at risk, taking the gun away from the boy. She was also a bit stunned that a child was carrying a weapon, though she didn't know why. It happened on the streets of Chicago all the time.

"He was hungry. You saw how he was dressed."

Blanchard shook his head.

"We've had thievery before, Jack."

"But not armed thieves. Would you at least admit that death or injury for our people is more probable here than in Des Moines?"

She sighed. "I'll talk to the medical team. We'll try to be more aware."

"Thank you. That's all I'm asking."

"What if you hadn't tried to stop him?" she asked. "Just let him take what he wanted?"

"First of all, Mel, I thought he was about ten feet tall when he was shooting at me in the dark. I didn't ask him how old he was."

"But still—"

"It's all hypothesis. Like, if the kid had gotten five or six slugs into me, would you have taken them out?"

Blanchard spun on his heel and walked away, heading for the hospital.

While he always maintained his composure in their arguments, she didn't think she'd ever seen him get mad before, but she was certain he was angry now.

She called after him, "You know I would!"

"Thanks," he called back.

The meeting was breaking up behind her, so Masters walked on over to the admin tent. Sam Delray was on a computer, entering budgetary data—probably trying to find money for the damaged equipment. Roberto Irsay had a laser printer torn apart, and Deidre Joliet was on a phone.

She went to the back corner of the tent, sat down at a side table, and picked up another phone, punching the button for the sixth of the ten phone channels they had.

Almost ten o'clock here, almost two in Chicago. She dialed the number.

"Justin, Swearingen, Halcourt, Noxon, Trickle, and Masters. How may I help you?"

"Lindsey? This is Melanie Masters."

"Oh, Mrs. Masters! I haven't heard your voice in so long. How are you?"

"Quite well, Lindsey. Is Greg in?"

"Ah . . . with a client."

"Would you interrupt him for a moment, please?"

"A very important client, he said. He didn't want to be disturbed."

"Tough. Disturb him."

"Ah—"

"Now, Lindsey!"

It took a couple minutes. Masters looked around the tent, but no one seemed to be paying any attention to her.

"Hello, Melanie. I'm afraid that I—"

"Why haven't you been returning my calls?"

"Because I'm busy. Like now. You shouldn't be calling me at work."

"And at ten at night? Who is she, Greg?"

"Get your head on straight, Melanie. I don't have time for romance, much less the headaches that come with them. Look at Gary Hart. Look at Melvin Reynolds."

"So where have you been?" she demanded, though she knew that for years he had spent three and four nights a week involved with one group or another.

"I have a committee. A campaign-strategy committee, and we've been very busy. The party has agreed to support me in a run for Dalgren's seat in the senate." He sounded extremely proud of himself. "As a matter of fact, Melanie, I *am* glad that you called. We have to be making plans of our own."

"Which are?"

"This is a very family-values-oriented electorate right now, the pollsters tell me. You and I have to put up a united front."

"Not possible for another six months, Greg."

"Well, what I needed to tell you was that I and a few others in the party have had some conversations with the director general—"

"You what!"

"He understands that, as a matter of hardship, you know, you'll have to give up your position early. It's—"

"You son of a bitch!"

She slammed the phone down.

Delray, Irsay, and Joliet were all looking at her.

The bastard!

Masters almost wished it were another woman, but politics could be a hell of a mistress, too.

Called the director general? The son of a bitch!

"Sam," she called. "What's the number in Geneva?"

Delray looked like he could have second thoughts about disagreeing with her. He thumbed through a notebook and read off the number for her. She punched it into the keypad, went through a couple receptionists and secretaries, and was gratified to have the understandably overworked director general accept the call without a prearranged time.

"Dr. Masters. I am truly sorry to hear that—"

"You have heard incorrectly, Director. I am not leaving my post."

"But that is wonderful!" He almost yelled, and his Belgian accent rolled across the satellite link. "I do not understand, however. There were so many people who called to tell me of dire circumstances in your home."

"They are not dire, Director. My husband wants to be a senator, and I suspect the senate is better off without him."

Whew! Hold the anger in, girl. We don't need to advertise a disagreement with Greg.

But you have probably disconnected from him pretty thoroughly, she thought.

"I will not explore that territory with you, Dr. Masters. I will be content with your decision to remain. It is so difficult to find people with your expertise who are willing to serve in hardship areas."

"Thank you."

"Is there anything else that I can do for you? Are you having any problems that I could address?"

Well, as long as she had him on the line.

"Money, for one."

"Ah, that is difficult."

She told him about the boy shooting up the hospital.

"Oh, that is terrible. Perhaps I can find another five or six thousand dollars for your budget. The equipment is quite necessary. I will notify Colonel Blanchard after I discover what is possible."

"Well, that's another thing. I'm afraid that Colonel Blanchard and I seem to be at odds."

"Yes?"

"He doesn't seem to understand the medical priorities, Director."

"In what way?"

"We should be dividing the unit and sending half of it to Mar Saba. We're not fully reaching all of the—"

"Quite impossible, Dr. Masters."

"But Blanchard doesn't understand—"

"The colonel fully understands the political situation, Doctor. And that is precarious."

"Rubbish! Who told you that?"

"Why, Colonel Blanchard, when I talked to him last night. I have also discussed the situation with high-level military leaders in Israel. It would be well, Dr. Masters, if you paid close attention to the colonel. I am certain he has your well-being uppermost in his mind."

She should have known that Blanchard would align support for his position early on. He was thorough, and he apparently had some help in the Israeli military. The old soldiers always stuck together.

"At any rate," the director general said, "I am most happy to know you will remain with us."

"Of course I will," she said.

Despite Blanchard.

And despite her back-stabbing husband.

There weren't too many places at Mercy Base where one could find privacy. Blanchard and Delray found one of them on nearby seats in the men's side of the latrine. It was a simplistic design. The urinals were two pipes driven into the ground at a slight angle and topped with large funnels. The commodes were planks with six holes bored through them, situated over six cut-in-half fuel drums. Once a week the planks were removed, the drums were saturated with fuel, and the waste was set afire.

Blanchard could have taken portable chemical toilets into the field with him, but they were more trouble to service over long distances than the typical military field setup.

"She was pissed," Delray said.

"I imagine."

"Do you know why?"

"When I talked to the director last night, he said she was resigning her position. It was news to me, but I was waiting for her to tell me."

"I didn't hear it all, Jack, but I got the impression it wasn't her idea. I also got the impression that she's staying with us."

"I'm glad of that."

"The way you two get along?" Delray grinned.

"The way we get along is okay as long as the job gets done. You met many who can do her job as well as she does it?"

"Nope. She's world class, but also a world-class bitch at times. I think, though, that maybe she's not so much angry at us as she is taking her anger out on us."

"She tries not to," Blanchard said. He didn't want to bring up Jillian Weiss's comment about husband problems. It was too much like gossiping.

"Could be. Anything else of import, Jack?"

"Yeah, a couple items you should know about. The kid with the gun?"

"I remember that one, somehow."

"Our gun."

"You jest!"

Blanchard told him about Jacob Talman's arms-supply company. "So we've got four stashed around. You don't have to worry about it."

"After this morning, I shouldn't worry?"

"They're all under lock and key now."

"Well, I suppose the conditions dictate the preparation. I sure as hell don't like it, though."

"No one does. The other thing is the guy with the flesh problem. It could be that he's a member of an extremist group called the Sword of God. I don't know if they'd try to come and get him back, or if they even know we've got him, but we want to watch for strangers."

"We see two hundred strangers a day."

"These would probably be carrying Kalashnikovs."

"I guess I'd notice that."

Blanchard stood up and pulled his jeans up. He zipped up and hooked his belt.

They left the latrine together, walking toward the admin tent. Automatically, Blanchard counted vehicles. Deuce-and-a-half gone to Atarot. Two ambulances out. One of the GP Hummers was gone.

"Heard back from the ambulances, Sam?"

"Not yet. I'll try the radio."

It was nearly dinnertime, served from six until seven-thirty, and Blanchard saw a brigade of people moving dinner trays from the mess hall to the ward tents. Dean Wilcox, Melanie Masters, and Ben Gordon came out of the hospital shedding scrubs. They stopped to stuff them in the laundry bag stashed outside the hospital. Both of them had been in surgery all afternoon. Seven surgical patients had been scheduled.

Wilcox headed for the showers, and Masters met them at the admin tent.

"Melanie, can I talk to you for a minute?" he asked.

She looked up at him, but her eyes were kind of foggy. Fatigued. He could understand it. The intense concentration of delicate surgery would have defeated him in about two minutes.

"I guess so. Yes."

"Come on."

Delray went on into the tent, and he led Masters out to his Hummer and opened the door for her. His and Delray's private meeting room didn't seem appropriate. Walking around the hood, he got in behind the wheel.

"I don't necessarily want to bring this up," he said, "but there's something I need to know."

She turned sideways in the seat to look at him. "Like what?"

"You were going to quit the team?"

Her lips pursed into a very angry red line. "The director told you that?"

"What else would he do?"

"No, I wasn't going to quit."

Blanchard didn't know where to go from there. "I guess he and I got our information wrong. Sorry."

"You were looking forward to it?"

"On the contrary. Losing you would be a hell of a loss to me and to the team."

She stared out the windshield. At nothing in particular, he thought.

"Some . . . people back home in Chicago thought I should quit. They intervened, and I countermanded their recommendations to the director."

"I see. Halfway, I see. I'm sorry if you've got problems, Mel, but I'm glad you're not leaving. And if I can help in any way, you just let me know."

She swung back toward him. "Attack Chicago?"

"Is that what it would take?"

"That's your normal response to a problem, isn't it?"

"There are other ways."

"Anyway, it's not your dilemma. I can handle it."

"It could be my problem when it affects the rest of the team."

"It doesn't."

"You don't yell? Snap at people? That affects others, Mel."

She shoved the door open and slid out of the seat.

"Go to hell, Jack."

Blanchard grinned to himself. At least she was calling him by his first name.

"A test?" Khalid Badr said. "Why should we need a test? You do not trust your Iraqi friend?"

"I trust him as I trust anyone," Kadar said. "Which is to say, with a grain of doubt." He thought that statement to be a proper education for his followers. His role was to be a teacher, as well as a leader. "We will make certain before we move to Jerusalem. If it should happen to fail on the day of need, would we not look foolish?"

Badr did not continue the argument, and Kadar slowly removed each of the cans from the plastic web and placed them on the plank table. He called to Oma Kassim: "Bring me a knife."

She found a paring knife in the cabinet and brought it to him. Slowly, he punctured each of the cans, used the knife to part the thin aluminum, and peeled the tops back. If any of the vials had broken and contaminated the soda, Muhammad would welcome them much sooner than planned.

"The tongs."

Kassim went back to the cabinet and found ice tongs. Kadar used them to probe the dark liquid, finally locating one vial at a time. He lifted them from the cans and placed them on a sheet of newspaper.

None of the glass vials were broken, and the rubber caps were all sealed with wax and tape. They were small, about four centimeters in diameter and twelve centimeters long.

Eighteen of them.

He carefully dried them off with a towel.

Visions of Sapir and Hakkar spun in his mind, and he said, "We must be extremely careful with them. I want the case, Abu."

El-Ziam handed him the small black plastic case, and Kadar packed seventeen of the vials into the cotton padding, laid a layer of batting over them, and closed the top. Rising from the table, he took the case into the back room and placed it inside the footlocker that he kept there. He snapped the padlock shut.

Back in the main room, he found the others staring at the remaining cylinder. They were likely remembering Sapir and Hakkim and were afraid to touch it. That was just as well.

He took the eighteenth vial and placed it in the Velcro pouch on his ankle.

"You will drive, Abu."

Everyone wanted to go along, but Kadar told them there would be nothing to see. He and el-Ziam went outside and crawled into el-Ziam's Fiat.

"Where are we going?"

"Near Mar Saba, there is a new settlement of Jews. We will go there."

"But, Ibrahim, there are Palestinians there, as well!"

"They have chosen to live with the infidels. They must have prepared themselves to live or die with the infidels. Drive!"

Seven

The IDF Guards manning the concrete and barbed-wire blockade on Highway 90 at the southern edge of Jericho frequently made it clear that they cared little for Palestinians who traveled so close to sundown, but tonight's harassment seemed far greater than the usual. Kadar and el-Ziam were ordered out of the Fiat while it was searched. A mirror on a wheeled trolley was even used to peer at the undercarriage. The beams of flashlights pored into every crevice of the car. They were both patted down by one guard, but Kadar's ankle pouch was not discovered. He was certain that it would be, and even more certain that his nervousness was apparent.

He survived, however, as he had survived many times in the past. Searchers were often reluctant to touch his lower left leg, the one with the deformation. The acute angle of the foot when he was standing and its bloated appearance—his left shoe was much larger than the right—gave them pause.

He was surprised by the intensity of the search. Something must have taken place in the last few days to cause a higher status of scrutiny at the border posts. He had not been aware of it while traveling *into* Jericho, but could now tell that it would be necessary to increase his own level of care.

"Where are you going?" one guard demanded.

"Where else? To Gaza City. Palestinians have free passage, do we not?"

"For what purpose?"

"There is a job," Kadar said. "I must be there early in the morning, and my friend has agreed to drive me."

Once they were back in the car, with el-Ziam shifting through the gears, Kadar said, "It appears that we must go on to Gaza City."

"Yes. They will call and report us to the border guards. We will be expected."

"One day, my brother, we will have the right to travel our country at will."

"Allah wills it," el-Ziam said.

When they reached the road to Jerusalem, el-Ziam made a one-kilometer jog to the east, then turned south again. This road was not as well-maintained and wandered through the desert to eventually connect with Bethlehem.

Ibrahim Kadar closed his eyes and rocked with the car. Like cinema images on the backs of his eyelids, he saw the dream flowing. A bright and soft morning sun shining on a land rich and lush. The wadis ran full with clear, sparkling water, and the fields were overflowing with wheat and lettuce. The shepherds tended flocks of sheep and goats and cattle that stretched from one hill to another. The cities were pristine, gleaming in the light of day, and the centerpiece of cities, Jerusalem, proclaimed to the world the righteousness of her Islamic people.

It was so promised.

But the promise could not be fulfilled until he had completed his work.

The Koran was the Word of God, and the Koran had identified Kadar's lifework for him. There could be no misinterpretation for a believer who had heard the words recited in the passion and beauty of Arabic, for the Word had been revealed in Arabic, and a translation to another language was in itself heresy. His duty, as he had clearly seen it, was to rid his land of infidels. In particular, the Jews were defined as the greatest sinners, for the prophet Moses had been sent by God to free the children of Israel, but the children had become proud and anointed

themselves as a chosen people. When God attempted to warn
them through His messengers, the messengers were put to death,
and though the Jews were the People of the Book since God
provided them with the scriptures, they had perverted their
privilege.

Kadar could not be certain, but he thought it possible that
he was a messenger of God. Certain of the revelations he had
experienced while studying the Koran, while disregarded by
the Imams when he had attempted to explain them, had convinced him of the correctness of his path. He had seen, also,
that spouting the words did not achieve results. The scholars
had not yet driven the infidels from his land. His father had
wanted him to be a diplomat, but he had seen the product of
diplomacy. Arafat had given away the most cherished of ideals
in exchange for promises that were empty. Only actions resulted
in desirable ends. If Palestine were to reach the fruitful promise
of its destiny, it must first be cleansed of nonbelievers.

He was also dedicated to the concept of the plague. The
land, beginning with the capital city, must be visited by a plague
so that the infidels, and even the believers who made commerce
with the money changers, were eradicated.

Only then could the land be reborn in the image God had
explained to his Messenger, Muhammad.

Allah Akbar!

Ibrahim Kadar was on the very brink of his own destiny.

A quarter moon was rising by the time they passed the ruins
at Hircania. El-Ziam drove at a steady but sedate pace, saying
that the car's shock absorbers were bad. Kadar knew something
was wrong. Every bump in the road translated to the seat he
was in. He bounced around, worried about the vial, and watched
el-Ziam fight the steering wheel. It seemed to him that the
researchers and scientists who had developed the formula in
Saddam's biological laboratories at Al Quaim might have had
the foresight to store it in more indestructible canisters than
the small glass tubes. Certainly, the Iraqis spent large sums of
money on weapons; why should they attempt to economize
with a simple container?

Five kilometers past the ruins, el-Ziam slowed and drifted
off the road to the right. He parked the car, then shut off the

lights and the engine. It was almost fully dark. The stars were bright, and the desert whispered to his ears with a tiny breeze.

"This is the Wadi en Nar," he said.

"Let us go." Kadar opened the door and got out.

The road to the Christian monastery at Mar Saba, located on the now dry Wadi en Nar, approached from the west. Here, they were four kilometers east of Mar Saba, about half as far east of the Jewish settlement, and there was no road to follow. There were, however, tracks along both sides of the wadi, the route for goats and sheep and nomads. The passages were slowly being widened by the increased foot traffic of settlers in the new village and would one day, no doubt, become yet another road.

Kadar had forgotten the possible need for a flashlight, but after fifteen minutes of stumbling along the trail, his eyes adjusted to the vague illumination from the sliver of moon, and he was able to avoid the shrubs and rocks alongside the well-worn rut. He did not always avoid stepping in the droppings of goats and sheep.

Twenty minutes later, as the two of them climbed a slight rise in the bank, he saw lights. This settlement of two hundred people had electricity. They needed it to run the giant electric motors that powered the water pumps for the four deep wells. Three of the wells, he knew, were dedicated to irrigation, and the settlement was surrounded by newly tilled fields smelling of damp loam. It would be years, however, before the imported fertilizers and black soils blended in with the native earth brought about a decent production of vegetables and grains. He knew little of farming, but he had read of the deterioration of the earth in some areas once fertile but suffering from centuries of unscientific agricultural methods. God would put that right, when true believers tilled the soil.

He stopped to survey his approach, and el-Ziam came up beside him. The two of them squatted beside the trail and studied the settlement. Like farmers everywhere, these people retired early. There were a few lights in some of the windows, blurred by curtains. At two points, at the far end, there were lampposts.

"Do you see them?" el-Ziam whispered.

"I see them."

A patrol of two guards moved slowly among the buildings. The beam of one flashlight darted about, and when it caught a wall, the silhouettes of the guards were revealed. Untethered dogs roamed about, barking at the guards as they passed.

"The dogs?" el-Ziam asked.

"People will think they are agitated by the patrol. If they come close, kill them."

"With my bare hands?"

Kadar did not answer. He rose to a crouch and moved off the trail down into the wadi. The fecund aroma of irrigated fertilizer drifted from the field on the other side of the trail. Following a parallel route, the two of them stayed low enough to keep their heads below the ridge. Two hundred meters along the wadi, Kadar drew to a stop and told el-Ziam, "Stay here. If they see me, you must create a diversion."

He climbed the slope two meters and peered over the edge of the wadi. He was directly opposite the center of the settlement. The trail here had widened to the size of a street, and as it continued to the west, it became a road to Mar Saba. On the far side, darkened structures lined the street, a cross street almost in front of him. He did not see the guards.

Rolling onto his side, he eased his knee up and felt for the ankle pouch. With his finger and thumb, he found the flap and pulled it, doing it behind the protection of the ridge so the ripping sound of the Velcro would be less noticeable. Easing the vial from the pouch, he clutched it firmly in this hand, then rolled back onto his stomach.

"Be careful," el-Ziam whispered. "Go forward in the name of the only God."

He had no other intention. Rising to his knees, he slithered his way to the top of the wadi, then rose to his feet and trotted swiftly across the road. His footfalls were almost silent in the soft dirt.

When he reached the first building, he put his back to it, melding with the shadows, and looked up and down the street.

There was nothing.

Sidling to the corner of the building, he peered around. The side street was a block long, leading to the center of the settlement. Houses crowded it, lining an earthen street with no sidewalks. There was no electric illumination on this street, but at the far end, in the center of an open plaza, was his target, shining eerily under the light of the quarter moon.

He saw no movements.

A dog barked to the west, hopefully marking the passage of the patrol.

It took him four minutes, moving cautiously and staying in the shadows near walls, to reach the plaza. He dashed across fifty meters of open space to slide to a stop in the protection of the concrete tank. It was round, perhaps five meters in diameter, and its walls were a meter high. On the east side was the pump house, but its motor was now silent. There was a forty-watt bulb shaded by a tin cover attached to the pump house, but it did not offer much illumination.

Kadar took his time, scrutinizing the entrances to the four streets leading to the plaza. On the northern street, he heard more dogs, but he did not see them.

Keeping his head below the top of the tank wall, he raised his hands so that the moonlight and the light from the pump house revealed the vial. It was stoppered with a rubber cork, then sealed with wax and some kind of dark plastic tape.

He realized he should have rubber gloves. A single drop . . .

Kadar had thought to pour just a portion of the vial here, but now feared the attempt to restopper the bottle and replace it in his ankle pouch. Perhaps, he thought, that was the reason for the miniature size of the canister. It was meant to be expended completely with one opening.

With his left thumbnail, he sought out the end of the tape.

His hands were shaking so badly he could not find it.

He stopped, took a deep breath, lodged his wrists against the rough edge of the concrete to steady them, and tried again.

Found the cut end of the tape and peeled it away, rotating the vial as he did so. The tape stuck to the end of his thumb, but he didn't want to touch the inside of it. Carefully, he lowered it to the tank top, stuck it down with his index finger, and pulled his thumb free.

Now the cork.

He could not just jerk it free; he might splatter the liquid.

Slowly, he twisted. Stuck tight! With additional pressure, it began to turn more and more freely, and he worked it out of the throat of the vial with infinite care.

He dropped the cork in the water.

Then he started to pour from the container.

What if it spilled over the lip as he poured? What if it dribbled onto his fingers?

He was instantly repulsed and quickly dropped it into the tank.

Then sank to his knees on the moist ground.

Allah, I am your servant.

Talman had barely settled into his bathtub—looking forward to thoroughly analyzing the aimlessness of his morning meeting with the Palestinians—when he sensed that something was amiss. He leaned forward to peer through the open doorway into his living room. The light on the telephone was blinking.

Sighing, he stood up, stepped out of the tub, and wrapped a towel around his waist as he made damp footprints on the carpet. He located the small toggle switch on the base at the back of the phone, switched it to the second line, and picked up the telephone.

"Comet," he said.

"Clarion. What is today's password?"

Clarion was the Shin Bet communications center.

"Crazy Legs," Talman said.

"The counter is Gypsy."

"What have you got?"

"A message from the Jericho border post. Ibrahim Kadar and Abu el-Ziam departed Jericho en route to Gaza City."

"Thank you."

"One moment. There was also a shooting at the Medical Assistance Team encampment early this morning."

"What! Casualties?"

"No casualties. Mr. Jack Blanchard reported the incident to the Palestinian Police as required, but said that it was only an attempted theft. The thief escaped."

Talman thanked the man for the information, then hung up.

He knew he would be notified when Kadar reached the Gaza Strip, but in the meantime, if the man did not follow his itinerary . . .

He sat down in the chair and began making calls from the list of numbers he had memorized. He called Blanchard first and got a few more details regarding the incident at what Blanchard called Mercy Base. Then he called a few of his agents along with a few who did not report to him, but who were situated along the route between Jericho and Gaza City, and asked them to watch for Kadar.

He was about to make yet another call when his other line rang.

He switched the phone.

"Hello?"

"Major Talman, this is Amin Rahman."

Yes. Well. Kiss the travel agency goodbye.

"What can I do for you, Chief Rahman?"

"Let us meet to discuss that, as well as what I can do for you."

So now we are to intensify our intrigues with back-channel meetings?

"Do you know the Blue Nile Cafe on Flowers Gate?"

"In the Old City?"

"Yes."

"I will find it."

Talman dressed hurriedly, but then took his time walking the seven blocks to the cafe. It would not do to portray himself as eager. Before he entered, he donned the reading glasses he rarely wore and settled them uncomfortably on his ears. That was the signal to Ya'akov Arif that he could be under surveillance and not to approach him with anything significant.

He stepped inside and looked around. As soon as Arif noticed him, he pulled the glasses off, folded them, and stuck them in his breast pocket.

Talman spotted Rahman's handsome profile at a table near the window, talking to two men standing beside the table. The man exuded charm, and Talman assumed he made friends wherever he went. He walked toward the table.

As soon as the deputy chief noticed him, he jovially bade his visitors goodbye, then stood up.

"Mr. Talman, I'm happy we could meet."

Talman was aware that, in public, Rahman addressed him as "mister." Preserving his true title?

Since he offered his hand, Talman shook it, then the two of them sat down. Rahman ordered coffee for both of them.

"Unless you wish to eat?"

"No, I have already eaten."

"Fine." He waved the waiter away.

"May I call you Jacob? And I am Amin."

"Certainly."

"To ease your mind, Jacob, I should tell you that I have obtained your superior's permission to meet with you. The telephone number I called you at is also not in general circulation. It will be my secret."

"Well, that does ease my mind. I am not certain, however, of the purpose of this meeting. Was that not why we met this morning?"

"This morning, I sensed some level of disapproval from you, Jacob. I would like to clear that up."

The waiter brought the coffee, and Talman sipped from his cup while considering how he should respond. The thought of being absolutely truthful never crossed his mind.

Rahman waited, and when Talman only shrugged, went on. "I would like to be most frank with you."

"All right."

"I was embarrassed by the shortcomings of my lieutenants. You knew that, of course?"

"I thought it was possible."

"Your organization, Jacob, has many years of experience behind it. Ours is youthful, and we have yet to acquire the skills necessary to it. Then, too, our organization is subject to a patronage, and it is one that I cannot often control. Do you understand what I am saying?"

"I do." The man was admitting that political pull had more influence than expertise in placing policemen in their positions.

"Do you also know how much I open myself up to you when I say that?"

He was looking for a little quid pro quo: I have revealed myself to you; now you must do the same.

All right.

"Amin, I am very reluctant to share information with you because I do not trust where it might go. Just a minute. Let us say that, with a little time, I might come to trust you very well. What assurances do I have that my information will remain with you? Or at least not be passed onto someone . . . with other objectives?"

"Such as?"

Talman gave him the name of one of the men at the meeting. "He is a paid informant of the Islamic Resistance Movement."

Talman had thought that the deputy chief had very fine control over his facial muscles, but he actually registered shock.

"That is true?"

"It is true."

While Rahman digested that tidbit, Talman scanned the nearby tables. The customers were primarily Arabic, and they were interested in the new deputy chief of police, but they all appeared to be consciously avoiding any appearance of eavesdropping on the conversation.

"I will discuss this with the president. The man will be gone by tomorrow."

"You might also wish to discuss with the president the man called Talib. He works for the Islamic Jihad."

Rahman sighed. "Are there others?"

"Not that I know in the group assembled this morning. Amin, I have just given you information sensitive to my agency. That is not what I am trained to do."

"I understand. I also think you would not attempt to mislead me simply to create chaos."

"My goal is to avoid chaos."

Rahman leaned forward in an unfortunate appearance of conspiracy. "There are two things you should know. The president does not appreciate, shall we say, having an error in judgment pointed out to him. Removing these two men from my headquarters staff will require diplomacy on my part."

Talman nodded.

"And secondly, within the police agency, I must move with

caution. I have given myself three years to slowly weed out the incompetents and replace them with people that I can trust. In the future, I hope they are people who would also merit your trust. I am constantly faced with the need to suppress corruption, but it is difficult to remain covert. If I am to have any success, over a long term, I must not get myself fired."

Rahman smiled.

And Talman smiled back. The admission of corruption was another surprise.

One never knew. This guy could turn out to be genuine.

"So, Amin, what are we discussing?"

"We have already accomplished much, Jacob. I am learning from you where the snakes lie in wait. That is what I would ask of you as we learn to confide in one another over the coming years, so that I can make the Palestinian Police Force a respected and able agency." Smiling as he straightened up, he added, "I intend for our relationship to last a long time."

"You want me to help you identify the bad people?"

"And the good, Jacob. I need to know both."

"And what are you doing for me?"

"If I cannot find a way to rid myself of the bad seeds, I will give them to you."

"Adnan Boshogi?"

"He is evil?"

"I cannot tell you, Amin. I rather think he is merely incompetent."

"Hmm. Boshogi is a trusted cousin of the president's wife. It is the reason he obtained the high-level position in Jericho. I think he would be difficult to remove."

"I mention him simply because he appears to be more a blockade than a facilitator. I have not worked with him, you understand, but I hesitate to do so because of my impression. Perhaps it is merely his attitude."

"Let me have a persuasive discussion with him. Occasionally, attitudes can be adjusted."

"On rare occasions, perhaps. My own would be difficult to sway, I admit. I am a stubborn man."

Rahman grimaced, then said, "I am glad you agreed to meet with me, Jacob. I think we might have initiated a process helpful to us both. And I intend to have the same discussion with your colleague Moshe Perlmutter tomorrow.''

Talman shook hands again as he left. Walking back toward his apartment, he felt somewhat uneasy. These changes could not take place overnight, and he wondered if he was being set up in some way. As soon as he got to his phone, he would call Isaac Stein and report his conspiring with the enemy.

And despite his questionable disclosure of the names of the informants on Rahman's staff, he still felt pretty good. If nothing else transpired, he might have at least created a little chaos.

He had lied about that, naturally.

She caught Sam Delray in the mess tent, one of the stragglers eating late, cooking his own meal after the dinner hour. He had a forkful of rice en route to his mouth when she asked, ''Where's Blanchard?''

''Ah, he's hit the sack already, Melanie.''

''This early? Why?''

Delray obviously didn't want to talk about it, but told her, ''There's a new schedule.''

''What new schedule?''

''Jack, Dickie, and I are taking turns serving as duty officer during the night.''

More military claptrap, she thought.

Then reconsidered. Blanchard was obviously taking the threat from the Israeli intelligence people seriously. She might not think much of his overreaction, but had to admit that he placed the welfare of the team highest on his list.

''Thanks.''

She left the tent and crossed the field to the first of the tents occupied by the men. The canvas sides were rolled up, but in the darkness she saw only the diffused lights of a couple bulbs shining through the netting. Knocking on the mesh didn't seem all that productive, so she barged right in. Toward the back of the tent, a couple men were playing chess across a bunk. On the left, Blanchard was sitting on his bunk polishing his Wellington boots. He was dressed in jeans, but that was all. She was surprised at the hard planes of his chest and stomach. It was not at all what she'd have expected in a forty-six-year-old, and she had seen a lot of forty-six-year-olds. Greg had a bit of a paunch, and he was four years younger than Jack Blanchard.

She was immediately sorry she'd made the comparison. She was not into making comparisons.

He looked up at her. "Problem, Mel?"

"No. That is, there's not a problem here. Can I talk to you?"

"Sure. Dickie's got a stool over there."

She looked to the back of the tent, where the chess players were watching her. Masters had steeled herself for two hours for this discussion, and she didn't want anyone else in on it.

"Let's go for a walk. Is that all right?"

"I can use the exercise."

She waited while he pulled on socks and running shoes, then picked up a dark shirt from the top of his footlocker. He buttoned it as they left the tent.

God, I don't want to do this, she thought.

She wasn't going to tell him everything, of course. But the anger had been boiling within her all day; all of the incidents of the past threatening to overwhelm her. Masters defied her own preaching; she often urged patients to seek counseling for various problems. But personally, she didn't confide in anyone. Several times during the afternoon, right in the middle of surgical procedures, she had felt as if her mind were on the brink of spinning out of control, and she had seriously considered searching out Jillian Weiss and talking to her. She had overcome that urge, but knew that she had to take action of some kind, and despite the medical demands facing her, she couldn't take action from Israel. Blanchard's attempt to talk to her before dinner had backfired, only increasing the level of her anger. It was directed at herself.

Now, after they were fifty feet from the tent, walking toward a perimeter light, she said, "I need to go home for a few days."

He didn't respond.

"A week, maybe ten days."

"I'll do whatever I can to cover for you, Mel. A few days away will probably be good for you."

"No, it won't."

"Look—"

"I absolutely shouldn't be gone, but I've no choice."

They walked in silence for a few strides. She stumbled on a slight rise she couldn't see in the dark. "Old cat eyes" grabbed her arm and kept her from falling. She immediately shrugged out of his grip.

Then Blanchard asked, "I'm a good listener, if you want to discuss it."

"There's nothing to talk about!" she blurted.

Then, unbidden, it came gushing forth.

And in no particular order.

"I've got to get rid of Greg!"

Blanchard knew who Greg was. It was in her file. He didn't know what form of termination she had in mind, however.

She slowed to a stop, then turned to him. He could barely see her in the dark, just a dim outline against the distant perimeter light. He thought she was trembling.

And he wanted to take her in his arms, calm her, console her. It was the last thing a sane man would do. She'd react like a mortar round reaching its impact point.

Inexplicably, she asked, a tremor in her voice, "What kind of car do you have?"

"Car?" What in the hell? "It's a five-year-old Chevy pickup. Glenda's watching it for me."

"Do you like it?"

"Yeah, I do. Otherwise, I'd have traded it off."

"I once went off on my own and bought a Mazda Miata. Bright red. Because I wanted to do it, and because it was fun to drive."

He almost said it was a cute car, then decided that wouldn't go over well. "Something happened to it?"

"Greg took it back to the dealer. Said the only thing I could drive was a Lincoln."

Greg's a real charmer.

"He got a vasectomy, you know?"

He didn't know, but he immediately heard all about it. The stupid bastard didn't even talk to her about it.

"I'm not going to have children. Like you have your Glenda."

Blanchard felt a wave of sadness wash over him.

"Did your wife pick out your clothes for you?"

"Yeah, she did, Mel. What the Corps didn't ordain. I wasn't much good at it."

"Greg selects my wardrobe for me. Nothing too sexy, nothing too trashy, the right degree of decorum. Greg chooses from menus. He decides what's on TV or not."

Jesus. How'd she get roped in by this guy?

"The only time he ever came close to hitting me, I'd gotten my hair cut short without his permission. He didn't like it."

The litany went on for five minutes. The SOB scanned the résumés—declaring his legal interest—of physicians who applied to her medical practice for associate positions. He wanted to make certain she worked only with those he approved. He took possession of her salary and profit checks and invested them for her; she wasn't capable of prudent investment strategies. Once at a reception he caught her talking to an eminent—and also handsome—plastic surgeon from New York, interrupted their conversation, and took her home. The bruises on her arm above the elbow had persisted for days. At a dinner party they were hosting, he took delight in informing her in front of their guests that she'd chosen the wrong wine. When he was the one who had selected it. He went over her credit-card statements with her monthly, demanding an explanation for each purchase she had made.

Blanchard understood her need to have some control in the PMAT. She didn't have any at home. He wondered if she was also a tiger around her medical practice.

She started to run down.

"Mel . . ."

She turned away, to face the perimeter. "You're wondering why . . . why . . ."

"I probably am."

Her head slumped forward. "I don't talk about these things."

"With me, it's okay. Think of it as privileged, Mel. Just you and me and the night, no one else ever."

"Because I love him." And after a moment, "Loved him."

"He was the hot catch?"

She whipped back toward him, as if she were going to take his head off, then relaxed a bit and said, "Mainline social family. Wealthy. The best circles, an automatic partnership in his law firm. My dad was a plumber."

"My dad wrestled a living out of a Wyoming ranch. Nothing wrong with ranchers, farmers, or plumbers."

He still wanted to wrap his arms around her, but refrained.

"Mel, is it okay if I call him a son of a bitch?"

She bristled for a moment, then said, "I've been doing it all day. He called the director general and resigned for me."

"Ah. You want to shock the son of a bitch?"

She didn't reply.

"From here? Without flying into old Chi-town?"

"How?"

"First, I've got to know if you really want out of that relationship."

Again, she turned away from him. Several minutes went by before she said in a voice he could barely hear, "Yes."

"Tell me what's going to happen if you and Greg end up talking with each other in some other lawyer's office."

"That scares me. It does."

"You have a lawyer?"

"Greg always—"

"Come on."

This time, he took her hand, turned her around, and led her back toward the admin tent. They circumnavigated it—he saw Roberto Irsay banging away at a computer—and went to the command Hummer. He dropped her hand reluctantly, opened the tailgate, and set up the satellite dish.

"I'm just a facilitator here," he said.

"I don't know if—"

"You listen to me, then talk to this guy, then you decide."

Blanchard had to go through information to get the home phone number, and while it was ringing, he told her, "You'd probably call this the good-old-boy network. Brett MacDonald is a retired brigadier general. He's also a practicing attorney in Evanston and teaches at Northwestern. He's tough as they come, and he doesn't take shit from anyone. Least of all some exalted legal letterhead."

He reached out, put an arm around her shoulders, felt some resistance, then pulled her close beside him and tilted the phone so she could hear both sides of the conversation.

After the fourth ring he heard, "MacDonald."

"Brett, Jack Blanchard."

"You prick."

"Prick?"

"You haven't called in a year, then it's in the middle of a damned good meal."

"You eat too late."

"I eat when I'm hungry. What do you want? You in trouble?"

"Probably, but it hasn't caught up with me."

"I heard you were fucking up the World Health Organization."

"That's exactly what I'm doing. In fact, I'm calling from some godforsaken place in the middle of the West Bank."

The tone turned soft. "Is it bad, Jack?"

"They need a lot of help, and we're trying to give it to them. I do have a personal problem, though. Another person's."

"What can I do?"

Blanchard gave him a quick briefing on Melanie's background and problem.

"Masters? Gregory Masters?"

"That's the one."

"A self-righteous asshole if I ever met one, and I've met a bunch of them."

"You want to help her out?"

"Be pleased to do so."

Blanchard passed the phone to Melanie and started to step away, but she pinned him against the tailgate with her hip. "You stay, Jack."

"Okay."

"General, this is Melanie Masters."

"Let's get off that track right away. I'm Brett. You're Melanie. You sure you want to do this?"

Blanchard saw her throat work as she swallowed. "Yes."

"Okay. I'm going to get Jack's numbers and fax you some crap to sign. You fax me the copies right back and get the originals in the mail. I want all your account numbers, auto registrations, addresses, and the like. First thing Mon . . . no, probably Tuesday morning, I'll have court orders and a private detective. We'll freeze all the accounts—"

"Why?"

"Your hubby's got a reputation for slick deals, Melanie. I wouldn't put it past him to try and siphon off some funds."

"He wouldn't . . . yes, he might."

"He'll damned sure try. And we'll put the private dick on your house, change the locks. He's not going to get in for a fresh shirt until he's got a judge's signature and an escort."

"I . . . do you want me there, Gen . . . Brett?"

"Hell, no! You're doing more good where you're at. Stay with it and let me take care of the details. You've got nothing to worry about, so don't."

MacDonald asked her some more questions, getting down-right personal, then hung up after she thanked him.

Blanchard turned around to lean inside the Humvee and set up the fax machine.

Masters clambered over the tailgate and sat on the sheets, her knees hugged up against her chest.

"He's something, isn't he?"

"Brett? Damned good man in a fight."

It only took a few minutes to get the machine hooked up, but he figured it would be a while before MacDonald found whatever it was he wanted to send through the ether.

"Jack? Thank you."

"Just here to help, ma'am."

"Don't do that 'ma'am' crap."

"All right."

"Do you think you could find my purse? In the tent? It's got all my account numbers."

"Are you okay, Mel?"

"I just want to sit here awhile."

By the time he got back with the purse, after being subjected to withering glances from Emma Wachter and Deidre Joliet in their tent, he found Masters sobbing.

She sat up and stuck her knuckles in her eyes.

"I'm having a crying jag. Sorry, I can't help it."

"I'm not much good with crying women," he told her.

"Fourteen years."

"I know." He perched a hip on the tailgate and figured on a long night.

"And I don't want any misplaced sympathy, either."

"I know that, too."

Omar Heusseni rested on his pallet in the sleeping room of Kadar's house in Jericho, staring at the discolored ceiling. He had much preferred living in Jerusalem, at his father's house, and not as part of a zoo where he had no privacy.

In the other room, shut off from him by a curtain, he could hear Oma Kassim and Khalid Badr panting loudly as they clawed at each other in the throes of passion.

Supposedly, she was Kadar's woman, but Kadar had momentous things on his mind, and he neglected her. Badr had been tending to the leader's oversight for several weeks now, and though Heusseni had once attempted to console her himself, she had laughed him away: "You are but a boy!"

She was no longer a girl. Once, Ibn Sapir had told him, she had been the most fiery of freedom fighters, risking heart and soul on daring raids against Jewish settlements and vehicles. It was said that she had killed many. But that was when she had been with the Islamic Resistance Movement, and she was no longer a girl. The fire had gone out of her.

He was not a boy, either. He was nineteen years old, the son of Ibn Sapir by a woman not Sapir's wife, and he had borne the name she assigned to him. She died when he was five, and he had spent the next fourteen years attending his father. He had fully expected to assume the mantle of leadership of the Sword of God upon his father's death.

That Sapir's death came far too soon was an unexpected development. The man had wasted away and died, but before he last closed his eyes, he had passed the baton to Kadar, explaining to Heusseni, "You are only a boy."

The humiliation he suffered was ceaseless. No decision was

his own to make. Kadar dictated when he would say his prayers, when he would eat, where he would sleep, who he would see. His heart ached for the small house in Jerusalem, where he had been able to come and go as he pleased and meet with his friends. There was life in Jerusalem; Jericho was endless death. He missed his friend Nuri.

Heusseni's existence revolved around cleaning the house, being sent on useless errands, shopping at the markets for Kassim while she and Badr explored each other, and sitting quietly in a corner while the supposed adults planned their endless, mind-numbing operations. To his mind, which had studied under the brilliant Ibn Sapir, the follies planned by Kadar, el-Ziam, and Badr were often notable for their lack of thought and the frequency with which they went unfulfilled. These three, he had decided long before, were more prone to talk than to action.

And Heusseni thought of this latest fanciful illusion of Kadar's as shortsighted and ineffective. Already, it had proven disastrous; one had only to consult with Ibn Sapir and Nuri Hakkar, if one could consult with them through some medium.

He had tried.

Heusseni was devout. He had prayed for his friend Nuri. In fact, he rarely missed his prayers, and he always offered intense prayer before embarking on the infrequent missions—his only important tasks—assigned by Kadar. They were chiefly missions of theft, at which he succeeded each time. For Kadar's purposes he had stolen food, ammunition, gasoline, explosives, and twice, automobiles.

He was an excellent thief.

In fact, he was a better thief than Kadar knew.

Heusseni had determined weeks ago that Kadar was going to prove himself impotent as a leader, and so he had begun to accumulate his own storehouse of tools. Under the floor of a farm shed outside of Jericho, a safe haven for the Sword of God, Heusseni had secreted eleven bags of ammonium-nitrate fertilizer and a half drum of diesel fuel obtained in the night from two different settlements. From the Israeli Defense Forces, he had obtained three Beretta semiautomatic pistols, an American M-16 automatic rifle, nine fragmentation grenades, four rocket-propelled grenades—though he did not yet have a launcher—and several mess kits. From Kadar's own armory, he had pilfered detonators and a quarter kilo of plastic explosive.

He almost had enough to start his own movement. Somewhere, Kadar had hidden money, and if he could find that, he might well go off on his own.

It was not that their ideals were different. Heusseni wanted as much as Kadar for the peace accords to collapse. Only total eradication of the Jews would fulfill the promise of the Prophet. And like Kadar, he thought that a continuing series of incidents that attracted international attention would defeat the Palestinian Authority.

They could not agree—if Heusseni had even been allowed to disagree with Kadar—on the method of attracting that critical attention from the world.

But as he thought of Kadar's simpleminded belief in annihilation by way of Iraqi biological warfare substances, and as he listened to Badr's hurried grunting and Kassim's little shriek of climax, he had a more profound thought.

Why should he wait? Why should he allow Kadar to assume what was rightfully Heusseni's?

He owned the means, and with the right target, he could prove to one and all that he was no longer a boy. Let them compare Kadar's pitiful and long-delayed exploit to what Omar Heusseni could achieve with a bag of fertilizer.

Let us then determine who was the true leader of the Sword of God.

A bus laden with farmers would not do, of course. That had become almost trite after the successive attacks of Izzidin al-Qassam.

No, the television had already identified his target for him.

One that the world would not applaud, but certainly notice.

And the world would force the damnable Israelis and the more damnable Palestinian Authority to make concessions to the true Palestinian movement.

Yes.

MONDAY, JULY 26

And slay them wherever you come upon them,
and expel them from where they expelled you;
persecution is more grievous than slaying.
                                        —Surah 2, the Koran

Eight

At a few minutes after seven in the morning, Blanchard walked over to the ward tent they were leaving behind and pushed through the opening.

Maria Godinez and Polly Brooks were going over instructions with the two Arabic women to whom they were entrusting the care of the remaining patients. He hoped their training was adequate since he was going to pay them for their services. It wasn't much, but the small stipend would help out their household budgets.

Seven of the beds were occupied, four with recovering cholera patients, two with men recuperating from surgery, and one with the young Arab, Nuri Hakkar.

To Blanchard, Hakkar appeared to be in extremely bad shape. Masters was going over him, prodding with a gloved finger, and the Arab didn't like it one bit. From time to time, he swung at her with his remaining arm, but there was absolutely no strength in it. The stubs of his legs and his right arm were reddened and infested with pustules. His stomach looked like raw meat. His lips were drawn back as much in distaste at her examination as in pain, Blanchard thought. Jillian Weiss was standing by to interpret, but it looked as if not much had changed in that process. Hakkar continued to maintain his silence. He refused to divulge so much as his birthplace. His only utterances consisted of epithets for the doctors and nurses attending him. Weiss had offered to locate an Arabic doctor or an Imam for him, but Hakkar hadn't responded to the offers.

Masters completed her exam, and she pulled a sheet up to his waist. The flattened sheet made the absence of his legs more prominent. He relaxed now, and the stub of his right arm and his left arm rested flat on the bed. He didn't have an interest in moving, or gesturing, and probably was too weak to do so anyway. The rest of his torso was a burnt pink color, coated in salve. His skin didn't seem connected to anything, and shifted over his ribs as he breathed. Brooks came over and placed a large dressing on the left side of his stomach and a smaller one on his right side, near his armpit. Dean Wilcox had told Blanchard those were areas where underlying musculature was exposed, and now even the muscles were deteriorating rapidly.

His eyes were the worst aspect. They were nearly opaque, and yet seemed to burn with a fever that would not be quenched. His head didn't move, but the eyes darted from Masters to Weiss, then back to Masters.

Blanchard was torn by conflicting values. Some of his memories were vivid:

Gunnery sergeant Abraham Hanover had the point, creeping forward along the trail with as much care as he opened a coffee can of his mother's peanut-butter cookies.

Blanchard, then a second lieutenant platoon leader, was behind him; his radioman, a lance corporal named Delecort, in close attendance. Overhead the triple canopy of the jungle leaked moisture, but it was hot and misty. The sweat rolled off Blanchard's face, pouring from beneath the helmet, making the dirt coating his face and neck itch against his skin. He longed to toss the helmet, but there was always that example to set.

Hanover jerked his hand up, and Blanchard froze. Behind him, stretched down the trail for forty meters, the rest of his platoon followed suit. Hanover, who had superb hearing, had noted something unusual in the undercurrent of the jungle symphony. Blanchard heard only the buzz of insects, the shrill call of birds, a monkey's chatter.

To his left, he detected movement and shifted his eyes. Snake. Big, some kind of constrictor, slithering along the lower branch of a tree. Its head was raised, waving back and forth, seeking the intruders into his kingdom.

Delecort, following Blanchard's eyes, saw the snake some five feet away from him, and almost involuntarily, he straightened his back and stepped off the trail to the right.

Snagged a trip wire.

Blanchard saw the wire in the same instant Delecort kicked it, yelled, ''Hit the deck!'' and burrowed his face in the slippery muck of the trail.

It triggered a Bouncing Betty, the charge leaping eighteen inches upward and spraying the air with a horizontal charge of shrapnel The fragments whipped above him with a whistle that stung his ears. Foliage ripped and shredded. Men screamed.

Delecort's legs were sliced off at the knees.

Hell gushed around them as an NVA company opened up with an intense cross fire from positions forward and to either side of the trail. Hanover, with a flesh wound in his upper arm, slithered backward and joined Blanchard. He provided cover fire while Blanchard worked on Delecort, fastening tourniquets above his knees, packing and taping Delecort's and Blanchard's own field bandages to the stubs of his legs. Blood was everywhere; his hands were drenched in it when he picked up his M-16 and joined Hanover in firing at ghosts in the green curtain.

It took forty-five minutes to back out of the ambush, slithering along the slimy trail, a moaning Delecort clamped to his back with web straps.

Blanchard lost one dead and seven wounded that morning.

None of them had been left behind. Marines never left a buddy, dead or alive, behind. And today, Corbin Delecort was president of his own software company in Palo Alto, California. Blanchard knew because he had checked.

That was one thing; this was another. In no way could Blanchard imagine a future in which Nuri Hakkar would have something to contribute. He was of the opinion that the young man would best be served by turning off the nourishment feeding his arm. Why prolong the agony?

But Masters was of another opinion, and her opinion was what counted.

"*Allalah ma'as-salama,* Nuri," she said and backed away from the bed.

Hakkar, of course, didn't bother with goodbyes.

The five of them stepped outside.

Under his breath, he asked Masters, "How long's he got?"

"I don't know. The vitals are fairly stable right now. It could be a while. He might even recover, Jack. Shall we go?"

"Why not?"

The convoy was ready to go. Most of the white trucks were assembled in a ragged line, their beds and their trailers laden with the essentials of Mercy Base. A military semitractor with a low-boy trailer, painted in the camouflage colors of the Israeli Defense Forces, was parked to one side. The bulldozer it had transported snorted diesel smoke as it leveled the remains of the base.

Parked next to the semi was a Palestinian Police Land Rover. The cops had shown up as they completed their loading and were sticking around to see them off.

Two of his vehicles were missing. Chao, along with a nurse and paramedic, had taken one of the ambulances on a tour of the wards left behind from earlier moves. This time, they would fold the tent at Site 1, having discharged the last patients there. If they hadn't already discharged themselves and disappeared. Chao was carrying the last cash payments for the conscripted Arabic candy stripers at Site 1.

Dickie Armbruster and Steve Mackey had taken another of the Hummers on to the Mar Saba site where they were supervising the IDF heavy equipment operators preparing the place for the arrival of the PMAT.

They began heading for their assigned seats.

"You want to ride with us, Mel?"

"No, Jack, thanks. Dean and Lars and I are going to work on our strategy during the trip."

She angled off toward a Hummer ambulance in the middle

of the pack, and Blanchard and Weiss continued walking toward the front of the convoy. Almost everyone was mounted up, and most were in cheerful states of mind. Drivers and nurses joked with each other. People laughed, sometimes a rare sound in this group. Everyone was looking forward to a few days of respite before the grind started all over again. Melanie Masters had been noncommittal about the change of venue.

In the past nine days, since Blanchard had hooked her up with Brett MacDonald, Masters hadn't once mentioned what was taking place on that front. To say that his curiosity was piqued was an understatement, but he wouldn't have asked her, and if he had called MacDonald, he'd have been shut down in an instant. The general didn't talk about his clients.

The only overt sign was that Masters had informed those who normally tended the telephones—primarily himself, Delray, Armbruster, and Irsay—that she wasn't accepting calls from Greg Masters. If she was in surgery or on rounds, especially, she wasn't to be bothered. Blanchard assumed that order originated with MacDonald.

And it was prescient. Greg Masters or his secretary had called over thirty times in the last week.

Masters herself had been more subdued. She was easier to get along with, though Blanchard thought she was probably in the trough of some depression. She called him Jack, but she didn't get any closer. He figured she was upset at herself for revealing so much of her personal baggage to him.

Weiss was looking at him speculatively.

"What's up, Jillian?"

"I wish I knew. We've been calling her Mellow Melanie."

"Don't look at me. I don't engage in social intrigue."

She stuck her arm through his and held onto his forearm as they followed the treaded tracks where the bulldozer had passed. "That's what makes you so lovable, Jack. Mysterious too."

"I've never pictured myself as lovable or mysterious."

"That's okay. You're not supposed to define yourself. That's what I do."

"Gosh, thanks."

"You just hang on," Weiss said, "she'll come around."

"Jillian—"

"I know about these things," she professed.

She was about to say something, but he stopped, dragging her to a halt.

A cloud of dust was boiling to the north, and as he watched, its origin slowly materialized. White Hummer.

He started walking again, Weiss still holding onto his arm. This could be a possessive woman, he thought, knowing she wasn't. She was just extremely friendly.

By the time they reached the command Humvee at the head of the column, he had picked out Armbruster's face behind the windshield of the approaching truck.

Armbruster locked up the brakes and slid to a stop next to them. A choking cloud of dirt rose about waist level.

Blanchard walked up to the open window.

"Something wrong, Dickie?"

"You had the phones shut down, Jack, and I didn't want to put this on the radio. No telling who's listening."

"What?"

"We've another bloody case of that necro-whatever-it-is. Two of 'em, in fact."

"That can't be."

Jillian released his arm. "Are you sure, Dickie?"

"I saw the first one, didn't I? I'm damned near an expert."

Blanchard pulled open the rear door. "Get in, Jillian. Let's go talk to Melanie."

He slid in beside her, and Armbruster drove down the column to stop next to the ambulance shared by the doctors.

Masters got out when he called to her, and he joined her between the vehicles.

"What is it, Jack?"

"Toxic epidermal necrolysis, according to Dickie. Two cases."

"No."

"Well, I don't know about Dickie's diagnostic ability."

"I do," Armbruster said, getting out of the Hummer and leaving its engine running. "I'm pretty damned sure of it, Doctor."

Masters looked at Blanchard.

He said, "Dickie, roll an op-unit out of the line. Get Perkins and Joliet. Jillian, you go with them."

Masters asked, "Are you coming, Jack?"

"I'd better stick with the convoy. We'll catch up with you later."

Ten minutes after that, the op-unit and Armbruster's Humvee sped away, and Blanchard crawled behind the wheel of his command unit. He had Tina Ambrosia and Washington Apt riding with him.

"*¿Que paso?*" Ambrosia asked.

"The same thing as Nuri Hakkar, I guess."

"That flesh-eating stuff?" Apt asked.

"It cannot be," Ambrosia insisted.

He didn't think so, either.

Masters promised him it wasn't contagious.

"This is Leila. I have to hurry."

"Go on," Talman told her.

"Kadar, el-Ziam, Badr, and the woman—I now know her name as Oma Kassim—are still at the house."

Kadar and el-Ziam had shown up in Gaza City last week, but had taken far longer to make the trip than might be expected. They had returned to Jericho on Wednesday afternoon.

"Heusseni?"

"That is what bothers me. I haven't seen him for two days, and he is usually the one who does the shopping. Badr has been shopping in his place."

"I'll check with the border guards. Thank you."

"It is good to hear your voice," she said.

"And I, yours. I will try to meet you sometime this week. I am supposed to talk to Adnan Boshogi."

"I would like that. Goodbye."

She hung up, and Talman immediately punched in the number for the Shin Bet communications center. He asked the duty officer to check with the border-security section for any record of Heusseni leaving Jericho.

Pluto, who was stationed in Hebron, had identified Heusseni as the son of Ibn Sapir. That gave Heusseni more importance than they had previously assigned to him, and Talman had asked Venus to keep a closer eye on him. Forty-eight hours' absence was not a very close eye, but he understood the difficulty of maintaining a round-the-clock surveillance when she was alone and two blocks from the house.

He briefly considered calling Rahman about the boy, but decided the time was not yet ripe for that. He had heard, through Isaac Stein, that Rahman had replaced two of his headquarters staff, and Moshe Perlmutter had reported having an interesting conversation with the deputy police chief. Who knew?

"Comet, there is no record of Heusseni leaving Jericho."

"All right, thank you. He has probably slipped through the cordon."

He called his agents to alert them, taking all of ten minutes to do so. Then he tried Blanchard's number, but there was no response.

That worried him, so he left his office and went upstairs to his apartment. He stood in the closet doorway, removed the cardboard box on the shelf that covered the radio, and turned the radio on. He dialed in the UHF frequency Blanchard had given him. When the digital readout displayed 241.0, he picked up the microphone and pressed the transmit key.

"PMAT commander, come in."

Static. He was about to try again when he heard: "This is Blanchard. Who've I got, over?"

"Your friend in Jerusalem."

"Gotcha. What's shakin'?"

"I tried your telephone, but I could not get through."

"We're on the move, heading for Mar Saba."

"I will keep that in mind. I am calling to tell you of a person to watch for." Talman described Heusseni for Blanchard.

"Is he dangerous?"

"It is possible. He is a member of the Sword of God, the son of its founding father, and he has slipped away from our surveillance."

"We'll watch for him. Remember, I told you about Nuri Hakkar?"

"Yes, with the . . . uh, disease." For some reason, Talman decided it was best not to air the specifics.

"We've got two more cases, though I haven't yet confirmed them."

"I thought that disease to be rare?"

"Me too, buddy. Anything else?"

"No. I am over and out."

He shut off the radio and went to his bedside table to retrieve a map. He had not been in the Mar Saba area for some time, though it was but eleven kilometers from his office, and thought it might be worth his while to spend an afternoon there. There were two new settlements he had not yet seen.

Bothersome, too, was the fact that the PMAT was going to be that much closer to Jericho—only twenty-four kilometers away. That much closer to the Sword of God.

It was taking much longer than he had anticipated.

Omar Heusseni had begun his work after midnight, and it was already eight o'clock in the morning. He had stopped only to say his prayers at dawn. Now, the sun baked his back as he worked. Oma had cut his hair several days before, and as usual, trimmed it too short, especially on the neck. He could feel the paler skin heating.

There was no one at home in the ruins of the farmhouse. It had been unoccupied for years, probably dating from the time the well went dry. Weeds had overgrown the yard, and the wooden shed where he worked leaned precariously from the direction of the predominant winds. It was small, meant only to hold tools, and it had no door. Several missing boards in the walls allowed the sun to splash rectangles of light on the wood floor. A section of the floor was now raised, propped against the inside wall. The opening revealed the pit Heusseni had laboriously dug several weeks before, when he first became disenchanted with Ibrahim Kadar.

The house was on a mental listing of Kadar's, and was shared with the membership; it was a refuge in time of need, but as far as Heusseni knew, Kadar had been there but once.

Backed up to the shed was the car he had stolen in Jerusalem yesterday. He would have preferred a van, but had had to settle for the eleven-year-old Mercedes sedan used as a taxi. In recent years private automobile ownership in Israel had skyrocketed, which not only overtaxed the rural highways and urban streets, but also drove prices upward for automobiles that were scarcely operating junk heaps. The Mercedes fell into that category, and its fenders revealed its heavy use in city traffic.

It was the mixing that was taking him longer than planned. The ratios had to be precise, and then the diesel fuel blended carefully with the fertilizer. He mixed slowly with a wooden paddle.

Just after eight o'clock, however, he completed the last bucket. He had spent his personal money for the twenty-four five-gallon plastic buckets with plastic lids, and he had enough material to fill twenty-one of them.

The mixing also had side effects. His nose stung and his throat was raw from inhaling the diesel fumes.

He walked away from the bucket and spent a few minutes drawing in fresh air. Then he went back to the car and opened the rear door. With a few minutes struggling, he was able to free the bench seat from its clips. He carried it around behind the shed and tossed it into the weeds.

Then he went back, opened the trunk, and began stowing the buckets inside the trunk, packing them tightly against each other. The balance of the buckets he placed on the floor of the backseat.

Then he began to deal with the tricky part. With a screwdriver he pried the lids off one bucket in the trunk, and two on the inside of the car. Using the razor-sharp edge of his knife, he cut a long slot, ten centimeters in length, in each of the lids.

Back in the shed, he dropped into the pit and retrieved the small blob of plastic explosive, the detonators, the wire, the plastic tape, the batteries, and the timer.

With extreme care, Heusseni stripped the plastic from the ends of the wire pair, twisted the ends with the leads of a detonator, and then wrapped the exposed wire with tape. Dividing the plastic into three balls, he shoved the detonator into one ball, tamped it tightly, then placed it in the fertilizer mix of the open bucket in the trunk. He replaced the bucket's lid, allowing the wire to exit through the slot he had cut.

He had to force the backrest of the backseat with the screwdriver in order to open a gap large enough to pass the roll of wire through. Then he shut the trunk lid, but softly, trying not to jar anything. He heard the latch click.

It took him another fifteen minutes to bury detonator-imbedded plastic explosive in two more buckets inside the car, then wire all of the leads together, finally throwing the roll of wire into the front seat. He went around to the passenger side and opened the door, wired the square six-volt batteries to the detonator leads, then attached one wire to the timing device. It was a small black box with its own nine-volt battery to power the digital clock. There were two terminals, and he left one unattached for the time being in the interest of his own safety. The batteries and excess loops of wire, he shoved under the front seat, leaving the timer close at hand.

Then he got in the car and started the engine.

The site at Mar Saba was located two hundred yards south of the Wadi en Nar, across the wadi from a Jewish settlement and less than a mile east of another settlement established by Arabs. Mar Saba was actually the site of a monastery, and neither of the settlements founded near it had been named. The Arabs called their village simply *"medina,"* meaning town, and the Jews referred to their own town as the *"kefar,"* translated as village.

She knew her charge from the World Health Organization was to treat West Bank Arabs in health distress. The Israelis were to take care of their own. Yet, she was not about to turn down anyone who came to her in an emergency.

A front loader and a small tractor with a scrapper blade were working the soil, preparing level areas for the tents and a sloped base for the showers. Steve Mackey was riding alongside the Israeli driver tractor, talking animatedly with him and making suggestions with a pointing finger.

"Why so far from the wadi?" Masters asked Armbruster.

"I don't want anyone sneaking up on us," he said as he drove past the location.

"God!"

"Doctor—"

"It's okay. I understand the mentality."

"Hold on."

She gripped the handle on the dashboard as Armbruster went over the edge of the wadi, fought a path across the rugged bottom, and then climbed the far side. The ambulance followed in their tracks.

On the other side he crossed a road, then drove down a street that was suddenly populated as people came out to watch them. He parked in a central square next to a concrete water tank.

As she shoved open her door and grabbed her bag from the floor under her legs, a contingent of three people emerged from a house at the side of the square and marched resolutely toward them. All three men wore the *kipa*, an embroidered cap signifying their orthodox views.

The rest of her team joined her as she met the villagers in the square.

"Dr. Masters," Armbruster said, "this is Mr. Laskov, the administrator. Dr. Masters is our chief of medicine, Mr. Laskov."

"I thank you for coming so quickly, Dr. Masters. This event is quite troubling."

"Where are the victims?"

"This way, please."

The house was apparently used as a village meeting space. There was a door, four windows on the street, and lots of space, maybe forty feet by thirty. The floor was concrete, and folding chairs were stacked against one wall. Beneath the windows, on thin mattresses laid directly on the floor, were three women and one man.

"Dickie, you told me two."

"And that's what I knew, Doctor."

Laskov said, "Since you left, Mr. Armbruster, two more people came forward."

She went to her knees next to the first pallet, that of a woman in her thirties. All of the patients were conscious, watching her, deep trouble spilling from their eyes.

"I'm Dr. Masters. What's your name?"

"Karen, Dr. Masters. What is it?"

"Well, let's take a look."

Joliet and Perkins moved up close, donning gloves as Masters did the same.

She introduced them as nurses.

"Dickie, you want to go get Mackey?"

"On my way."

"Cale, would you and Deidre take histories on the others. Especially any contact between the four of them?"

"I can help with that," Weiss said and went around the pallets to begin talking to the man.

Masters looked up at Laskov, and he quickly realized he should be elsewhere. He ushered his two colleagues away and out the door.

This wasn't the time to be worried about privacy, and she quickly unbuttoned the woman's blouse. She wasn't wearing undergarments, and her chest, breasts, and stomach were rough and reddened with rash. As Masters went through her examination, she questioned the woman about her history and the onset of the rash.

"You first noticed the rash two days ago?"

"Yes, Doctor."

"Anything else?"

"I have been coughing. I may have a vaginal infection. There is an itch."

There were often secondary infections associated with what was also known as scalded-skin syndrome.

"When you cough, have you noticed anything special about the mucus?"

Fear in the eyes. "It is reddish."

Blood, then.

"Any pain."

"Some. It is not too bad."

She changed gloves three times as she moved to the others. All of the symptoms were there, and more worrisome, all seemed to be in the same stage of development. The man had a yellow exudation around his eyes, and she wiped it away carefully with a tissue. Ocular lesions were common with the disorder.

When she was finished, she, Perkins, and Joliet moved away to consult.

"Toxic epidermal necrolysis," she confirmed.

"This is amazing," Joliet said.

"What about contacts between them?"

"Karen is the cousin of the man, though they haven't seen each other for several days," Perkins said. "Other than that, no close relationships. They tend to meet each other throughout a day, frequently when they are getting water."

"As soon as the hospital gets here, we want to set up for serum analysis. We're looking for leukocytosis, elevated levels of alanine aminotransferase, as well as fluid and electrolyte imbalances. Urinalysis—watch for albuminuria. We'll do Gram stains of the lesions. All of that will only confirm the diagnosis, I'm afraid."

"Should we begin treatment?" Perkins asked. "We don't have much with us."

"Do what you can to start. As soon as we can get it, we want to start high-dose systemic corticosteroids. Let's get IVs under way, also, assuming an electrolyte imbalance. Keep replacing fluids. As soon as we get the wards set up, we want them out of clothing. Minimal contact with fabrics in order to maintain skin integrity."

"Monitors?" Joliet asked.

"Arterial blood gas levels, serum protein, electrolyte, hematocrit and hemoglobin. We want to watch vital signs and urine output."

"I'm getting awfully low on prophylactic antibiotics," Jillian Weiss said.

"Get hold of Dickie, tell him what you think you need, and send him to Jerusalem to scrounge from the army and the hospitals."

"I'm good at that, I am," Armbruster said as he and Mackey edged their way through a crowd that had gathered in the street outside the door. Through the windows Masters saw that they were forming into some kind of line, as if she were opening up shop right away.

Mackey glanced at the four patients.

"You wanted me for a reason, Melanie?"

"Steve, this disease is not contagious. It usually is the result

of a reaction to such drugs as penicillins, butazones, sulfon-
amides, barbiturates and such. Some researchers say it might
reflect an immune response. I need to know how four people
came down with it at one time. They're all in the same stage
of development.''

"Was there a mass vaccination? The whole town at once?''

"I don't know. We'll check.''

"Common contacts?''

"The major one,'' Perkins said, "is that water tank out there.
They meet there when they're getting water.''

"I don't see this as being transmitted by bad water,'' Masters
said.

"Still, it's our only source right now,'' Mackey told her.
"I'd shut it down until we know for sure.''

"Talk to Administrator Laskov about that. He'll balk, I'm
sure.''

"Okay.''

Masters tried to prepare herself to talk to the patients. This
was the worst part, trying to ease their levels of anxiety while
explaining what they had, and what she was going to do about
it. She would deal with it realistically. If they asked, she would
tell them they had a seventy percent chance of recovery. She
had to avoid giving them any false hopes. And if they asked
further, she would tell them there was a strong chance that, if
they recovered, there would be a good deal of residual scarring.
That was a tough one, for it often interfered with a patient's
desire to get better. Body image was a powerful part of the
psyche.

Armbruster and Weiss tried to get out through the doorway,
and he called to her, "Doctor, can you come here?''

She walked over, smiling for Laskov and several others who
were gathered there.

"Until we get the clinic set up, probably late tomorrow
morning, we won't be doing any screening.''

Not one of them paid any attention to her.

The man next to Laskov pulled up his shirt.

"Doctor, have you seen a rash like this before?''

* * *

Ibrahim Kadar did not have a telephone. He thought of it as a minor inconvenience, and he walked down to the post office to make his call, using *asimonim*—the public-telephone tokens—to pay for it.

The major inconvenience was that no one answered when he called. He beseeched Allah's temper upon the nonrespondent and left the post office. Walking down the street, he entered the cafe of Leila Salameh and took a table near the door.

She was the only one who worked there, and she was attending to a couple at another table, the only customers in midmorning. He waited patiently, scanning bottles accumulated on the counter near the door to the kitchen. He was always alert to the possibility of intoxicants being sold from any restaurant. It rarely occurred in Jericho, but he knew that they were readily available in Jerusalem. In Jerusalem! The holiest of cities!

It was a practice that would soon vanish forever.

Finally she approached him.

"How may I serve you?"

"Coffee, only, Madame Salameh."

"I have just received the freshest of oranges."

"An orange, also, then."

He spent twenty minutes peeling and eating his orange and drinking the strong coffee, left the correct change on the table, and went back to the post office.

This time, the man answered the telephone. He was an uncle of Khalid Badr; one who did not approve of Badr's activities, but who was always in need of money. In exchange for appropriate amounts, he was able to overlook his disapproval long enough to perform small tasks of intelligence gathering and other chores.

Both of them knew that Shin Bet listened in on their conversations, so both were circumspect.

"You took your trip?"

"I did."

"And did you enjoy yourself?"

"Immensely. Everywhere I looked, I saw reddened skin."

Wonderful! Kadar had been so worried since that night he

spent each evening after prayers and before bed examining his own skin minutely for any signs of deterioration. So far, nothing untoward had appeared.

"I am happy for you," he said. "There is another matter. You know the son?"

"The son? Oh! You mean Om—"

"That is the one. Have you seen him?"

"Not in several weeks. Is he well?"

"I do not know. He went away on Saturday, and I worry about him."

"I will watch for him and tell others."

"Thank you, my brother. *Allah Akbar!*"

He replaced the telephone and wandered out of the post office.

While he was pleased that the attack on the settlement appeared to be under way, the disappearance of Heusseni was irritating in the extreme. The son of Ibn Sapir had very little sense, and he likely nursed some useless grudge against Kadar for assuming his father's role.

Impatient and imprudent, Heusseni could well act in some disruptive manner that would interfere with Kadar's plans.

If the youngster ever came back, he might have to kill him. Even believers were subject to death if they interfered with the divine purpose of Allah.

Omar Heusseni was nervous. Oma Kassim had done this before, and he wished he had her experience to guide him.

He had angled the rearview mirror down, and as he steered the old car along the highway, he kept taking surreptitious glances at the floor of the backseat. The buckets had not moved.

He was driving cautiously, afraid of creating a jolt that would prematurely detonate the explosive mixtures. He did not know how sensitive they were. In the future he would study more, and experiment with various bombs out in the desert.

The road curved to the left, toward the south. Soon, when it curved to the right, headed to Bethlehem, he would have to leave the asphalt and rely on Allah's good graces. That was the part of his plan that worried him excessively.

A pickup truck came up behind him quickly, blared its horn, passed, and soon disappeared over the lip of the hill ahead of him.

Heusseni maintained his steady forty kilometers per hour. The speed limit was eighty kilometers per hour, but he took no chances with bumps in the road.

He had already reconnoitered the encampment of the World Health Organization, and he knew what to do when he reached it. He would drive into the camp, park the car, connect the wire to the timer, and set the timer for ten minutes. Then, he would walk away. It was so simple.

Once he had reached the camp.

However, getting to the camp was the problem. It was about six kilometers from the paved road, and the Mercedes was not designed for travel across the desert. He feared getting stuck, and worse, he feared the consequences of smashing a wheel into an unseen crack in the surface. The explosion would be tremendous, but lament of laments, he would be the only one to hear it.

If, indeed, he heard anything.

He followed the pickup to the top of the hill, and as he cleared it, he was startled by what he saw.

Two kilometers away, just pulling onto the pavement and headed his way, was a long line of white vehicles.

He was too late!

They were leaving.

The first of the military-type vehicles was much farther ahead of the others, coming at him, not fast, but rapidly enough.

He must think!

Yes!

Oh, yes!

He would not have to chance the sand.

Allah was so good to him!

Careful to maintain his speed, he reached beside him in the seat and connected the final wire to the timer.

He switched on the timer.

Heusseni examined the road ahead. Most of the convoy was now on the pavement. The lead vehicle was a kilometer away.

Heusseni set the timer for three minutes, then shoved it under the seat so the he would not be tempted to change it.

As soon as he passed the lead vehicle and reached the first of the main body, he would simply park the Mercedes in the middle of the road, get out, and run for the ditch at the side of the road. He would bury himself as deeply as possible.

They would think him sick, or in need of relieving himself. By the time they sensed danger, when the approximate middle of the convoy had reached the automobile, it would be far too late.

As he drove on, his mind kept the count.

Two minutes and fifty seconds.

Blanchard tried to maintain a half mile lead on the rest of the vehicles. If he spotted trouble, he wanted to deal with it early on.

In his rearview mirror he saw Delray's Hummer—on the very end of the column—bite into asphalt. Okay. They had about five kilometers of paved road before they'd leave it again and cross the desert for Armbruster's new site near Mar Saba.

It was another of the endless sunny days, the temperature hovering somewhere around thirty-seven degrees Celsius. Using that scale, it always sounded better than one hundred degrees Fahrenheit, which was the average July temperature. Every day had been average, and he'd have given his bottle of scotch for a good mudslinging downpour.

A pickup went by moving at a good clip. The front seat was packed with four people . . . and maybe a kid. He watched it in the rearview mirror for a few seconds.

No big deal.

Ahead, he saw a blue Mercedes coming, not fast, just lolling along.

Counted heads.

One, the driver.

When it went by, the driver didn't even look at him, kept staring straight ahead.

A taxi.

Out here?

Taxi drivers didn't waste time at slow speed.

The face?

Familiar?

What had Jacob Talman said about . . .

He glanced in the rearview mirror and saw the Mercedes's brake lights flaring. It was slowing down.

"Hang on, kids!"

Blanchard stomped the brake, whipped the wheel hard left, and hit the accelerator. The Hummer slid broadside on the pavement for a few seconds, clawed for traction, found it, and slid its tail around. He spun the wheel to center as he started through the gears.

Forty.

Fifty.

"What's going on!" Apt yelled.

"Mother Mary, pray for me!" Ambrosia told him.

Sixty-five.

The slowing cab was a quarter mile ahead. The first vehicle in the column, a deuce-and-a-half with a tanker trailer of gasoline, had almost reached it.

He came off the accelerator, downshifted.

Two hundred yards.

The Mercedes was almost stopped. Was the driver's door opening?

Downshift.

The Humvee fishtailed as he bled off the speed.

Into first gear.

He was doing twenty miles an hour when the Humvee slammed into the back of the Mercedes. The driver's door slammed shut, throwing the driver back into the front seat. A pair of huge white eyes appeared over the back of the seat, staring through the rear window at him.

Blanchard tromped on the accelerator pedal.

The heavy sedan wasn't helping him, but it was in drive and it couldn't resist the power and momentum of the big truck.

The driver shot upright, grabbing the wheel by the time Blanchard was back up to thirty miles an hour. He snap-shifted into second, losing bumper contact for an instant, the truck jarring the sedan when it smashed into the bumper again.

Then, forty.

He kept his eye on the driver's hands. The driver tried to steer into the approaching trucks flashing by on Blanchard's left, but Blanchard kept the pressure on, the wider bumper of the Hummer maintaining control over the narrower sedan, and the Mercedes wouldn't turn for him.

He lost contact for another few seconds when he shifted up a gear, then the Humvee's big bumper slammed into the car once again. His eyes huge in the rearview mirror, the driver stared at him as he tried now to steer off the right side of the road.

Belatedly, Blanchard realized that Ambrosia was screaming.

The two-way radio was alive with every other driver trying to call him. "Jack! . . . what's goin' on? . . . hey, man!"

Delray's Humvee went by, the man slowing to a stop, to turn and follow him.

The road ahead started to curve east for the run into Bethlehem.

"Time to lose this sucker!" he yelled.

The two of them were doing almost fifty miles an hour when Blanchard put both of his feet on the brake pedal and stood on it, gripping the bottom arc of the steering wheel with both hands to add to the pressure.

The fat tires of the Hummer left thick black streaks on the pavement as it slewed back and forth. Blanchard fought the steering wheel, trying to keep it straight, then came off the brake and shifted to neutral as they rolled off the hard surface and onto the verge at the beginning of the curve.

The Mercedes went straight off the pavement and out into the soft desert sand. The driver kept the wheels straight so it didn't roll. It bogged down within a couple hundred yards.

In fact, it wasn't even stopped when he saw the driver's door fly open and the body tumble out of the car, rolling over and over. The man was on his feet in seconds and running.

The Arab was about fifty feet from the car when the car, then the man, disintegrated.

The orange-and-black ball of flame took over the whole horizon, stunning his eyes. Ambrosia's scream went off the register.

And the wall of sound and concussion and heat hit the Humvee, treating it like a paper airplane.

It flew.

Nine

Armbruster and Weiss had left for Jerusalem in search of supplies, and Masters had villagers running throughout the settlement gathering mattresses wherever they could borrow or steal them. Perkins and Joliet were using any scrap of paper to take down names and histories and get people sorted out in the assembly room.

Masters stayed by the door, taking one patient at a time, making a diagnosis, and passing them on to the nurses. Her count was at twenty-seven when Laskov interrupted her.

"Doctor—"

"Mr. Laskov, I am busy."

"There is no one tending to the radio in your vehicle. A very agitated man demands that you respond."

Oh, hell! Blanchard! She didn't want to talk—Damn it! She needed them here as fast as possible, anyway.

"Hold on for just a minute, Mr. Yakov," she said to the man sitting in the folding chair in front of her. "I'll be right back."

Stepping through the door, she was dismayed at the length of the line. It was wrapped halfway around the square. Men, women, children.

Babies.

She wanted to cry when she saw the babies.

Trotting across to the ambulance, she pulled the door open and reached in for the microphone.

"Blanchard!"

"This is Sam, Melanie."

"Sam. We need you here fast. We've got an . . ." She hesitated to say epidemic, especially over the radio. She released the transmit button.

And Delray broke right in, his bass voice taking command. "Melanie! Listen, damn it! We've had a terrorist attack."

What! Oh, my God!

"You wouldn't believe what Jack did—"

She jabbed the transmit button, overriding him until he let her talk.

"Where's Blanchard? I want to talk to him."

"Melanie, shut up! They've got Jack in the op-unit. Ambrosia's dead. They're working on Apt in one of the ambulances."

Shit, shit, shit!

"It's going to be a while before we get there. I've got the Palestinian cops on the way, and I left a message on the Shin Bet guy's machine."

Masters couldn't believe it. Everything happened so suddenly. Her heart beat so rapidly, she could feel it. She forced herself to regain some degree of calmness.

"Sam, who else was hurt?"

"Just those I gave you."

"How bad is Jack?"

"I don't know. Dean's in there with him. Lars is working on Apt."

"All right. Leave the op-unit and the ambulance, and get the rest of the team up here."

"Melanie, I can't do that. I've got to get things under control here. Everybody in the whole damned unit's in shock."

"Sam. You know the Hakkar case?"

"Hakkar? Sure."

"I've got twenty-seven of the same, and I'm still counting."

"Ah, fuck!"

Another voice broke in. Armbruster's. "Sam, I've been listening in. I'll turn around now and be there in twenty minutes."

"Dickie," she ordered, "you and Jillian get those supplies. Now!"

"Oh, bloody hell! Roger that, Doctor."

"Sam, are we clear? I need every nurse and every EMT immediately. When you get here, start setting up ward tents. We'll need at least five or six of them."

"Six?"

"At least. I've got to get back."

She closed her eyes for a moment. Unbelievable. Two crises at once. And with the unit packed up and on the move. And Blanchard.

Oh, God, no.

She felt her throat close up, blinked back a tear.

"And Sam, you tell Dean to radio me as soon as he knows about Jack."

"Wilco."

She found a handkerchief in her pocket, dabbed at her eyes, then pulled her gloves back on. They'd run out of gloves long before, and she was having to use the same ones over and over. Walking back to the community room, she saw two more people get in line. This couldn't be happening.

When Blanchard opened his eyes, he couldn't see. The brightest damned sun he'd ever encountered was trying to sear his eyeballs.

Hot. The sweat was rolling off him.

Pain. His head throbbed, through and through. Never been a hangover like it.

And noise. None. He couldn't hear.

Or could barely hear. There was a voice, far away, drifting in slowly over a boiling sea, like a barely heard foghorn.

The volume came up.

"Jack, can you hear me?"

To the left? He rolled his head that way, and then had to squeeze his eyes shut as a bolt of lightning shot through his brain.

When the pain subsided, he tried opening his eyes again. Now he could see, but dimly. A face was taking shape, slowly coming into focus. He saw behind the face first and realized he was in an op-unit. He'd been staring up at the operating light.

The face firmed up. Wilcox.

"Can you hear me, Jack?"

"Yeah." His mouth felt gritty. Hot and dry and gritty. It seemed to work funny. His head pounded. His voice was far away, on a distant shore. "Yeah, I can now. What the hell's going on, Dean?"

"You don't remember the explosion?"

The words sounded funny, barely audible.

"The what? The . . . oh, shit, yes! Tina and Washington! Are they . . ."

Blanchard half closed his eyes, trying to get around the pain in his head, focusing on Wilcox's mouth, which looked infinitely sad.

"Tina didn't make it, Jack. Washington's got a broken hip and quite a few cuts. Lars is with him."

"God damn. What . . . how?"

"The Hummer was blown a couple hundred feet across the highway, Jack. I don't know how many times it rolled, but Tina was ejected, and it rolled over her. You and Washington stayed with it."

"He's going to be okay?"

"Sure thing. You want to hear about you?"

No. Not if he had to live with this head. Blanchard closed his eyes again, squinching them tight. His head hurt like hell, but he couldn't detect pain in other parts of his body. "You have some water?"

"Here, Jack, over here."

As slowly as possible, he rolled his head back. Wilcox shut off the overhead light, and he saw Polly Brooks bending over him. She had a glass of the most beautiful water, and she dipped a sponge in it, then dribbled a few drops on his lips. He sucked at it, ran his tongue around his lips. Then she gave him a steadier stream.

"How's that?" she asked.

"Needs to be cut with some scotch."

"You're going to be all right," she said.

"Not with this head."

"Concussion," Wilcox said. "You're going to have a head-ache."

"I came to Israel to hear, 'take two aspirin'?"

"You also hit the steering wheel, I think. A couple times, hard." He felt Wilcox's light touch on his stomach. The hand moved to his thigh, and Blanchard realized he didn't have any clothes on. "There's going to be some nasty blue showing up on your tummy and thighs. It's a bad bruise, and you're going to have sore balls, too."

"More water, Jack?"

"Jesus, yes."

She dribbled more water for him, and he swallowed several times. He didn't know why he was embarrassed. She was a nurse.

Wilcox's face came back into view. "Black eye, too, though I don't think it'll be too bad. The worse was a bunch of little glass punctures and cuts in your left arm."

"Glass?"

"Plastic glass from the side window, I imagine. Polly and I took out about five dozen shards. Some cut fairly deep, and we put in twelve stitches. That's all the visible stuff. Now, I want to get your cooperation for a little bit."

"Can I have my clothes? It's getting cold in here."

Brooks grinned at him, then draped a sheet over his midsec-tion. Wilcox spent about ten minutes poking him, pressing cool fingers into his gut, and tapping in various places while demanding responses. Wilcox checked his eyes with a penlight.

"Have you guys been talking louder than normal?" he asked.

"Yeah. You've got some loss of hearing, Jack, but I'm pretty sure it's going to come back."

" 'Pretty sure' is real reassuring, Dean."

"Give it some time. And plenty of aspirin. We gave you some shots that should ease the headache in a little while. But you'll begin to notice your stomach when the painkiller wears off. The rest of you is fairly fit."

"I have this overwhelming urge to sit up," he told them.

"To see if you can?"

"Yeah."

"Okay."

Brooks and Wilcox got their arms under his shoulders and helped him up. The change in attitude sent a new wave of pain rocking and rolling through his skull, and for a minute he thought he was going to throw up.

The nausea passed quickly, and he looked around.

Maria Godinez was standing at the foot of the gurney. She had taken to wearing long-sleeved blouses to hide her own wound.

"Hi, Maria."

She smiled. "I am glad you will be all right, Jack."

"Where are we?"

"About fifty yards from what used to be your Humvee."

"What about the Mercedes?"

"I haven't been over there," Wilcox said, "but Bob Timnath said he couldn't even find the hood ornament."

"Everyone else?"

"Okay. We've got Apt in the ambulance next to us, and Sam took the rest of the team on to Mar Saba. There're cops all over the place out there, now. Israeli army guys came in a helicopter. A couple of them want to talk to you pretty bad."

"This still the twenty-sixth?"

"It is. Why?"

"I'm going to remember it for a long time."

Jacob Talman did not know the deep voice that left the message on his machine, and the man was in such a hurry that he failed to leave his name. He guessed it to be Delray. The date/time stamp told Talman that the call had come seventeen minutes before.

He called the comm center first and left messages for Stein and Avidar, neither of whom could be reached. He asked that Avidar order the army units on the scene to not question witnesses until Talman arrived.

The Palestinian Police had jurisdiction over many of the

towns and settlements in the West Bank, but the Israeli army
continued its control of the roads.

He was out of his chair, digging for the keys in his pocket,
when he thought of Rahman. He put in a quick call, mentioning
an emergency, and was patched through to some radio receiver.

"If you are calling about the attack, Jacob," Rahman said,
"my unit in the area has already notified me."

"That is all I had, Amin. I am on my way to the scene."

"As am I. I have a helicopter. Go to the YMCA Stadium
on David Hamelech Road, and I will pick you up."

Talman hung up.

Rahman had a helicopter. That is where the money went,
for frills. Talman had no helicopter, and the IDF wanted quadru-
plicate documentation of an impending nuclear event before
they would allow him the use of one.

But then, Talman was not the equivalent of a general, either.

He might have been derisive of Rahman's appointment to a
political position, but after their meeting at the cafe, Talman
had done some background investigation of the man. Talman
learned that Rahman had trained with the French police acad-
emy and had served with Interpol for fifteen years, specializing
in antiterrorism campaigns. Jacob Talman's level of trust in
the Palestinian had come up another notch.

It took him a few minutes to drive to the stadium, about six
blocks west of his office on David Hamelech Road, to use his
ID to get into one of the vacant parking lots, and to park
the Toyota. Four minutes later, a small Aerospatiale Alouette
appeared over the top of the stadium, spotted him in the parking
lot, then settled to the ground, raising little whirlwinds of dirt
and debris. Ducking his head, he ran to it and crawled into the
backseat with two of Rahman's assistants.

Rahman, sitting in the left front seat opposite the pilot,
pointed to a headset, and Talman pulled it on.

The helicopter lifted off.

"I have just had a report, Jacob," Rahman said over the
intercom, which helped to overcome the racket of the turbine
and rotors. "There is one dead, a female medical technician,
and two injured."

"Do you know the names, Amin?"

"No. One of the injured is the medical team's administrator."

Blanchard. This was not a good omen.

"There is some confusion at the scene," Rahman went on. "A large number of witnesses, the rest of the medical team, left with a large number of vehicles and without authority. As to authority, I am afraid the police commander is in conflict with the army commander."

"This will happen frequently in the future, Amin."

"I fear as much. Let me say this: I acknowledge your authority. May I sit in on the interviews?"

"By all means, Amin."

A few minutes later, Talman saw Bethlehem a few kilometers away through the right-side window, and two minutes after that, the pilot went into a bank over the highway. Two of WHO's trucks were pulled off the road to the east. Another was upside down, also on the east side of the highway. An IDF helicopter was on the ground. There were four Palestinian Police Land Rovers. Six or seven civilian vehicles had halted so their drivers could view the carnage.

There was not a great deal of carnage, he noted with relief. In addition to the overturned truck, on the other side of the highway was a burnt circle in the sand. A crater perhaps three meters deep identified ground zero. Shrubs and weeds and a few twisted trees were blackened up to a hundred meters away. A number of men crisscrossed the area, looking for relics.

"It looks better than I expected," Rahman said.

"We still have one dead, a person assisting the Authority," Talman reminded him as the pilot landed near the IDF helicopter.

"Believe me, I am quite saddened," Rahman told him.

You should be in the hospital," Jacob Talman told him.

"I am in the hospital," Blanchard said and tried a grin. "I carry it around."

His mouth was working better, he thought. But his head throbbed steadily, and he looked ridiculous. Polly Brooks had tied an ice bag on his forehead with a few wraps of gauze. His stomach muscles and upper legs ached fiercely, and he had trouble bending over or standing up, though he had only tried that exercise once. Wilcox was right; his genitals ached, too.

Adding to his discomfort, while Brooks had helped him back into his jeans, which were sliced in various places from when they'd taken them off him, he was also wearing a green operating-room smock. His shirt was suitable for use as confetti. No shoes. One of them had disappeared. No socks, either.

Talman looked down at his feet.

"Never been blown out of my socks before, Jacob."

"I thought it was only a saying."

He was sitting in the front seat of the ambulance. Washington Apt, under sedation, was in the back with a paramedic. Bob Timnath stood by on the driver's side with the other nurses, Wilcox, and Svenson.

Talman had just introduced him to Amin Rahman, who was some kind of Palestinian Police chief. He looked like he ought to be some kind of movie or TV star, and Blanchard automatically distrusted good-looking men.

"Dr. Wilcox told us of your exploit, Jack," Talman said. "You are fortunate to be alive."

"If you were wearing this body, you'd rethink that statement," he said.

Rahman, standing behind the Shin Bet operative, smiled.

"Still, I need to ask you some questions."

"First things first, Jacob. I have to send the others to Mar Saba."

"We need to talk more with them."

"Do it later. I'll explain in a minute."

Talman looked back at Rahman, who shrugged.

"Dean, I'll keep Bob to drive this thing. The rest of you go look for Melanie."

"On our way, Jack. Don't do anything strenuous. I want to see you tonight."

"So do I," Polly Brooks added with a smile.

"Be damned careful," Blanchard said.

Rahman spoke up. "I will have them escorted."

He issued an order in Arabic, and a few minutes later, the op-unit pulled out behind a Land Rover.

The ambulances didn't have backseats in the driving compartment, so he couldn't offer them a place to sit down. Talman and Rahman, surrounded by a phalanx of army and police officers, stood around the wide-open passenger door.

"Jacob, we need a little privacy for a minute."

"I will ask Amin to stay."

"Whatever."

The two of them issued orders, and the crowd dispersed.

"How did you anticipate this attack, Jack?"

"I recognized the driver."

"There is nothing left of him."

"Good."

"How did you recognize him, Mr. Blanchard?" Rahman asked.

"From Jacob's description. Omar Heusseni."

"Ah!" Talman squatted down and rested on his heels.

Rahman looked to the Shin Bet officer.

"The bastard son of Ibn Sapir. At one time, we thought him the heir apparent."

"The Sword of God," Rahman said.

"Yes."

"They are resident in Jericho," the deputy chief said. "I will have Boshogi question them."

"May I sit in on that?" Talman asked.

"Certainly."

Through the buzz of his headache, Blanchard wasn't quite sure what they were talking about, but he had another nagging question.

"What about Tina?"

"Ambrosia?" Talman said. "There must be an autopsy. The body is being transported to Jerusalem."

"I want one of my doctors present."

"Of course. I will arrange it." Talman looked off to the side, staring into some private distance. "This is an outrage, Jack. An operation conducted against a humanitarian group. We will, however, attempt to downplay the importance for reasons we have discussed with you. I know the young woman died, but if it were not for you, many more would have died. The media onslaught could not have been contained, if that had happened. This might not be the direction you would take, should a reporter contact you, but I would ask you to consider the broader ramifications. If you like, I will have General Avidar speak with you.''

Rahman studied him with very direct, very dark eyes. They did not plead, but they seemed to ask understanding.

''I've never much cared for reporters, Jacob. I'll talk with the rest of the team.''

''Thank you. Now, you said you would explain something?''

''Toxic epidermal necrolysis.''

Rahman looked confused.

''The flesh-eating disease,'' Talman told him. ''Nuri Hakkar, also of the Sword of God, has contracted it.''

''It sounds vile,'' Rahman said.

''It is,'' Blanchard said. ''The last time Dean Wilcox talked to someone at Mar Saba on the radio, we had forty-one cases of it.''

Talman's mouth gaped open. ''Oh, Lord!''

''An epidemic?'' Rahman asked, his face suggesting his horror.

''Doctor Masters can explain it better, and both of you should talk to her.''

Blanchard was tired of talking. His mouth was dry again, and he was almost tempted to take the sleeping pills Wilcox had given him, to dive under the surface of the pain in his head. He hadn't ever been big on pills, though.

He tried to bend down to pick up a canteen on the floor, and his stomach protested.

''Hold on!'' Timnath said, reached over, and picked up the canteen. He unscrewed the top and handed it to Blanchard.

''Thanks, Bob.''

He took a long swallow.

''Jacob, can we continue this later?''

Talman stood up. ''Certainly. I will know where to find you.''

''One other thing, Jacob. I need the communications gear out of the Humvee, whatever's left of it.''

''I will arrange for that, also.''

''Crank it up, Bob. Hey, how's Washington doing back there?''

"Fine," the paramedic said. "He is secured to the gurney."

"We in a hurry?" Timnath asked.

"Just a mild one. Don't bounce Washington around."

While Timnath backed around and got them back on the highway, Blanchard scooted down in his seat and rested his head against the back of it. He took several deep breaths, then another couple swigs from the canteen. The water was lukewarm, but tasted as if it had just been scooped from an oasis. He thought of the pharmacy in his old hometown, the ice-cream counter, cherry Cokes, ice-cream sundaes.

He couldn't sleep, especially after Timnath left the asphalt again and headed overland for Mercy Base. He knew the EMT was trying to be careful, but the terrain played tricks on visual perception, and it was a rough ride. Every little bump transferred directly to his stomach and created spasms. He worried about Apt, and was glad the electrician was knocked out.

He didn't know what time it was. Bothersome, but no big deal for some reason, and he didn't lift his arm to check his watch. The whole episode had flashed past in seconds, or years. It didn't seem to make a difference.

When they finally reached the encampment, he was surprised by how much progress had been made. Tents were up, and more were going up. There were more people working than he had in the entire unit. Two men were assembling the showers. Blanchard understood Delray's prioritization. When the doctors and nurses and EMTs came off duty, they were going to need showers badly. One of the two-and-a-half-ton trucks was missing. The medical supplies. He guessed it had been moved over to the settlement.

Timnath eased to a stop next to several parked vehicles, and Delray appeared at Blanchard's door and pulled it open.

"You don't know how damned happy I am to see you sitting up, Jack."

"If that's what you call this. Where we at, Sam?"

The Aussie knew what he was asking. "Sixty-four cases."

"Shit."

"Yeah. Bob, what kind of shape are you in?"

"Good, Sam."

"I want you to take Washington to Atarot Airport. I've

arranged a medevac. You may get a radio call to stop for supplies somewhere. We're suddenly damned short of everything, and they're turning Jerusalem and Tel Aviv upside down.''

"Will do."

"Don't talk to reporters about any of this," Blanchard advised him. "And Sam, you'd better get that word out to everyone. Send any queries to me."

"Good deal," Delray told him.

Delray helped Blanchard out of his seat. His stomach muscles were definitely cramped up now. It hurt to stand up straight, which he couldn't maintain. And it wasn't just the stomach.

"Oomph," he said.

"Dean said your Don Juaning was going to be on hold for a while."

"I wish to hell I was a Don Juan, so I could dream about what I was missing. Where'd all the labor come from?"

"I recruited some villagers, and the Israelis sent an army platoon to help us get set up. That was after I threatened to broadcast the problems here, not knowing your new policy. The army also promised more tents and cots, but they're not here yet."

"You're finally learning to administer, Sam."

"Due to the press of need, we don't have sleeping quarters. I grabbed those tents for wards. Thinking ahead, huh?"

"I was considering a nap, buddy."

"I recalled Lon Chao to help Melanie, so I've got his ambulance over here."

"I should probably—"

"No, you shouldn't. You've got the duty tomorrow."

Delray watched him as he hobbled toward the ambulance, which was parked away from the camp, near the wadi. He still couldn't quite straighten up, and he knew he looked like some kind of apparition in the surgical greens and bound-on ice bag. Wilcox had taped his jeans together in a couple places.

When they reached the vehicle, Delray opened the rear door to give him ventilation. The gurney was gone, but a padding of blankets had been spread across the full width of the deck. There were five skimpy pillows piled at the side.

It looked like heaven.

"The thermos has ice water. Dean said to keep you drinking."

The thought of more water prompted another need.

"I'm going to screw up Steve Mackey's planning."

"Go ahead. I'll watch out for women."

"It doesn't matter. Polly's spread my limitations far and wide by now."

He stood at the side of the truck and urinated, then rezipped his torn-up jeans and braced himself for the next step.

"You want anything to eat, Jack?"

"Not for two weeks."

Climbing inside was an experience he wouldn't remember as the good old days, but he finally stretched out and rolled onto his back. Blanchard normally slept on his side or stomach, never on his back. Neither of the two positions seemed attractive.

"Go to sleep, matey. I won't wake you for dinner."

He heard Delray's footsteps recede, disappearing into the cacophony of building camp—yells, calls, orders, revving engines, sledgehammers driving tent pegs, a bubbling generator—then poured himself a glass of ice water. He drank it all, put the plastic glass out of the way, and closed his eyes.

He was asleep in seconds.

It was dark when he awakened, and the first thing he realized was that his headache had subsided to a dull throb.

The second thing he realized was that he wasn't alone.

Someone was lying beside him, on his left.

"Anyone I know?" he asked of the darkness. He strongly suspected he would hear Weiss respond.

"Thank you, Jack."

"Mel? Hi. Thanks for what?"

"For what you did. Protecting all of those people. My people. Our people."

She sounded utterly fatigued. Her words slurred.

"I hurt when I think about Tina and Washington," he said. "I should have stopped and shoved them out."

"You didn't have the time."

"I might have."

"Don't worry about mights. Sam told me. You should hire him as a publicist."

The ice in the ice bag had melted, and the rubber bladder sloshed on his head. He reached up and tried to find the gauze with his fingers.

"What are you doing?" she asked.

"Trying to get rid of this damned bag Polly saddled me with."

"Wait."

She found the light switch and turned on the overhead light, then moved into a cross-legged position and helped him peel off the gauze.

"Quite a shiner you have."

He touched his left eye. It felt tender.

"I don't even know what I hit."

Masters reached over him to retrieve the glass he'd pushed aside, and he could smell the mixture of sweat and medicine with which she was coated. Her breast brushed his cheek. Then she poured him a glass of water.

"Drink."

"I'm—"

"Or Dean'll have you carrying around an IV."

He drank, then she took the glass and poured herself some water.

She didn't look good at all. Her eyes were darkened and baggy. Her blouse was bedraggled, having been soaked with perspiration, then drying on her. Her chestnut hair was tangled and matted. Her shoulders slumped with exhaustion.

"What's the count?" he asked. "Not that I'm trying to objectify."

He'd had his fill of body counts long before.

"One hundred and seventy-one. We think that's all."

"Not contagious, right?"

"Not contagious. This had to be spread by some carrier."

"Biological warfare, Mel."

"That's what your Jacob Talman thought."

"You talked to him?"

"Him and some Palestinian policeman."

She reached up and turned off the light, and he heard her scrambling around, then settling down next to him.

''We don't have beds yet, so we're sleeping where we can. Do you mind?''

''Not in the least.''

Within two minutes he heard her breathing go soft and regular.

Felt pretty safe with him. Of course he was in no shape to go practicing sexual assault. In any degree.

Blanchard woke up once more in the night, but couldn't get an angle on his watch to see what time it was. Masters's head was on his left arm, her own arm thrown across his chest, and her left leg flexed and resting on his thigh. She was snuggled up tight against his side.

His left arm was asleep, and the weight of her leg aggravated the bruise on his leg. The hospital odor and sweaty aroma of her hair was in his nostrils.

He didn't mind a bit.

Ten

The Western Wall, or as the pious knew it, the Wailing Wall, was one of the retaining walls of the Temple Mount, the holiest place on earth for Jews. The precinct was also known as *Haram esh-Sharif*—the Noble Sanctuary—to Arabs, and after Mecca and Medina, was their most important shrine. Christians, too, laid a sympathetic claim to the area, for it was here that Jesus was presented in the Temple, debated with the scribes, and tossed out the money changers.

It was called the Wailing Wall as a result of Jewish lament after the Temple was destroyed. The first Temple, built by Solomon in 950 B.C., lasted for 400 years until it was razed by Nebuchadnezzar. The Second Temple was completed in 516 B.C., but suffered damage over the centuries, and was rebuilt again by Herod in the half century before Christ's birth. Herod outdid the earlier attempts by enlarging the structure atop Mount Moriah, having to build substructures on the steep slope, including the retaining walls and the area in the southeast corner known as Solomon's Stables. The Temple itself was constructed of white marble and was generously clad in gold. Herod's magnificent achievement only lasted a hundred years, until the Romans destroyed it in 70 A.D.

Now there was a large, open space in front of the Western Wall marked off with railings, and the most important ceremonies of the Jewish faith took place there. It was equivalent to a synagogue and utilized by the strongest believers who would not go on the grounds of the Temple Mount since the location of the Holy of Holies—only entered by high priests—was unknown as a result of the destruction.

The Western Wall was where army recruits were sworn in. Jacob Talman had been sworn in at the Wall.

He was not very devout, however, and since his *bar mitzvah,* had been less than scholarly about his faith. It was present, but he would never be accused of being overly ardent. His faith, he supposed, had been supplanted by his rampant nationalism. He was, in fact, often offended by the extreme activities and declarations of the fundamentalist sects of his faith, and that was one of the reasons he devoted his allegiance more to his country than his religion.

Not that all his contacts with the overly righteous were unfruitful. Some, he nourished.

At five-thirty in the morning, there were few visitors to the Wall, and Talman strolled past them, working his way downslope toward the Porat Yosef Synagogue. He had not reached it when a figure clad in black and wearing *peiyot*—side curls—joined him. He also wore the *streimel,* a felt-trimmed hat. His face was lined with the wisdom of the ages. They walked in silence for a while, passing by the synagogue.

Beit Horon was, to say it mildly, an ultraconservative. His group, and others like it, frowned on such conveniences as television or computers or newspapers, and they lived their lives strictly according to the most rigid principles of religion. Those beliefs did not prevent them from voicing political views, and despite their relatively low numbers, the ultraconservatives held sway in the Knesset. Beit Horon's was one of the more strident voices in condemnation of the peace plan. When Jews were the predominant population of Israel at eighty-five percent, he saw no redeeming value in giving away land to a minority simply because of their screams and their violence. God would not have done so, and as Horon's only mentor, God was tough to circumvent.

Jacob Talman understood his philosophy to some extent and treated him with respect. Horon was not an informant as much as a sounding board. He kept Talman abreast of developments among the far far right in these monthly meetings. Talman, naturally, served the same purpose for Horon.

"There will be many deaths," Horon said. He spoke in Yiddish since Hebrew was considered by members of his group to be a sacred language suitable only for religious purposes.

"Do you think so?"

"Absolutely. Has it not started at Mar Saba?"

Horon's tentacles ran far and deep. He either knew of the problem, or he was probing for details or confirmation.

"I know of no deaths," Talman said.

"A baby, not yet four months old, died in the night."

"By what cause?" He did not know about the baby, and he did not know how the old man would know, unless, as he had always strongly suspected, some of Horon's more sinful followers used the telephone.

"It is unknown, but a strange malady afflicts the entire community. The World Health people are overwhelmed."

Time for admissions. "There appears to be widespread disease, yes. What do you make of that?"

"It is punishment, Jacob, intended to demonstrate the error of our decisions as a people. I choose to interpret this punishment as relative to the formulation of the peace plan. There are numerous similar episodes recounted by the prophets."

"That settlement includes Arab families," Talman countered.

"A few, but simply an accident of place. A kilometer to the southwest is an Arab settlement. Is it affected?"

"No, Beit, it is not, though we continue to examine it. My interpretation of events is different from yours, though."

"How is that?"

"I believe the settlement was the target of biological warfare."

"It is still punishment, is it not? Can you argue that, Jacob? No one questions God's methods."

"What will you do with your suppositions?"

"The evidence is hardly supposition, Jacob. Later this morning, the issue will be raised in the Chief Rabbinate."

That body, incorporating the Supreme Rabbinical Council along with the chief rabbis of the Sephardi and Ashkenazi communities, was the primary authority relative to Jewish law. The rabbinical courts, separate from the secular courts, were subject to its jurisdiction. The influence of the council permeated all layers of government.

"And then?"

"Very likely, it will be carried to the Knesset."

"Either action will attract the attention of the media," Talman said.

"So? Is that not good?"

"It is terrible. There will be panic."

"It is time for panic. Many decisions of the misguided past must be overturned. That which is not ours to give away must be reclaimed."

Such was Horon's power that this single man could subvert the policy decisions made in haste at ten o'clock last night. Representatives of the Council, the army, the Palestinian Authority, and the health ministry had met with General Levi Avidar, Deputy Chief Rahman, and Talman. In concert with dozens of telephone calls to departmental ministers, that group had determined that the settlement at Mar Saba was to be the subject of a quarantine and total news blackout. Under penalty of extreme censure, no one was to utter the phrase "toxic epidermal necrolysis."

When—there was no conjecture about "if"—the media became aware of the blockade, if the correspondents wanted to infer a massive outbreak of measles, which was a skin disease after all, no spokesperson would correct them.

A company of Israeli infantry, since the settlement was Jewish, had been dispatched in the middle of the night, along with a cadre of health scientists who had mobile laboratories. A search for necessary medical supplies to augment those of the PMAT was launched, and it was soon discovered that a Brit by the name of Armbruster had already wheedled most of those supplies from willing civil servants at four hospitals, three clinics, and the army depot. He had left a stack of IOUs behind

him, and at Talman's recommendation, it was agreed that the
debts would be canceled. The man was, after all, working in
favor of the afflicted. Still, necessary materials were in short
supply, and quiet orders for additional medical inventories had
been placed in France, Italy, Greece, and Spain.

"Beit, my friend, have I ever encouraged you to change your
politics or your convictions?"

"No, Major, you have not."

"And I will not make the attempt now. I would ask, however,
that you delay your speech by ten days."

"For what reason?"

"Until you have more complete information. I would not
want you to suffer from adverse publicity, should your information be inaccurate. This is a sensitive matter, and I assure you
that it could affect the well-being of all our citizens."

Horon considered. He, too, did not wish to lose credibility.
While Talman was not telling him so specifically, Horon might
well think that his information was incomplete. Which it was.

"What do you offer in return?"

"I will provide you with every minute detail."

Horon took only a minute to consider the deal. "Seven
days."

"Very well. Seven."

He had hoped to get five, and would have settled for forty-
eight hours.

Talman walked back to his car, which was parked on Chain
Street near a public telephone. He called the communications
center, which routed him directly to Avidar.

The general answered himself, "Avidar."

"Major Talman, sir. I have spoken with Horon."

"And?"

"He is aware of some aspects of the situation at Mar Saba.
He was to address the Rabinate this morning and the Knesset
this afternoon."

"Damn! "

"I have secured a week's delay."

"I may have misjudged you, Jacob. Are you certain you are
not a prophet?"

"I sincerely doubt it, sir."

"What did you have to give up?"

"Details."

"Well, in a week, they will probably be widespread, anyway. Did he mention the attack on the medical team?"

"No, nor did I, and it may have been contained. Amin Rahman and I impressed the need for secrecy on everyone at the scene, including civilian spectators. Relative to that event, I am to meet with Boshogi in Jericho at nine o'clock to interview Kadar."

"I hope Boshogi does not screw this up. Does he have any evidence to link the Sword of God to the attack?"

"According to Rahman, none. All we will succeed in doing, I think, is to put Kadar on notice."

"Will they conduct a search?"

"I cannot say."

"What is your view, Jacob, of Amin Rahman?"

"At this point, favorable, sir. I have higher hopes than I have had."

"Good. So do I."

Avidar hung up, so Talman did the same.

Unlocking the Camry, he went in search of breakfast and nearly found it before he changed his mind. Instead he decided to make the drive to Jericho earlier than he had planned for his morning meal.

He stopped at the security checkpoint outside Jericho and asked the guard to contact all of the guard posts for Jericho. No one reported Kadar or his associates as having left the town.

He drove on to the café and parked outside it. It was eight o'clock, and Leila Salameh was opening the shutters and the door. Neither her face nor her eyes revealed one spark of recognition as he approached the entrance. Two Arab men came off the street with him, and she welcomed them all to her humble establishment.

It was humble. Seven tables with four chairs each. No counter or booths. Two ceiling fans struggled. The only decoration was an intricately woven rug, which hung on one wall and added yellows, bright blues, and blazing reds to an otherwise ecru environment. Talman suspected that the rug was chosen to give Leila a spark of hope in her otherwise somber days.

Talman took a table positioned under a window to catch the mild breeze it offered and waited. She took an order from the Arab men first, which was to be expected, then came to his table. She was wearing an ankle-length black skirt and her customary overblouse. Her face was scrubbed clean, and her hair shone with radiant reflections. With her back to the Arabs, she gave him the ghost of a smile, barely revealing the defection in her lip.

"*Sabah el-kher,*" he said in Arabic.

"*Boker tov,*" she said. "Good morning."

"If it is possible, I would like two eggs scrambled, biscuits with marmalade, coffee, and orange juice."

"It is quite possible. It will be a moment."

"There is no hurry."

Unfortunately, the Arabs were in no hurry, either. They probably did not have work to go to, and they lingered over endless refills of their cups, talking with animated heat about one subject or another. Talman's breakfast was excellent, garnished with slices of pineapple, apple, and strawberries. Leila probably assumed he needed more fruit in his diet. He ate it all.

The Arabs were still there by the time he had to leave, so he was unable to talk to her. He hoped his presence was reassuring, and assumed it was by the private smile she gave him when presenting the bill. He paid in shekels and kept the bill, stuffing it in his pocket as he left.

In the car, he read the note: Unknown Arab visited Kadar at seven A.M.

Of course. He expected no less.

Boshogi's headquarters was on the same street, near the edge of the town, and the environment was what he had presumed it would be—hostile. There were four uniformed policemen and Boshogi waiting for him, per Rahman's orders, he assumed.

Boshogi was constructed on the same principles as a pear, with the center of gravity low and centered between his bulbous stomach and his gigantic buttocks. The short legs had quite a task, keeping all of it balanced and upright. The coating of whiskers on his jaws was not thicker than the last time Talman had seen it and still had not produced a chin of significance.

After forced pleasantries, they went outside to the cars, and Talman followed them to Kadar's house.

It was an unremarkable house. Stucco was falling in large chunks from sun-dried brick walls. The roof was of red tile, and many tiles were missing.

The woman called Oma Kassim answered the door, and Boshogi spoke in Hebrew for Talman's benefit. In fact, Talman spoke limited Arabic in addition to Hebrew, Yiddish, and English, but he never told anyone of the ability. It was a language in which his principle role was one of listener.

"Ibrahim Kadar."

The woman appeared much older than her years. Once, she would have been quite beautiful, Talman thought, but the beauty had been buried in bitterness and anger. She surveyed them all with evident disdain. She said nothing, but backed away, leaving the door open. A minute later, the diminutive Arab appeared, limping.

"Policeman Boshogi, what do you want?"

"I have a warrant to search this house."

Two surprises, there. One that Boshogi had thought to get a warrant. And second, that the Palestinian Police were actually using written warrants.

Kadar, with a sharp, hatchet-nosed face and black hair cut long, studied the policeman for a long second. He also wore a thick black mustache and affected the unshaven look, his beard a short stubble on his lean cheeks. After apparent deep consideration of Boshogi's intent, he waved away the warrant extended to him. "The Jew may not enter my house."

Boshogi did not know quite what to do, but after a moment's confusion, said, "You have no say in the matter."

He did not bother to introduce Talman. Then again, the seven o'clock visitor was likely to have provided Talman's name to Kadar.

Following Boshogi, they bulled their way into the small living room. The woman stood in the doorway to the kitchen, and men Talman recognized from their pictures as Abu el-Ziam and Khalid Badr were seated at a table. El-Ziam had inflamed eyes and a bushy black beard. Badr was bland faced and overweight.

The commander of police for Jericho shooed the woman, el-Ziam, and Badr outside, and sat Kadar down. He took the chair opposite Kadar and started firing questions at him.

They were expected questions. Kadar's location at various times. What of Omar Heusseni?

Talman walked slowly through the house as the questioning went on, watching the haphazard search conducted by the four uniformed officers. He listened to the responses. Kadar's eyes followed him wherever he went.

Kadar was here, where else? Heusseni had disappeared days ago. No one knew where he was.

The search turned up nothing of value. The questioning was complete in twenty minutes.

Boshogi looked to Talman. "Well?"

"Come in here, please."

He led the way into the sleeping room, containing mats on the floor separated by boxes. One was an old military footlocker. Since it was locked, the searcher hadn't bothered opening it. Talman pointed it out.

"What?"

"Your man did not open it."

"Kadar!"

The leader of the Sword of God came to stand in the doorway. "Whose is this?"

"It is mine."

"Unlock it."

Sneering, Kadar crossed to the locker, inserted a key in the cheap hasp, and opened it. Boshogi bent to riffle through the contents while Talman watched.

Nothing but clothing, a pair of shoes, one of them specially constructed for Kadar's deformed foot.

Talman went to the kitchen and stood looking around. An old wardrobe at the end served as a pantry. Its contents were scattered by the policeman's search. There was a narrow table shoved against one wall, littered with the remnants of breakfast, and an icebox was placed next to it.

Against the outside wall was a cabinet with an old enameled sink and single faucet. Next to it stood an iron, wood-fired stove. Talman had watched the policeman sweep the soaps and cleansers from the cabinet beneath the sink earlier, leaving the doors standing open. The boxes were now on the linoleum floor.

He squatted in front of it and studied the interior. Boshogi and Kadar came in and watched him.

An old piece of linoleum had been cut to fit and laid inside the cabinet to protect the wood from spills. He found the edge and lifted it, then pulled it out.

Glanced at Kadar as he did so.

The man's face was less stoic now.

"*La!* Get this Jew out of my house!" he said.

"One minute," Boshogi told him, interested now.

A few centimeters from the front edge of the cabinet floor, he found a large crack. He used the blade of his pocketknife to pry up the inner board. It came free easily, revealing the deep base of the inside of the cabinet. He supposed it was large enough to secrete several weapons, but there were none there now.

There were several bundles of currency, however. He lifted them and riffled the bills.

"About fifty thousand shekels, I imagine," he told Boshogi as he stood and threw the bundles on the table. "A large amount for a kitchen."

"I do not trust banks," Kadar said.

"Who does?" Talman asked him in return.

He edged past the two men and left the house. There was an older Fiat parked next to the house, but he supposed that it had been sanitized also and did not bother looking it over.

Boshogi came out, followed by his underlings. He stopped next to Talman.

"Well, Major?"

"I think our purpose has been served, Chief Boshogi."

"It has?"

"Yes. Kadar knows that you are watching him with more intensity now. If he has unsavory activities in mind, he will now curtail them or alter his plans."

"Yes, that is good."

"Thank you for your cooperation. *Shokran.*"

"I am at your service at any time, Major." The echo in his words said exactly the opposite.

Talman went to his car, started it, and turned toward the main street. He would dearly have loved to hear the ensuing conversation between Boshogi and Kadar. He supposed the topic would center on the insufficient amount of the bribe Kadar had paid Boshogi for advanced warnings. He also wondered if Boshogi had learned anything about searching houses. None of the sleeping mats had been moved, and it was a wooden-floored house, suggesting a crawl space beneath. If there were a trapdoor, though, he thought that nothing would have been discovered. Anything incriminating had been removed much earlier.

Ibrahim Kadar was livid with rage. Not even his followers knew of his cache of funds, and the insolent Jew had gone right to it. Before el-Ziam, Badr, and Kassim reentered the house, he stuffed the currency in his pockets.

He had barely hidden his treasury when Boshogi's nasal voice startled him.

"I think we must confiscate that as evidence."

He whirled around. "Evidence! Evidence of what?"

"We will decide."

He snapped one bundle from his pocket, peeled off five thousand shekels, and handed them to the dirty son of a goat.

"There. There is your evidence."

"Good day to you, Brother Kadar. I am happy you had a chance to meet Major Talman. He is very interested in your activities."

"You will tell me when he comes again." He made it a statement.

Boshogi flipped the currency with his thumb. "Perhaps."

Brother! His true brothers served him infinitely better.

Except perhaps, Heusseni. He wondered where Heusseni had disappeared to. It was difficult to find a much better thief. It was clear from the questions Boshogi asked, however, that the Jews did not have Heusseni in captivity.

* * *

Blanchard had finally gotten his way. Mercy Base was surrounded by Israeli soldiers. A whole company had set up camp next to the compound, and an orderly rotation of sentinels was dispersed every four hours to posts on the outskirts of the settlement and the medical facilities. Barbed-wire fencing was being installed by army engineers. Access to any of the settlement's telephones had been cut off by midnight, and only the satellite channel link in the admin tent was open. Delray and Blanchard were controlling that, too. Phone calls to families in other parts of the world were monitored. Delray had had to agree to that condition presented by Rahman and Talman before he was allowed to set up the equipment.

Despite her feeling of incarceration, Masters was a little relieved. She had not yet admitted to Blanchard that he was right, but the shock of the attack and of Ambrosia's death was a heavy burden. She felt like a political pawn, and with the staggering number of cases in the wards, certainly the result of some biological attack, she knew she was in the middle of a war.

It was not a good feeling, but there was nothing she could do about it except perform as she was trained.

And that, she was good at. The Israelis apparently agreed, for they had provided five army doctors and a dozen nurses to assist the PMAT, leaving Masters in charge. They realized that hers was a *Palestinian* assistance team, and to make up for her help, they would provide food, medical support, and security. There was also an Israeli team of health officials and scientists working out of large vans in the settlement. They had sealed off the water wells and were conducting tests. The domestic wells at the Arab village to the west were also being tested.

Off-duty soldiers were helping the PMAT staff erect the last of the tents. The admin tent and the mess hall were up, as was the clinic. By noon, they expected to have the hospital and a couple of the residential tents up. There were eleven ward tents, and the whole effect was less uniform than before. There weren't many perfect lines, and Blanchard probably didn't approve of the less-than-military appearance, but he hadn't said so. The WHO white tents were interspersed with the desert-camouflage tents provided by the army.

Masters left the mess tent, where she had gotten herself a tall plastic glass of iced tea, and walked to the admin tent.

Irsay was at one of the computers, laboriously trying to interpret Perkins's, Weiss's, and Joliet's handwriting on scraps of paper as he entered medical and family histories for each of the patients. He had been at it most of the night.

Jillian Weiss was updating her pharmaceutical records, also. She and Armbruster had performed splendidly, begging and threatening every medical administrator they could find, and returning with the Humvee packed with glucose, corticosteroids, antibiotics, and anything else Dickie thought might be useful one day. Armbruster had unloaded, checked on Blanchard, then gone back to Jerusalem.

Blanchard and Delray were at their desk, wading through paper. Delray was on a phone to Geneva. Blanchard looked pale, and he had a jug of ice water at his elbow. He was hunched over, as if sitting up straight were too much to attempt.

"Jack, you should go find your bunk."

The modest-hero bit could go too far. Then, again, maybe he was entitled to it. There were a hell of a lot of people who were very grateful to Blanchard. She was.

"I will, later, Mel. If they ever unpack it."

"Use mine."

He grinned, appearing a bit comical. The eye was nicely black and blue now.

"By yourself."

They had awakened in the ambulance this morning at about the same time, somehow entwined. She had apologized for inflicting pressure on his injuries, but he had said, *"De nada,"* and fortunately, not mentioned it since. She had helped him walk to the showers—he still didn't walk very well—and had the distinct feeling that he was going to invite her to join him. He didn't, and he looked a lot better in the fresh clothing Perkins got for him.

She felt better after her own shower, asking him through the partition if she could have an extra minute.

"Take five," he had told her. "I'm taking them."

She pulled a director's chair across the floor to their desk and sat down. A long sip of her tea helped take the edge of heat off. The oscillating fan stirred the papers.

Delray hung up.

"The director general talked Israel into sending us two more doctors—specialists of some kind in bacteria—and four EMTs. It's only for a couple weeks. They're digging into the inventories in Alexandria and will airlift more supplies to us. He said he'd find the money somewhere."

"You told him we're under a vow of silence?" Blanchard asked.

"I did. He concurred."

Blanchard turned stiffly toward Masters. "You talked to the Israelis?"

"Does your neck hurt?"

"No more than the rest of me. Every muscle picked today to tighten up, and I figure it's either a conspiracy or a strike."

She shook her head. "We'll get Polly to give you a massage. She's quite good."

"Maybe later."

"Okay, the health department. I felt sorry for those guys. They're all dressed in rubber suits, in this heat, collecting samples. But they're not taking chances, and that's good. The water tank is sealed off with plywood."

"They think that's the source, then?"

"It's the common denominator. Cale mentioned it first, and I think he's right. They'll also be going house to house, examining every one. I imagine every home will be drenched with some kind of antibiotic spray."

"So what can they find?" Delray asked.

"Traces of the bacteria. Or maybe traces of the carrier. The bacteria had to be suspended in something."

"What about, say, an aerial spray?" Blanchard asked. "When I think warfare, I think of delivery systems."

"No one remembers an aircraft in the vicinity for quite a while, and certainly not one that came close to the settlement."

"What about the timing, Mel? Is there some kind of gestation period?"

"That's an unknown, Jack. This defies what we normally

expect of the causes, generally a drug reaction or possibly an immune response. If I were to guess, I'd say that well had to be contaminated at least a week before today, and probably longer. But we don't know how long it takes from contamination until the first symptoms appear. Tomorrow, the health ministry people will have an interview team here. They're going to try to map out when any member of a family went to the well, or drank water from a well source that another family member had collected. If they get reliable data for a couple weeks, they might be able to pinpoint when it started.''

"Can you tell anything from the symptoms?''

"They're all in about the same stage, though some might be a little more pronounced. Someone may have not had contact with the water until, say, a day after other members of the family.''

"Is there anything at all promising?'' Blanchard asked. "I need a little positive-attitude adjustment.''

Looking at his battered condition, she could certainly understand that.

"We're catching it early, if that helps. Hakkar was far advanced by the time we got to him. With these people, despite the large number of them, we're probably within three or four days of initial symptoms. With the treatment protocol under way, I expect a high percentage of recoveries. There will be scarring in some, in varying degrees, but we're going to get them back.''

"Percentages?'' Delray asked.

"Twenty percent? We might lose that many. Thirty-four.'' She was suddenly overwhelmed by the numbers and lost the objectivity she was trying to maintain.

"God, it's terrible! We lost the baby last night.'' She had cried when she heard the report.

"That was quick, wasn't it?'' Blanchard asked her.

"She was already in a severe stage of pneumonia. This didn't help.''

She brushed at her eyes with her fingertips, then took a quick drink of tea to keep her throat from swelling.

"You okay, Mel?'' Blanchard asked.

"I'm all right, Jack.''

"Anything else we can help with, right away?"

"No. We're trying to get the wards settled down, set up the routines of examinations, changing IVs, and so on. We're running more medical tests, and we're sending them to Jerusalem for analysis. Our lab equipment is too primitive for the tests I want. Lars is working with Del Cameron on menus for the wards, and we're going to need to resupply the kitchen as soon as they're done."

Blanchard wrote himself a note.

"Robin Hood's back!"

Masters swung around to look at the front flap, where Armbruster had appeared. He was carrying a huge bolt of fabric, and he brought it to her and held it out for inspection.

"What do you think of that, Doc?"

"Cheesecloth. You've got a bolt of cheesecloth."

"Bolt, hell! I've got thirty bolts. Three thousand yards."

"Whatever for?"

Armbruster bowed his stubbled head. "You know me, how modest I am? Well, I got to thinking about all those poor people lying around naked."

They had divided the wards into male and female. The infant children were with their mothers. To avoid any sloughing of the skin, they were forced to lie naked in their beds.

"And you got cheesecloth for them? That's wonderful, Dickie!"

"It might help a little in the dignity area."

"Where in the hell are you getting this stuff, Dickie?" Blanchard asked.

"I'm making some of the best contacts of my life. I ever retire from WHO, I've got it made in the black market. Hell, I've got a trailer load of soft drinks and fruit juice. I've got two gross of surgical greens, a hundred pillows, four hundred sheets. One guy gave me two quarts of Dewar's, for those of us who need that kind of preventative medicine."

"How are you swinging all this?" Delray asked.

"Well, if they push me, I just sign the tab."

"How?"

"Jack Blanchard, what else?"

* * *

"Ammonium nitrate."

"One of the simple jobs, eh?"

"That's right, Jack. Nonetheless, very effective," Talman told him.

Blanchard switched the phone to his left hand and sipped from his water glass. He was taking fluids damned near as fast as he could, at Dean Wilcox's urging. He hoped something started working on his muscles. Every damned one of them was sore, and it was all he could do to stay in the canvas chair. His stomach and groin ached with wild abandon, but he had refused Wilcox's painkillers. He didn't like stuff that might slow down his thinking.

"You talk to the Sword of God people, Jacob?"

"I listened. It wasn't my jurisdiction."

"Anything surprising?"

"They have more money than they should have. There were no obvious connections to Heusseni's undertaking. He may have been operating independently."

"You didn't expect to find anything, did you?"

"Not really. I wanted to observe the relationship between Kadar and the Palestinian policeman."

"You have worries in that regard?"

"Let us just say I was not impressed. How are you doing?"

"I've been counting muscles and sinews. I have been overendowed with them."

"Yes, I know. Take heart, my friend, tomorrow is always the better day."

"Tomorrow's not a problem. Today is."

"A massage often helps."

Blanchard thought of Masters's suggestion. He might have taken her up on it if she had offered the service, but he had reservations about asking Brooks. He didn't know why. The memory of Melanie beside him in the night was quite clear.

"Look, there's a reason why I called you, Jacob. Except for a few lost boxes—which we always lose in a move and find later—the camp's pretty well set up. Since I'm not moving around much, I've had some time to think."

"Think of what?"

"There's a Sword of God source you haven't tried to question yet. Nuri Hakkar."

"Hakkar? That is true. I have not thought of it. Probably because he is so ill."

"He's damned sick, for sure. I don't know how much time he's got left, and that's why I thought that, if you want to interview him, you'd better make it quick."

"Will he talk to me?"

"I doubt it. He won't talk to any of the medical staff."

"Then you raise a hopeless possibility."

"What I was thinking, what about Rahman? He's Palestinian, right?"

"Hmm. Let me call him."

"Jacob, I want to go along."

"Ah, Jack . . ."

"I remember paying some dues here."

"I will call you back."

At noon, Del Cameron brought him a thick roast-beef sandwich from the mess hall, along with a bag of potato chips. He ate it all, recalling that he'd missed two meals the day before. Then he spent ten minutes hobbling out to the new latrine, which with all of the people in camp—a company of infantry, for God's sake—was well used already. It took him ten minutes to get back, so he wasn't making much progress in the walking category.

At one o'clock Jillian Weiss came by.

"I could give you a massage, Jack. That would help you a lot."

"Are you a masseuse, Jillian?"

"No, but I'm willing to learn."

He thanked her, but passed. The thought of intentional pressure on any part of his body wasn't a welcome one.

At one-twenty, Armbruster told him he'd secured the weapons in Blanchard's locker. "With all those randy conscripts out there, I doubt we'll need them."

"You said all?"

"Yeah. Somebody delivered the comm gear out of your

Hummer. They very kindly delivered the Uzi that was under the seat, too.''

"Nice touch on somebody's part," Blanchard said.

"Thought so, myself. I've got a couple guys installing the equipment in two-four-four. That'll be your new command vehicle."

At one-forty, Talman called and said they'd pick up Blanchard at three o'clock.

When he hung up, Armbruster asked, "What's that about?"

Blanchard told him.

"Do I need to dress up for this trip?"

"What the hell? You can go, and you look fine."

Rahman's helicopter, marked on the side for the Palestinian Police, landed south of the army camp a few minutes after three, and Armbruster walked out to it with Blanchard.

"The next time you're out scouting for supplies, Dickie, see if you can requisition a golf cart."

"Getting bloody soft, aren't you, Colonel?"

Over the bleat of the rotors and the whine of the turbine, Blanchard practically shouted as he introduced Armbruster to Rahman and Talman, then let Armbruster help him aboard.

The chopper lifted off, dipped its nose to the south, and picked up speed.

On the headphones, Rahman asked if they could use first names, then said, "This was an interesting idea of yours, Jack. Do you have an approach to suggest?"

"Keep in mind, Amin, that I always stick my nose in where it's not wanted, but yeah, I've got a suggestion. First of all, the guy's in sad shape. Both his legs and one arm have been amputated."

"Yes. I will attempt to get my mind around that obstacle."

"Then, he's fairly hopped on painkillers. According to his chart, they've been giving him morphine in heavy doses. He may not be entirely coherent."

"Go on."

"He professes not to speak English or Hebrew, and he won't say much to our interpreters, but in that kind of dreamland he's in, he might talk to a native Arabic speaker. As long as he doesn't figure out who you truly are."

"I will remove my coat and tie."

"Good."

A few minutes later, they touched down near the single tent left standing at the site. Blanchard, Armbruster, and Talman got out and leaned against the chopper as the rotors wound down. Rahman shed his tie and suit jacket and walked across the field to the tent. One of the local women who was tending the patients came out and talked to the deputy chief for a few minutes before he went inside.

The remnants of their passing were still evident—rectangles in the ground where tents had stood and where the bulldozers hadn't bothered leveling. A water trailer with a bucket hung from its spigot was still parked next to the tent, and several trash bags outside it held the empty containers of MREs they'd left behind for the patients and native staff.

"You trust this guy, Jacob?" Blanchard asked, trying to straighten himself up. Whenever he was standing, he tried to overcome the tendency of his stomach muscles to double him over.

"I'm beginning to, I think."

"I don't trust anyone, any man, that good-looking."

Talman smiled. "He had a reputation when he was with Interpol in Paris. Since returning to Gaza, however, he has married and has sired three children."

"Interpol?" Armbruster echoed.

"For fifteen years. Rahman has a more global view than many in his agency."

About twenty minutes later, Rahman reappeared at the flap of the tent and walked out to join them.

Talman asked, "Amin?"

"He died."

Blanchard had been expecting it, but the blunt statement took him by surprise.

Talman appeared instantly suspicious.

"And no, I did not help him to that end. I did learn some things."

The afternoon sun was merciless, and the four of them moved closer to the helicopter, seeking shade.

"He was delirious, but mildly so, I believe. I talked to him as a family member might, and he ranted and raved against the Jewish oppressors. I asked him about Ibn Sapir, and he told me that Sapir died of the same malignancy that affected him. The skin disappearing, tearing off in great hunks as Sapir scratched at himself. His colleagues, and he would not identify them, buried Sapir in the desert and took Hakkar to Kiryat Arba.''

"That is all?" Talman asked.

"That is all. It does not tell us much."

"Oh, I don't know," Blanchard said. "This Sapir was a Sword of God type, too?"

"The leader before Kadar," Talman said.

"Two bloody rare cases here, a hundred and seventy there," Armbruster observed, aiming his thumb over his shoulder to the north.

"I'd say the Sword of God has its hands on something devastating," Blanchard said. "Sapir and Hakkar may have mishandled it."

"Where would they obtain such a thing?" Rahman asked.

"Not far from here, if I had to guess," Blanchard said.

Rahman sighed. "Yes. Saddam is rumored to have many more chemical and biological weapons plants than have ever been revealed."

"Certainly," Talman said, "it should justify an around-the-clock surveillance of the house in Jericho."

Rahman nodded slowly.

"I already told you of my observations this morning, Amin," Talman said.

Blanchard didn't know where that was coming from, or where it was going, but thought he wouldn't intervene.

"I think," Rahman said, "I will give Adnan Boshogi a new assistant."

"That is a wonderful idea," Talman told him.

Armbruster waited until that conversation was apparently over, then produced a handful of latex gloves and said, "Gentlemen, in light of expectations, I secured an extra body bag to that water trailer. If I could get Mr. Talman to help me, we might make it easier on the other patients by removing Mr. Hakkar."

"I will help you, also," Rahman said. He also called to the pilot, and the four of them left Blanchard standing in the shade of the Alouette.

He felt pretty damned useless. When he got back to Mercy Base, he was going to crawl into his bunk and try to get over this.

He might even give Polly Brooks a call.

Gregory Simpson Masters, Jr. flew United to Washington, the Concorde to Paris, and El Al to Tel Aviv. He was not a frequent international flier, and by the time he disembarked, he was jet lagged beyond belief. The exhaustion, coupled with his mood, created an attitude quite unlike his normal demeanor.

The past ten days had been utter hell. He'd been locked out of his apartment; he'd been humiliated by his brokers and bankers calling, wondering why his accounts were frozen; he'd been unable to concentrate on the problems of his clients; and he'd been forced to cancel three meetings with his political backers. If they caught wind of his troubles, they'd be bailing out as soon as they could get him to admit to them. His father was already suspicious. Gregory senior had heard something, somewhere, and Masters had been unable to tell him that Melanie had filed for divorce.

He'd told his father that they were having a little spat. His father told him to unspat her, and do it damned fast. Otherwise, he could kiss the senate goodbye.

It was totally unbelievable. That fucking ex-general had tied up everything except his Lincoln Continental and the cash in his pocket and his office. Just *bang!* overnight. He didn't know who had sicced MacDonald on him. Certainly, Melanie had never met the man. But she had just as certainly agreed to everything MacDonald suggested because she would never have dreamed it up on her own. Her signature was on the papers filed with the court; Masters had checked to make sure.

And then, for her to refuse to talk to him on the phone! Utterly un-fucking-believable! She was under someone's thumb, and Masters was damned well going to straighten her out.

He knew, though, that he would have to subdue his rage—

at both MacDonald and her—and sweet-talk her out of this. Nothing was unrecoverable, after all, but it really pissed him that he'd had to cancel a whole series of meetings with important clients to make this foray to Israel.

He left the terminal and signaled for two cabs. He sent his luggage to the Hilton in one, and took the second to the American Embassy on Hayarkon Street. It was after five by the time he reached it, and in his fatigue, he was snappish with the receptionist. She finally located some trade attaché who was still in the building.

"Yes, Mr. Masters, how can I assist you?"

"I want you to find my wife."

"Sir?"

"She's an American, a doctor, heading up a World Health medical team somewhere in the West Bank. I need to know where she is so I can visit her."

"Ah, yes! The Palestine Medical Assistance Team. Yes, of course." He picked up a telephone and tapped a four-digit code. "While I'm calling, could I see some identification, sir?"

"What the hell for?"

"Anyone could ask for Dr. Masters. She's an important person to us, and to the World Health Organization."

Melanie important? Irritated, Masters dug out his passport and his driver's license. The flunky looked them over, then handed them back. He swung around in his swivel chair, turning his back to Masters as he spoke with someone. It seemed like an awfully long damned conversation. He heard only snippets: ". . . yes, her husband . . . here, now. . . agitated . . ."

He finally turned back to face Masters and replaced the handset.

"We will have to wait a moment while calls are made. It shouldn't be too long."

Masters got up and walked to the window to stare out at the city. Rotten city. The streets were too narrow. Bad planning, all around.

The phone rang, and the flunky answered it. This was a shorter conversation.

He turned when he heard the phone put down.

"Ah, Mr. Masters, we've got something of a glitch."

"Glitch? What do you mean, glitch? Where is she?"

"Ah, at the moment, the medical team is located in a classified area, and she cannot be reached."

"That's impossible!"

"Not according to the Israeli army. What they will do is get a message to her, and have her call you. Where will you be staying, sir?"

Shit! The bitch wasn't returning his calls. That's why he had come all the way to this godforsaken country!

"Sir?"

"At the Hilton."

"We'll be in touch with you as soon as we know anything."

The sucker was talking to him as if she was sick or something. Incommunicado, shit!

The flunky got up and walked him to the door, then firmly shut it as soon as he was standing in the corridor.

Damn her! Now she had a whole fucking army protecting her. What did she think he was, some goddamn serial killer?

Eleven

There were many patrons in the post office, most of them wanting to use a telephone, and Kadar was forced to wait twenty-five minutes while endearments and inconsequential news of relatives were shared over the wires.

These people had no concept of history or world events and what they could mean to their lives. They would whittle away daily at the length of their lives and not raise one hand to protest the injustices delivered on them by the Jews.

Unfortunately, they could not know that the man standing in their midst would soon deliver to them their destiny. If only they had the capacity to understand, Ibrahim Kadar would not have to wait in line for a telephone.

Soon, however, he would have all the telephones he needed, and assistants running to answer them.

When he finally reached the head of the line, beseeching Allah that the telephone on the other end would be picked up, his prayer was answered, and Khalid Badr's uncle said, "Yes?"

"What of Heusseni?"

"There is nothing. No one has seen him."

This might not be as strange as it seemed. Earlier, he had thought it possible that Heusseni had been apprehended in the act of removing property from one person or another, and sequestered in some jail. With the visit of Boshogi and the Jew, asking questions about the youngest member of the group, he had changed his mind. Heusseni had likely attempted some foolish deed, been recognized, and was now the subject of a manhunt. He would have buried himself in one of the safe places.

"And of the settlement?"

"I attempted to visit once again, but was turned away by soldiers. The area has been secured, and travel into the village is forbidden."

"This is joyful news. Send the message."

"But—"

He hung up; he was in no mood for protests.

Walking back to the house slowly, for his foot bothered him today, his outlook on life was as bright as the sun that blessed his land.

As he came in sight of the house, the brightness dimmed considerably. Abu el-Ziam came up the street from the other direction, driving his Fiat. He slowed and turned in to park beside the house. El-Ziam was not the immediate problem, however.

The arrival of the car had attracted someone's attention apparently, and Kadar saw movement across the street from his house, a mere shifting of a silhouette in the garden next to a house. The garden was protected by a low wall, and fruit trees kept it in shadow.

He was walking on the same side of the street, and he quickly switched directions and walked up to the front of a house three lots this side of the garden. Instead of approaching the door, he veered to his right and darted into the narrow alleyway between houses. It took a few minutes to circle around behind the garden, and crouching, sidle up to its rear wall.

He knew her, but who . . . ?

From the café. The woman called Leila Salameh.

And why would she be spying on his house? There was no question that she was spying. She was on her knees next to the house, staying low behind the wall and under an orange tree.

Kadar pulled up his pant leg, ripped the strap loose, and withdrew his knife.

Blanchard handed the telephone to her. "Jacob Talman, Mel."

The ex-Marine appeared much better this morning. There was more color in his face, and he moved with a shadow of the fluid grace she had come to expect from him. He was maybe at eighty-five percent of where he should be.

"What does he want, Jack?"

"I've no idea."

She pressed the phone to her ear. "Yes, Mr. Talman?"

"I am sorry to bother you, Doctor, but I have a message from your embassy, the United States Embassy, that I have been asked to pass on to you."

Talman spoke as if he were reading from a memo. "Mr. Gregory Masters is at the Tel Aviv Hilton. He asks you to telephone him." He gave her the telephone number and the room number.

Shit!

"Thank you, Mr. Talman."

"A moment, Doctor. Needless to say, perhaps, but the conditions at Mar Saba are such that . . ."

"I understand," she said. "I won't mention them."

She handed the phone back to Blanchard and sank into Delray's chair. Lon Chao and Maria Godinez were working at computers on the other side of the tent, and Bob Timnath was filing records as they came off the printer.

This was not the best of worlds. She knew Greg would be difficult to deal with, primarily because he wouldn't understand this country or what was happening in it.

"Mel?"

She smiled, but probably not with full effort. "Both ORs are scheduled. Dean's got an appendectomy, and Lars had an emergency cesarean section. Lon and I are next up."

There was a long line at the clinic, people from the Arab village to the west, and despite the quadrupling of their ward capacity, they were handling the workload. She had the doctors and nurses from the Israeli army tending the necrolysis wards, and that was primarily a wait-and-see task at the moment. The patients there were consuming medical supplies rapidly. The PMAT staff was concentrating on the kinds of problems for which they had come to the West Bank, and they already expected to fill an additional three tents. Particularly troubling at the moment were three cases of typhoid fever. That infectious disease signaled other problems, and Steve Mackey's team was currently at the Arab village performing an evaluation.

"Yeah," Blanchard said. "I read the chart. What else is bothersome at the moment?"

She already felt humiliated after spilling half her life history on him, and she was not going to involve him further. And inexplicably, she instantly broke that resolution and said, "Greg's in Tel Aviv."

"Brett MacDonald must have really gotten to him."

"I don't know."

"You want to see him?"

"I should, I suppose."

"How have your face-to-face meetings gone in the past?"

It didn't take her long to recall the way he always dominated her. "Not well."

"Any reason to expect the future will be different?"

"I think . . . I don't know."

"Grab a phone over there." Blanchard glanced down at his own telephone. "Line two. Let me have the number."

Masters told him the Hilton phone and room numbers, then got up and crossed to the medical desk to pick up the receiver after Blanchard dialed the number.

The response was gruff at first, then softened. "Hello! . . Melanie?"

"This is Colonel Jack Blanchard. I'm the medical-team administrator."

She had never heard Blanchard introduce himself with his former title. He might be using it to intimidate, she thought.

"Oh. I need to speak to my wife, Colonel."

"Mr. Masters, you need to understand that we've got a couple hundred patients, more coming, and four doctors. Dr

Masters is scheduled for surgery all day long. Is there something I could help you with?''

''Ah . . . there is an emergency, Colonel. You'll have to get her out of surgery.''

''What is the nature of the emergency?''

''That is private. Get her on the phone.''

''No.''

One thing Greg Masters reacted poorly to was being told, ''No.'' Masters couldn't recall a time when he'd ever accepted it.

She could imagine the struggle he was making to keep his voice civil. ''Where are you located, Colonel? I'll rent a car and come there.''

''That information is classified by the Israeli government, I'm afraid.''

''Is this some kind of conspiracy?''

''Sir?''

''Listen, if I have to get the police involved, or the prime minister, I'm going to see my wife. And I'm going to see her today!''

''Oh, you're one of those.''

''What? One of what?''

''An ugly American.''

''Listen here, goddamn it! I've . . .''

''I'll pass your message on, Mr. Masters,'' Blanchard said and hung up.

He looked over at her. ''Sorry. I blew it.''

She realized then, that no matter the legal procedures taking place in Chicago, and how strong Brett MacDonald made her appear, she wouldn't have had much more success than Blanchard. Greg steamrolled over everything in his path.

''Thanks for trying, Jack.''

''Toward the end there, I discovered I didn't like him. My antagonistic side comes out once in a while.''

''It's okay.''

''You don't have to see him.''

''I probably do. I'm sure he won't leave until I do.''

''Well, you're not going anywhere without me tagging along.''

* * *

Kadar sat on the wall, one leg thrown over it, when the woman called Leila suddenly stood up. She was about twelve meters away from him, separated from him by only rows of beans, tomato plants, and a few trees, and he did not want to lose the element of surprise, so he froze in place.

It was another automobile. A light-blue sedan, it parked in front of the garden, and its engine died. The driver, an Arab that Kadar had never seen before, settled back against the cushion and stared at Kadar's house. It was obvious that he did not care if he was seen by anyone in the house.

The woman looked at the car for a few seconds, then walked across the garden to a wooden gate in the wall. As she let herself out, Kadar noticed that she carried two bowls, one filled with tomatoes, the other with onions and cucumbers.

So. Perhaps she only harvested the garden for her cafe.

But judging by the way she had watched el-Ziam drive up to the house, he did not think so.

She was a puzzle piece, but if a piece did not fit, it should be thrown out so as not to spoil the rest of the picture. He would have to deal with her, though with the car parked in the street now, it would have to be later.

After she disappeared behind the corner of the neighboring house, he pulled his leg back, slipped to the ground, and replaced the knife in its sheath. He walked through the back-yards of three houses, then again turned to the street and crossed it. Walking to his house boldly, he ignored the man in the car and pushed the door open.

"Ah! There you are!" Badr said. "I have something to tell you!"

"Who is the man across the street?"

Khalid Badr looked instantly disappointed that he could not deliver his news, but both Badr and el-Ziam went to the front window, standing to either side of it, and peered around the curtain. Kassim came to the door of the kitchen to watch them.

"This is the man I was going to tell you about," Abu el-Ziam said. "He is the new assistant to Boshogi. I saw him at the police headquarters and asked about him."

"This is the Jew's fault," Kadar said. "He has forced changes in the police."

"Boshogi will no longer help us?" Badr asked.

"It is doubtful. What have you learned, Khalid?"

Badr, who was short and overweight, always enjoyed recognition. He smiled broadly, revealing two dead teeth. "On the road to Bethlehem?"

When the wait became too long and tried his patience, Kadar sighed and said, "I know of the road."

"There was a large explosion, a car bomb."

"How did you learn of this?"

"My cousin. He was traveling the road with his family, and he had passed the car, then the convoy."

"Convoy? What convoy?" The man did not know how to tell a story.

"The Palestine Medical Assistance Team. They have all-white vehicles. He recognized them immediately."

Kadar waited.

"So? Are you going to tell me what happened?"

"I do not know. My cousin was several kilometers away, and he saw it only in the rearview mirror. He heard it, however. He said it was very loud. Also, it was colorful, he said."

"Was the convoy damaged?"

"Again, I do not know. He thought it strange because nothing was mentioned in the newspaper."

"Then it was probably a failure, and no one would claim a failure."

"I think it was Omar," Badr said.

There was a momentary silence. Neither Kassim or el-Ziam wanted to respond, perhaps because it was so infrequently that Badr came up with an insight.

"Ah . . . it cannot be," Kadar told him.

"The Jew was here the very next day, asking about him."

This was true.

"It is no wonder it was a failure, if the boy was involved. He is naive, a simpleton."

"Still," el-Ziam said, "whether or not it was Omar, it remains a beautiful target. The World Health Organization's efforts have been often featured in the world news. I have heard of it on the radio.''

This was true, also. Kadar would keep it in mind.

''Let us assume a fifty percent probability that Omar made this stupid move, operating without supervision,'' Kadar said. ''Tell me how that affects us.''

''We have a new policeman across the street,'' el-Ziam said, ''making no effort to conceal his interest in this house. We have been invaded by the police, also, and if not for Boshogi's warning, the Jew would have found weapons and the vials in the house.''

''We do not need the attention,'' Kadar agreed. ''Omar Heusseni may well have brought this on us, but no matter. The time has come for all of us to leave Jericho.''

''Now? Today?''

''We will go after darkness. We must retrieve the weapons, and we must walk.''

''But my car!'' el-Ziam complained.

''It will be here when we return. When we return in triumph! You will get a new car,'' he promised.

El-Ziam looked skeptical.

It was a problem with his followers. They lacked his own faith and optimism.

''Oma,'' he told his woman, ''you will shop for what you need and prepare all of the food in the house to be taken with us.''

She only nodded. She did not talk as she had when she was younger and more avid. At one time, her only goals in life were to make love most of the day and kill Jews when she was not making love. Lately, though, she had been demonstrating little of either interest.

''What of the policeman out there?'' Badr asked.

''If he is still here tonight, you will have the chance to dispatch him.''

''But he is an Arab, Ibrahim!''

''Obviously misguided, Khalid. Otherwise, he would be assisting us.''

''Perhaps you had better . . .''

"I will be otherwise occupied. There is another loose string to tie up."

Kadar was thinking of the woman at the cafe.

By five o'clock all of the radio and television stations had broadcasted the proclamation. By six o'clock special editions of newspapers in several languages were available on the street, and Jacob Talman left his agency to buy one. He stood on the street and read the lead story. The details were scant, but the words of the message received by the television station were repeated in both Hebrew and in Arabic—the language used in the message—and he assumed the format was also the same:

A PLAGUE HAS DESCENDED UPON THE JEWS.
BY THE HUNDREDS, THEY ARE DYING AT MAR SABA,
AND THEY WILL DIE ALL AROUND THE HOLY OF HOLIES,
UNTIL THE RIGHTFUL OWNERS RECLAIM IT.
ALLAH'S WILL BE DONE WITH THE ASSISTANCE OF
HIS RIGHTEOUS SERVANT,
THE SWORD OF GOD.

There goes the neighborhood, Talman thought, remembering the phrase from some American television program he had once watched late in the night. And there goes, also, the carefully managed secrecy. The media would swarm around Mar Saba, attempting to verify the message. "Plague" was generic enough, but if any correspondent got an inkling of what was actually taking place, and managed to get the word on the air or in print, the streets would fill with panicked people.

He went back to his office and called Stein and Avidar, but had to leave a message in both instances.

The general called back fifteen minutes later.

"I know, Jacob. This cat has left the bag."

"I called Jericho and spoke to Boshogi, sir. He said there was absolutely no evidence with which he could arrest the members of the Sword of God. He believes it is a fake message because he has heard of no problems at Mar Saba. I did not enlighten him. I did go out briefly to speak to Beit Horon, and he also considers the message a hoax. That is, he knows that something is wrong at Mar Saba, but would as soon not attribute it to Kadar. I rather think that . . . well . . .''

''Tell me.''

''Horon may think his people are the only ones capable of visiting plagues upon the land.''

The general harrumphed, and Talman wasn't certain whether it was a stifled laugh or a rebuke. He asked, ''Boshogi. Is he doing anything at all?''

''He tells me he has established a twenty-four hour surveillance on the house.''

''We will have to accept that for the moment, then. I have a call placed to Amin Rahman, but he has not yet returned it.''

''How will we respond to the message?''

''Colonel Stein has gone to the encampment, and he will be the spokesman. We will acknowledge an outbreak of a disease, but we will not identify it.''

''Can we get away with that?''

''Who knows? He is to work out a story with Dr. Masters.''

''And the hundreds of dead?''

''There are only one hundred and ninety-five people in the settlement to begin with, Jacob.''

''There has been one death. A baby.''

''Then, we will admit to that. We will not lie,'' the general said.

Talman saw where Levi Avidar was headed. ''You would like to give the impression that the Sword of God is taking credit for what is probably a natural disaster?''

''We will attempt that approach, yes. Any journalist worth his title should dredge up the misbegotten events attributed to the Sword of God and draw the inescapable conclusion of the band's incompetence.''

''According to the paper I have just read, they have not done that yet. But, as to incompetence, we know better, do we not sir?''

''If they're behind Mar Saba, Jacob, they've proven themselves dangerous.''

''I will go to Jericho tonight,'' Talman said.

"One moment, Jacob. What do you know about this man in Tel Aviv, this Gregory Masters?"

"Very little, sir. He is apparently the husband of Dr. Melanie Masters. Because of the quarantine, the army would not let him know where she is, and I carried a message at the army's request."

"The man has been raising inordinate hell, calling everyone possible in the Knesset, the Cabinet, and every ministry. You don't know what his problem is?"

"No, sir. Just that he wants to see his wife."

"Well, you'd better make arrangements for that to happen, Jacob."

"I will see what I can do, sir."

He called Blanchard immediately after Avidar hung up, but he had to wait five minutes while the administrator was tracked down.

"Yes, Jacob?"

"Do you know a man called Greg Masters, Jack?"

"Shit. You mean he's gotten to you?"

"He has apparently ruffled some feathers. Dr. Masters should go see him as soon as possible."

"Ah, Jacob. There's a messy divorce in the works. That information is between you and me."

"Oh, damn. She won't see him?"

"Let me see what I can do."

"Thank you. I would like to shut him up, if possible."

"It's tough keeping some things quiet, Jacob. Your Colonel Stein is here, trying to stick his thumb in our dike."

"The reporters are there?"

"By the battalion. The army sent another company of body-guards for us."

"We may lose control of this situation," Talman admitted.

"I sincerely hope not."

"What of the patients?"

"Almost every one of them is deteriorating," Blanchard told him. "But Mel says that's to be expected. The treatment should take hold in the next couple of days."

"Tell her I wish her well."

Talman replaced the telephone, then went up to his apartment to retrieve some currency and his Browning nine-millimeter semiautomatic pistol. He rarely carried it, but he thought his trip to Jericho should have some offensive capability.

He was tired of being reactive. Lately, his days seemed full of sudden ugly surprises.

Blanchard walked back to the wadi, went down one side and up the other, and into the village. On the north end of town, Colonel Stein and Masters were holding an impromptu press conference near the roadblock the army had created.

The conference broke up before he reached it, and he ran into Stein and Masters. He turned around to walk back to the encampment with them.

"How'd it go?"

"Reporters are very suspicious," Stein said.

"And rightly so," Masters added. "I'm not at all comfortable with this."

"With what?" Blanchard asked.

"We said it was an epidermal infection. When they asked about the quarantine, the colonel told them we were protecting against the possible spread of the disease."

"That's right, isn't it?" Stein asked.

"It's not contagious."

"How else are you going to explain the number of cases we have, Doctor?"

"Maybe with the truth, Colonel Stein."

"The truth shall free us all?"

Before she could jump on that statement, Blanchard said, "Dr. Masters has a thing about military expediency, Colonel. Don't hold it against her."

She was about to turn on him, fire in her eyes, as they reached the wadi, when he said, "Mel, we've got a bit of a problem."

"What? What now?"

"The guy in Tel Aviv. He's been jangling some high-place nerves."

"Oh, damn him!"

"We can do whatever—"

"I'll drive over there."

"Let me go in your place. I can straighten him out real quick."

"Oh, no! I don't want your antagonism rearing its head. You'll end up in jail."

Privately, Blanchard appreciated her concern.

Stein watched this exchange with a straight face. He had to be puzzled, but he *was* an intelligence officer and didn't give away much.

"Compromise?" Blanchard suggested.

"Okay. You can drive me."

"Are you planning on going tonight?" Stein asked.

"Yes," Masters told him.

"I'll write a quick pass for each of you. We're strengthening our road patrols, and you might be stopped."

They crossed the wadi, and Masters went to make a last quick tour of the wards. Blanchard and Stein found Delray and Armbruster in the mess tent, and Blanchard briefed the two of them quickly while Stein wrote out his passes.

"You sure you're up to this, Jack?"

"No sweat, Dickie. I feel pretty good today."

"You walk with a hitch in your get-along," Delray said.

"And that eye looks like shit," Armbruster added.

"I appreciate your candor," Blanchard told him. "Colonel Stein, are you going back to Jerusalem?"

"I think I'll wait and see what the journalists do, first."

Blanchard left in search of Masters, found her at the clinic, and asked, "Do want to change before we go?"

"Hell, no. I'm not dressing up for Greg, and he can damned well see what we're going through."

She was wearing jeans and a Cubs T-shirt, and there were a few splotches of blood on the shirt. Blanchard wore a similar costume, though bloodless.

He found the Humvee that Dickie Armbruster had converted to the new command vehicle, checked the gas level, then cranked it up.

"Let's try to not run into car bombs, please."

"Do my best, Mel."

He drove down through the wadi, which was developing a road of its own from all the traffic through it, then through the village, and out on the road north. They were mobbed by the reporters as they passed through the military checkpoint, but he maintained a steady five miles an hour, and they fell by the wayside.

The half-dozen Israeli soldiers at the roadblock seemed disappointed that he didn't run over a few of their oppressors.

It was twelve kilometers into Jerusalem, and he threaded his way through the city until he could join Highway 1, the modern highway connecting the capital with the seacoast city. He got up to speed and settled in with the traffic. The knobby tread of the tires whined on the pavement.

"Be there in about an hour," he said.

"What would you do in my place, Jack?"

He had to roll the question around in his head for a couple minutes. He didn't think he was much good at this.

"First, you need to assess the situation, Mel. What's Greg's objective?"

"Objective? He wants to reconcile."

"Why?"

"The family—his family—doesn't react well to scandal. I don't think there's ever been a divorce."

"That's all?"

"Well, then, I suppose he's feeling a bit humiliated by this experience. Brett said he went through the roof when he was told that the revenues from my practice, that Greg invested, were to be audited. That would bother him."

"Anything else?"

"The political thing, I guess. He's concerned about his appearance before the voters as an outstanding family man."

"So, you've given me three reasons for his being here courting you."

"Yes."

"Not one of them mentioned love."

After that, she was quiet for a time, as faster cars overcame them and passed. Blanchard watched each carefully, though with more difficulty as daylight waned.

"You're correct, Jack. I don't think love is part of the equation. On his side."

"You know where you stand, then, and you know what you have to do."

"What?"

"Hit low, hard, and fast. Don't give in to any wishful thinking. Back away and see if this is one of the battles that ends the war."

"You've been leading me with some kind of war strategy?"

"Or a variation thereof. It's all I know, Mel."

The city of Tel Aviv-Jaffa and its outlying suburbs housed 1,500,000 people, and during the day its white high-rises contrasted nicely with the azure waters of the Mediterranean. Blanchard recalled that the *Yafo* part of the city, situated to the south, was founded by Japheth, Noah's son, after the flood in Jewish tradition. That made it fairly old, but it was difficult to tell with the massive building programs that were under way.

At night the streets were well lit, and it might have been any metropolis in the world. He came into the city on Quibbutz Galyyot, racing the Hummer with a few hundred other, but smaller, vehicles. The lights were on at the Bnei Yehuda Sports Ground, and there were several thousand people milling around there. He didn't know what was going on, but sometimes, life seemed to go on, no matter what crises he was himself facing. They passed the complex and went onto Hayarkon Street, which fronted the sea, and he turned north.

People were out, doing normal things—window-shopping, hunting for their dinners armed only with a Mastercard. On his left, the darkness of the sea was broken by the lights of shipping, mostly commercial freighters and tankers, he thought.

He found the Tel Aviv Hilton on Independence Park without any trouble. He'd stayed there a few times. He also found a parking place and put the Humvee in it.

"Stay in the truck," Masters commanded.

"You bet. I'll think about where I'm taking you to dinner. Afterward."

She gave him a long look, as if amazed at his willing compliance, then got out of the truck. As soon as he saw her disappear into the lobby, he slipped out and locked the doors, then went over to stand next to a taxi rank.

Not five minutes later, she reappeared at the glass doors, pushed through to the sidewalk, and spotted him.

"You don't obey very well."

"I like to be close to the action."

"Come on, then."

Inside they found an unoccupied elevator, and Blanchard punched the button for the seventh floor.

At the fourth floor, she said, "I'm scared."

"It's okay. We all are."

They got out on the seventh, and Blanchard checked the plastic signs for the right direction. It wasn't too far down the plush and hushed corridor. He noticed Masters was careful not to brush his arm or touch him in any way.

She knocked on the door.

It took him a couple of minutes to get the door open.

Well, shit, there's the problem right there.

Greg Masters was too good-looking, more handsome than Amin Rahman, even. Not a big guy, maybe five ten and a hundred-forty-five, but trim. Probably a result of massage rather than strenuous workouts, he guessed. A finely shaped face, smooth aquiline nose, dark-brown, limpid eyes. His hair was full, curly, and exquisitely styled. The teeth were the product of expensive orthodonture, even and very white. The smile was wide, sincere, and just a hair trigger away from a sneer. This was a guy who sneered regularly. Smooth, accomplished, socially poised and acceptable, and very aware of his position.

Where Amin Rahman had fought his way to the top, Blanchard figured Greg Masters had been pushed to the top. Or dropped on it.

He was wearing suit pants, a white shirt with an expensive tie pulled loose, and carrying a heavy glass of something amber

The smile widened even further. "Melanie! My God, I'm glad to . . ."

Lost the smile when he saw Blanchard.

"Greg, this is Jack Blanchard. He drove me in."

"Uh, yeah, we've talked, Colonel."

He reached out with his free hand, grabbed Masters's wrist pulled her into the room, and started to shut the door in Blanchard's face.

Blanchard caught the doorknob and forced the door right back at him. The measure of muscles didn't last long.

"You can wait in the hall, Colonel. This is private."

"I get claustrophobic, Greg. Besides, I'm thirsty."

Blanchard stepped inside, spotted the bottle of Black Label on the dresser, and crossed to it. He didn't look back.

Uncasing two glasses from their plastic wrappers, he dropped ice cubes from the plastic bin into them, then poured scotch. Water from an insulated pitcher on a plastic tray topped them off, and he took one back and handed it to Masters, then stood next to her.

"Thanks, Jack."

The male half of this duo watched his performance with something like incredulity, feeling outmaneuvered probably. Two against one. Blanchard tipped his glass to the man, then took a long sip. Good going down.

Greg Masters didn't know where to go from here. This was a guy accustomed to battling all day long with words, but physical confrontations were foreign concepts. Blanchard outweighed him by nearly forty pounds and had a good four-inch reach on him. Physical wouldn't be fair, but it wouldn't come to that. Masters wouldn't test him on a bet. If he couldn't intimidate with words, he was lost.

The lawyer backed off, sat on the edge of the bed, and studied them. Was that the faint aroma of distaste on his face as he noted their jeans and T-shirts?

"Where have you been?"

It was a practiced question, Blanchard understood, one for which he expected an immediate answer.

"Classified," she said.

"You can tell me. It's not going to be repea—"

"Classified."

"I see," he said, taking another and longer look at Blanchard.

"What *do* you see?" Masters asked him.

"The, uh, two of you . . ."

"Have been working hard all day. We help people, Greg. You've been making noises like you're important, and we've driven all this way to see what's so important. Do you want to tell me, so we can get back to work?"

Blanchard was proud of her. If she'd melted even a little, it might have all gone to hell. He supposed they'd argued before—most married couples did. But he also supposed that Greg Baby had never seen her as resolute as this.

"Melanie, I didn't come all this way to argue. We've got to straighten out whatever is wrong between us . . ."

"What do you think that is, Greg?"

"For the life of me, and I've been thinking very hard about this, I don't understand what the problem is. We've done so very well, darling, and . . . don't you want to sit down?"

"I don't have time to sit. What's the rest of your pitch?"

"God, Melanie! Our future is at stake. Don't call it a pitch, for God's sake."

"Our future? Or yours? What did you have in mind for me?"

"Darling, you've got a terrific reputation, and this stint in Israel won't hurt you a bit. We can use it to—"

"I'm tired of using, Greg. Maybe that's the problem."

Blanchard sipped his drink.

"Melanie, surely there's some way . . . some arrangement we can make in order to avoid all of this legal fuss."

He wasn't at his courtroom best, if indeed, he was a courtroom lawyer. His eyes kept darting between Masters and Blanchard, and Blanchard figured he was a paper lawyer. Paper tiger.

"I can understand why you'd want to avoid the legal entanglements, Greg. Brett tells me you've screwed up badly. You ignored your father's advice, didn't you?"

Now he came off the bed, advancing on her. Blanchard put one foot forward, and he stopped abruptly.

"Goddamn it! You're making accusations about things you know nothing about!"

"We'll find out, I guess. Greg, there's nothing more to say. Pack your bags and go back to Chicago."

"Shit! I know what you're up to! I'm going to slam you with a countersuit that'll leave you shaking in the wind."

Masters sipped her drink, then smiled at him.

Blanchard was proud, again, so he smiled, too. All she needed was a bit of a threat to erase any thought of wavering.

The attorney looked at him, and the red flush rose out of his collar and suffused his face.

"And I'm going to name you the goddamned correspondent, Blanchard!"

"Nothing would make me happier, Greg, old man, but I'm afraid you're pissing up a rope. You're the only one who'll get wet."

Blanchard finished his drink and placed the glass on a table near the door.

"Thanks for the drink."

Masters set her glass next to his and opened the door.

"Try to get used to it, Greg. It's over. Go home."

Blanchard closed the door behind him. When they reached the elevator stack, Masters sagged against the wall.

"That's the hardest thing I've ever done in my life."

"I thought you did fine, Mel."

"Only because you were there."

"You're used to talking back to me. Some of it just rubbed off on Greg."

She tried to give him a little smile at the joke, but it didn't come off.

"What are you thinking?" she asked.

She probably wanted feedback on the confrontation, but he didn't feel very professional at that level, so he said, "Dressed the way we are, I'm thinking hamburgers, thick slices of onion and tomato. Some fries and a beer."

"Be serious, damn it!"

"I didn't get mad. Didn't even think about slugging him."

"Jack!"

"I was serious about the burgers. But, hell, Melanie, I'm no expert on this stuff. Gut-wise, I don't think you've heard the last from Greg. However, I don't think you'll have to face him again if you've got me in tow."

She smiled grimly and pushed herself off the wall. "Let's go find those hamburgers."

Shortly after midnight, Ibrahim Kadar slipped through the kitchen window, which was on the side of the house, hidden by a cedar tree, and lowered himself gently to the ground. He helped Kassim out next, then took the backpacks from Badr. They contained a few changes of clothing and the food that Kassim had prepared for their journey.

Badr and el-Ziam came next, and the four of them crossed the side yard to the shadows of the neighboring house.

"Go," Kadar whispered.

They slid along the wall of the house, then disappeared into the dark. They would retrieve the weapons and the black plastic case from the cache in a house a block away, then make their way south, slipping away from the town through an orchard that escaped continuous surveillance. He had warned el-Ziam about the care required of the vials, evoking pictures of Sapir and Hakkar.

Kadar had changed his mind about the policeman. At four o'clock a replacement had arrived for the unknown officer sitting in the car. Kadar knew the replacement, and as expected, he appeared to have gone sound asleep by ten o'clock.

He had not changed his mind about the woman. The more he thought about it, the more convinced he was that she spied for someone. It might be Hamas; it might be the Islamic Jihad; it might be the Jews. It did not matter.

He moved stealthily down the alleyway until he was a block away, then crossed between houses to the street. The car was still parked opposite his house, and he could detect no movement within it. The policeman smoked cigarettes with the same frequency as Abu el-Ziam, and surely, if he was awake, there would be the telltale glow of a lit cigarette to give him away.

Crossing the street quickly, he walked on to the next alleyway, then worked his way down it to the back of the cafe. He had to be careful of the trash that littered the ground. Cans and offal and discarded boxes would be lethal as the source of noise.

Next to the kitchen at the rear of the cafe was a small apartment for the owner, but the only entrance was a door to the kitchen. He stepped around several garbage cans and, feeling with his toes in the darkness for obstacles, moved up to the door. There was a small pane of glass in its upper half, and light shone through it. The single apartment window was dark.

Easing up to the window, he looked through it. She was not asleep yet, as he had planned on. Instead, he could see right through an interior doorway of the kitchen to where she sat at a table reading a newspaper. Her back was to him. From time to time, she looked up, but always toward the front.

There was a radio on somewhere, issuing Arabic music.

Bending quickly, Kadar retrieved his knife.

His hand found the knob of the door and tested it slowly. The use of locks was not widespread, and this one was not locked, either.

Gently, he pulled the door open, then slipped into the kitchen.

He went quickly to the other door, finding a place to the side of it, in front of a refrigerator.

She continued to read.

The only light was from a bare bulb in the ceiling directly above her. He looked through the front windows, but saw nothing in the darkness.

Placing one foot out, he stepped through the doorway.

Then moved his damaged foot to the front.

He was three meters away from her.

Positioning the knife in his right hand so that he could grab her hair with his left and lever her head back, he would then rip the knife across her throat.

He took another step.

Then another.

A front window exploded.

She yelped, started upward from her chair.

His plan evaporated, but he successfully drove the knife into her back.

Twelve

Talman was too damned late.

He knew it.

He had parked his car off the main street, a half block from the cafe, then walked to Kadar's house. The Palestinian policeman who was supposed to be watching it was sitting in his car reading. Talman had taken up a station several houses away and watched both the car and the house. There was activity in the house, judging by shadows passing over the drawn curtains, but nothing definable.

At eleven o'clock, when he was assured that the policeman was visiting the Land of Nod, he had moved closer, using the trees and the shadow as cover, until he found a position below a sidewall window. There was still movement, and there was conversation, but he could make out the importance of neither. He rested his back against the stuccoed wall and waited.

Close to midnight, he nearly had a heart attack when the window above his head swung open, and he had crept away toward the front of the house when a figure emerged and dropped to the ground. Talman lay flattened on the ground, hugging it dearly, hoping the shadow of the tree protected him from the sparse moonlight.

More figures appeared from the window, then all of them moved across the yard. He heard a short, sharp, whispered command. They melted away toward the rear of the house.

Talman rose to his hands and knees and crawled rapidly after them.

They split up; three shadows creeping to the south, the other darting across backyards. He was torn but for a moment, then climbed to his feet and followed the singular figure.

Within a block, he lost it in the darkness. Cursing himself for a fool—three people would have made more noise and improved his tracking—he worked his way slowly along the sides of sleeping structures back toward the main street. Though he searched madly for his adversary, he could not find him.

When he had reached the main street once again, and saw the light shining in the windows of the cafe, Talman walked in that direction. He did not hurry, cautious of a peril lurking in every inky recess of doorways, windows, and alleyways.

He had almost reached the cafe when, through a front window, he saw Leila sitting at a table under a light. And immediately behind her, Ibrahim Kadar.

Without conscious thought, Talman ripped the Browning from his pocket, flicked off the safety, cocked it, and fired.

The window shattered.

Leila yelled.

The bullet went who knew where, because Kadar leaped forward, arm outthrust.

This time, he aimed.

Fired again.

The gunshot echoed down the silent street. Cordite stung his nostrils.

Kadar dodged away, went to the floor.

Talman raced up to the window, slammed his back to the wall next to it, then spun to look inside.

He did not see Kadar.

Leila was sprawled facedown on the table, blood spreading rapidly on the back of her white blouse.

He heard another door slam. At the back of the cafe.

To hell with Kadar!

He took four steps to the door, tried the handle, found the

door locked, then raised his foot and kicked the door near the latch.

It flew open, the simple latch ripped away from the jamb.

Shoving the gun into his pocket, Talman reached the table in seconds.

"Leila!"

No response.

The source of the blood bubbling on her back was high, between her shoulder blades, to the left of the spine. Looking around, he spotted a stack of towels on a counter and retrieved several. He ripped her blouse from hem to neck, and packed a towel tightly against the wound.

Holding it in place, he levered her back in the chair and got an arm under her legs. He held the towel in place with his right arm as he lifted her.

He was damned if he would take her to an Arab doctor in Jericho. If someone suspected she was spying, she would not survive the night.

Lurching with her weight, he trotted out the front door.

A few people had gathered on the street, but none offered help.

It took him a second to orient himself, to remember where he had parked his car, then he ran for it. His breath was coming in deep gasps by the time he rounded the corner and ran the twenty meters to the car. He lowered her legs to the ground and fought the key out of his pocket. The lock eluded him a moment, then he found it and jerked the door wide. He shoved her into the front seat and followed, keeping her upright and pressed against his chest with his right arm so he could keep pressure on his towel bandage.

He had to use his left hand to start the car and shift, but five minutes later, he skidded to a stop at the guard post.

The soldier took one look inside and raised his rifle.

Talman shoved the door open. "She's ours, you fool! Get a Jeep!"

He had to yell one more time and produce his credentials before a sleepy-eyed sergeant appeared to assess the situation.

Alarmed, the sergeant asked, "Do you want me to drive you, Major?"

"Yes, but get your Jeep. Where we're going, we'll need four-wheel drive."

"Melanie! Emergency!"

Masters's eyes flashed open, but it was dark. She rolled her head sideways and saw the flashlight aimed at the floor.

"Jillian?"

"It's a knife wound, deep. We've only got EMTs on duty."

"Coming."

She rolled onto her side, slipped her legs out of the bed, and stood up. Peeling the nightgown over her head, she tossed it aside, then pulled on the jeans and sweatshirt she'd left out on her camp stool. Her running shoes were on the floor, and she stepped into them without socks. She didn't bother to tie them as she followed Weiss through the front flap.

"Where?"

"They took her to the hospital."

"Her?"

"Some friend of Mr. Talman's, I think."

Timnath and another paramedic had her on the table in OR 1. Talman and some Israeli soldier hovered nearby. The OR light was bright enough to hurt her eyes.

"Bob?"

"It's deep, Doctor. May have nicked the heart. Vitals are erratic."

"I need an OR nurse and an anesthesiologist."

"Cale's on his way," Weiss said. "I sent Roberto for Dr. Gordon."

"Mr. Talman, I need to keep this room sterile."

Talman's eyes looked dark and ferocious. There was a tremendous amount of blood all over his shirt.

"Of course, Doctor. Would you . . . could you . . . she's very special."

"Everything we can. Let me see, Bob."

She leaned over the table as Timnath pulled away the bandage he was using as a compress.

"Looks innocent enough."

"Sharp blade," Timnath said. "We may have to break a rib to work in there."

"All right. I'm going to wash up. Have Cale prep her as soon as he gets here."

"I'm here," Perkins said, pushing through the flap. He already had scrubs on.

"We want X-rays. Get a blood type."

She followed Talman and the soldier out of the OR into the lab.

She pulled paper slippers over her shoes as she asked, "You don't know her blood type, Mr. Talman?"

He turned to her. "No."

"Her name?"

"No."

"And yet she's special?"

"Absolutely. I can make one call and get all of those things for you."

"Please do. Her whole history, if you can. Quickly."

This was one crazy country, she thought.

It took them most of the night to walk to the safe house. It was a disaster of an old farmhouse, part of the roof missing, the door hanging on one hinge, the glass from the windows long ago broken or stolen.

They made the trek slowly and with extreme caution because they were carrying the Kalashnikov assault rifles, three kilos of C-4 *plastique,* detonators, and the vials with them. It was the entire arsenal of the Sword of God, and without Omar Heusseni's expertise in requisitioning supplies and materiel, likely to remain slim.

Until Jerusalem was abandoned by the Jews, and Kadar was recognized for his prophecy. Then the coffers of the Sword of God would be awash in contributions.

The wooden floor of the house was splintered and broken, with gaping holes. It did not make an attractive bed, but they settled down on it, using the backpacks for pillows, and waited out the night.

Kadar could not sleep; he was too excited.

He had rid the world of one more spy, but the narrowness of his own escape from death was still with him. His blood pumped through his veins with fiery abandon. The echoes of the shots aimed at him still rang like phantoms in his ears.

He had not told the others of the event. He had no idea who his attacker might have been. He knew he had erred in not examining the area around the cafe before making his entry. It would not happen again.

In the darkness of the house, with the breathing of Kassim, Badr, and el-Ziam in his ears, he moved his lips in silent recitation:

> That then is God your Lord:
> there is no god but He,
> the Creator of everything.
> So serve Him,
> for He is Guardian over everything.

Allah's will would not be thwarted. Kadar had survived the vicious attack by the unknown predator for a single purpose: to fulfill his destiny.

Kadar felt much better knowing that.

At dawn he rose and carried his backpack outside. The expanding light made the old house and its broken fence stand out in sharp relief against a barren field. He did not know why the house stood abandoned, but suspected an old family feud. Its existence had long been known to him, probably foreordained by Allah, and he had kept it as his reserve.

He did not have his prayer rug, and unfortunately, they had neglected to bring water with them, but he would not be denied his ritual. Begging God's forgiveness for his lack of preparation, he simulated the washing of his hands, dipping his hands three times into an imaginary bowl. He could almost taste the water as he imagined the rinsing of his mouth, again three times. In his mind, he washed his face, cleansed his beard of foreign matter, and then stooped to clean his feet.

"There is no god but God, and Muhammad is His messenger."

Standing and facing toward Mecca, Kadar raised his arms and intoned, *"Allah Akbar!"*

He recited the first passage of the Koran, then bent forward to lodge his hands on his knees, *"Allah Akbar!"*

He paused for a moment, standing upright, to meditate about the power of his vision and the strength he would need to pursue it, then lowered himself to his knees and stretched forward on the dusty earth. Face into the dirt, he pronounced his prayers, then repeated the exercise of prostrating himself twice more.

"There is no god but God, and Muhammad is His messenger."

His prayers completed, he sat on the canted stoop and rummaged in the backpack for the portable radio. He tuned it to a Jerusalem station broadcasting in Hebrew. He already knew the Arabic stations would be supportive; he wanted to know what the Jews were saying.

At the moment, nothing. It was only music.

Badr came out and headed off behind an outlying shed to attend to his morning ritual before his own prayers.

A moment later, he called, "Ibrahim! Come look at this!"

Resigned, Kadar pushed himself to his feet and walked to the shed, then around it.

Badr urinated noisily into the weeds. "See this!"

Badr pointed with his free hand at an old car seat and a steel barrel.

"This is wonderful, Khalid. What do you make of it?"

"Omar."

The fool was seeing Heusseni in everything. Still, Kadar walked over to the barrel and bent over it to sniff.

"Diesel fuel," he said.

"Exactly."

It was possible. Kadar had once shown this house to Heusseni.

The two of them went back around the leaning shed and looked through its open doorway. There was nothing inside but trash.

Badr went in, dropped to his knees, and searched the floor. Excitedly, he said, "Here! The dirt is thinner here. Look! A crack!"

He took out a pocketknife and worked away at the crack in the floor, finally edging up a board, then a whole section of the floor.

"I told you," he said proudly.

Kadar returned to his backpack and retrieved a flashlight. He allowed Badr to drop into the shallow pit with the flashlight and watched as the beam played around.

Plastic buckets, the smell of fertilizer.

"And here! There are two cans of gas. A box."

Badr reached under the floor, pulled out a box, and placed it at Kadar's feet. He squatted to look into it. There were detonators, fuse, wire, connectors, and batteries.

Another cardboard box, and when opened, they found tinned food.

"Oma will be pleased," Kadar said drily.

"This pleases me," Badr said as he rose from the pit with two bundles of oil-soaked rags. He peeled the rags away to reveal an M-16 automatic rifle.

In all, they recovered the M-16, three Beretta revolvers, ammunition, five sticks of dynamite, fragmentation grenades, rocket-propelled grenades, the gas, and some food from the pit.

"You will believe me?" Badr asked.

"I believe you, Khalid. Omar was here."

The little thief had been stealing from the Sword of God. It was sinful.

While Badr carried the cache to the house, Kadar listened to the radio news.

The item was not even headline news. The end of the newscast was almost upon him before it was mentioned.

"Officials in Jerusalem have branded the proclamation of the Sword of God, which was widely disseminated yesterday, as fraudulent. When interviewed, Dr. Melanie Masters, chief of medicine for the Palestine Medical Assistance Team, said only that there was an outbreak of a skin infection and that she saw nothing to worry about at this time. A spokesman for the army suggested that the Sword of God might well be claiming responsibility for what is truly an act of God.

"And our research has revealed that instances in which the

Sword of God has been suspected have been ill-planned and bumbling efforts.''

Kadar kicked the radio so hard it soared through the air for ten meters, then hit the ground with a loud *THWACK*. Plastic panels broke off. It also quit working.

The idiots!

This Dr. Masters! A fraud! What would she know of anything? The doctor was not even a man, who might have the knowledge to understand.

Claiming God's acts! A blasphemy! The Sword of God served God's wishes.

Did they not know what was coming? He had given them a horrendous sampling.

Or had he?

He did not know for certain that the batch of bacteria provided by Majib Khabanni was the same as the first, the one that had killed Sapir and disabled Hakkar. Perhaps Khabanni had misled him. Kadar would truly appear as the close relative of a goat if his weapon turned out to envelop the populace with impetigo or measles.

The misbegotten son of the devil!

Unbuttoning his shirt, he reached inside for one of the bundles pressed close to his stomach. He peeled off a sheaf of currency, replaced the bundle, then went inside and handed the money to el-Ziam.

''You will catch a bus to Jerusalem. In the American Colony section, there is an alley off of Kalad Ibn el Waleed, and a few meters down the alley is a garage with blue trim. Inside is a Dodge van. Bring it back here.''

He detested the necessity to keep giving away the locations of his refuges, even to members of his movement. The refuges were fast becoming extinct. The garage, in fact, was the last within Jerusalem.

''A van? That is wonderful!'' el-Ziam said. He was softened by modern living and hated walking farther than necessary. He had complained throughout the night.

''Complete your devotions first, then walk down to the highway. And on your way back, fill the van with gasoline and buy newspapers.''

"Of course. Do we need the van right away?"

"We must personally examine the effects of our handiwork, Abu."

At seven-thirty, a very haggard Jacob Talman sat in Blanchard's administration tent with Blanchard and Rahman. Talman was wearing a Denver Broncos short-sleeved sweatshirt that Blanchard had given him, but his chinos were still speckled with dark-brown bloodstains. The deputy police chief had arrived by helicopter, and Blanchard had given him a cup of coffee, topping off Talman's and his own mugs for about the tenth time.

"Do you want anything else, Amin? Some breakfast?"

"This will do nicely, Jack."

Talman was about to say something when Weiss popped through the front flap.

"They're closing now," she announced.

Talman asked, "How . . . ?"

"We'll know in a little while, Mr. Talman."

Blanchard introduced Weiss to Rahman, and the two rattled for a bit in fluent Arabic, then Weiss left.

Blanchard had been up since before one o'clock, when Irsay woke him to find out if some guy named Talman was allowed to use the communications gear. He hadn't shaved yet, and the stubble on his cheeks bothered him. The one aspect of his morning that looked promising was that his headache was finally gone. He didn't want to dwell on it for fear that it would come back. Just to haunt him. He was finding some muscles that didn't complain when he stretched them.

"Did you go to Jericho, Amin?" Talman asked.

"I did. Boshogi's officer who was watching the house is no longer a policeman."

"It wasn't your man, then?"

"No. He has to sleep sometimes, and he was off-duty. He will still be there to watch Boshogi."

"In the meantime, we've lost track of the Sword of God."

"I am afraid that is true."

"Damn it! I knew I should have followed the other three."

"But then, Jacob," Blanchard said, "you wouldn't have been there for Deborah."

Blanchard had been present when her medical records were faxed to Mercy Base, had seen the surprise on Talman's face when he learned her name was Deborah Hausmann. When he asked, Talman only said, "We do not always know one another."

"I have issued," Rahman said, "an alert to arrest Kadar on the charge of attempted murder. I have also told all units that anyone discovered to have allowed his escape will face charges. He will not be welcome in Gaza or in Jericho."

"I appreciate that," Talman said. "The army is also looking for him."

"And what, Jacob, do you think of Kadar's threat?" Rahman asked.

"His threat?"

"In the message sent to the television station."

Dickie Armbruster came in carrying a mug of coffee in one hand and a thick egg, pancake, sausage, and bacon sandwich in the other. He ate many of his meals between two pieces of bread, and he didn't seem to care about the Jew or the Arab watching him eat. He kicked a canvas director's chair across the tent next to Blanchard and sat down.

"I assumed, Amin," Talman went on, "that the message was a lunatic's claim to fame. I did not read it as a threat."

"Oh, the threat is there. Remember the part about 'reclaiming the holy of holies'?"

"He wants Jerusalem."

"Don't we all?" Rahman said, but with a smile.

"This guy has what, three or four followers?" Blanchard asked. "I don't see him storming the ramparts."

"He may be a very patient man," the chief said. "He will wait until all are dead, then raise his flag."

"Bloody hell!" Armbruster exclaimed. "He'd use this necrolysis crap on the city?"

"I won't claim him as a brother," Rahman said.

Blanchard felt the revulsion creep into his mind. He'd been

through the necrolysis wards, and he'd seen the fear in the eyes of every patient. They were frightened of what was happening to them, watching the skin peel off of its own accord, absolutely uncertain if their futures were to be counted in hours or filled with scar tissue. One child, ten or eleven, who could not be commanded to stop scratching at his rashes, had his wrists restrained to the side of the cot. His torso was a hell of ripped skin and blood-filled pustules. He cried twenty-four hours a day.

"Before you leave," Blanchard told Rahman, "I want to take you through the wards."

"I saw Hakkar."

"I want you to see one hundred and seventy Hakkars. And think about four hundred thousand of them. Jesus, there aren't enough doctors on the whole continent to meet that kind of disaster."

"Thirty percent fatal," Armbruster reminded them. "That's a hundred thousand dead."

"How damned bright is this Kadar?" Blanchard asked. "I think he's missing some serious brain cells."

"From what is in his file," Talman said, "he is not intelligent, though there may be some feral cunning. Judging by some of his exploits, I think he may also lack common sense. In the past he claimed to have had visions, and some have said that he has a large share of ego."

"For his ego, he's got to kill a hundred thousand people?" Blanchard asked.

"Many of these fanatics," Rahman said, "truly believe that what they do, they do for the greater glory of God. It is often not explainable."

"I'd be happy to explain it to him," Armbruster said. "Maybe with a mouthful of frag grenade."

Rahman stood up. "Take me to the wards now, Jack. Then I will fly to Jerusalem and meet with General Avidar."

"I'll run you through," Armbruster said, standing. "I've got to go over that way, anyway."

The two men left, and Talman said, "I am quite scared, Jack."

''Me too. This isn't the kind of shit that's easy to fight.''

They sat in silence for a while.

Polly Brooks and Sam Delray came in with one of the army doctors, poring over a requisition form. Their utilization of medical consumables had skyrocketed, but the Israelis were covering most of it since it was a Jewish settlement. Still, Delray was swamped with paperwork. Blanchard felt guilty about falling behind on his share.

Brooks gave him a broad wink and asked how he was feeling.

''Good. Great.'' Her massage *had* worked little wonders for him.

A few minutes later, Masters and Wilcox appeared. Wilcox had been rousted out of bed by Masters a half hour into her surgery to assist. Both of them were still in surgical greens, and looked exhausted.

Talman hopped up and gave Masters his seat. Wilcox sat on the desk.

''If we get her blood pressure back up, we'll be out of the woods,'' Masters said. ''The blood-volume loss was substantial, but we've replaced that.''

Talman's shoulders slumped as he visibly relaxed. Blanchard felt for him.

''The internal damage was also substantial. We repaired the lung and hundreds of small vessels. The aorta was punctured, as was a lower chamber of the heart.''

''Good as new, or better,'' Dean Wilcox said. ''Melanie was a champ.''

''Not without your help, Dean.''

''I can't thank you both enough,'' Talman said.

''Frankly, Mr. Talman, I don't know how you got her here in time.''

''I prayed all the way.''

''And what is the relationship, if you don't mind?''

Talman didn't even hesitate. ''Lei—Deborah is a spy for her country, Dr. Masters. She works in my service.''

Blanchard watched her face. Despite the fatigue, he thought it paled a trifle.

''Does . . . uh, what was she doing?''

''General Avidar will kill me for telling you, but she was

watching the Sword of God for us. It was their leader, Ibrahim Kadar, who attacked her.''

"And she does this regularly?''

"Living in an apartment behind a cafe. She has been living the life of an Arab for two years.''

"That takes dedication.''

"Yes, Doctor, it does.''

Masters stood and headed for the entrance. "We won't let her get away from you.''

"Thank you. Can I see her?''

She stopped at the flap and looked at her watch. "Give it a couple hours. They'll have her in one of the wards.''

Wilcox also stood. "I'm headed for a shower.''

"Use six gallons, Dean,'' Blanchard told him.

"I want to see you sometime this morning. How's the head-ache?''

"Gone.''

"Cross your heart?''

Blanchard crossed his heart.

"The eye looks better, too. About like a white-and-black terrier I had as a kid. And maybe we can get a few of the stitches out.''

Blanchard heard the turbines of Rahman's Alouette powering up. A few minutes later, the rotors beat the air, and it took off.

Through the mesh of the tent, he could see a line starting to form at the mess tent, and he turned to Delray, who was at the far end of the tent. "Hey, Sam. How's the food holding up?''

"We're way in the hell over budget. Everybody and his brother has been visiting at dinnertime.''

"The army units?'' Talman asked.

"Well, some of the guys and girls show up now and then for a snack, and we don't turn them down.''

"I will ask for some assistance for you.''

"And I'll thank you, Jacob,'' Delray told him.

"You want a bite to eat?'' Blanchard asked Talman.

"I probably should. I must wait to see . . . Deborah. And my car is in Jericho.''

"We'll get an egg, then I'll take you to your car.''

They only made it halfway to the dining tent, though, before an army private came running up to them.

"Are you Mr. Blanchard?"

"Guilty."

"I'm from the north roadblock. We don't have a way to contact you."

"You have a problem, Private?"

"There's this guy yelling and demanding to be let through."

Oh, shit!

"Wouldn't call himself Masters, would he?"

"Yes, sir. Gregory Masters."

He probably figured out the location from the news reports.

They walked through the empty settlement together, to the blockade on the northern edge. Blanchard saw that army engineers were stringing barbed wire on orange steel stakes. The whole damned place was really going to be isolated.

Greg Masters was standing outside his rental car in the middle of the road, steaming. He must have been steaming, his face was that red. Two Israeli soldiers were standing close at hand, as if afraid he was going to bolt and leap over the lowered barrier that blocked the road. They kept their submachine guns at port arms.

Blanchard and Talman ducked under the barrier and approached the car.

Masters didn't look happy to see him, and Blanchard noted that the lawyer hadn't shaved this morning, either.

"Greg, old buddy. Nice to see you."

"I want in, Blanchard."

"You probably wouldn't like it."

"You've got my wife in there."

Blanchard glanced at Talman.

Talman said, "We could let him in."

Masters grinned.

Blanchard said, "But, then, we couldn't let him out."

"That is true," Talman agreed.

"You can't do any such thing," Masters protested. "You're only a guest in this country, Blanchard. I want to see someone with real authority."

Talman produced his credential folder and flipped it open.

"Talman, Jacob. Major, Israeli Defense Forces. Do you want to be incarcerated, sir?"

Judging by the speed with which he got in his car, Blanchard didn't think so.

As he backed away, trying to get turned around, Talman asked, "Did I take the right approach, Jack?"

"Absolutely. I'm beginning to enjoy this joker."

Thirteen

It was the next morning before Talman found Deborah Haus-mann in a state that was not too groggy to know who he was.

The tent where they had placed her was full. There were twenty steel-framed cots, and nineteen of them were occupied by Arabs. A nurse or paramedic was working with someone halfway down the right side. There was no place to sit, so Talman stood at the foot of her bed for ten minutes before her eyes flickered open.

He thought she'd been awake a few times before because her face showed no confusion or fright about her surroundings. He moved around the end of the bed and up to her left side.

She glanced sideways at the movement, then smiled. "Comet."

It was a whisper.

"Venus."

"I always appreciated that, you know."

"What?"

"Your assignment of the code name. One does not always feel pretty working in a kitchen and drab costume."

He grinned, and she patted the edge of the bed. Not too briskly, he noted.

He perched his hip on the very edge. She raised her hand, and he took it. It felt warm and trembly in his own.

"Dr. Masters said it was you who brought me here."

"Did she tell you anything else?"

"Other than about the knife wound and the surgery, she said nothing. And I remember very little. My whole back feels dull. My head buzzes with whatever they have given me."

He told her what he had seen.

"Ibrahim Kadar?"

"Yes. And I am a terrible marksman. I apologize."

"For nothing," she said. "Will I go back to Jericho?"

"No. I have already spoken to Colonel Stein."

"Did he say what I will do?"

"You are not to worry about it. I may teach you to operate a computer during your convalescence."

She gave him that nice smile, and he appreciated the slight deformity of her lip. "You have learned my name. I know because Dr. Masters used it."

"It is a pretty name."

Her face turned serious. "You would like to debrief me."

He shrugged. "Whenever you are ready."

"I think he—Kadar—must have seen me watching the house."

"When was this?"

"In the morning. I purchase vegetables from an old woman across the street, and I spent some time in her garden. It has been my excuse for watching the house."

"Did you see anything interesting?"

"I saw el-Ziam return from somewhere. In a Fiat. There was a policeman who parked almost in front of me, but I had not seen him before. And earlier, while el-Ziam and Kadar were gone, a man visited the house."

"Do you know the man?"

"Only by his picture. It was Amin Rahman."

"You must understand that, in times when the country faces a crisis, the country comes first," Menachem Strauss said.

"This doesn't seem like much of a crisis to me. You people are always killing each other off," Greg Masters said.

Strauss frowned deeply, adding even more lines to his heavy face, and Masters figured he'd better tone down his comments. The old man was supposed to be the premier attorney in Israel when it came to government affairs, and Masters was shelling out 250 dollars U.S. for this forty-five minutes.

"What appears in the newspapers is frequently only the tip of the iceberg, Mr. Masters. The citizen is not always aware of the total ramifications of an incident, and the government's concern with security is paramount. Justifiably so, I might add, though I am often at odds with many administration policies. If this Major Talman did not want you at Mar Saba, then would agree with Major Talman."

"He threatened to put me in jail! No hearing, no trial."

"His prerogative under the circumstances, I imagine."

"So what are you saying?"

"I know of no court which, upon your petition, would enjoin the government from keeping Dr. Masters away from you."

"She's being kept against her will."

"Yes. So you said."

"She doesn't belong to the Israelis. She works for the WHO."

"A welcome guest in the country."

Jesus. This old bugger wasn't giving him any help at all. If his father hadn't found out about the divorce action and raised so much hell about Brett MacDonald's injunctions and court orders and told him to get her back at any cost, Greg Masters would have grabbed the first plane for Paris. He should be back home anyway, trying to get the finances straightened out.

"Who in the government could I talk to? Perhaps persuade to help me out?"

"Ah!" Strauss's face showed both relief and encouragement. "Now, we are talking influence. Quite often, that is the prudent course of action."

Okay! This was more like he was accustomed to. A little word here and there, a little grease, got a hell of a lot accomplished.

"I don't have any clout here."

"Unless you have something to trade."

"Like what?"

"Anything is possible. You may know something you don't think you know, but which is important to someone else."

That was how Greg Masters's world worked.

"Have you got a name?"

Strauss sucked his upper lip while he thought. "You might wish to speak with Beit Horon."

"He's important?"

"He knows a great many people who have influence."

"What's his phone number?"

"Oh, he doesn't use the telephone."

Jesus Christ! These people are truly backward.

"I thought that I would not get out of Jerusalem," el-Ziam said.

Kadar and el-Ziam stood beside the Dodge van in the farm-yard. Kassim and Badr watched from the doorway of the house.

"I expected you back yesterday, Abu."

El-Ziam got out of the car. "It took forever to find the garage with the blue trim—it was more than a few meters down the alley, and then by the time I found the newspapers and other supplies, the roads out were blocked completely."

"Completely?"

"There is a large sign. There will be no passage in or out of Jerusalem between eight o'clock at night and six o'clock in the morning. It is a temporary measure, the sign says. The soldiers were everywhere."

"There were no exceptions?"

"I watched for a while, but only two military vehicles were allowed to pass. All others were turned back, and I did not attempt an exception."

Moving to the back of the vehicle, el-Ziam opened the rear door.

"This morning, you were allowed to pass?"

"Without problem, Ibrahim. They barely looked at me, or at anyone departing. However, all of the cars and trucks entering the city were examined in detail. I saw it as I waited in line to leave."

"What were they doing?"

"It is unheard of. They had little computers, and I think they were entering license numbers. Perhaps names, also. They were careful to compare pictures on identification papers. And in the little house at the side of the roadblock, they had bulletin boards filled with pictures."

"Did you see yours?"

"I was much too far away, Ibrahim."

He reached into the van and withdrew a bundle of news papers, handing them to Kadar. Then he pulled out mattress pallets. "Oma! Khalid! See here!"

The man wasted Kadar's money on frills that would do nothing for the cause. Kadar was deeply offended, but held of expressing his derision for the moment. He would need el Ziam this afternoon, and he did not want a sulking assistant.

Kassim and Badr rushed to help him unload the mattresses Such waste!

"And see here! A propane stove, so we will have hot food And water! Ten gallons of it. Ibrahim, you should have men tioned water to me. It is as necessary to us as life itself."

But Kadar had already wandered away, scanning quickly through the papers. They were all the same; the Sword of God was examined and then cast aside as a cartel of fools. The incident two years ago was mentioned often. Sapir had issued a claim of responsibility before Nuri Hakkar rammed a bu with a carload of dynamite.

There was something wrong with the detonator, however and the bomb did not detonate, though Hakkar was able to run away from the crash.

And what about Sapir's attempt to burn down the building where the Knesset met. He had safely eluded the guards and reached the walls of the structure, saturating the wooden door with gasoline, then spreading the Sword's tracts around the grounds as he slipped away. The igniter worked as promised on the timer, and the flames leaped to life.

But a guard simply turned on the lawn-sprinkling system and doused the fire.

There were other miscues and backfires, and they were al

mentioned. It was as if the writers and editors, both Jewish and Arabic, laughed at them.

The shame was almost too much to bear.

That was the leadership of Ibn Sapir, not of Ibrahim Kadar.

The Sword of God was now honed, its edges sharpened to razors, and despite the small size of his band, the world would know of his power.

Unless another disaster was in the making. What if Khabanni had entrusted him with biological weapons that only created measles? His friend had told him the Iraqis were upset with the accident of Sapir and the original vials. Majib Khabanni could be unaware that the scientists had filled the second delivery of vials with something less than potent.

Even now, the army and the Jews in the halls of government could be laughing at the wilted blade of the Sword of God.

He threw the papers to the ground angrily.

But wait!

The Jews were strengthening the walls of Jerusalem. That had to tell him something—that they were afraid.

And they were afraid of him!

Unless it was simply a ruse to draw him in.

No.

Well, perhaps.

He had not anticipated having a problem reaching the city. This was a setback, but surely one that he could overcome if he thought about it for long enough.

In the meantime, he had to know for certain what was taking place at the Jewish settlement near Mar Saba.

Whirling around, he marched to the house, went inside, and found his backpack. He came up with the three pistols Badr had located in the pit. They were well oiled, and there were two full magazines for each. They were Beretta .380-caliber semiautomatic pistols. As an afterthought, he also took the small plastic box to which he had transferred the vials. He pushed it into the pocket of his jacket. He didn't want Badr or Kassim investigating the secret weapon without his knowledge.

He stood up and handed one of the semiautomatic pistols to Badr. "That is yours. Take good care of it."

Beckoning to el-Ziam, they went out the door, and he gave one of the pistols to him, also, along with two of the magazines.

"Where are we going, Ibrahim?"

"To Mar Saba."

"I understand that the settlement is blockaded. It will do us no good."

"We will go to the Arab village, Abu."

He rammed a magazine home, then snapped off the safety and primed the weapon. Without warning, he raised it and fired several rounds at the shed.

Badr and Kassim rushed to the doorway.

"Rehearsal, only," he told them.

He unbuttoned his shirt and pushed the muzzle of the weapon under his waistband. The other magazine he dropped into his jacket pocket.

With Kadar giving frequent directions, they left the farmyard, drove a kilometer to the pavement of Highway 458, then turned south for five kilometers to Highway 1. From there they drove west toward Jerusalem, but a kilometer short of the first road-block, they intersected the road leading back east to Mar Saba.

Squinting his eyes, Kadar studied the road leading into the city and saw that the lines of traffic were badly tied up. The cars barely moved, and the lines reached almost to where they planned to turn off. To the left and right of the roadblock, he saw the tiny figures of walking soldiers. El-Ziam was correct; the city was under siege, but from the inside out.

El-Ziam parked the van near the monastery when they reached it, and they both got out. The sun was hot, and the whole region felt as if it were sucked dry of any moisture. A couple kilometers to the west was the Jewish settlement, and Kadar could tell from the tracks in the road that it had received many visitors lately. Most likely, they were the vile reporters who had scorned the Sword of God and who were soon to know the folly of their ways.

To the southwest was the Arab settlement that was his destination.

"You will wait here," Kadar ordered.

"But, Ibrahim, your . . ."

"Many among our people are lame, Abu. I will certainly go unnoticed."

As usual, the response was a look of skepticism.

"How long will you be?"

"Two, perhaps, three hours. How am I to know?"

He began walking, dragging his foot after him.

It did not take him long to reach the village and find that it was typical of such places, built out of whatever materials came to hand. The three streets were narrow. It might have housed 200 or 300 people, and many of them were out and about. Quite a few were men of working age, but who obviously had no jobs to go to.

Near the center of the town was a communal kitchen, and soldiers and civilians labored there, cleaning. Large drums of disinfectant were being unloaded from a pickup. They were being directed by men in civilian clothing, and Kadar felt a prickly sense of anticipation. This was obviously a consequence of what had been discovered at the other settlement.

He stopped an old woman and asked where the clinic was located. She pointed east, but gave him no other help. He trudged on through the town and down a path that had been taken by many feet.

When he came over a small rise, he saw the encampments. There were two. On his left was the medical team's collection of white and camouflage tents. Directly to its south was a smaller group of tents and vehicles that obviously belonged to the army. There seemed to be a great many guard posts surrounding both bivouacs, and a wall of barbed wire two meters high was all but complete.

Worse, he came upon a line of people stretching from one of the tents clear up the trail. There must have been ninety people in front of him, most sitting or reclining on the dusty ground. A few, already tended to by the medical people, came walking back toward him.

It would be all right. Allah respected patience, and Kadar had much to give.

He got in line.

* * *

Blanchard and an army captain named Dietz, who commanded one of the two companies assigned to their security, walked the perimeter together. They went clear around the settlement, Mercy Base, and the army's tents, stopping at each post. Dietz gave each noncommissioned officer (NCO) in charge two sheets of paper containing pictures of suspected terrorists. The Sword of God was not the army's only concern, Blanchard deduced.

When they were done, Blanchard invited the captain to lunch, but he claimed other duties and wandered off toward them. It seemed as if everywhere he looked, he saw cammo fatigues. It wasn't much fun getting back into military harness, but Blanchard was glad they were there. He and Armbruster had talked about their relief, especially after the incident on the road.

Blanchard walked back to the mess tent, got in line, and was rewarded with a toasted cheese sandwich, potato chips, and milk.

The pantry is getting too damned low.

He carried his tray to a back corner where Armbruster and Talman were sitting with Weiss and Brooks.

"How are you doing, Jack?" Brooks asked. "Ready for another massage?"

"Are you kidding? What you did to me was downright painful. The Marquis de Sade's got nothing on you, Polly."

"Brought you around, didn't it?"

"It did that." He dodged around one of the oscillating fans, stepped over the bench seat, and sat next to Weiss. "You mind, Jillian?"

"I'm looking forward to it." Under the table, she rubbed her leg against his own, then grinned at his discomfort.

"What'd you think, Jack?" Armbruster asked him.

"Jacob's army knows what they're doing, Dickie. Looks pretty tight to me. Most of the barbed wire is up."

"Melanie hates that, you know?" Weiss chimed in. "She's calling it Mercy Concentration Camp."

Talman winced at that description.

"She knows what's at stake, Jillian."

"Oh, I know. But she doesn't have to like it. I don't like it, either."

"I think we ought to move the clinic outside the perimeter," Armbruster said. "Cut down on the traffic in and out."

"That's a good idea," Talman told him.

"How are we fixed for tents, Dickie?"

"We're out, but I can probably scrounge one from Dietz."

"Why don't you set up outside the perimeter this afternoon, and we'll move the clinic personnel in the morning. The one we vacate can become another ward."

"Done, Colonel."

Blanchard took a large bite out of his sandwich, chewed, then asked, "You getting to know everyone, Jacob?"

"I am, indeed. Everyone in your group is very helpful."

Blanchard had given him a dedicated telephone line and a chair in the admin tent since it looked like he wasn't going to leave until Deborah Hausmann was doing back flips. He'd spent most of the morning on the phone.

"Any sign of this bloody Sword bunch?" Armbruster asked him.

"None. They have dropped out of sight. Unless they got across the Jordanian border, however, they will surface again. We will find them."

"What about the thing Rahman mentioned?"

Rahman's name seemed to bring out a tic in Talman's left eye, but he said, "Appropriate measures have been put in place. In fact, since you bring it up, I should tell you that your resupply vehicles going into Jerusalem will need special passes."

The intelligence officer reached into his breast pocket and came up with a thin sheaf of blue-and-green plastic cards. He counted off two . . .

"I've got five trucks scheduled this afternoon," Armbruster said.

. . . then three more and gave them to Armbruster.

"The cards will change at least weekly, though the change will be unannounced. I will see that you get more when they do change."

"Why don't you give me one for the command truck, Jacob? Just in case."

Talman handed him a card, and Blanchard looked at it. It was a simple plastic card with blue-and-white diagonal stripes of varying widths. He used his pen to print his last name in one of the white stripes, then put it in his wallet. His knit shirt didn't have a pocket.

"As long as you've got plenty," Polly Brooks said, "I think we all need one."

"Right!" Weiss agreed. "How are we supposed to get R&R?"

"You can ride with me," Blanchard said.

"Lovely."

After lunch he and Talman went back to the admin tent where he found himself face-to-face with about two dozen terrorists. Sam Delray had tacked Captain Dietz's most-wanted posters to the center tent pole.

"I'm getting tired of seeing these guys, Jacob."

"You are not the only one."

Delray was on the phone, trying to track down some urgently needed something or other. Chao sat before a computer, running a diagnostic program.

"My problem," Blanchard said, "is that my people are so damned good, I sometimes don't have anything to do."

"They may be doing that for you," Talman said. "How are you feeling?"

"Don't let the black eye fool you into thinking I'm A-one. I still ache in places where there were never places before. Getting better, though."

"You should take Miss Brooks up on her offer."

"I should."

His first massage had been exquisite, but Blanchard had never been fond of other people touching him—irrational as that might be, and he hadn't totally relaxed.

"I will be here until five o'clock, if that is all right with you?"

"Sure. What happens at five?"

"We will airlift Deborah to an army hospital in Jerusalem."

"I'm happy she's coming around, Jacob."

"As am I. I hope everything else we are doing goes as well."
Blanchard didn't think Talman's downcast face reflected much hope.

Beit Horon didn't like riding in the car, Greg Masters thought. He sat primly upright in the passenger seat and kept his face very stern and stoic. In the backseat, his face fragmented by the jiggling rearview mirror, Masters could see Deputy Minister Tayar, a member of the Council and a representative of economic ministry. By his side curls and black clothing, he was obviously closely aligned with Horon, perhaps of the same fundamental sect.

Whatever the connection, Horon hadn't had as much trouble getting Tayar away from his desk as Masters had had running down Horon.

This damned country was so strange, and there were a hell of a lot of strange people running it. Back home, he'd have known exactly who to call to accomplish some small favor. The men he knew were hard and ruthless, but predictable.

Horon had grilled him for forty minutes, and Masters, because he didn't *really* know what was going on at Mar Saba—the nature of the problems had never crossed his mind—had exaggerated a trifle. He didn't want to lose Horon's attention. He'd portrayed Melanie as an *international* expert in communicable diseases; he'd *suggested* that Melanie slipped him information that the disease threatened to decimate the entire population of Israel; and he'd *implied* that the death toll was considerably higher than reported.

"That is not what Jacob Talman told me," Horon had said.
Talman! Beit Horon seemed to know everyone.
Masters had admitted meeting Talman and *intimated* that Talman and an American army colonel were in charge of the cover-up.

"We should inspect this site," Horon had said.
"That's my only interest, sir, to see if my wife is all right."
And here they were, bearing down on the roadblock of the Mar Saba monastery.

He braked to a halt at the barrier, and a soldier moved up to his window.

Tayar leaned forward and handed the guard a blue-and-green card, along wit his identification card.

The soldier didn't seem to like it. "Minister, I have no orders . . ."

"Get your superior," Tayar ordered.

"Yes, sir."

He was back in a minute with a lieutenant.

Who was also nonplussed. "Minister, I have a list of people who are allowed into the area. I am afraid you are not on it."

"Do I have to call your general and demand your removal, Lieutenant?"

"Sir . . ."

"Do I not have the passcard?"

"Yes, sir, but—"

"Raise the barrier. Now!"

The officer stepped away from the window and signaled another soldier.

The barrier rose.

Masters engaged the transmission and drove forward.

He was in!

Now, he'd see what those sons of bitches Blanchard and Talman had to say. Tayar and Horon could deal with them while he did what he had to do.

He thought he'd put Melanie right in the car and get her out of this damned country on the first flight. Without Blanchard around, she wouldn't put up a fuss.

Kadar had almost reached the gateway to the compound, and he was beginning to feel a little nervous. Ahead of him were but four people. As the people seeking medical attention reached the opening in the fence, a guard asked them a few questions, then directed them onto the line standing in front of a white tent some ten meters inside the fence.

The box with the vials in his coat pocket seemed suddenly to enlarge, to stand out, to be instantly noticeable. The Beretta pistol in his waistband grew, as well, becoming visible beneath his loose shirt.

In the time he had been standing in line, he had searched the interior of the encampment for any sign of people afflicted with the disease, but he had seen nothing. There was a large number of people going in and out of tents, most of them dressed in green blouses or white laboratory coats, but he could not clearly see what was in the tents. Of one thing he was certain, there were many tents, which apparently contained patients.

Once he was inside, it should not be difficult to get a look into several of them. The two rows of five tents that stood a little apart from the others seemed to offer the most promising venue.

The line shuffled forward one space, and he moved ahead.

Outside the near tent, apparently the clinic, was a table at which two people were seated. They spoke to those in line and filled out forms. The exchanges were in Arabic, and he caught enough fragments of their speech to suppose that they were collecting names and medical histories.

A woman and a boy, her son, were released at the gate and moved to the end of the next line, inside the compound.

These people were treated like cattle, herded here, then there. There was a defined lack of respect, and it was enough to make him vomit.

As he watched, a trio appeared from the interior of the camp and walked with determination toward the table. One was the Jew who had invaded his home, Talman. Another was a big man, an American, wearing jeans, a safari jacket, and a blue baseball cap. The third person was a woman dressed in a white laboratory coat. She was probably a nurse.

The man in front of him was released, and Kadar took a step forward.

The guard began to study his face, and Kadar pointed to his left foot.

"Go on, then. To the next line."

He shuffled forward, emphasizing his limp, until he was within five meters of the table. He moved close to the man ahead, shielding his face from Talman's sight.

He strained to listen to the conversations taking place.

Through an interpreter, the woman in the white coat was talking to someone in the line. She introduced herself as the chief physician, Melanie Masters, and assured the man that they were working as fast as they could. Everyone would be seen; everyone would be treated.

The doctor who belittled him! The Masters who said his supreme weapon was of little consequence! A nonbeliever! She will die a thousand deaths, each more horrible than the one before.

The big American man interrupted her.

"Oh, shit! Jacob, look there."

Kadar glanced to the right, around the shoulder of the man in front, and saw three figures marching rapidly this way. Another American and two men in black.

Ibrahim Kadar wished he knew what was going on.

His task, however, was to see what was inside those other tents.

He turned his head and looked behind him, saw a private soldier walking away from the gate.

Mumbling his Hebrew so as to not seem too fluent, he called to the man: "Is there a place I might relieve myself?"

The soldier looked a little disgusted, as if patients were not supposed to have bodily functions, then said, "On the other side of the camp. You will see it when you go around the hospital tent."

Keeping his back to the group in which Talman stood, Kadar walked away, his limp less noticeable now. When he reached the large tent that was apparently the hospital, and got around the corner of it, he breathed a long sigh of relief. He could hear people talking inside the tent, but they seemed intent on whatever they were doing. He moved across the front of it and waited at the corner.

When he saw his chance, he would walk over to the rows of tents where patients seemed to be kept.

* * *

Damn him!

Masters excused her way through the line and started toward Greg.

Talman and Blanchard followed, Talman saying, "Let me talk to them, if you will, Doctor."

He took longer strides and got in front of her by the time they reached the three men.

"Minister Tayar, it is good to see you. Mr. Horon, how are you?"

Greg smiled at her.

"Who are you?" Tayar asked.

"Major Jacob Talman, sir. May I present Dr. Masters, chief of medicine, and Mr. Blanchard, the team administrator."

"Dr. Masters," Tayar said, "precisely the person we want to . . ."

Greg stepped forward and put his arm around her shoulders.

"Get away from me!"

"Look, darling, let's you and me go somewhere and talk. Just the two of us."

"Get your goddamned arm off me!"

She shrugged loose from him and backed up a step, right into Blanchard. She didn't move, but stood right in front of Blanchard, practically on his toes.

Greg hesitated, but then backed off.

Tayar and the man named Horon looked confused.

Tayar finally said, "I want to know exactly what is going on here."

Sounding resigned, Talman said, "Minister, if you and Mr. Horon will come with me, I will explain the situation. . . ."

"Explanations are not adequate," the minister said.

"And I will show you the patients. Meanwhile, Mr. and Mrs. Masters can have a few minutes to themselves."

"Wonderful!" Greg said.

Talman took his fellow Israelis and walked toward the wards.

Blanchard said, "Let's get out of the middle of the compound. We can go down by my Hummer."

"You stay here, Blanchard!"

"Not on a bet, Greg, old buddy. I'll let you talk, but you

don't get out of my sight. All right, Mel? Otherwise, I'll just pick him up and throw him over the fence.''

She couldn't think of any way to make Greg leave that didn't result in some disruptive scene. Delray and Weiss were looking their way from the admin tent.

She spun on her heel and started walking to where the vehicles were parked, her path taking her between the hospital and the administration tent.

Greg swung in beside her.

''It's going to be all right, darling. It's going to be great. See what a little influence can do? Got me right in here.''

''What did you tell them, Greg?''

''Just what they needed to know.''

She reached the vehicle and walked around it to the back, Greg trailing along.

Blanchard went and sat on the running board of one of the big trucks, about twenty feet away.

''What does it take for you to understand that I don't want to see you again.''

''I think you're being a little impetuous, Melanie. We haven't had a chance to discuss what our future is going to be like. The party is going to run me—''

''Not if they have to pay me back.''

''What! What are you talking about?''

''Brett tells me that the preliminary audits suggest you gave my money away to damned near every political cause in the country.''

''Your money? Melanie, it gets comingled; it—''

''That's bullshit. You knew exactly what you were doing.''

''Who knows? A few bucks here, a few—''

''Over half a million, you son of a bitch! You were throwing my money around, trying to buy yourself an in with the party.''

''Mel—''

''I'm not worried about it, Greg. I'm getting it back. Right out of your precious campaign fund, or out of your stocks and bonds.''

He looked stricken. And it was about time.

She thought for a minute he was going to hit her. His right

hand started coming up, and the motion brought Blanchard to his feet.

Greg glanced at Blanchard, then dropped his hand.

Just as her head was jerked backward, yanked hard by her hair.

She felt cold steel against her throat.

She nearly collapsed, visions of Deborah Hausmann flashing through her mind.

Blanchard didn't see him until the last instant.

He came out from behind the Humvee, grabbed Masters by her hair, and laid the flat side of an ugly five-inch blade right against the side of her throat.

Blanchard got six steps closer before the small Arab barked, "Stop!"

His voice was cold as ice, dead as a cemetery.

Greg Masters had taken three steps back before the command froze him.

"Easy, now," Blanchard said.

He couldn't see the man's face; it was blocked by the spread of Masters's hair, but he felt abruptly chilled.

"You will do exactly as I say, and exactly when I say it. Otherwise, the woman will spill her blood into my earth."

"No one needs to get hurt here," Blanchard said.

"You don't need me," the lawyer whined. "I'm not part of any of this."

"Be quiet!" The head came around to stare at Blanchard. "Who are you?"

"Blanchard. I'm the guy you want. I run this camp. Let her and the man go."

"I will give the orders."

It was Ibrahim Kadar. His picture was on the tent pole. How in the hell . . .

He backed up between the parked Humvees, pulling Masters with him, and the knife disappeared for long enough to open the back door.

Backing clumsily, he slid inside and jerked her in with him.

"You, Blanchard. You will drive. The other man gets in front."

Blanchard took a step forward and looked down the side of the truck. Kadar had his head sticking out, and now he had an automatic pistol aimed this way.

"Get in, Greg," Blanchard said.

"Not me! This has nothing to do—"

Blanchard took one step toward him, got a fistful of expensive necktie, and jerked. The attorney came flying forward, and Blanchard got behind him, shoving him alongside the Hummer. He opened the front door, pushed him inside, grabbed his belt under the skirt of the jacket, and heaved.

Greg Masters ended up on his face in the passenger seat, scrambling to get upright.

Blanchard got in and shut the door. He angled the rearview mirror so he could keep an eye on Melanie. Her face was ashen, and Kadar had a firm grip on a hank of her hair. The terrorist pulled his door shut.

"Start the engine."

The key was in the ignition, and Blanchard kicked it over. Automatically, he checked the gauges. Christ, a full tank.

He shifted his head a little so he could see Kadar's face in the mirror.

"Where to, Kadar?"

"You know me?"

"Doesn't everyone?"

The face looked pleased. A goddamned egomaniac.

"There is a vehicle gate to the west. We will go that way."

Blanchard reversed, backed out of the line of vehicles, and headed for the gate.

"Everyone must look calm."

Blanchard gave the soldier on the gate a ferocious look, but was waved through. Security always looked for the threat from the outside, rarely from the inside.

He shifted to second and felt the tires dig into the loose sand.

"Now, wh—"

"Keep going. Straight ahead."

So, they were going for the Bethlehem highway. His mind raced, looking for gaps in Kadar's actions. His eyes kept flicking to the mirror, checking on Melanie. The little son of a bitch wasn't letting go of her.

And he remembered Hausmann.

He wouldn't take any rash steps, but give him an opening, and—

"Stop!"

Blanchard checked the outside mirror. They had just gone down a slope, and Mercy Base was no longer in sight. He eased to a halt and sat quietly. Out of the corner of his eye, he saw Greg Masters huddled against the door. His hand was inching forward, reaching for the door handle.

"You touch that handle and she gets hurt, Greg, I'm taking your balls off one at a time."

"Be quiet!" Kadar yelped.

In the mirror he saw Kadar go to his knees, move the pistol to Melanie's ear, then peer into the back of the Humvee. With his free hand, he rummaged through the boxes, then came up with several rolls of two-inch tape.

He taped Melanie first—hands, knees, and ankles, then shoved her to the floor. She landed with a thud and a tiny yelp.

Then Blanchard, appearing to fear him more than Greg Masters. He wrapped several loops around Blanchard's right wrist, then leaving a few inches of slack with several bands of tape, bound it to the gear shift. He did the same thing to Blanchard's left wrist, binding it to the steering wheel with just enough slack that he might be able to turn the thing.

Turning to the lawyer, Kadar said, "Get out."

He reinforced the order by slamming the pistol into Masters's cheek.

"Don't kill him! Please!" Melanie yelled from the floor.

Blanchard thought that was exactly what Kadar had in mind. Masters, he could use. Blanchard, he could use. The male Masters was deadweight.

"You know who this guy's father is, Kadar?" Blanchard asked.

Kadar stopped jabbing with the automatic. A Beretta .380, Blanchard noticed. Put a pretty decent hole in Masters.

"He's a close friend of the President of the United States.

Remember Libya? You want American fighter-bombers scattering bombs around here, go ahead and kill him.''

"You lie!"

"Shoot him, and let's find out."

Turning to Masters, Kadar said, "Open the door. Get out."

As Greg slid out, so weak kneed he almost went to the ground, Kadar slipped between the bucket seats and followed him out. It took about two minutes for him to use the rest of his tape on the guy who should never have left Chicago.

A big chunk across his mouth. His wrists bound together behind his back with about ten wraps. His elbows pulled tight enough before taping that Greg tried to scream through his gag. Kadar shoved him to the ground, where he landed on his face, then wrapped adhesive around his ankles and knees.

Kadar might have shut the front door, then gone for the back, and if he had, Blanchard was prepared to dig holes with all four tires, leaving the terrorist with Greg.

But he climbed back over the passenger seat, then into the back.

"I will put a bullet in her head if you do not obey me."

"I'm all ears, Kadar."

"Let us go."

"Where are we going?"

"I will tell you when we get there. If you do not answer to Allah first."

Fourteen

Greg Masters lay as quietly as possible until the sound of the engine died away. It took a superb control of his will.

Then he rolled his head to the side. He was having trouble breathing. His nose was full of dust, and he couldn't open his mouth to relieve his desire for air.

The heat sizzled around him. He could feel the sun bearing down, and wished he didn't have his suit coat on. Sweat rolled off his face in huge beads and dripped on the ground. He felt something crawling up the inside of his leg, and the leg twitched, but his knees were bound so tightly he couldn't crush it.

Ants.

Now he saw them. A hundred red-bodied, evil things skittering around, approaching his face, exploring.

He rolled frantically, attempting to get away from them, but his constraints made it difficult. His shoulders ached from the position of his elbows.

That fucking Blanchard!

He wouldn't be here now, except for that bastard!

The silence was deafening. He couldn't hear anything except the air whistling through his nose.

He felt something crawling on his hand and struggled to

smash it against his back. Missed. It disappeared, crawling, then he felt it again, moving up his forearm.

He was on his side, looking up the slope. The encampment was back there somewhere. All he could see were the tracks left behind by the truck.

How far was it? A mile and a half? It couldn't be over two miles.

Squirming, he rolled to his left, and landed on his back, his arms and hands trapped beneath him. Levered his feet out, and rolled again, onto his side. He figured the gain was eighteen inches. How many inches in two miles?

Could he roll the whole distance?

Uphill, it was even more difficult.

He had to get help soon. He could fry here in the sun.

The perspiration rolled into his eyes, stung them, made his vision blurry.

Jesus!

He was going to die here, in some unnamed desert.

Because Melanie thought she had to be an independent thinker.

He loved her, but damn it, anyway! She had to stop thinking about herself and consider his needs, too. And—

Christ! Some fucking *terrorist* has her! Let's keep that in mind.

His mind was flying in so many directions he couldn't concentrate. First things first. He was going to die in this damned desert.

He had another thought.

He could hop.

He pushed over onto his face, doubled himself until he got his knees under him, then got his torso upright. With a few little hops, he found himself standing.

There was great elation in that. He was back in control.

He bounced around until he was facing uphill, then, toes together, took a little hop. Then another.

He was going to make it!

And his left toe caught a clod of dirt, and down he went,

landing on his left shoulder. The pain screamed down his arm and into his elbow.

Masters started crying.

Because he was driving, Blanchard knew exactly where he was. They traveled less than fifteen kilometers from Mercy Base.

"Turn here," Kadar said. "To the left."

He braked, shifted down with his restrained right hand, and fought the wheel around with his left. The tape tether was short and didn't give him a lot of agility in swinging the wheel for ninety-degree turns.

It was a narrow, twin-rutted road.

"You're lucky we didn't get stopped when I didn't signal my turns," he said.

"What!"

"Forget it."

Blanchard had been trying to evaluate his captor. The guy had zilch in the way of practical sense. He seemed to operate on pure instinct. From what he could see in the mirror, Kadar was nervous, almost a suppressed hysterical condition. His movements were jerky, but not uncoordinated enough that he might lose control of the weapon. None of it made him less dangerous. Just unsophisticated.

Blanchard had seen it before:

The son of a bitch was going to skin him alive!

Starting with his face.

Unfocused beyond the gleaming steel of the Ka-bar waving in front of Blanchard's face were frantic black eyes and a mouthful of browning, rotting teeth. Behind the NVA noncom were the two youngster soldiers of his patrol, grinning in anticipation.

Blanchard backpedaled in fear, smashed against a tree. The Viet came after him.

Feinted with his left leg.

The knife went for it.

Stuck.

Blood gushed.

Put all his strength into the upswing of his right leg. The steel-toed jungle boot drove the bastard's testicles back into the body cavity.

The scream could have blown teeth out. The Ka-bar went flying.

Blanchard went down diving forward, landing on the guy's gut with his shoulder, forcing the air from his lungs in a spittle-drenched spray. The two soldiers scrambled for their assault rifles.

Blanchard's groping hands found the holstered Tokarev pistol, and he rolled off the retching body, spinning sideways, punching off the safety, hoping the pistol was cocked, with one in the chamber.

Found the trigger.

Blasted off two shots that sent the soldiers running for cover.

He didn't hit anything worthwhile, but they left their weapons behind.

Rookie recruits.

It took him twenty seconds to snorkle his way facedown across the fetid, packed underbrush of the trail to the knife, angle it in his hands enough to slice the nylon rope of his wrists, then his elbows. His left shoulder popped back into the socket audibly, and the pain put a black path across his vision.

The North Vietnamese was trying to rise, tears streaming down his face, his hand searching erratically for any weapon. He might have yelled out.

So Blanchard cut his throat.

He'd seen Kadars before.

Kadar kept his automatic trained downward, toward Masters, and Blanchard had consciously avoided abrupt movements of the steering wheel. He dodged chuckholes carefully. If he could help it, there weren't going to be any accidental trippings of the trigger.

He was worried about her. She hadn't signed on for this kind of thing; in fact, she had been in near denial as to the possibility. She had to be frightened.

"Mel?"

"Okay, Jack." Her pitch was high. The vocal cords were stretched as tight as her nerves.

"Be quiet! Do as you are told."

A mile down the road, driving slowly, he came upon a dilapidated house.

"Park next to the house, around to the side."

A man and a woman appeared in the open doorway briefly, dodging back inside when they saw the Hummer. He braked to a halt next to the house.

"Shut off the motor."

"You're forgetting something, Kadar."

He couldn't shut off anything he couldn't reach.

Kadar leaned forward to grab the key and turn it. The engine died.

The two from the house came out, apparently after recognizing Kadar, and there was a spate of angry repartee conducted in Arabic as Kadar threw open the door and shoved Masters out. Blanchard felt his muscles hunch up. He was on the verge of tearing at his restraints and doing something, anything, to protect her.

Probably die.

He forced himself to sit still and keep his mouth shut.

While they were taken inside, Blanchard thought he picked up the other names—Khalid and Oma. Khalid had a beat-up Kalashnikov AK-47 that still looked operable, and he kept it trained on Blanchard during the transfer.

Kadar found wire—old and frayed lamp cord—to tie Blanchard, then retied Masters. He pulled the tape off her knees. They were shoved into a corner of the only room in the house, sitting side by side on the rotten wooden planks of the floor, and the ends of the wire binding their wrists were looped around joists below the flooring and twisted tight. With his roll of white two-inch tape, Kadar spun a few wraps around Blanchard's ankles.

The three moved to the other side of the room where a pot of something boiled on a propane camp stove set on the floor. They sat on mattresses, and Kadar jabbered excitedly, as if he had just pulled off the world's greatest stunt.

It would be less great if the Israelis got some surveillance airborne and spotted that nice, bright, white Hummer sitting in an abandoned farmyard.

"Jack . . ."

"Wait," he whispered back.

Keeping an eye on Kadar and his pals, he checked Masters out in his peripheral vision. She was about fifteen inches from him, and her white coat was gray with smudges from the floor of the truck and the ground where she'd been rolled. The dirt was streaked across her face and caked in her hair. Her lips were set in a small straight line, her upper lip drawn in. She was looking into his eyes with her own combination of defiance and fear.

Good. We'll work on the defiance part.

Keeping his movement imperceptible, he shifted his buttocks and worked his way toward her. He had to shift his arms to the left as the wire tether came taut.

Masters imitated him, and they were soon pressed together, shoulder, hips, and legs. He hoped the contact eased her fears.

His arms were numb by the time it turned dark. The woman named Oma found a kerosene lantern and lit it after several tries, then put it on a box at the far end of the room. It left Blanchard and Masters in shadow.

A half hour after the sun went down, and after the two men had gone outside to offer prayers—he heard their chanting— Blanchard heard the rattle of an old car pulling in, and a few minutes later, another man burst into the house.

There was a decidedly heated exchange between Kadar and the newcomer, who was obviously pissed at something.

Blanchard took advantage of the loud argument to whisper, "Think positive thoughts, Mel."

"Thank you for Greg."

Blanchard hadn't thought about Greg since the guy hit the ground, and then only with a misgiving that he hadn't let Kadar have his way. He didn't respond.

"Are they going to kill us?" she whispered.

"If they were, it'd be all over. No, they need us."

"For what?"

"I'll figure it out in a little bit."

* * *

Talman had had the devil's own time convincing Tayar and Horon that the nation's best interest rested in keeping the outbreak of toxic epidermal necrolysis at Mar Saba under wraps.

Both men had been appalled by what they saw in the three men's wards they visited under his leadership. The pleading eyes were worse than the ravaged, red skin and the open sores. The children cried from something they did not understand. They longed to move about, and the nurses and aides had to caution them to remain immobile. Talman would always remember acres of cheesecloth.

Outside the last tent, Dr. Wilcox had explained, "We have seen this on rare occasion, gentlemen. It is a streptococcus disease one normally associates with strep throat or impetigo. The invasive form that attacks the epidermal tissues normally intrudes through an open wound. It is extremely rare, and it is not contagious.

"What we are seeing here, however, suggests that someone has devised a carrier to spread the disease, probably through water in the village, since the laboratory has isolated strains of a matching bacteria at the water tank. Worse, a lack of immunity or open sores do not seem to be requirements. The bacteria is evidently ingested, absorbed into the bloodstream, and transferred from blood vessels."

"It is warfare?" Tayar asked.

"Biological warfare, yes."

"The madman of Iraq," Horon spat. He was apparently ready to believe in a man-made event rather than one delivered from heaven. Such was the impact of a visit to the wards. "He has extensive laboratories."

"Perhaps," Talman said. "We may never know."

"You do think that this Sword of God sect is responsible?" the minister asked.

"I am all but certain of it."

"We must let the world know," Beit Horon proclaimed. "They must be exposed for the filthy vermin they are."

"Three things deter me, Beit. Also, they deter the executive committee of the Cabinet and the defense ministry, so I do not really count. One is the panic that would be created. The second is the irreparable damage to the Palestinian Authority's chances of obtaining foreign aid. The Authority would fall apart."

"And well done," Horon said.

Tayar's head bobbed in agreement. The two of them would put the peace plan into a coffin and bury it at sea if they could swing enough votes to obtain the boat.

"Thirdly, we suspect that Jerusalem is the next target of the Sword of God."

Tayar's eyes widened.

Horon appeared immensely saddened, more so than he did normally. He turned his hoary head toward the tent.

"Like that?"

"Like that. Nearly half a million people, Beit. We need to run Kadar to ground, and if the people are running through the streets in hysteria, that might not happen." Talman switched his eyes to Tayar. "Those roadblock passes should not be used quite so haphazardly, Minister."

Tayar said, "Why has this not been brought before the entire Knesset?"

"You can answer your own question, I think, Minister."

Sigh. "Yes. Information leaks."

"Now, what am I to do? I have confided defense information to a deputy minister not in my chain of command, as well as to a civilian. If I followed the policy laid upon me, I would place you both under house arrest. That would cost me man-hours in guards."

Wilcox said, "After hearing all of this, I feel like I should be under arrest, also."

"I'm afraid you're not going anywhere for a while, Doctor."

Horon said, "We have known each other many years, Jacob."

"We have."

"My word is my trust."

"I know that. I am prepared to let you return to Jerusalem, but you cannot speak of this to anyone."

"I will agree."

"Plus, you must rally your followers to seek Kadar. I will give you pictures."

"That, I most assuredly will do."

"Minister Tayar, I know how inviting it is to use information to gain political leverage. But you cannot talk to anyone. Not even those in the defense ministry."

"Not defense?"

"I am not certain how many have been informed."

"But this . . . the loss of Jerusalem . . . could have a devastating fiscal impact. That is my charge."

"No one. We will know in ten days whether or not we have been successful."

"Ten days. I agree to that."

"Very well. You may leave, but I hold you to your word."

Horon looked around. "We must find Mr. Masters. He drove us."

Explaining to the two men how Gregory Masters may have used them simply to get himself into the encampment, Talman walked with them along the perimeter in search of Masters. They had no luck.

"He may have gone with his wife. I will have you driven," Talman said.

They stopped at the administration tent, and he called Captain Dietz over the sound-powered telephone installed to connect the guard posts and Blanchard's office. Minutes later, a Jeep picked up the two men in black, and Talman breathed easier.

He called Isaac Stein and reported the incident. Talman was not about to take full responsibility for Tayar. Beit Horon, he felt he could trust.

He made other calls, checking in with all of his sources, and with one of the women at the travel agency. She was not an agent, so she could not tell him if there were messages on his hidden telephone.

At four-thirty, Armbruster brought him a cup of coffee, and the two of them talked until five, when the helicopter was supposed to arrive.

It did not.

He placed another call, and he learned the helicopter was to be delayed an hour.

At six, with the sun starting down in the west, the medical evacuation helicopter landed in the army compound, and Talman accompanied Deborah Hausmann as she was wheeled on a gurney from the ward tent to the landing zone.

She smiled up at him and took his hand.

He squeezed hers. "At least, you are going where there is air-conditioning."

They had reached the helicopter when Armbruster came running up and signaled to him.

Talman released her hand and met Armbruster.

"We may have a problem, Major."

"What is that?"

"No one's seen Jack or Dr. Masters all afternoon. Greg Masters is gone, and his rental's still parked in the village."

"You have checked the camp?"

"Under every bed."

"Blanchard would never leave without telling you?"

"Me or Delray. He never has."

Talman released his second major sigh of the afternoon and went back to Hausmann. They were transferring her to the helicopter's stretcher.

"I am going to have to stay awhile, Deborah. I will come later."

"It is good to hear my name. I will wait for you."

He liked the sound of that. Giving her a thumbs-up, he backed away and rejoined Armbruster.

"Is there anything else significant missing, Dickie?"

"Yeah. The command Hummer."

So they went to talk to Captain Dietz, and the commander polled his guard stations and came up with a corporal who had been on the western gate all afternoon.

"Sure, sir. Mr. Blanchard drove out around two."

"Who did he have with him?" Talman asked.

"A woman in a white coat, a man in a suit, and some Arab."

"Bloody hell!" Armbruster shouted and started running.

Talman turned to go after him as Dietz called, "Major! May I come?"

"Let's go!"

Armbruster had a Humvee running by the time they caught up with him. They piled in, and Armbruster spun the tires in a wide circle, heading for the gate.

Outside the gate, Armbruster coasted to a stop, and they scanned the ground. Most tire tracks veered off to the southwest, aiming for the intersection with the pavement that led back to Mercy Base's last site. Another well-used track turned left and followed the fence line around the encampment and the stricken settlement.

One set of tracks led directly west.

"What do you think, Dickie?" Talman asked.

"It's the best shot in a hurry, Major."

"Go ahead."

Armbruster slapped the gearshift, and they were soon making forty kilometers per hour, bouncing over the rough terrain. They hadn't gone two kilometers, and were heading down an incline, before Armbruster locked up the brakes.

"What!"

"Over there, by that bush."

With the slant of the sun almost in his eyes, Talman had thought the discoloration a rock.

But no, it was not a rock. It was a man in a gray suit, trussed like a chicken.

And waving his head madly, afraid he would be missed.

Or perhaps run over. Armbruster slid the truck to a stop alongside him, and Talman and Dietz were the first out, the captain producing his knife to cut the bonds.

"How the bloody hell did you end up like this, Mr. Masters?" Armbruster asked.

The man yelped as the Brit ripped the tape from his mouth, leaving a white rectangle in a sea of red skin burned raw by the sun. He started gasping, and Armbruster held a canteen over him and dribbled a few drops in his mouth.

Talman squatted down, and he and Dietz watched the show.

Masters grabbed Armbruster's wrist, but the Brit yanked the canteen away.

"A little bit at a time. I asked you a question."

"Arab guy . . ." he choked out.

Armbruster sprinkled water on his face, then gave him a small sip.

"Blanchard called him something like Kadar."

"He's still got Blanchard and the doctor?"

"They're probably dead by now. Gimme that!"

Dietz helped him sit up.

"Uh-uh. Not so fast," Armbruster told him. "What happened to you?"

"He was going to kill me, but I got away."

"We can see that, Mr. Masters," Talman said. "How did you manage it?"

"Opened the door and jumped out . . . must have been going forty."

"And barely wrinkled your nice suit," Armbruster observed.

SATURDAY, JULY 31

An eye for an eye . . .

Fifteen

"Once they reached the pavement, they could have gone either way," Talman told Avidar. "There were no tracks to follow."

"There are no results from the air search, Jacob?"

"No, sir. After nine, visibility became impossible. The road search continues, and we have ten units out."

Not counting the medical-team rebel faction who would not listen to him, and who were roaming the countryside in their own uncoordinated search.

He checked his watch. One-twenty in the morning. Delray and Weiss were on this end of the tent with him, helping with the telephones and radios. Captain Dietz was manning the sound-powered phone, staying in touch with army operations. On the far end of the tent, one of the doctors, Chao, and a nurse were not doing anything but waiting. With them was Gregory Masters, his face coated in a clear salve, but the white space (where the bandage had been) made his face look like a red beet with a wide rectangular mouth. His tie was gone, and he wore his suit pants, which were stained with grime. Masters, after his treatment by the doctors, seemed to remember he had a wife, and that his proper role was one of grieving husband.

Talman could not understand how some women made
choices.

Despite Talman's objections, Armbruster and two men
named Timnath and Perkins had taken three Humvees and other
members of the medical team out to search. They already had
the passcards Talman had been so free with earlier.

"The army's feeling," the general said, "is that the white
Humvee is too recognizable, that they will have hidden it and
taken the hostages in another vehicle."

"That seems likely," he agreed.

"There have been no sightings at any of the approaches to
Jerusalem."

"That is the word we have gotten also, sir."

"The leadership is receiving pressure from the media, Jacob.
Primarily, they want to know why the roadblocks are so firmly
in place around the city. Some are questioning the relationship
between those and similar blockades at Mar Saba. Soon, someone will have to give in to them."

"I understand, General."

"You must find this Kadar very soon."

"I have talked to my people, sir. They are out in force.
Moshe Perlmutter has alerted his agents, also, in case Kadar
attempts to flee to the Gaza Strip."

"Have you talked to Rahman?"

"No, sir." Talman hesitated to mention his suspicions of
the deputy chief. His appearance at Kadar's house in Jericho
was still unexplained, and Talman had not had time to investigate it further.

"I will call and brief him," Avidar said.

"Very well, General."

Avidar abruptly changed the subject. "How is Hausmann?"

The general had a genuine concern for everyone working
for him, which was one of the reasons Talman appreciated him.

"She will recover, sir. Thanks to Dr. Masters."

"I know. We will do all we can, Jacob."

Delray looked up as Talman replaced the receiver.

He shook his head, "There is nothing new, Sam."

Through the netting of the tent wall, he saw headlights appear
to the east. They were moving at speed, and they dimmed as

they got closer, finally disappearing altogether as they came up to the gate. This was done not to blind the guards, and anyone who did not shut off their headlights would lose them to gunfire.

A few minutes later, a Humvee pulled up beside the tent, and Armbruster and the Argentinean named Irsay came in.

Weiss poured them coffee from a Thermos sent over from the mess hall.

"Anything, Dickie?" she asked.

"No, ma'am. We've got these handheld halogen lights, and we've been cruising the roads, shining them to the side, looking for tracks leaving the macadam. Those Hummer tires leave a distinctive footprint, but we haven't seen one."

The radio crackled, and Delray answered a call from Perkins, who was searching to the south. They had not found anything, either. The reports coming into Dietz from the army units were similar.

"You don't think they went right on into Jerusalem, Major Talman?"

"I have had the guard posts polled, Dickie. No one has seen a white Humvee."

Talman was suddenly concerned about that, though. Kadar not only had Blanchard and Masters, he had Blanchard's pass-card.

He grabbed the phone and punched the number for his communications center.

"Lorna Doone," he said. The code of the day.

"Box elder."

"This is Comet. We need to change the passcards."

"Hold on, please. I will speak to the duty officer."

Nearly ten minutes went by before the communications specialist came back to him. "They will start right away, Comet."

"How soon?"

"New distribution will be made to government officials and military units before the change can be issued to the security posts. The estimate is five-thirty."

Four hours. It would have to do.

"Thank you."

When he hung up, Armbruster said, "I'm going to bust my way into Jerusalem before the color of my card changes."

Weiss said, "I'll go with you, Dickie."

And Masters stood stiffly and said, "I want a ride to my hotel in Tel Aviv."

"Not with me," Armbruster told him.

"Well, then, I'll just take my car."

"But you don't have a passcard," Talman said. "You can't get out of here, much less through Jerusalem."

"I want out of this hellhole. Give me a card."

"I am fresh out of cards, Mr. Masters."

Talman found that he could enjoy telling this man, "No."

With the first drone of aircraft engines in the distance, Kadar had remembered the white truck. Yelling to el-Ziam and Badr, he had raced outside with mattresses and blankets, and they had covered the truck with them. They were an odd assortment of browns and grays, and turned out to be effective camouflage. In the back of the truck, they found sheets—which were too white and would attract attention—and three olive-drab army blankets.

He was going to put them over the van when el-Ziam mentioned the tracks of the big truck tires. Abu el-Ziam was still unhappy with Kadar because he had been left sitting in the sun at the monastery for hours without knowing what was taking place. It did not seem to matter that Kadar had no way to send a message to him. But he still remembered the tracks, and he took the Dodge and drove it up and down the long lane into the farmyard several times to obliterate the tire tracks. Then they parked the van under a tree and covered it with the blankets.

Several times before the sun went down, helicopters and small airplanes passed by, but none directly overhead. Army vehicles and another of the white trucks passed on the road at the end of the lane several times. Kadar wondered at the extent of the search; it seemed too intensive for a couple foreigners. He had thought them important at the time he had decided to take them. The doctor, especially, might be able to get him pas the Jerusalem roadblocks before she paid for her simpleminded remarks to the media.

It seemed he was correct in regard to their importance; the government would not devote so many resources to the search if he were not.

After he finished his prayers, he told this to the others as they sat on the wooden flooring near the door. The lantern was dimmed to its lowest setting. Badr got up frequently to look out the glassless windows to reassure himself that the arrival of the IDF was not imminent. The two prisoners were motionless in the far corner. They had not said one word since being tied.

"Why would they be important?" el-Ziam asked.

"The medical team has had free run of the West Bank. And they have an international following because of the work they do for the Palestinians. The media will be highly interested in the disappearance of these two. That is why the government tries so hard to find them."

Kassim, who rarely spoke anymore, as a result of Kadar's teaching, spoke now. "Do we not do our brothers a disservice? These doctors help our people."

"They are infidels," Kadar claimed. "They are filthy, and they will be discarded as soon as we have used them."

She diverted her eyes downward, rather than debate him.

To change the subject, Badr asked, "You think they can get us into Jerusalem?"

"Let us find out."

Kadar picked up the lantern. He carried it to the corner and saw their faces come into the light. They had moved close together. The woman was frightened. The whites of her eyes were prominent, and her mouth held a downward cast.

The man, who had said his name was Blanchard, gave away nothing. His face was stoic, and only his eyes followed Kadar's movements. This was not a good sign, Kadar thought. He would rather see open defiance, disdain, or fear. A face that disguised its feeling suggested danger. He would either be careful with this man or kill him quickly, rather than take unnecessary risks.

If he proved useful, he would stay alive.

For a while.

Reaching out, he grabbed the back of Blanchard's head and jerked him forward so he could see the bonds. He moved the light to see better. The wires were secure.

Pulling the woman forward by a handful of her hair, he checked the wire on her wrists, also. She yelped when he yanked her hair, and the response gave him some satisfaction. From his days in training, Kadar had always appreciated a telltale response from his foes.

He gave the lamp to el-Ziam to hold, and settling to his knees next to the woman, said, "Your name is Masters."

She nodded.

"Answer me."

"I didn't know it was a question."

He slapped her, throwing her head sideways and echoing in the room.

"Melanie Masters," she blurted.

He had seen the tension go into Blanchard's shoulders when he slapped her, but the American said nothing. Kadar might have expected a curse or expletive.

Kadar said, "The government is searching for you. Why?"

"My birthday, tomorrow. No one wanted to miss it."

Kadar stood, retrieved his knife, moved over their legs, and squatted next to Blanchard. He used the point of the blade to tap Blanchard's nose lightly.

"I will not have you mock me."

"You may have to put up with it, Kadar. No Jerusalem without the two of us."

Blanchard acted as if he were in command, and that was *not* the truth.

"I will do whatever I wish to do. It is my country."

"That's why you're hiding, right?"

"Why would you think I wanted to go to Jerusalem?"

"To use the bacteria."

Kadar offered a puzzled look. "Bacteria? What bacteria do you speak of?"

El-Ziam confused the interrogation. "See! You see! They know everything!"

"Be quiet, Abu," he said in Arabic, then returned to English. "Tell me."

"Shit, Kadar, old ass. You're stupider than Israeli intelligence figures you are."

The man was flirting with the loss of his nose. Kadar's hand twitched, and a small slice dribbled blood.

"Jack!" Masters yelled.

"You gave yourself away when you attacked the settlement," Blanchard said. "Hell, everyone in the army knows what you've got. You couldn't plan your way out of a pile of goat shit."

"I told you!" el-Ziam shouted.

Kadar pulled the knife back to his right shoulder, ready to slash . . .

"And you're sure as hell not going to Jerusalem without me."

He hesitated.

"Prove this."

"In my wallet."

Blanchard leaned toward the woman, and Kadar pulled two folders from his hip pocket. One contained a photo identification card, and the other was a wallet.

"The blue-and-white card."

He found it in one of the pockets of the billfold.

"Hey!" el-Ziam said. "That is what they were using at the roadblocks."

"What?" Kadar said in Arabic. "You did not tell me of this."

"I did not think of it. It was not required to leave the city, but those coming in were showing cards like that to the guards."

He turned the card over and saw Blanchard's name printed in ink.

"See the name? Only I can use that card," Blanchard said.

The blood was dripping from his nose to his upper lip. Kadar called out to Kassim and told her to get a towel and a Band-Aid for him. He stood up and walked across the room, then outside into the night. The stars were very bright.

El-Ziam followed him.

"What are you thinking, Ibrahim?"

"They will know that Blanchard has this card."

"That is true."

"And they will change the card very quickly."

"Perhaps by morning."

"We must move tonight."

"I think the danger point is high now," el-Ziam said. "They know all about us."

Kadar thought that Blanchard had been attempting the old adage, "Divide and conquer," and he had hit some nerves for el-Ziam. Abu wanted to think he had been correct in decrying the test at Mar Saba as unnecessary.

Perhaps he should allow his second in command to voice an opinion, even if he were not to follow it.

"What would you have us do, Abu?"

"Kill them. Then we will go to Jordan."

It was probably the appropriate course to take.

Dr. Melanie Masters couldn't help being critical of the Arab woman's nursing. She used an old rag to wipe Blanchard's nose and mouth, then slapped a small Band-Aid over the wound.

The woman was probably less than thirty, but acted much older, as if life had been a monumental disappointment for her.

Blanchard said, "*Shokran.* Thank you, Oma. I appreciate it."

Masters thought she probably understood English, judging by the momentary pause and look at Blanchard, then she picked up the lantern, rose from where she squatted, and walked away.

"How did you know her name?" she whispered.

"I'm a good listener. I told you that once."

"You're a terrible negotiator. You almost got yourself killed."

"How are you doing, Mel?"

"I'm scared to death. My heart rate has doubled," she said.

It was true. She could feel her heart beating; her pulse sounded like a train in her ears. She had been frightened before—near auto accidents, noises on dark streets, but never anything like this. Knowing that this man, this Kadar, might kill, and not knowing if, or when, had her nerve endings sensitized. Any little creak or jolt spiked her blood pressure.

''Please, Jack, don't do anything foolish. I don't know what I'd do without you.''

''I'm going to be around, Mel. I want to make sure this guy takes us with him.''

''You do?''

She couldn't believe that.

''If he thinks he doesn't need us, that's bad. If he tries to take us to Jerusalem, I might find an opening.''

In all the hours of darkness—and she didn't know what time it was now—she had been nearly overwhelmed by the awful things that could happen. And the worse scenario was being alone, without the strength Blanchard seemed to give her. She'd never have believed in a million years that she would ever think that way.

The light came toward them again, and she was relieved to see that it was Oma. The woman carried a dipper and placed it against Masters's lips.

Masters clamped her lips together.

''Drink. *Mai*—water.''

She parted her lips, and Oma tilted the ladle. Her mouth had been so parched, she could barely whisper to Blanchard, and the warm liquid trickling into her mouth was paradise.

Abruptly, it pulled away, and Oma gave the balance of it to Blanchard. Then she turned and went back to where one of the others sat watching her.

''A little kindness goes a long way,'' Blanchard said.

''God, that was good.''

''The guy sitting over there? That's Khalid. The one with the bushy beard who went out with Kadar is Abu.''

''*Abu* means father.''

''So maybe he's a daddy.''

''What's going to happen to us, Jack?''

''Hey, babe, we're on the winning side. Don't forget it.''

''It's difficult to be very damned optimistic. I don't know how you do it.''

''It's supposed to wash off on you.''

It was, and it wasn't. Her moods seemed to vacillate rapidly.

''What's he doing? Kadar?''

''He's out there trying to figure out how he's going to use

me to get him through the roadblock when the whole damned country's looking for me.''

"Can he figure it out?"

"No. But he's going to try, anyway."

"Maybe he'll just give up?"

"Did you take a close look at his eyes?" Blanchard asked.

"Yes," she sighed. "You're right."

Blanchard had tried to shift around enough to get a look at his watch, but couldn't quite manage it. His best guess was that it was about two o'clock in the morning. Give or take an hour or two.

He had hoped, too, that Masters would go to sleep, but she didn't. Every once in a while, he could feel her changing positions, trying to relieve the cramps she must be feeling. On top of his last few days' battle with his musculature, this wasn't helping. And despite his years of practice, he wasn't able to get a few winks, either.

Kadar wasn't predictable enough that Blanchard felt he could take his eyes off him for a minute. Whenever he was around.

The exalted leader had returned to the room earlier, and all four of them were debating something or other. Probably their upcoming vacation in Jerusalem.

Oma spoke at length and with some heat, the first time he'd seen her exhibit anything more than passivity. Kadar shouted her down.

Abu wasn't faring much better. The man's voice got loud when he was angry, but Kadar didn't let volume deter him from whatever course he'd chosen.

After about ten minutes of imposing his will, or his stubbornness, Kadar got up and came over to the corner.

He didn't say a word, just shoved Blanchard aside and reached down behind him. A couple minutes later, Blanchard was free of his tether, though his hands were still wired behind him. Kadar shoved him aside roughly and started working on Masters's wire. Kadar was a small man, though relatively strong. He seemed to think he was a hell of a lot stronger than he was, though.

The weapons reinforced his strength, of course, and Kadar liked the knife. A man of the blade.

Blanchard couldn't see the knife, but the pistol was stuck in Kadar's waistband. He might have tried for it but for Melanie. Abu was standing by, too, but he wasn't armed as far as Blanchard could tell.

Blanchard's arms were asleep, and his legs felt numb. It took him some time to respond to Kadar's order to stand up. The Arab jerked Masters to her feet. Abu kept an interested eye on Melanie. Where Kadar appeared to be almost asexual, Abu gave away hints as to his thoughts. Blanchard didn't like them a bit.

He was keeping a catalog of such things. At some point in time, Blanchard was going to refer to that catalog as he paid his debts.

They were going somewhere. Oma and Khalid were gathering backpacks, shoving clothing and bits and pieces into them. Blanchard, who had been trying to keep track, saw his wallet and ID folder go into one pack.

Kadar grabbed the wire fastened to his wrist and shoved him in the middle of the back. Blanchard immediately stepped into a hole in the floor, stumbled, but caught himself. All he needed was a sprained ankle.

He looked back for Masters. She was in Abu's loving care. He gripped her upper arm with too much willingness as he led her across the floor.

They reached the doorway.

Oma called to Kadar, and Kadar whipped back on the wire, tugging Blanchard's arms backward. He felt it clear to his shoulders.

Khalid picked up two assault rifles and stood a few feet from the woman, rifles cradled in one arm, the shoulder straps of two packs held in his other hand.

Oma gushed a stream of Arabic.

Kadar methodically lifted the pistol from his belt, snapped the safety off, raised it, sighted, and shot her in the forehead.

Masters screamed.

The gunshot reverberated around the walls, numbing Blanchard's ears.

Oma's body crumpled backward, crashing to the floor. The packs she had been holding were still clutched in her hand. In the light from the lantern on the floor, Blanchard saw that her eyes stared straight up at the ceiling.

Khalid and Abu didn't move a muscle. Khalid's face went completely blank.

Shit! What an asshole!

He was more convinced than ever that Kadar was psychotic. Not a feeling in him. And if he was setting an example, it had taken hold.

Masters had collapsed to her knees, and Abu began fighting to get her back on her feet, murmuring something to her in English.

"Outside!" Kadar ordered. "Khalid, get the other packs."

Blanchard stepped through the doorway and let Kadar push him around the corner of the house to where the Hummer was parked. Khalid came out, and Kadar spoke to him. Dumping the knapsacks and weapons on the ground, Khalid pulled the mattresses and blankets off the truck, then opened the tailgate.

He crawled into the back and started throwing out boxes and sheets and towels. He tried to remove the communications gear, but it was bolted down and wouldn't move even after he bashed at it with his fists and feet. It took him three tries, but he ripped the satellite dish from its cable and tossed it aside.

Abu came up with Melanie and forced her up on the tailgate, then inside. Khalid pulled her farther in and shoved her down against the back of the rear seat.

"Jack!"

"Just do as they say, Mel."

Abu ran off, then came back with three army blankets and more of the backpacks. He tossed them inside, and Khalid stored them. Then came the Kalashnikovs.

Then Blanchard felt Kadar's hands working at his wrists, and in a few minutes, they were free. He rotated his shoulders, attempting to get some feel back into them and into his arms. He rubbed his wrists where they were chafed by the wire.

"Do you understand what is happening here?" Kadar asked.

"You can't drive, I'll bet."

"She is dead the instant you stray from what I tell you to do."

"That much, I can figure."

"Get in and start the motor."

"Got a suggestion for you, Kadar."

"I do not need your suggestions."

"We aren't going far if you don't give me the passcard and my ID."

The suggestion resulted in a flurry of activity as they searched through the packs.

At two-twenty-five in the morning, Captain Dietz answered the sound-powered telephone.

Talman looked up from where he was resting his head on the desk.

Dietz covered the mouthpiece with his hand. "It is the road-block on Herzog. They say they have a white Humvee attempting to go through."

Talman came out of his chair and crossed to the table where the army captain sat.

"Who is driving? Do they have identification?"

"A man named Perkins. He has the passcard, and he says he is a nurse. The guard is skeptical."

Talman said, "Ask him if the man sounds like he comes from the southern United States?"

Dietz repeated the question into the phone, then said, "The sergeant only knows that he doesn't sound like a Brit. Or like most Americans."

"It's probably the right man. Double-check his ID and let him through."

For most of the way, all Blanchard could think about was the Uzi hanging under the driver's seat.

A glance in the rearview mirror was all it took to dissuade him from trying for it. He could see Kadar's head in the back, poking up from beneath the blankets that covered Masters,

Abu, and Khalid. It was a tight fit back there, but he had no doubt that the Beretta was pressed against Melanie's skull.

He drove at Kadar's dictated forty-five kilometers per hour, and he didn't pass any other vehicles. The civilians probably figured they couldn't get past the roadblocks, anyway. And he was just as happy to not run into any military vehicles. They might have tried to stop him, and that would have resulted in some deaths. He didn't try to forecast whose.

He had the side windows wide open, forcing air to the cramped back end. He had to speak above the windstream.

"You sure you want to try the main road, Kadar?"

"Do as you are told."

Kadar was thinking an attempt at one of the smaller entrances into the city would look more suspicious. He was probably right.

Blanchard had started off by hoping there weren't other Hummers out and about. That would make him stick out like a hammered thumb. Now, he hoped he was only one of many. It would make the passage easier if the guards weren't overly suspicious of the white truck. Any glitch at all in this process was not in the best interest of Masters.

He saw floodlights coming up. The Israelis had the place lit up pretty good.

The roadblock was farther into the city than he had expected. A few blocks of outlying buildings passed by before he had to slow for the barrier dropped across his lane of traffic. All of the city streetlights were on.

"Almost there, Kadar, old chap."

"I can see. I have eyes. You will speak loudly enough for me to hear. And you will remember, her death comes before all else."

Kadar's head disappeared from the rearview mirror, and the blanket was pulled over him. Just another load of dirty laundry back there.

He could imagine Melanie's fright. Some cruddy hand clamped over her mouth. Put that in the catalog.

Braking to a stop, he watched a soldier move toward him from the side of the road. They had a portable shed over there.

"Good morning, Sergeant."

"Good morning, sir. Another one of you?"

Somebody had been through.

"Afraid so."

The sergeant gave him a thorough exam. They wouldn't have pictures of him or Masters out yet, he didn't think, but certainly their descriptions had been circulated.

"Do you have a passcard and ID, sir?"

"Sure do."

Blanchard reached under his left thigh for the card and his ID case. If the sergeant asked for a driver's license, he'd had it. Kadar had kept his wallet.

He passed them through the window.

The guard looked them over carefully, looked again at Blanchard as if checking the photo on the ID, and started to say something. He knew damned well half of his military was looking for a man named Blanchard.

Blanchard shook his head with violent and negative exaggeration.

The man's eyes went wide, and he reached for the pistol on his web belt.

Again, Blanchard shook his head, with his left forefinger against his lips.

A quizzical look.

"Tell you what, Sergeant. In view of the circumstance, why don't you check with Major Talman?"

"Major Talman?"

"I imagine he's at your headquarters or out at the medical unit."

"Please shut off your lights and wait here, Mr. Blanchard."

Blanchard shut off the headlights. The sergeant signaled someone, and three soldiers appeared to stand to the side and front, all with Uzis aimed at the truck. More precisely, they were aimed through the windshield at Blanchard.

It was in Talman's hands now. He thought the intelligence man would understand the situation immediately.

Which gave him two choices.

Save Blanchard and Masters by letting the Humvee through.

Or waste Blanchard and Masters, and save 400,000 of his countrymen.

For a patriot and a pragmatic military man—like he thought Talman was—it was an easy decision.

In Talman's place, Blanchard would have voted for the city.

Sixteen

And this was supposed to be a damned civilized country. Gotta piss in a funnel stuck in the ground.

Masters left the latrine and aimed himself back toward the center of the camp.

And walk 150 yards to do it.

In the dark, too, he lamented. There were a few lights on in the ward tents, where he'd been warned not to go. As if he wanted to see a bunch of sick people. There was a light in the mess tent, but he couldn't face the putrid coffee, and he'd only finished half the spaghetti he'd been given for dinner.

He didn't want to go back to the cot he'd been given in a tent full of people who snorted, yelped, and breathed through their noses with shrill whistles.

He felt like hell. His face burned; his legs were bruised; his arms were stiff. It was too uncomfortable to sleep. He longed for his own bed, but even that was denied him. Damn Brett MacDonald and his locksmiths.

He had looked around this place. What the hell Melanie saw in it, he couldn't fathom. Maybe she'd never gone to Girl Scout camp. It was for the goddamned birds.

But maybe this experience with the terrorist would straighten her out. Masters had no doubt she'd be released soon, and hopefully, have learned a valuable lesson. She would be ready for Chicago and clean sheets and her expensively furnished office.

Nagging him, at the back of his mind, were the accusations she'd made. Sure, he'd made lots of contributions. He didn't know the total, but it was expected. One had to give a little to get a lot in return. And maybe he'd made them out of her accounts. It didn't matter; they were a team. They were supposed to work together.

That could all be straightened out. It was a detail. What was important was for her to pack up her crap and head for the airplane with him. They had to get out of this rotten country, back to where people knew how to treat each other. She could straighten out ex-damned-General MacDonald before any of it hit the newspapers.

Masters found himself standing at the back of the administration tent, and he figured he might as well get one disagreeable chore over with. Middle of the night here, so it must be daylight in Illinois, right?

He shoved aside the curtain and stepped inside. A few people were gathered at the front end, but he ignored them and sat down at one of the telephones. He punched a button for a vacant line and keyed in the number.

"Hello?"

"Dad, it's Greg."

"Gregory? Yes, where are you? Did you and Melanie reach a resolution?"

"Well . . . I'm at the medical camp, but there's this little bit of a problem."

"There is no problem that can't be fixed. Do I have to do it for you?"

"It's not that, Dad. Melanie's been—"

The line went dead.

Masters looked at the hand holding the reset button down, and followed the arm up to Talman's face.

"What in the hell do you think you're doing?" Masters demanded.

"You were told there is an information blackout, Mr. Masters."

"Yeah, but this doesn't count. This is my father. Now, take your goddamned hand off the phone."

"You are barred from using the telephones, sir. You will please leave the tent."

"Listen, you shit! I know my damned constitutional rights!"

"Then, you should have stayed where your constitution is in effect."

Jesus! They take away every personal right I'm entit—

"Major. For you."

Talman looked back to where other phones were ringing and said, "Dr. Svenson, could I ask you to keep this man off the phone?"

"Certainly, Major."

Even the doctors were on his case, now.

Talman took the telephone from a lieutenant who had replaced Dietz on the military line.

"Major Talman."

"This is Sergeant Myerson, Major. I have the duty at the Jericho Road security checkpoint."

"Yes, Sergeant. Go on."

Another Humvee wanting through, he thought.

"There's a white Humvee with the WHO logo here . . ."

Must be Armbruster.

". . . driven by a man named Jack Blanchard."

Whatever fatigue he had been feeling evaporated instantly. His eyes cleared. He pressed the receiver tightly to his ear, so as to not miss any nuance.

"I thought that was the guy you were looking for, Major. He looks a little like the description, except he's got a black eye and a bandage on his nose."

"Indeed, it is, Sergeant. Is there someone else with him?"

"No, he's alone, but he's acting strange. Shaking his head when I talk to him. He told me to call you."

Blanchard would be under duress, of course. Masters was at

risk somewhere, perhaps even in the Humvee. Blanchard was letting Talman make the decision.

It was very nice of the man. Would that Talman could return the favor.

"He has the passcard, Sergeant?"

"Yes, sir, though someone wrote his name on it. The ID looks right. It's him."

Would Kadar be rash enough to attempt to breach the block-ade this way?

Yes.

Then he would be in the truck. As would the bacteria.

Talman felt his heart clutch. This should not be his decision, but he felt the press of time. Jack Blanchard, whom he now thought of as his friend, was sitting there, waiting. Waiting on an execution order, as it was. Levi Avidar was far out of his reach. If he told Myerson to hold the vehicle, there would be many deaths due to gunfire, certainly those of Blanchard and Masters.

To let them through, however, meant the potential death of hundreds of thousands.

And Masters. She who had saved Deborah Hausmann for him.

Two weeks ago, there would have been no question of his decision. Arabs threatening Israel deserved bullets. He was becoming soft.

If he were at the roadblock, it would be easier to decide. He would feel as if he had some control. As it was, he did not know the capabilities of the soldiers in place.

He turned to look back at Gregory Masters, who was arguing about the telephone with Lars Svenson. The man probably wouldn't even grasp the gravity of this decision. Talman held the life of the man's wife clasped tightly in his hand—which was sweaty—and Masters argued about a damned telephone.

"Sir? Major, are you still there?"

"I am here, Sergeant. Do you have a vehicle?"

"A Jeep. Yes, sir."

"Do this. Give Blanchard his papers back and allow him through." As he talked, he lifted his foot and toed the lieutenant on the knee to get his attention, and mouthed, "Get me a car."

Then to the sergeant: "The streets are not crowded?"

"No, sir. Not at all."

"Then, you and one other man follow him. Stay very far back. Do not use your headlights. Try to determine where he goes, but do not risk being seen."

"Ah, yes, sir. I understand."

"What is your radio frequency?"

He jotted it on a piece of paper as the sergeant recited it.

"I will be in touch with you shortly."

Talman dropped the phone on the desk.

"Jeep on the way, Major," the lieutenant said.

"Good. You find a secure line and call General Avidar and tell him Blanchard is in the city. Don't put it on the air. Tell him I can be reached on this frequency." He handed the note over.

Talman saw lights headed his way from the army encampment.

"Blanchard's in the city?"

Good God!

He turned to find Masters right beside him.

"I heard that."

"I will be finding out, Mr. Masters."

"I'm going with you."

"No—"

"She's my wife, Major! You've denied me everything else, but damn it!"

This much was true. Perhaps the man simply hid his feelings well. Americans were known for that. American men.

"Very well, Mr. Masters. But you are not to interfere with any operations we may conduct."

"Got my word."

He led Masters out of the tent, and the two of them crawled into a Jeep driven by an enlisted man.

"Through the village and out the Mar Saba road, Corporal. As fast as you can."

Under the blankets in the back of the truck, it was unimaginably cramped with four bodies. The blankets threatened to suffocate her, and Masters felt as if she were near the end of her endurance. The fear that this could go on for days or weeks—thinking of the Iran hostages—was overwhelming.

One of the pigs—and she didn't know which one—was pressed up tightly against her back, his stomach prodding her in the back. His left arm was under her head, and his hand clamped her mouth shut. That didn't help her breathing. His other hand had a firm grasp on her breast, and he kneaded it roughly. The retard was probably excited by all of this. His odor made her want to gag.

She was repulsed by him and horrified for Blanchard. If anything went wrong, Kadar and his men would start shooting, and anything could happen. She wondered where the bacteria was.

Blanchard was a good actor. She had been listening intently, and his voice had sounded cheerful enough, though she was aware that something was wrong. He had asked the guard to call Talman. The wait seemed interminable.

She heard boots on the pavement.

"Mr. Blanchard . . ."

"Yes, Sergeant."

"I spoke with Major Talman, and everything is fine. You go right ahead. And drive safely, sir."

"Thanks, Sergeant."

The engine growled, and she felt the truck moving.

The man behind her snickered.

The conflict raged within her. She felt a welcome sense of thrill that Blanchard had gotten them through without bloodshed. And on the other end of the fulcrum was Kadar with his batch of bacteria. People were going to die, and she was an unwilling participant in the process.

A few blocks later, the blanket was pulled aside, and a welcome breeze boiled over the seat.

She shook her head violently, and the man took his hand from her mouth.

"Get your filthy hands off me!"

He laughed and squeezed her breast hard.

The one they called Abu.

With any good fortune, one day she would operate on him.

* * *

Ibrahim Kadar slapped el-Ziam on the side of the head with the butt of the pistol. It was just hard enough to get his attention.

In Arabic he said, "Remove lust from your mind, Abu. She is an infidel, filthy."

"But, Ibrahim—"

"For now, we have much loftier goals."

El-Ziam muttered a curse under his breath.

Kadar got his knees under him and raised his head enough to see through the windows, checking behind them first. There were no cars following. The streets were particularly void of traffic, probably as a result of the curfews and blockaded roads.

Allah! You ride with me!

Ahead, through the windshield, he saw a few headlights and some taillights. Workers going between home and work, he thought.

Pushing himself over el-Ziam and the woman, he rolled into the backseat.

"Thank you," Badr said. "I may breathe again."

"Just stay where you are, in case I must come back."

He lowered himself to the floor behind Blanchard and peered ahead over the American's shoulder. To remind him who was the commander, he jabbed the muzzle of the pistol into the man's neck.

Blanchard barely flinched.

"I got you through, Kadar. Let the doctor go."

"I decide who will do what. You will turn right at the next intersection."

"Good idea. You don't want to stay on the main drag."

"What! What do you mean by that?"

"This truck sneaking around the back streets won't catch anyone's attention, will it?"

He was right. A vehicle as recognizable as this one would normally be seen only on the primary streets, accomplishing some errand.

"Where we going?" Blanchard asked.

"You will know it when I tell you. What are you doing!"

"You told me to turn right here."

"Stop! Back up and get on Herzog again."

Blanchard stopped the truck, backed up, and returned to the street.

Kadar took a quick glance to the rear.

What was that!

A shadow flitting under a streetlamp. No. Another car. It turned off.

"Want to take a ride past the Knesset, Kadar? It's well lit up."

He looked to the left. Most of the government buildings were lit. It spoke well of the Sword of God and its leader. The country was in turmoil, looking for him, and he went where he pleased.

Soon—a month—and this city would be a dead one. And soon thereafter, it would rise again from the ashes, a stronghold of Islam.

"You will go straight."

Another car, a civilian sedan, went by, going the other way, the driver looking curiously at them. With the lack of traffic tonight, others would notice the white truck immediately. When he looked to the side streets, he frequently saw military and police vehicles. They were out in force.

They continued to the northeast, and the street became Aza, then Agron, then Hativat Hatzanhanim. He almost ordered Blanchard to turn left on Shivtel Israel, but he saw a police car and a police van parked halfway down the block. The policemen were standing next to the cars, talking to each other.

As they approached the Damascus Gate—properly Bab el-Amud, the Gate of the Column, to Arabs—he said, "You will turn left onto Nablus Road."

"Shekhem Road, you mean?"

"It is Nablus to me."

"Nice job Suleiman did, huh?"

"What are you talking about, Blanchard?"

"You haven't taken the tour, Kadar? Suleiman the Magnificent built the gate in 1537. Kinda divides the Old City from the American Colony."

Such things meant little in the grand scheme.

"Be quiet!"

There were more automobiles traveling the street Blanchard
turned onto. He settled lower, to keep his head from becoming
an obvious silhouette, and took another quick look to the rear.

A car followed them.

It was larger. A van. He watched carefully for three blocks,
then it turned off.

His absorption with what was behind almost made him forget
what was ahead.

"Turn here!"

Blanchard made the turn belatedly, went half a block, then
went left, again to the east, at Kadar's direction. Three more
blocks, and they intersected Kalad Ibn e Waleed. He ordered
a left turn, then shortly thereafter, a turn into the alley.

"Right on the edge of the American Colony?"

Kadar did not answer, but the answer was simple. Americans
demanded garages, and there were more garages in this area
for rent.

They bumped down the roughly paved alley for sixty meters.

"Stop here, and shut off the lights."

Blanchard braked, and Kadar said in Arabic, "Abu! Open
the door."

El-Ziam tumbled over into the backseat, got out, and went
to raise the garage door. In the darkness of the alley, the opening
was a bare rectangle of blacker blackness. A flare of light
spilled outward when el-Ziam turned on an interior light.

"You're damned fortunate it's a double garage, Kadar, old
boy. We'd have to take the fenders off for a single."

"Just drive in!"

"You sure? We didn't take any evasive maneuvers to lose
our tail."

Involuntarily, Kadar looked back over his shoulder. There
was only darkness and the dimly lit street behind them.

"There is no tail, as you call it."

"Whatever you say."

Blanchard let out the clutch, turned the wheel hard, and
pulled inside the garage. He shut off the engine, and el-Ziam
closed the door.

Badr shoved the woman over the backseat.

"See! We are safe!" he exclaimed.

"Don't count your chickens," Blanchard told him.

Kadar could see Blanchard's eyes in the rearview mirror. They did not look servile enough.

Greg Masters was in the back of the Jeep with both hands firmly clinging to a grab bar. The idiot corporal took turns on two wheels. There were no side doors, and the wind rushing inside brought tears to his eyes. The engine scream was loud enough to drown out any polite conversation, but the radio made it even worse. The static nearly overpowered anything remotely intelligible, and if it was intelligible, only Talman and the corporal understood it because it was in, he thought, Hebrew.

Talman kept the microphone in his hand and occasionally spoke into it. He did so as they approached the roadblock at better than seventy miles an hour, and the barrier rose and they blasted through without stopping.

Well, nothing like having the top cop take you home, he thought.

He leaned forward between the seats and shouted, "You can drop me at any decent hotel, Major."

Talman turned and stared into Masters's eyes. They were like dead pools.

"I thought you were worried about your wife."

He was, of course. But, hell, he'd never dealt with terrorists before. That's why they had armies, right?

"I have faith in you guys. And what the hell? I don't know how to go about this. I'm probably just in the way."

"Exactly," Talman said and turned to face the front.

Maybe a couple miles farther along the boulevard, the corporal jammed on the brakes, and they slid to a stop next to another Jeep which was parked at the curb. The driver climbed out and saluted.

Talman returned it offhandedly.

"I'm sorry as hell, Major."

"What happened, exactly?"

"The Humvee made a turn to the right, and I speeded up so as not to lose it. All of a sudden, it came backing out onto

Herzog, and I was afraid they'd seen me, so I turned off. I waited a minute, then got back after them, but I never saw them again.''

Talman nodded, seeming to accept this shitty excuse, then said, ''Go back to your post, Sergeant. I will take it from here.''

He said something to the driver, and they tore off again, screeching around corners, dashing into narrow streets through what Masters thought was called the Old City, then sliding to a stop in front of a large glass window.

''Come with me, Mr. Masters. Corporal, you can return to Mar Saba.''

Stiff as he was, it was difficult getting out of the cramped rear of the Jeep, and Talman didn't even bother to help. He crossed the sidewalk and unlocked a glass door. Inside he found a light switch and turned overhead lights on.

It was a damned travel agency.

Masters followed him inside.

''Have a seat at one of the desks, Mr. Masters. I have to make telephone calls.''

''Jacob!''

Masters damned near dropped his load when the voice spoke from behind him. He whirled around to find some guy dressed in black.

''Hello, Moshe. Come in,'' Talman said.

The newcomer looked quizzically at Masters, and Talman introduced them, though with apparent reluctance.

''I heard the transmissions on the radio,'' Perlmutter said. ''It is unfortunate.''

''Yes. I have to get something under way, and soon. What are you doing in Jerusalem, Moshe?''

''I came looking for you. I have the information you were seeking.''

''Please, Mr. Masters, have a chair. We won't be long.''

They went into a cramped office and closed the door behind them.

He didn't feel like sitting; he'd been sitting all day.

He did feel like the most unwanted son of a bitch in the valley. These bastards had just lost Melanie, and they were treating him like shit.

What he really wanted was a drink, and he went to the door and looked up and down the street.

It didn't look very inviting. Like something out of *Casablanca*. It was dark, and the shadows of doorways could be hiding anything.

There probably wasn't a bar open, anyway. It was a backward damned place.

Besides which, his face would draw laughs, and he didn't need that.

He really ought to call his father. The old man didn't react well to being hung up on, and he still had to tell him what had happened to Melanie.

He went to a desk with a computer on it, picked up the phone, and punched a button for one of the lines. It was dead. So were the other three lines.

What a hell of a way to run a business.

He gave Perlmutter the only chair in the office and sat on the desk.

"You looked into Rahman?"

"I did, Jacob. Following the line of inquiry you suggested. You said you would tell me why you have this sudden new interest?"

"One of my agents saw Rahman enter Kadar's house in Jericho shortly before the Sword of God went on the run. Rahman did not stay long."

Perlmutter ran his hand through his smoky hair and stared up at Talman. His eyes appeared huge in the magnified lenses of his glasses.

"All right. Everything I could find out about his background matches exactly what we have in his dossier."

"And his family?"

"His ancestors and his offspring are all accounted for, and in the file."

"But you checked into extended family? That is not in the file."

"Yes. None seem to have done as well for themselves as Rahman has. There is one, a sister-in-law—his wife's sister.

who ran wild early. From age twelve, I am told. She was
associated with Hamas for some time, then dropped out of
sight.''

"The name, Moshe?"

"Oma Kassim."

"Yes. I thought it would be something like that."

"Would he be compromised?" Perlmutter asked.

"I cannot answer that." Talman handed Perlmutter his keys.
"While I consider the answer, open the bottom drawer. Inside
is a phone. Would you call the general?"

"Not Stein?"

"I think I had better confess to Avidar."

"Confess? Are you joking, Jacob? Confess to what?"

"To fucking the city of Jerusalem."

The interior of the garage was diminished considerably by
the presence of the Hummer. And it wasn't much of a garage
to begin with.

The wall studs were exposed; there were two 100 watt bulbs
in ceramic ceiling fixtures; and there was a six-foot-long workbench at the end of one bay. A few mechanics tools had been
resting on it, but they were scattered on the concrete floor now,
wiped away by one swath of Kadar's arm.

Blanchard was sitting on one end of the bench, his arms tied
behind him once again, and then further tied to the back leg
of the bench. His right leg was snugged up against the front
leg of the bench with a few turns of wire. Masters was in the
same shape, at the other end of the bench. She frequently looked
at him, and he gave her smiles of encouragement every time.

The left side doors of the Humvee were open, and Abu sat
on the front seat. He kept staring at Melanie, and Blanchard
didn't like the attention she was getting. Khalid and Kadar had
spread the army blankets on the cement floor and were spreading
out their belongings. Khalid loved his Kalashnikov, Blanchard
could see.

Kadar opened a plastic box on the floor, and sat staring
lovingly at whatever was inside. He had his own love, and
Blanchard was damned certain what it was.

He was beginning to regret his success at the roadblock. Back in the run-down farmhouse, the city had appeared to be filled with more probabilities for escape. Now he thought he should have let the IDF sergeant take a look through the truck, find a mob of terrorists, and open up with his handgun. He'd have died, of course, and Melanie's chances wouldn't have been all that great, but the other soldiers would surely have taken out Kadar and company.

It would be over now, though with less than spectacular results.

He'd thought for damned sure Talman or somebody would put a shadow on them, but unless they were outside in the alley right now, waiting for the proper moment, that scenario didn't look too promising. Already, it was daylight. The gaps around the garage door let the morning peek in. Another hot, bright day in store. It would become blistering hot in here by midafternoon.

If Masters knew what he was thinking, she probably wouldn't be impressed. She'd think his nationalism had transcended itself to a fifty-year-old nation.

But Blanchard had spent some time in the wards, talked to the people through Weiss or Irsay, and seen the combination of agony and hope in their eyes. He had heard the children screaming and crying. No one should die that way. No one should suffer that way, even if they didn't die.

And no city should go through it.

"Why don't you just open it up, Kadar?" he called. "Take a swig and see if it works on a godlike figure like yourself?"

Kadar shot to his feet instantly. He moved pretty well for having the clubfoot.

He came over and stuck his face in Blanchard's. The drill-instructor routine, but with bad breath.

"You have a smart mouth, Blanchard."

"Unlike yours, mine's connected to a smart brain."

Khalid and Abu were interested now. They got up from where they were sitting and sidled over to watch the debate.

"Jack!"

Shut up, Mel. We're moving the attention over this way.

"You cannot talk to me like this." His face had darkened like storm clouds moving in. He reached down to the floor and came up with a turnover handle for a three-quarter-inch socket-drive set. Heavy, long bastard.

"I can talk to you any way I want, Kadar. You need me."

"Need you! What for?" He slapped the heavy handle against his left hand.

"To get you to the water supplies."

The man's eyes nearly popped.

"You think we didn't figure that out? Every pump house and water main in the city is under twenty-four-hour surveillance. You'll never get there on your own. And you'll need a doctor who's concerned with water purity as cover, too."

Let's give you a role, Mel.

"This is preposterous."

"Of course it is. Give it a shot on your own. Hell, you couldn't even get into the city without me. And I'm not even Israeli."

He lifted the handle, then seemed to consider the consequences if he really did need Blanchard. Tossing the handle to the floor, he spoke to the others in Arabic.

Abu grinned, stepped around his boss, and drove a roundhouse right fist into Blanchard's stomach.

Blanchard grunted.

Masters yelled, "Kadar, you sadistic bastard!"

Kadar issued another order, and everybody waited while Kadar found his roll of tape and taped Melanie's mouth. As an afterthought, he ripped off another six inches and pressed it hard over Blanchard's mouth. It was going to be tough coming off, Blanchard thought, because of his day-old growth of whiskers.

Then Kadar said, "Beat him."

And they did.

They took turns, and they took care to stay away from his face, but they had a hell of a good time landing blows against his ribs, stomach, and upper arms. It took them about fifteen minutes before they tired, but by then, Blanchard was back against the wall of the garage, on the ragged edge of consciousness.

Seventeen

"Major, this is Dickie Armbruster. Captain Dietz told me to call you."

"Yes, Dickie?"

"Any word on my people?"

His people. Everyone was claiming Blanchard and Masters.

"They're in the city," Talman admitted.

"Bloody hell! With Kadar?"

"We assume so. I will tell you about it later."

His discussion with General Avidar had not gone well. The commander was definitely unhappy, on the brink of firing Talman on the spot. "The whole truckload should have been killed immediately!"

Talman said he knew this.

Avidar relented, perhaps because Talman knew so much about the operation, which appeared to be coming to a head. It would be difficult to replace Talman at this late date. Fire him later. The general had accepted Talman's recommendation to abandon the roadblocks and begin sweeping the city in the search for the Sword of God and its captives. The city police department had been rallied in force, also. At this point, Talman did not hold out much hope for Blanchard and Masters. They no longer were of value to Kadar, now that they had gotten him into the city.

"I believe I've got something for you," Armbruster said. "Jillian and I were taking a sweep to the north of Highway 1 and spotted Humvee tracks on a side road."

A little late, Talman thought.

"So we checked it out, right? And we found the body of a woman."

"A woman?" Please, not Masters. No, in that case, Armbruster would have been bristling, ready to commit mayhem.

"I've never seen her before, but she's Arab, I think. Shot through the head."

"Where are you now, Dickie?"

"At the farm." He provided directions.

"Stay there."

"Hurry it up, will you, Major? I've got better things to be doing."

Talman's car was still at the Jericho checkpoint, but Moshe Perlmutter's was parked on the street. As the two of them emerged from his office, Greg Masters leaped to his feet. He had moved to a chair by the window when Talman's two employees arrived for work.

Masters looked even more ridiculous in the light of day. His face was beginning to peel around his whiskers, and the white splotch across his mouth seemed brighter.

"You will stay here, Mr. Masters."

"Bullshit!"

"Or I will have you arrested."

He and Perlmutter went out, crossed the street, and walked to where the agent in charge of the Gaza Strip had parked his Volkswagen Jetta. They crawled in, and Perlmutter eased away from the curb into traffic. It seemed like a normal day; the street was choked with automobiles and the sidewalks were crowded with people. Abnormally, though, he frequently spotted police and military patrols.

The people on the streets did not seem to notice them, but then, they did not know the dangers. They were just people.

All of whom were at risk.

"So?"

"A body has been discovered, Moshe."

The roads out of the city were now wide open, and Perlmutter stayed with the flow of traffic; there was not much else he could do. Talman used Perlmutter's cellular telephone to report the incident to Colonel Stein.

On impulse, he called Rahman, who must have been sitting next to his telephone, it was picked up so quickly.

"I have been hoping you would call, Jacob. Rumors surround me like flies, and I do not know which ones to swat."

"Can you take your helicopter to a place near Jericho?"

"Certainly."

"I will meet you there." Talman gave him the directions.

It was nine-thirty by the time they reached the ruined house. There was a Dodge van parked in the yard, and next to it, a white Humvee. The tailgate was down, and Armbruster and Weiss sat on it, watching them pull in. The pharmacist appeared fatigued. Armbruster was shaving with a portable electric razor. Brits always presented a respectable image.

He slid off the tailgate as Perlmutter parked next to them. Weiss only nodded a subdued greeting.

Talman opened his door and got out. He looked around, and to the right side of the house, he saw cardboard boxes, mattresses, sheets, and towels scattered over the ground. A small satellite dish rested on its rim against the wall.

"Most of those were in Jack's Hummer," Armbruster said. "I took one of the sheets and put it over the body. Seemed the decent thing to do."

The forensics investigators would disagree, but Talman did not think a great deal of evidence was necessary to point toward Kadar. He wondered if Blanchard had shot the woman in some kind of fight. Sergeant Myerson had reported Blanchard wearing a bandage on his nose.

He and Perlmutter stepped inside the house. The dust on the floor had been repeatedly disturbed. A propane stove was on the floor, surrounded by discarded paper and sacks. The body was beyond it.

Perlmutter approached and lifted the sheet. Talman went around him to look.

"Do you know her, Jacob?"

"Oma Kassim."

"Ah. That is why you called Rahman."

"It was the only assumption to be made."

They took a look around the room, noted the markings and disturbed dirt in the far corner where it appeared that hostages had been held, then went back outside.

"You know this is where they were held, right?" Armbruster asked.

"It seems apparent, Dickie. The woman was a member of the Sword of God."

"They disenroll them rather severely, Major."

Talman told him the details of Blanchard's entry into the city during the night.

The ex-SAS sergeant took the news grimly, but seemed to understand Talman's decision. Talman presumed the man had dealt with Irish terrorists before.

"We're going to Jerusalem. Any problem with that?"

"No, Dickie."

"Do I need one of your new passcards?"

"The roadblocks have been taken down."

"We're off, then."

He slammed the tailgate, and he and Weiss climbed into the truck. After he got it turned around, it took off in a rush of noise and a cloud of dust.

Perlmutter called the army investigators, then the two of them sat in the front seat and waited for Rahman.

Twenty minutes later, the rackety helicopter landed in the field on the other side of the house. Rahman walked around the house, and Talman signaled with a nod of his head, then took him inside and lifted the sheet to show him the body.

He watched Rahman's face closely.

It sagged a little, perhaps in sadness.

"Oma Kassim," he said.

"Yes."

"She is . . . was my sister-in-law. My wife's youngest sister." Rahman rotated and went outside.

Talman followed him, keeping his silence. They stood next to each other in the dirt. Moshe Perlmutter watched them from his seat in the Jetta.

"I knew she was a confederate of Kadar. I have been keeping watch on her."

"You chose not to enlighten us."

"There . . . was the hope that I could persuade her to leave Kadar. I believe she had become disenchanted with him, but was indecisive about her future. I would have helped her. I tried to help her."

"She was disenchanted?"

"You had to know her when she was younger, Jacob. She was fiery, the blood of her Bedouin ancestors running in her veins. She embraced causes with all her being."

"And what changed her?"

"I do not know. If I look back, and believe me, I have composed charts of the timing, I believe it may have started with the death two years ago of a lover who belonged to Izaddin al-Qassam. Then she went to Sapir, and when he died, I think she lost heart. The last times I saw her, she moved with the zest of a ninety-year-old."

Talman waited.

"I saw her several days ago in Jericho. Another of my attempts at convincing her to return to Gaza. She would have had a home with my wife and myself."

"I was aware of the visit."

Rahman swung his head to look in Talman's eyes. "That is why you have not called me."

"You can understand my dilemma."

Rahman nodded. "I have let my personal motives interfere with my professional conduct. I apologize to you."

"The affliction is with all of us, Amin." Talman described his torment over allowing Kadar into Jerusalem. "I like Jack Blanchard, and Dr. Masters saved the life of Deborah Hausmann. I allowed those concerns to dictate my decision."

"Then we must both atone for our shortcomings, Jacob. What must we do?"

"I am afraid that Kadar will be received well in the Arab community of Jerusalem. Some may assist him, not knowing what he is about. I need your help."

"You will have it, to whatever extent I can manage." Rahman's eyes changed, softened. "Jacob, she should not be left like that."

"The medical examiner—"

"There is the cleansing . . . the wrapping . . . the . . ." Rahman's voice drifted away, and he turned slightly to face to the east.

"I will talk to the examiner, Amin."

Khalid sat on a blanket near the garage door, a weapon cradled across his lap. He stared into infinity, lost in a private dream. Kadar and Abu were apparently both asleep in the Hummer, Kadar in the backseat and Abu stretched out in the back.

The heat was building up inside the garage, and Masters felt the perspiration dribbling down her back. She was still wearing her lab coat, and it was grimy with the hours of captivity. The sounds of traffic on a nearby street could be heard, but other than that, there hadn't been another noise for hours.

And for the past hour, she estimated, she had been working on the tape across her mouth, following Blanchard's example, rubbing her cheek against her shoulder, catching the edge of the tape, worrying at it.

Blanchard had freed his gag a few minutes before, and he was watching her, nodding his head in encouragement.

Her cheek felt raw from the chafing, but finally, a large corner of the tape did raise. She pressed the adhesive against the fabric of her coat with her mouth, then slowly pulled away.

A bit more. Press it down again.

Pull.

It came half away from her mouth, and she switched to her left shoulder, and worked it completely free. The tape stuck to her shoulder.

"Good girl," Blanchard whispered.

"Are you all right?"

"A few sore spots. I'll get Polly to work on me."

"Stop provoking them, Jack."

"Gives me something to do."

She knew Blanchard had been trying to divert Abu's attention from herself.

"Is that true?"

He knew immediately what she was talking about.

"The water supplies? I hope to hell so, Mel. Talman or someone should have figured it out by now. Anyway, it gives us an excuse for staying alive."

She closed her eyes and imagined the bacteria suspended in the rushing water mains of the city. Into sinks, tubs, showers. Cooked with food. Frozen into ice cubes for the tourists at the hotels. The wards at Mercy Base were horrific enough; hundreds of thousands afflicted with the same disease terrified her. There wasn't enough medical support in the world to meet the crisis. A hundred thousand could die. Surely more, if they couldn't treat them all. Jerusalem would be a ghost town.

"Mel, I hate to ask you this."

"What, Jack? Anything."

"I don't want to leave you alone, but we've got a chance if I do. When Kadar gets ready to act, you give him some excuse for staying behind."

"What if he wants us all to go?"

"Then that won't work."

"What *will* work?"

"Something. I'm working on it."

As soon as Talman and the other guy left, Masters was out the door and gone. One of the women told him he shouldn't leave.

He ignored her.

The first cab he found had an asshole of an Arab driver who didn't understand English, but they finally found the word Sheraton in common, and the driver got him to the Sheraton Jerusalem Plaza on King George Street.

He checked in, took the elevator to the fifth floor, and found his room. He first called the Hilton in Tel Aviv, and told them to find a taxi and send his luggage to Jerusalem. Then he took a long and very hot shower. It seemed as if he couldn't get the damned desert out of his pores.

Then he ordered shrimp and lobster sent to his room, along with a bottle of gin. He ate sitting at the table in a hotel bathrobe and luxuriated in the absence of dirt.

When he was sated, he mixed a second drink and called his father. It didn't matter that it was the middle of the night there.

"H'lo."

"Dad."

"Greg! What the hell happened? I tried to find you all day long."

"It's a long story, Dad. Look, some terrorist group has kidnapped Melanie. That's what I was trying to tell you when this army guy cut us off."

After an uncomfortable silence, Gregory senior asked, "Is she all right?"

"I don't know. They're still looking for her."

"Goddamn it, Greg! Melanie is an American citizen. They can't treat this kidnapping lightly."

"You'd be surprised how lightly they treat it, Dad. Hell, I've been threatened with jail—"

"By whom?"

"The damned army commander. I don't know what in the hell he does, but he apparently swings some weight."

"Why?"

"Damned if I know. They're trying to keep everything hush-hush."

"To hell with that! I'm going to call the senator, then a couple people I know in the State Department."

"Good. I think some pressure would help."

"You raise hell over there."

"I've tried. They don't listen."

"Call the embassy first. If that doesn't work, get hold of someone from CNN."

"Good idea, Dad."

The dial tone sounded in his ear, and he got up to look for telephone directory. Since he already knew how the embassy worked, or didn't, he decided to go right to CNN.

* * *

Kadar awakened at two o'clock. He crawled out of the truck and looked at the captives. They had loosened their gags, but he decided to overlook that fact since they were not screaming their foolish heads off. Both of them watched him in obvious disapproval. They were like vultures, and soon they could perform as vultures do. He would give them bodies.

Badr was sound asleep, his head cocked to one side as he leaned back against the garage door.

He crawled back in the truck, and reaching past the sleeping figure of el-Ziam, retrieved his knapsack. Unzipping it, he reached in for the packets of money and began counting it out. When he had what he felt was adequate, he snapped a rubber band around it, then put the rest back.

Backing out again, he first went to check the bonds of his hostages. Blanchard had been working at his, but unsuccessfully.

"If you want Abu and Khalid to play with you again, you will try to get loose."

"Why don't you untie me and all three of us will play?"

Kadar walked down the garage and kicked Badr on the thigh. His head jerked upward, his eyes flashed as they tried to envision where he was, then belatedly, he jerked the rifle from his lap.

"Get up, Khalid. I have work for you that will keep you awake."

The man struggled stiffly to his feet, and Khalid took the AK-47 from him, then gave him the money.

"Go buy a car for us."

"What? Why should we buy a car? I can steal it, Ibrahim."

Khalid Badr did not have Heusseni's particular skills in the profession. He would end up in the clutches of the police, and Kadar would have neither the car nor the servant.

"We will not attract attention, Khalid."

"Perhaps you should purchase the automobile."

"I am too well known. It must be you."

Badr looked at the money, then shoved it into his pocket. "I will buy it if I do not find something suitable for stealing.

Kadar shrugged in submission. "And buy rubber gloves. Twenty pairs of them."

Badr lay on the floor in front of the door, and Kadar raised it enough for him to slip outside. He pulled it back down and locked it in place.

Looking back at Blanchard and Masters, he saw that they were very interested in what was taking place. But mystified by it, also.

That was just as well. Blanchard always acted as if he knew everything, but he was sadly mistaken.

It was Ibrahim Kadar who could foretell the future.

And he knew it was a dismal future for Blanchard, Masters, and the Jews of Jerusalem.

Talman and Perlmutter flew with Rahman in his Alouette helicopter to Atarot Airport, where Talman commandeered the temporary offices of Levi Avidar. He assumed the general would prefer to find new secret offices in the future over having Rahman present at Shin Bet's communications center or head-quarters.

There were six telephone lines available in the two small offices and the large single one, and all three of them spent several hours making calls. Talman designated one line, called the communications center, and left it open for any reports on the progress of the search. The Shin Bet communications technicians were staying in open contact with the army units conducting the search. He called all of his agents for reports, but the outlying districts seemed unaware of anything momentous in the making. They had heard of the mysterious blockade of Jerusalem, then the even more mysterious retreat of the army.

He called Sam Delray at Mercy Base and told him where he was, in case any of the medical team needed to find him.

Colonel Stein was out, so he called Levi Avidar.

"What is the situation, Jacob?"

He reported the death of Oma Kassim.

"She was of the Sword of God?"

"And a sister-in-law of Amin Rahman, General."

"I see."

"We have worked that out, I think. Rahman is here, on a telephone, attempting to persuade his people to help us."

"That is good. Where is 'here'?"

"I have set up a center in your office at Atarot. Perlmutter is also present."

"That is fine, Jacob. I will send technicians to help you."

"Thank you, sir."

"I went to the hospital to meet and talk with Deborah Haus-mann. She understands why you are unable to visit her."

"I appreciate that, General."

"You concentrate on what you must do."

"Find Kadar."

"Exactly. And if it means . . ."

"I will not make the same mistake again, sir."

"I will be at this telephone. You call if you need assistance Or a final decision."

After the general hung up, Talman returned to calling every one he could think of. He telephoned one of his agents in the city and had him deliver a message to Beit Horon. He kep checking in on the open line to Shin Bet.

"What is the status?"

"There are now two thousand army personnel and over a thousand city policemen involved in the search, Major. The concentration is currently in the Muslim Quarter of the Ol City, as well as in the western district."

Yes. The army and the ministers would want the area aroun the university and the government buildings—the Hakirya dis trict—searched first.

At four-thirty, the door to the office opened without th courtesy of a knock, and he looked up to see Armbruster.

"Dickie?"

"Sam Delray said you'd be here, and I figured out I wasn making much headway on my own. Have you met Cale Perkins Polly Brooks? Bob Timnath? You know Jillian."

They all filed into the room, and Talman wondered wher he was going to put all of them. One of them carried a sac of what looked like soda cans, and another had a tall stack c boxes balanced against his chest.

"I hope you like pizza, Major."
He realized he hadn't eaten since . . .
He couldn't remember.

It was dark outside when Khalid came back and banged on
the garage door. Abu opened it for him, then helped him with
two mesh sacks he was carrying. From the chatter and Kadar's
agitation, Blanchard assumed Kadar had forgotten to order
food, and Khalid had taken it upon himself to do the shopping.

The two lieutenants spilled the bags out on one of the blankets
and began pawing through the goodies. There were a large
number of rubber gloves, and when he saw them, he took a
quick glance at Masters.

She nodded. The implication was not lost on her.

He figured she must be as hungry as he was. And his mouth
and throat were so dry he could barely swallow. Each of them
had been released in late afternoon and allowed to relieve
themselves in the corner on the other side of the Hummer.
When Melanie asked for water, it turned out that Kadar had
none.

This was a master planner.

Blanchard had refrained from making an appropriate comment because, at the time, he wanted to pee, but not in his
pants.

Now he spoke up, "Kadar."

When the man looked up, he said, "Give the doctor something to drink. Please."

Kadar considered the plea for all of three minutes before
muttering something to Abu, who picked up two wide-mouthed
bottles of juice and brought them to the worktable. He twisted
off a cap and tilted the bottle to Melanie's mouth. She drank
hungrily, and finished it in about ten gulps. Abu managed to
cop a few quick feels.

Blanchard got the other bottle. It was a citrus mixture of
some sort, but it was cool, and it relieved his throat.

Abu got carried away with himself, found a loaf of pita, and
ripped off chunks to stuff in their mouths. He got some sexual
excitement out of that exercise, too.

The three Arabs took their time eating, talking among themselves, and Blanchard thought, screwing up their courage.

Blanchard had no idea of the time, but thought it was around midnight, when Kadar came over and stood in front of them.

"You," he said to Masters, "are going with the others. You will do this because I will kill Blanchard if you do not do exactly as I direct."

In the weak light from the overhead bulbs, Blanchard saw the gleam in Abu's eye. The bushy-faced Arab was imagining a bit of recreation in addition to his chores.

Blanchard would have preferred to get Melanie away from Kadar if he thought she'd have any chance at all of escaping Abu and Khalid. He didn't see much of a hopeful percentage in that happening, though. Melanie would treat wounds before she'd inflict them.

"For what reason?" Masters asked him.

"If you are stopped, you will identify yourself as a doctor. You are examining water facilities for purity."

"That won't work," she said.

Kadar was quick to take offense. His face reddened, and he said, "It will work if I say it will work."

"I don't have my purse."

"Purse? What is this of the purse?"

"I have no identification with me. There is nothing that says who I am or that I am truly a doctor. Who is going to believe this dirty lab coat, in the condition it's in?"

Good girl, Mel! You've been thinking about this.

Kadar considered this for a minute, then turned to Blanchard. "You will go."

Old Abu lost his grin. He wasn't very interested in Blanchard.

"And if I say no?"

"You have already experienced the wrath of my companions."

Those idiots couldn't punch their way through a Japanese house. Blanchard thought he might have a cracked rib, and his stomach and arm muscles were sore, but Abu and Khalid didn't know much about swinging a fist. A problem when one didn't grow up in America.

"And I have the woman. I will not kill her, but I will carve your name in her forehead. The scars will show forever."

"Untie me so I can work the cramps out."

"When it is time."

Kadar turned and went back to the blanket to settle on his knees next to Khalid. Blanchard watched closely as he removed the black plastic box from his pocket and picked at the clasp until it opened. One by one, he lifted clear small vials from the box, along with cotton batting. He lined them up on the blanket, and Blanchard counted seventeen of them.

He took a quick glance at Melanie, who nodded.

Selecting four of the vials, he wrapped them in some of the batting, then handed them to Khalid, who obviously did not want to take them. He did finally, putting them in the pocket of his work shirt and buttoning the flap. He took four pairs of the rubber gloves and shoved them in the back pocket of his jeans. The gloves were bright yellow, intended for household chores.

Kadar said something in Arabic, and Khalid and Abu picked up their AK-47s and ejected the magazines, checked them over, then, rammed them back in place. They ran the bolts and set the selectors to some mode of firing.

Then they got up and climbed into the rear seat of the Hummer.

Kadar came to the workbench, told Blanchard to lean forward, and spent time untwisting the wire around his wrists. When it came undone, Blanchard felt the tingle of increased circulation. The wires hadn't been clamped too tight, but tight enough.

"You will untie your leg yourself," Kadar said, pulling his pistol free.

It was difficult to get to, sitting on the bench like he was, and his fingers felt clumsy. Bending over didn't help his bruised stomach muscles. After a few minutes of forcing his fingers to grip and untwist the wire, his leg came free, and he pushed himself off the bench.

He was dizzy for a moment, and he spread his legs to maintain his balance. He tried a few tentative steps.

"Where are we going?" he asked.

"You will go where Khalid tells you to go. Get in the truck."

"You'd better give me my ID and passcard."

Backing away slowly, but keeping the Beretta trained on Blanchard's midsection, Kadar reached his pack and bent to rifle through it. He came up with the folder and the card, and and tossed them at Blanchard's feet.

He picked them up and slid them into his hip pocket. "What about my wallet? They might ask for a driver's license."

Kadar got that, too, but only gave him the license. The sucker didn't want him running around town with money, having a good time.

"Get in."

He turned and winked at Melanie, and she gave him a smile that he thought was a lot braver than she felt.

He climbed behind the wheel. The keys were still in it.

Abu let him know where he was by jamming the muzzle of the rifle into Blanchard's neck.

Kadar went to the corner, shut off the lights, then opened the garage door.

Blanchard pulled his door shut, hit the ignition, and revved the engine. Slapping the shift into reverse, he backed out, turning tight to avoid running into the garage on the other side of the alley.

He pulled the lights on as the garage door was going down, and the last thing he saw was Melanie's face.

She wasn't smiling now.

Her face was the picture of anguish, and he hoped it wasn't the last thing he would remember about her because he was going to remember for a long time.

Eighteen

After turning the lights on, Kadar sat cross-legged on the blanket and leaned back against the wall. He felt good, perhaps a little on edge, worrying about how el-Ziam would carry out his instructions.

But it was good.

It was under way.

Soon, within weeks, after the incubation period, the world would know his power and the power of Allah.

One man against the multitudes! Oh, how they would cry his name!

Zionism would fall for allowing Jerusalem to die, as would the corrupt state of the Palestinian Authority, and in the search for leadership, his people would seek out the most powerful.

And he would do all he could to help them. It was his destiny:

In the Name of God, the Merciful, the Compassionate.
Praise be to God, the Lord of the Worlds,
The Merciful One, the Compassionate One,
Master of the Day of Doom.
Thee alone we serve, to Thee alone we cry for help.
Guide us in the straight path

The path of them Thou has Blessed.
Not of those with whom Thou are angry
Nor of those who go astray.

The *Fattiha,* the Lord's Prayer of Islam, was the opening surah of the Koran, and it was recited for each new beginning. This, indeed, was a new beginning, and Kadar closed his eyes while he recited it to himself.

What truly impressed him about Khabanni's weapon was that it worked like a neutron bomb. Only people died. Important things, like the Temple Mount and its treasures, would be unaffected. All that was required was an army of labor to remove the bodies to the desert and burn them. That army would rally to his cause, and they would march victorious into *their* city, and Islam would spread throughout the land. Whatever remained of the Jewish nation would wither before their advance.

Oh, glorious day!

He almost shouted it aloud, then remembered the woman.

He looked up to see her staring at him. She sat silently on the bench, but the set of her mouth and the look in her eyes told him of her disdain. He could wipe it away in seconds, replace it with abject terror if he chose to do so.

A few well-placed jabs of the fingers.

One of the tools on the floor.

Or even a drop of the bacteria placed in her mouth. Let her experience the revenge of Allah, lingering over days and weeks.

Yes! Revenge!

A woman who did not know her place, who strutted with self-important airs, who claimed to be a learned one and yet spoke lies to the people, should be one of the first to taste the vengeance of Allah.

But there was plenty of time. He would use her as the lever against Blanchard. Or perhaps she would serve another purpose before he had completed the dispersal. A new image had come into his mind recently, an image of early ritual, and he wondered if his new beginning should not be celebrated with a rite taken from the days of greater glory.

He looked over at her.

Yes.

She would be a fitting sacrifice. An American from the satanic America. An infidel deserving of Allah's attention.

There was no hurry. El-Ziam would soon return, and Kadar would have a more complete picture of the security conditions present in the city.

And there was the . . .

But wait!

The Jew, Talman, would have determined by now that he was in Jerusalem simply because he knew Blanchard was here. The search would have intensified.

Abu el-Ziam and Khalid Badr were not absolutely reliable. He should have left one of them here with the woman and gone himself to accomplish the task. Surely, if they were stopped, el-Ziam and Badr would mount a ferocious resistance, but Kadar thought that it would be short-lived.

And if Blanchard escaped unharmed, or at least, still able to talk . . .

Blanchard knew where the garage was.

Kadar berated himself for not blindfolding Blanchard before approaching the garage. Blanchard was driving, so the thought had completely slipped his mind.

Abruptly, he started patting his pockets, then found the key to the car Khalid Badr had stolen. To his good fortune, the key had been in it, otherwise he would be required to hot-wire the ignition, and that was something at which he was not adept. Had the key not been in it, it was unlikely that Badr could have stolen it.

He should bring the car to the garage, bring it inside.

Unfortunately, Badr had not told him what kind of car it was, nor the color. He had also not mentioned where he had parked it, though it must be close by. He would have to go around the block, searching for a lock which fit his key.

Pushing himself to his feet, he glanced at the woman.

She would scream her foolish head off if he left her alone.

Kadar walked over to her, stepping carefully around the tools littering the floor. The roll of tape was on the floor under the bench and he picked it up.

"What are you doing?"

"We must insure your silence," he told her, then ripped off a long piece of tape, placed it over her mouth, and wrapped it clear around her head. It would tear out hair when it was removed, but she would not rub this gag away.

He was pleased with the change in her eyes.

The superiority was gone.

Some of Amin Rahman's assistants had arrived earlier, but by then Talman had commandeered the office suite next door—belonging to the operations department of an air-freight company, along with its eight telephone lines. The deputy chief had moved his people in there, and Talman had assigned the IDF army technicians to telephones in Avidar's space. Perlmutter was supervising them. The PMAT personnel were not much help except for Weiss, since she knew the languages, but they were so intensely following every report that flowed in that he wouldn't ask them to leave.

Air traffic for Atarot was unaffected by Talman's crisis. Through the windows in the outer office, he could hear the scream of jet engines as airplanes took off.

Rahman came from the hall and sat down with Talman and Armbruster.

"I have six hundred policemen coming from Gaza City."

Talman made himself a note. "I will inform the army patrols so they will not think that an invasion is imminent."

Rahman smiled grimly. "I should deploy them to the Muslim sector?"

"If you would, Amin. They will be more likely to get responses from the citizens. Perhaps you could split them up and also cover the Armenian Quarter?"

"I will inform the commanders."

Weiss stuck her head through the doorway from the larger office and said, "Major, there is a Colonel Stein on line two."

"Thank you." He punched the button. "Major Talman, sir."

"A warning, Jacob. Do not talk to any reporters."

"Fortunately, I have not seen one, Colonel."

"That is because they are all here. That is, they are down the hall, laying siege to General Avidar. The leader seems to be a CNN correspondent, who claims he has inside information from Gregory Masters. He is looking for corroboration, he says.''

"Oh, my God! I forgot all about Masters. He is supposed to be at my agency.''

"Apparently not. My report says he is now registered at the Sheraton Hotel.''

"Should I have him picked up, sir?''

"We're a little late, I think, Jacob. You have an advantage in that the reporters seem to be unaware of your presence at the airport. What of the search?''

Talman looked at the large map of the city he had tacked to the wall. Pins with colored heads denoted the areas where the search was under way or completed. The army headquarters had a more detailed map, of course, but he wanted to have a general picture for himself.

"The Jewish Quarter is all but complete, sir. Perhaps five percent of the city. Whoever is in command of the search started there since it is an obvious target of Kadar. But other sectors are undergoing door-to-door examination. Hakirya,''—the university and government region—''Ramat Eshkol, and Kirya Shmuel all have large concentrations of troops.''

"General Schweiss has responsibility for the search,'' Stein informed him. "But no sighting of Kadar?''

"Not a trace.''

"All right. Keep me informed. Oh! One other thing.''

"Sir?''

"The scientists think they have a method for cleaning areas contaminated with the bacteria.''

"Think they do?''

"Many tests are required, I understand. But they have an antibiotic in granular form with which they are treating the water tank at Mar Saba. If it clears the bacteria, we may have some hope of restoring the water source.''

"But nothing of a preventative nature?''

"I do not think so, Jacob.''

"Thank you, Colonel.''

Talman replaced the telephone and told the others of the development.

Polly Brooks, sitting with Timnath on the couch at the side of the room, said, "It's not going to help those people in the wards."

"No, Miss Brooks, it's not."

"I just called. Three people died earlier. A woman and two teenagers."

Talman shook his head in sadness. "I am sincerely appalled."

"Let's get this bloody sucker," Armbruster said. "I feel about as useful as a . . ."

He flashed a look at Brooks and gave up his colorful image.

Instead, he looked at the map. "This is a rotten city to search."

Rahman agreed with him. "It is not a perfect grid, is it, Dickie? However, you are accustomed to towns not laid out in the classic American way, are you not?"

"In Ulster, and all over England, people simply added streets wherever they thought a street might be useful, and they've done it over the centuries," Armbruster said. "It is the same here, and there's not much logic to it."

"So you mount a search by a different rationale than just marching over ground, right?" Talman asked.

"I can't fault your people, Major. We'd probably do it the same way, by target priority. You've covered the Jewish sector, and you're working on the government area. I'd think Kadar would go after them first."

"But you're worried about something?"

"I get the feeling that once an area's been cleared, and the troops move on, there isn't much preventing Kadar from sneaking into the clear area."

"That bothers me, also," Rahman said.

"We're leaving guards behind, according to what I've been told," Talman said. "But I suppose you're both right. That may be inadequate. Do you have anything I could suggest to the search commander?"

"I think we may have to conscript the people. Maybe send an airplane over to drop flyers Alert them somehow, Major, and get them working for us."

"I've been trying to find Beit Horon. He could help in that regard."

"How much do we reveal, though?" Rahman asked. "If we tell them the true nature of the emergency, we may create the chaos we are trying to avoid."

"Can you rally the Muslim community, Amin? I mean, they may not like hunting one of their own."

"I can but try. The trouble is, most do not understand what is at stake, either in the form of the threat or in terms of foreign aid to the Authority. It may depend upon what we decide to tell them."

"I'll call Avidar and see how much he wants to reveal," Talman said. "But I think the answer will be 'nothing.'"

They were on the major artery of the Jericho Road, headed south through the eastern fringe of the city. There were a few vehicles out, mainly trucks hauling produce and other goods. Headed for market, Blanchard guessed. He had seen two military patrols, but they had been ignored.

Approaching the intersection with Suleiman, he asked, "Where are we going?"

"I will tell you."

"Sometime soon? Should I turn here?"

"No!" The muzzle of the AK-47 reinforced the negative, jabbing in behind his right ear. Abu was going to make him mad sooner or later.

He breezed on through the intersection. Above on the right and a few blocks ahead, he could see the lights around the Temple Mount. They would be passing to the east of it.

On the west side of the mount was the Jewish Quarter, so he figured they were bypassing that. Or coming around to enter it from the south.

Blanchard had all but completed his inventory of military goodies. From a mirror view, when passing under a streetlight, he thought the communications gear in the back was a loss. He knew the satellite antenna was gone, but the top black box was tilted, probably kicked by Khalid and Abu when they were hiding back there.

The instrument-panel radios were intact, he thought. They were turned off, but the microphone still hung in its clip.

He followed the curve of Jericho Road to the right.

What remained for him to check on was whether Armbruster had installed *all* of the equipment from the wrecked command Hummer into this one.

"Abu, I've got to adjust the seat."

The man could have said no. He gave a little twitch with the barrel of the rifle, and Blanchard assumed that was to be taken as approval.

He used his right hand to search for the seat-adjustment lever.

And the Uzi that was supposed to be hanging under the seat.

He found the lever.

But not the Uzi.

So he just scooted the seat back a couple inches.

"All right! Now we're getting somewhere!" Masters said aloud.

He swirled the gin in his glass, listening with satisfaction to the click of ice cubes, and watched the television screen.

In the middle of the night, the CNN channel had abandoned its routine news reports and jumped live to its reporter at an Israeli army headquarters.

Masters had told his story to the same reporter, and the man had even shown up at the hotel and taped the interview with Masters. He fully expected to see himself on the screen shortly.

The on-camera talent barely got to make his own introduction before the view switched to three guys in uniform emerging from a doorway and advancing on a podium. The Israeli flag hung on a standard to the rear. The bright lights for the camera made the men squint their eyes.

The voice-over introduced the viewers to the silver-haired distinguished man who stepped up to the microphone: ". . . General Levi Avidar of the IDF."

The reporter had said something about Avidar, something about him being head of an intelligence outfit, but it was against Israeli law to identify him as such. What a crock of shit!

"Good morning, ladies and gentlemen. A very early morning."

A little titter in the group.

"I will make a statement regarding the overall situation, and then General Schweiss will brief you on the current search.

"Yesterday afternoon, a man who claims to be the leader of a terrorist group called the Sword of God, Ibrahim Kadar, kidnapped two foreign nationals. We presume he is assisted by two known associates, Khalid Badr and Abu el-Ziam. Pictures of the three will be provided to you. A fourth associate, Oma Kassim, has been found shot to death, but the circumstances around her death are not yet known.

"The victims of the kidnapping are Dr. Melanie Masters, chief of medicine, and Mr. Jack Blanchard, program administrator, for the World Health Organization's Palestine Medical Assistance Team. They were abducted from the team's encampment near Mar Saba."

What! The son of a bitch didn't even mention my name!

Masters was truly offended. If he hadn't put up a struggle, he'd be one of Kadar's victims, too. Not to mention that the publicity wouldn't hurt his political chances, either. This damned telecast would be beamed all around the world. Sure, the first concern was Melanie, but he had learned to take advantage of every opportunity, and international news was an opportunity if he'd ever seen one.

"The Sword of God has not yet claimed responsibility, but it is believed the hostages are alive and located somewhere within the city of Jerusalem."

The view switched to photographs of the terrorists. One by one, they were shown on the screen. Kadar didn't look very impressive, just shaggy. The full-bearded one, el-Ziam, looked merely unkempt. Badr's eyes were vacant, as if he were slow witted. Masters hadn't seen the last two, of course, but looking at Kadar's picture, he thought he might have missed an opportunity. One fist in the face could have leveled Kadar, and then he wouldn't have to be subjected to all this shit.

"I know you have all noted the search teams combing the city, and I'll let General Schweiss explain the mechanics of the search."

Avidar stepped away from the podium as a voice yelled from off camera.

"General! What does this have to do with the quarantine a Mar Saba?"

He stepped back to the microphone.

"Beyond the fact that Dr. Masters is in charge of treatment I have no ideas about a relationship."

"And why is there a quarantine? No one has answered tha question."

"I am not a medical expert, miss. What I have been told i that the primary well in the village is contaminated and it ha affected most of the people living there. The medical personne have responsibility and the proper expertise, and your question are best directed to them."

"But . . . but, we aren't allowed—"

The CNN reporter interrupted. "Dr. Masters's husband say that dozens of people are dying, General."

The son of a bitch! Dr. Masters's husband! I've got a name goddamn it!

"I don't know where he gets his information," Avidar said "Not from the same place I get mine. There have been fou deaths." He referred to some papers he held in his hand, the provided the names and ages of the four victims.

"The Sword of God issued a statement about a plagu descending on Mar Saba."

"The Sword of God is composed of people who did not g past secondary school, sir. They wouldn't recognize a plagu and this is not a plague."

"Dr. Masters's husband said that he was threatened wit prison if he left the quarantined area."

My name, damn it!

"Is he in prison?" Avidar asked.

"No."

"Is he at Mar Saba?"

"No, he is in a hotel."

Avidar shrugged, then said, "Our priority concern is wit the hostages held by Ibrahim Kadar. That is where we ar directing our efforts."

He walked away from the podium.

One of the other generals came forward to explain what the army and police were doing about Kadar.

One reporter, who identified himself as being with the *London Times*, asked, "What effect is this kidnapping going to have on the peace accords and the relationship with the Palestinian Authority, General Schweiss?"

The third man stepped forward, and proved not to be a general at all, but the chief of the Palestinian Police.

"We do not anticipate any change in relationships, sir. In fact, in unprecedented cooperation, the Palestinian Police Force is working side by side with Jerusalem police and the Israeli Defense Forces in this search. Some six hundred officers have joined the search, and more are being organized. Deputy Chief Amin Rahman is in charge of the operation and is working closely with IDF commanders. We do not condone the actions of Ibrahim Kadar or his organization."

There were a lot more questions, and when the conference ended fifteen minutes later, the CNN reporter hadn't run one inch of his interview with Masters.

Following the press conference, the CNN anchorwoman reported some background on Melanie and on Blanchard's military career. So he was a Marine colonel, so what? Big fucking hero! If he was so great, why were he and Melanie in the clutches of some crackpot like Kadar?

In neither report was one mention of Greg Masters and his anguished wait for word of his wife.

Bastards!

As far as he could tell, no one was going to accomplish anything of value.

He would have to do it himself.

Clicking off the TV, he stood, shed his robe, and headed for the bed. The first thing in the morning, he'd get out there and kick butt.

They were no longer on the Jericho Road.

In fact, Blanchard wasn't quite sure where they were, except that it was south of the Old City. There'd been a sign a block back, but it was in Hebrew and didn't help him a bit.

The road wasn't paved, and though there were houses (a
darkened at this time of the morning) along both sides of th
street, none of them issued a curious spectator. The road wasn'
in the best of repair, either. He was dodging chuckholes an
eroded cracks, and holding his speed down.

There weren't any streetlights, either, and the Hummer'
headlights washed the faces of the buildings as he swerve
around the pitted street. Several blocks ahead, he saw a groupin
of bright lights and maybe some high fencing. He suspecte
they were nearing a water-treatment plant.

Not good.

He hit a small hole, the truck bounced, and the muzzle c
Abu's rifle raked down the back of his neck. He felt lucky th
damned thing didn't go off.

His thoughts kept flashing to Masters.

Damn. I was just getting to like her.

Running around in the night, looking for water, wasn't hel
ing her a bit. He tried to think of things he could do for he
but finally shut off that train. He had to do for himself, first

For lack of time, and for the conviction that he wasn't helpin
either of these assholes get anywhere near water, he picked th
first large chuckhole he saw coming up and steered toward i

The right wheel slammed into it, the fender went dow
Blanchard bounced upward in his seat, Abu shoved the rifl
forward as he tipped sideways, and Blanchard felt hard ste
bang his skull.

And he heard a strange thud. Almost directly under him.

"Watch where you go!"

Was it a rock hitting the floor pan?

"Sorry," he professed to Abu.

Then worked his left foot backward, arched his ankle, an
slipped his toe under his seat.

And felt something solid.

It moved when he pushed with his toe.

He hoped Armbruster had merely hung the Uzi in a differe
position, and that he was playing footsie with lethal hardwar

He moved his foot to the clutch, then shifted to first ge
and let the Hummer slow some. Dropped his left hand off th
wheel and let it dangle between his legs.

Nice big crack in the road.

He whipped the wheel left as if he were trying to avoid it.

In the mirror he saw both Abu and Khalid leaning to the right.

Leaning forward, he reached down, found the muzzle with his fingers, gripped it, and sat back as he pulled it up between his thighs.

Kept checking the mirror.

His captors regained their balance and stared forward through the windshield.

The lights were closer now, a block away. Squat, flat-roofed buildings surrounded by chain-link fence and swamped in light. Filtration ponds.

Not one damned guard in sight.

Fumbled the gun around, found the safety, found the trigger.

Kept it low, between his legs, in the dark.

There.

He coughed aloud to cover the sound of the safety clicking off.

"This is unexpected," Abu said, probably to Khalid. "There are no security precautions."

"It may be a trap," the cautious Khalid said.

"Stop here. We will watch for a while."

The emphasis was a jab with the gun.

Blanchard clutched and let the Humvee roll to a stop.

Then he let the clutch pop loose, tromped the accelerator, twisted in his seat to throw his back against the door, and brought the Uzi up.

Both Abu and Khalid were tossed backward against the backseat when the Hummer leaped ahead. Khalid put one round from his Kalashnikov through the roof.

Blanchard fired a burst of three into Abu's right chest, extremely conscious of what was in the left buttoned pocket of his shirt.

Abu squealed as he died, his finger tripping off a short burst from the AK-47, which shattered the plastic of the rear-door window.

As he tried to get his assault rifle in position, Khalid took a second to pass horrified eyes over his dying partner, which was his last look.

Blanchard put three rounds into Khalid's shocked face. Blood and gore went everywhere. The right rear-quarter plastic window shattered.

The engine had died, but the echo of the gunshots still reverberated around the cabin. Cordite stung his nose, and white smoke filled the interior.

Pushing himself upright, Blanchard reached around the seat and checked for pulses in the two bodies sprawled on the back seat.

There was blood everywhere. Abu's chest gurgled—lung punctured. Khalid had no face, and locating his carotid artery swamped Blanchard's hand in blood. No pulses.

Nice result for a left-handed hip shot. He'd never fired lefty before, but he hadn't had the time to switch. Plus, the range was about two feet. Difficult to miss.

He got to his knees and searched through Abu's pockets, found the vials still secure in their batting, and reached over to put them in the glove compartment. He wiped his bloody hand on Khalid's pants.

Lights came on in the nearby houses when he grabbed the microphone.

He clicked the radio on, got a carrier wave . . .

And then had another thought.

He didn't particularly want two battalions of trigger-happy soldiers bearing down on one garage in one alley. Not with Melanie inside.

Repositioning himself in his seat, he cranked the engine to life and whipped around in a U-turn. A few heads peering through windows. One guy had started out his front door, but reversed direction as soon as the truck lights found him.

He didn't worry a hell of a lot about chuckholes on his way back down the road, and he kept the accelerator floored in second gear.

Hang on, Mel! One lone cavalry on the way.

When Jericho Road came up, he skipped the stop sign and hit pavement in one screeching slide, straightened out, and gunned it up through the gears. He passed two semi-trucks and a blue Buick before reaching the left turn onto Kaled Ibn el Waleed. Coming from the other way on Jericho Road was an army Jeep, and he saw it whip in behind him, a block back, accelerating after him.

Please, God, don't let them have a siren.

He took the turn into the alley at minimum speed, locked up the brakes, and killed the ignition.

Grabbing the Uzi, he slid out and ran down the alley, counting the garages.

Three ... four ... five ...

The blue-and-white one had its door up and the lights on.

And it was empty.

Nineteen

Blanchard stood in the open door of the garage and felt sick. Nothing.

The tools were scattered over the floor, but the workbench was conspicuously vacant. The blankets and backpacks were missing.

A frightened command in Hebrew bounced off the garage doors of the alley.

He couldn't interpret it, but he knew what was wanted.

Crouching, he laid the Uzi on the floor. Then he held his arms to either side.

Two soldiers, who looked old enough to have just left their high-school proms, moved out of the dark. They had their own versions of the Uzi. Aimed at his back.

"Anyone speak English?" he asked.

Apparently not.

Taking care to move his hand slowly, he risked jumpy nerves to reach into his hip pocket and come up with his ID. He heaved it toward the closest soldier, who retrieved it. He was careful to keep his weapon aligned on Blanchard.

"Ah! Blanchard! Jack Blanchard!"

The relief was evident in the voice, and Blanchard lowered his arms and turned to face them so they could see his face.

"Jack Blanchard," the other one agreed.

When he smiled, they smiled back, so he walked back to the Hummer.

Opening the door, he reached inside for the microphone. He pointed to the back, and one of the soldiers opened the rear door.

Blanchard flipped on the overhead light.

The soldier gagged.

The other one took a look, his face went red, and he pursed his mouth.

"Anyone standing by at Mercy Base?"

The response was instant.

"Jack! That you?"

"Me, Sam."

"You all right? Where's Melanie?"

"I'm fine, and he's still got her. Is Talman there?"

"He's at Atarot. They've got some office there."

"Okay, that's where I'm going."

"Jesus, Jack! Tell me what happened."

"Promise to update you later, Sam. I've got to get moving."

He tossed the mike back inside, shut off the interior lights, and slammed the doors shut. Going back to the garage, he picked up his Uzi, then pulled the door down. Who knew what kind of evidence was still in there?

The soldiers had regained some composure by the time he got back to them.

"Atarot?"

"Airport? Yes."

"Take me there."

With a little sign language, he got them all in their Jeep, backed out of the alley and on the way to the airport.

They had a red light behind the grille, and the driver was happy to use it, though there wasn't any traffic worth worrying about.

They also had a radio, and they used it, so anyone with an interest was standing outside the office building when the Jeep pulled up and parked.

Jillian Weiss flew into his arms and kissed him full on th
mouth.

Armbruster stood on the curb next to Bob Timnath an
nodded slowly at him. Polly Brooks came up right behin
Weiss, giving him a hug that inflamed the back of his neck
where Abu had frequently rested his rifle muzzle.

"Hey, guys! We've still got work to do."

"I am certainly glad to see you, Jack," Talman said. "Yo
are alone?"

Rahman stepped off the curb and offered his hand, an
Blanchard shook it, relieved to not get into Arabic hugs.

"Khalid and Abu couldn't make it." Blanchard briefl
explained their fates.

"But Dr. Masters . . . ?"

"Kadar's still got her."

"So. Nothing has changed. Moshe, will you call Genera
Avidar, Colonel Stein, and the search commander and brin
them up to date? I will go to this garage."

Most of them wanted to go to the garage.

Kadar had not been gone long after Blanchard drove awa
with Badr and el-Ziam. He was back in fifteen minutes, drivin
a rusty blue Saab into the garage. He seemed in a great hurry
and Masters wasn't certain why.

The first thing he did was untie her leg and push her off th
bench. He didn't untie her wrists, and her arms ached to sprea
and release the tension on her muscles. It was all she could d
to stand upright as the feeling returned to her leg.

"Stand there. Do not move," he ordered.

With the tape stuck fast across her mouth, she wasn't abou
to answer him. The only thing that gave her hope was that h
seemed to want her alive. She no longer hoped for more tha
that.

So she remained in place while he gathered blankets, bundle
and knapsacks, tossing them in the back of the car. Then h
got a very puzzled look on his face, finally smiled as if
himself, and pulled one of the packs back out of the car. H
came up with a pencil and a piece of paper. He spent tin

composing, kneeling on the floor, pushing the pencil around, developing Arabic characters.

He looked like a child, completely immersed in the pictures he was drawing.

And while he was, Masters looked down at the floor. The tools were spread over the concrete floor. At her feet was a burst packet of . . . what? Allen wrenches, she thought they were called. She shoved them around with the toe of her right foot.

Her left leg was numb after being tied in the same place for so long. Hot needles of recirculation shot through it. She balanced on her left leg.

Kadar took his piece of paper over to the wall and impaled it on a nail halfway driven into a stud.

"Come here."

She followed him to the back of the car, where he opened the trunk.

"Get in!"

She shook her head negatively.

"Whore! Do as I say!"

His right hand caught her on the nape of the neck, gripped it so tightly she wanted to scream, and shoved her forward. Her knees slammed into the bumper, and she tilted forward and landed on her shoulder inside the trunk. He scooped up her legs and shoved them in behind her. She barely had time to squirm her feet out of the way before he slammed the lid.

Within a minute, the car started, and she felt it moving.

She was in a half-fetal position, her knees bent, and she braced her feet in anticipation of sliding around. It didn't happen; Kadar drove conservatively.

She had never been afraid of the dark, but this seemed so total. It would be exactly what Kadar wanted, of course, so she fought the urge to give into the terror.

All she could think of was that Harry Houdini had once said the secret to his success was that locks were designed to keep people out, rather than in. But in the blackness of the trunk, she couldn't even see the latch of the trunk lid, much less get at it with her hands tied. She kept working her wrists, but didn't feel one bit of slack.

She worried about Blanchard. What if they killed him? She would be left all alone, and she didn't know if she coul cope. Masters was surprised at how much Blanchard's strengt bolstered her.

And her family at Mercy base—Dickie, Jillian, Sam, Lars Dean, Lon, Deidre, Polly . . . They would be worried, and sh didn't want to cause them pain.

Greg. What an ass he made of himself when he was out c his element. He thought the entire world ran by the rules h had learned from his father, and it did not. There was a pa of her that still loved him, but it was the part that had adore his easy charm, his comfort with the elite, his ambition. Sh had felt so complete letting him deal with the details while sh concentrated on her practice, her continuing medical educatio and her fit in the medical society.

She knew he wasn't responding well to her strike for indepe dence, and she suspected he wouldn't handle her abductio well, either. A year ago she could have predicted him. Toda he was a cipher. She didn't know what he would do. It mad her fearful, both for herself and for him. She didn't want hi to be hurt in any way.

Masters didn't want herself hurt, either, and she realize she had been relying heavily on Jack Blanchard. He had th experience, and he appeared so cool, so composed, so full c potential for retaliation against Kadar. And now that he wa gone, her resolve had waned.

She couldn't even remember how many hours had gone b At least thirty. Hostages were supposed to grow close to, begi to identify with their captors over time. She couldn't imagin that occurring with her. They were such pigs. The memory c Kadar shooting Oma stayed with her, making him much mo frightening.

Thirty hours.

From the initial appearance of Kadar, she had assumed h captivity would be short-lived. It was simply a mistake in tim to be corrected shortly.

Now, she was beginning to wonder. For strange and unex plained reasons, Arab terrorists hung on to their hostages fe abnormal lengths of time. Years.

She couldn't face that.

And she didn't know what she could do about it.

Jack, don't do anything foolish. Come back to me!

After ten minutes the car drew to a stop, and the engine was shut off. She heard the door slam and waited for the trunk lid to be raised.

It stayed in place, and she heard footsteps receding. A hard surface, concrete or asphalt. She thought they were still in the city.

It was very quiet.

She struggled with her bindings. This would be the perfect time to get away!

Another fifteen minutes went by, then she heard footsteps. She held her breath.

The lid popped open, and Kadar stood there, grinning down at her. His white teeth in the dark bewhiskered face were almost Cheshire catlike in appearance. It was all an Alice adventure. Wasn't it?

It was still dark out. There was a streetlamp a block away, but the narrow street they were in was cramped with buildings butted one to another, and darkness wrapped all of it. Masters blinked her eyes.

Kadar reached into the trunk, got his arm under her back, and roughly pulled her out of the cramped space. He stood her on her feet, slammed the trunk, and staying behind her, grabbed her wrist and shoved her ahead of him.

Over the curb, across a sidewalk, and then staying in the shadows, they walked for a half block. When they reached his destination, she found it was a concrete-faced structure, the door recessed deeply. Kadar reached around her, prodded the door open, and then pushed her into the blackness inside.

She stumbled over something soft, fought to keep her balance, and then recognized what she knew all too well. The acrid tang of fresh blood.

She wanted to scream, but the gag restrained her. She rotated, prepared to dash past Kadar, in an attempt to reach the street.

The door closed, eliminating the graying rectangle of light from the street.

A few seconds later, an overhead light came on.

She looked down and saw the body. A middle-aged man pajamas, his throat gashed wide open.

Immediately she knew there was no hope for him.

And none for her.

Talman decided he had a question.

"Jack, I assume they had the bacteria with them?"

"Oh, shit! Left it in the Hummer."

He understood how Blanchard might have other things his mind, namely Masters.

"Let's go!" Armbruster yelled, heading for one of the Hur vees parked at the curb. Blanchard spun around and race around the front of the truck for the passenger side. The Amer can was still carrying an Uzi submachine gun, but Talma thought he wouldn't mention it at the moment.

"Come along, Amin," Talman said. To the two soldiers, I said, "You will follow in your Jeep."

He and Rahman crawled into the back of Armbruster's truc and when the dust of Armbruster's rapid departure settled, I looked back to see the other Humvee behind them, follow by the army Jeep. Timnath, Brooks, Weiss, and two oth PMAT personnel were in the second WHO truck.

The supposedly well-oiled IDF response team was certain peopled with strangers, Talman thought. Looking at Rahma then himself, he thought of Neil Simon's *The Odd Coup* Nothing fit here.

Rahman asked, "Jack, the woman at the farmhouse? I you . . . ?"

"Kadar shot her, Amin. I think she was arguing with hi but it was in Arabic so I didn't get the gist of it. He just pull out a Beretta and put her away. Her name was Oma, I think

"I see. Thank you."

Blanchard looked back at Talman, but Talman just shrugg his shoulders. He would explain it later.

"Dickie," Blanchard said, "you don't know how happy was to find this Uzi under the seat."

"I don't pray much, Jack, but I was praying you'd rememb to look. Where the bloody hell are we going?"

"Grab a right, here."

Between giving instructions to Armbruster, Blanchard
related the story of his kidnapping. The part where Gregory
Masters was involved did not agree with what Masters had
said, but Talman did not question Blanchard's version.

"You say you counted seventeen of the vials?" Rahman
asked.

"Right, and four are in the other Hummer. And, Jesus! That's
another thing! Do you know when we got close to that water-
treatment plant, there was absolutely no security on it, Jacob?"

Talman groaned. Another slipup. "Does your UHF radio
have two-thirty-seven-point-four on it?"

"I can find it."

Blanchard handed him the microphone over the back of the
seat and punched in the new frequency.

The communications specialist monitoring the radio patched
him through to Colonel Stein.

"I just heard about Blanchard from Moshe, Jacob."

"He is here with me, and he makes an excellent suggestion,
Colonel."

"Which is?"

"We should deploy guard units to every water-treatment
facility, pumping station, and water-main access in the city."

"Absolutely! This should have been obv . . . ask Mr. Blanchard if he would like to take your position in military intelligence,
Jacob? Or mine?"

Blanchard shook his head, but he was not yet smiling.

"This is the street, Dickie. Slow down a little, and grab the
second alley."

Armbruster turned into the narrow alley and abruptly braked
to avoid running into the other Humvee parked there.

They spilled out of the Humvee as the other vehicles pulled
up behind them.

Blanchard led the way, pulling open a door and turning on
the overhead interior lights.

Talman looked in at the bodies. Flies swarmed about them.
The aroma of spilled blood, urine, and simple body odor was
overwhelming.

Armbruster said, "That's a picture worth putting in my scrap book. I'm sorry I don't have my camera along."

Blanchard opened the dashboard compartment and retrieved a bundle of cotton. He brought it around the truck and pulled the batting apart to show Talman, Rahman, and Armbruster the vials.

"I think we want to be damned careful with these things," Blanchard said. "In the second before I shot Abu, I recall thinking I didn't want to hit him in the pocket."

"I am thankful you did not," Rahman said.

Talman turned around and waved to one of the soldiers, who trotted up to him. "Call your headquarters and ask for an army forensics unit, city police, and the medical examiner to be sent to this address. They will need an ambulance."

"Yes, sir."

The soldier ran back toward his vehicle as Blanchard rewrapped the vials. He offered them to Talman, who took them with great reluctance. He placed them in his shirt pocket and buttoned the flap.

"Where is this garage, Jack?"

"Down this way."

The entourage followed him, and Talman observed Brooks and Weiss as they glanced inside the truck. Weiss gave a thumbs-up after seeing the dead terrorists. Brooks simply looked sick. Weiss was a true Israeli, import or not, he thought.

Blanchard approached a garage door, bent to grab the handle and pulled it up. The light inside was on.

"Dickie," Talman said, "would you keep everyone outside? The investigators will want the area to remain uncontaminated."

"Sure thing, Major."

Talman did not have to say anything to the others since they had all heard his request.

Except for Blanchard. He marched right inside.

"Jack . . ."

"I've been here. Look at this paper on the wall. That wasn't here before."

Blanchard stepped carefully and crossed to the paper.

"Amin, this is in Arabic. Could you interpret?"

Rahman glanced at Talman, and Talman sighed and nodded. The deputy chief entered the garage and joined Blanchard.

"It says, 'Go to the place before Jericho.' "

"What the hell does that mean?" Blanchard asked.

Staying out of the garage, Talman walked over to the left side of the doorway. He said, "I would assume it is a message to el-Ziam and Badr, for when they returned. It would tell them where Kadar had gone."

"To the place before Jericho?"

"Before the group moved to Jericho, they had a headquarters in Jerusalem," Talman said. "That was under Ibn Sapir."

"Do you know where, Jacob?"

"I believe we may have the address of a headquarters. Whether or not it is the right one is open to interpretation."

Blanchard moved down the garage to the workbench. He stepped carefully around the tools as he went. He examined the bench as if it were under a microscope. Again careful to disturb nothing on the floor, he crossed to the other side.

"This is where Melanie was tied. There's no blood. I think she's all right."

He stepped away, looking down, then froze in place.

"I'll be damned!"

"What is it, Jack?" Talman called.

Pointing at the floor, he said, "She left a message."

"What?"

Talman could no longer resist. He strode inside to stand next to Blanchard. On the floor, Allen wrenches had been aligned to form characters:

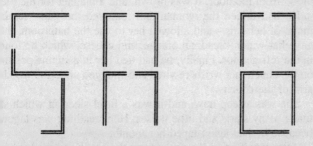

"What in the world does that mean, Jack?"

"I'm damned if I know. S-A-R? Search and Rescue?"

Rahman left the paper on the wall to come over and loo
Armbruster came inside, too, and squatted down to study tl
wrenches.

"Hell, Colonel," Armbruster said, "that last letter's a ꞁ
And she left a space for the missing letter. It's a Saab."

Talman studied the characters and decided Armbruster cou
be right.

"I will get a message out right away," he said.

"Every damned Saab in the country," Blanchard said. "W
want them all."

"Of course, Jack. I will see to it."

"What's more important," Blanchard said, "is that sl
hasn't given up."

"And," Armbruster added, "we've not given up on her.

The house was familiar to Kadar, of course. When Ibn Saị
commanded the Sword of God, it had been his residence.
belonged to a cousin of Sapir's, who rented it to anyone wi
enough money, and it was the only place Kadar could think
go which el-Ziam would remember when he read the crypı
note in the garage.

There was one small bedroom, a tiny bath, a kitchen, and
living room, all furnished adequately by the former tenant. T
tenant now resided in one of the two wardrobes in the bedrooı
and Kadar had not bothered to clean the copious amounts
blood from the floor. It was brown, and a magnet for the fliఁ

He had untied the woman and removed the gag—teari
much of her hair—and allowed her to use the bathroom, th
gave her water, bread, an orange, and cheese, which he fou
in the refrigerator. Finally, he had tied her in a supine positi
on the couch, her wrists rewired and snugged up to the wood
arm of the couch.

She was asleep now, and it was a fitful sleep in which s
made many starts and little noises. Her breathing was labor
because he had again taped her mouth.

After transferring the packs from the car, Kadar had tried

leep on the bed in the other room, but he could not. He was
oo keyed up. The colors seemed more vibrant, shivering in
ime to the pulse of his blood. He kept rising and going to the
mall window in the front wall of the living room and parting
he curtains.

By daylight he was convinced that el-Ziam and Badr would
ot appear. Either they could not interpret the note he had left,
r they had been captured at the water-treatment plant. If it
vas as fortified as Blanchard had claimed, then he could under-
tand that. He hoped they had been able to disperse the bacteria
efore they were caught, but he knew that was wishful thinking.
Neither of the two were stable enough that he could indulge
n hope:

> Praise be to God, the Lord of the Worlds,
> The Merciful One, the Compassionate One,
> Master of the Day of Doom.

The words kept rolling through his mind, reminding him of
is purpose and his proper role before Allah.

Either way, it meant he had lost Blanchard. He should fulfill
is promise to the man and kill Masters. Females were less
aluable as hostages, anyway. Who in Islam would trade any-
ling of value for a woman?

After his sixth trip to the front window, where he found the
treet coming alive with pedestrians and automobiles, he turned
way in disgust. He would have to do this himself. He almost
egretted shooting Kassim, but she had turned suddenly stub-
orn, telling him—ordering him!—he should not kill the Jews.
. stupid woman!

He looked at Masters, still asleep, and then his eye caught
le television. It was small, its screen barely a hand span.
'rossing to where it sat on a small walnut table, he turned it
way from the couch, then sat on the floor. He did not want
le woman, if she awakened, watching any program in which
le might be featured.

He clicked it on, then turned the sound low. It took a few
inutes to warm up.

Four people talking, a breakfast show.

He turned the channel selector until he found CNN, immedately entranced because it was his own picture on the screeAn anchorman reported in English:

"... Kadar is considered to be armed and dangerouAuthorities describe him as a fanatic with limited intellectupowers ..."

I will memorize this face. After the revolution, he must bcondemned.

"... once again, the latest break in the case came early thmorning when the medical-team administrator, Jack Blancharoverpowered two of his captors who were followers of KadaKhalid Badr and Abu el-Ziam were killed in the confrontation.

Jack Blanchard also is condemned. Certainly, the Jews winot charge him with murder, as they should.

"Spokesmen for the government and the Palestinian Authoity have announced a cooperative venture in the pursuit Kadar. The Palestinian police chief denounced Kadar adenied that Kadar has any affiliation with recognized Palestinigroups, even the extreme dissidents. He said that Dr. Masteis considered a true humanitarian without political associatiowho has served Palestinians in the West Bank exceptionalwell. As you saw on the taped segment, the Palestinian Authoity has urged all Arabs living in Jerusalem to assist in the searfor Kadar and Masters.

"In international developments, the prime minister hacknowledged the receipt of a strongly worded message frothe United States State Department, and British, French, anItalian diplomats have pledged their assistance ..."

Kadar shut off the television.

His brothers had turned against him. It was unimaginableBut then, the sycophants of the Palestinian Authority did nspeak for all his brothers, had not yet done so. And not one them understood the significance of what he was doing fIslam.

There was not one word of the bacteria. They only sougthe woman.

He looked over at the sofa with renewed interest.

Perhaps she *was* of value. If other nations protested habduction, he may have underestimated her importance.

Instead of a lever against Blanchard—since Americans were entirely too sympathetic toward their women—she might still serve him as a shield.

The loss of el-Ziam and Badr was not a setback. They had served as a burden.

The goal was achievable, and it was close at hand.

Until Weiss came back from one of the airport's restaurants with a plate piled high with scrambled eggs and pancakes, Blanchard had forgotten he was hungry. She placed it on the desk where he was sitting and picked up his coffee cup to refill.

"Eat, Jack."

"Jillian, you're an angel."

"I've been trying to tell you that."

She got coffee for both of them from the urn, then sat opposite him. Dickie Armbruster sprawled in a chair at the side of the desk, his feet resting on the edge of a wastebasket. On his face he had a scowl that Blanchard had never seen before.

Blanchard had thanked everyone else from the team for their concern, then sent them back to Mar Saba. He made a million promises to keep them updated through Sam Delray. Armbruster was allowed to stay simply because of the scowl, and Weiss convinced him he might need an interpreter.

He spread butter on the pancakes with the plastic knife, then poured the plastic container of maple syrup over everything. With his first bite he thought of Kadar's lack of concern for food, and Melanie's hunger, and his appetite diminished. He put the fork down.

Armbruster knew what he was thinking.

"Like Jillian says, Colonel, you've got to eat. Dr. Masters will get her feast when we get her back."

"While it's warm," Weiss reinforced.

Blanchard picked up the fork and forced himself to shovel it down—not tasting it now—while trying to interpret the half-dozen conversations taking place on the phones in this office and the two connecting offices. Most of it was in Hebrew, so he didn't have much success. He knew the suite next door was even worse. When he poked his head in there earlier, the dialogue was all in Arabic.

Before he finished, a police officer came in with the statement typed up from his taped interview, and without bothering to read it, he signed off on it.

"Jillian . . . ?"

"I've been listening to them, Jack. Nothing important yet. Someone said the owners of seventy-some Saabs have been contacted, but there are no promising leads."

The identification of the car hadn't been released to the media. No one wanted Kadar ditching the Saab. No matter what year, color, or model it was.

He heard a voice he thought he knew talking to Talman in the outer office and excused himself to check on it. When he passed through the doorway, he saw Avidar leaning over the desk, looking at some paper Talman had.

"Hello, Levi."

The general straightened. "Jack! It is good to see you. In more ways than one."

Avidar came around the desk and they shook hands. He was still as short, and still as distinguished, as Blanchard remembered. Little more silver in the hair, but no dullness in the bright blue eyes.

"It's been a long time, Levi."

"Much too long. I am happy, however, that your skills have not diminished."

"I wish I hadn't killed both of them. I didn't know Kadar was going to scoot."

"Hindsight has never helped anyone. You know that."

"Where are we at?" Blanchard asked.

"General Schweiss has control of the search, as you know. There are over two thousand soldiers committed to it, as well as a similar number of policemen. Deputy Chief Rahman now has twelve hundred of his policemen in the city. There is a fairly decent search line now stretched from north to south across the city and moving east. Much of the southern part of Jerusalem has been scoured, and those units are moving north out of the Jewish and Armenian Quarters of the Old City."

Blanchard knew how much of a role logistics played in a

mammoth operation. All of those men and women had to be fed, watered, and relieved from time to time.

"And on the intelligence end?" He was convinced a slip of someone's tongue would be more productive than the physical search. There were too many nooks and crannies in Jerusalem.

"There is nothing significant as yet. Jacob is pressing for information about the car, and all of our assets are turning over the rotten logs, looking for maggots who might know something about Kadar."

"I appreciate all you're doing, Levi. I feel damned helpless at the moment."

"We will soon have another decision to face, I think."

"The media?"

"Yes. Already there are minor questions concerning the size of the manhunt. Some begin to wonder if one American doctor is worthy of the millions in resources we are pouring into the operation. They will start to suspect another motive."

"I hope it doesn't come to that."

"As do I. Panic achieves nothing."

Talman answered a ringing phone, spoke for a moment, then stood. "General, I have located Beit Horon. I will meet him in fifteen minutes."

"Good. Do what you can, Jacob."

"I'll go with you," Blanchard offered. He wanted to be doing *something*.

"I think this meeting is best held in privacy, Jack."

He grabbed his jacket on the way to the corridor.

"Is Moshe Perlmutter here?" Avidar asked.

"Through that office, then the one to the left."

Blanchard called through the doorway. "Jillian, Dickie, let's go for a ride."

"Damned right!" Armbruster said.

"They have a radio here?"

"They set up something in the next room."

"Get a frequency, would you?"

While Armbruster darted into the back office, Jillian found her purse, and then the three of them went into the hallway and down it to the glass doors. They emerged into a late morning that was bright with sun and heat, and dim on potential.

It got worse.

Greg Masters was leaning against the fender of the Humvee. The fire had gone out of his face, but his nose and forehead were peeling, and the white splotch across his mouth made him appear as if he were leering. He was wearing an expensive suit.

"I knew you'd be around here, Blanchard, as soon as I spotted the truck."

"Appreciate your concern, Greg, but we're in a hurry."

Armbruster came up with a key and unlocked the door.

Masters stepped in front of Blanchard as he went around the front of the truck. For a little guy, compared to Blanchard, Masters was awfully damned short of memory or brains. Blanchard couldn't recall meeting anyone so confrontational with so little to back it up.

"What is it you want, Greg?"

"My wife, what else?"

"There're a lot of people looking for her. Talk to someone in charge."

"You got her into this, Blanchard, and believe me, you're going to pay."

Blanchard nearly laughed out loud. He did grin.

"Anything happens to her, you and anyone connected to this medical-team crap are going to curse my name."

"It's all right," Armbruster said from behind the driver's door. "We already do."

"Plus, I'm going after you for causing the estrangement between—"

"For God's sake," Weiss blurted. "Get real, Masters!"

"You know," Blanchard told him, "if you really wanted to help, you'd go find some TV reporter and offer yourself in exchange for Melanie. If you could convince him how important you are, Greg, Kadar might take you up on it."

Blanchard stepped around the man and got in the Hummer.

Weiss climbed into the back, saying, "Sheesh!"

As Armbruster backed out of the parking slot, Blanchard watched Masters. It looked as if he was taking the suggestion seriously.

Twenty

The military and police forces were conspicuously apparent on the streets now. Vehicles and walking pairs were everywhere and moved at a seeming turtle's pace to the east. Talman slowed his borrowed Jeep to observe them as he drove west on Ramban. They appeared to be stopping at every house and business, talking to the inhabitants, but not necessarily invading the premises for a personal inspection.

That would have been the policy set by Schweiss. Unless the circumstances or residents provoked suspicion, privacy would be recognized. Despite his misgivings about missing the less than obvious, or for inexperienced soldiers to misinterpret the demeanor of a resident, Jacob Talman would not have conducted it otherwise.

He followed the curve to the north, then crossed Hanassi Ben Zvi and drove west on Ruppin Road. The Israel Museum was on his left, and he turned into the drive leading toward it, but found a parking place far short of the sprawling complex of buildings and pavilions that made up the museum. Sliding out of the Jeep, he walked the other way, to the west, toward the Shrine of the Book.

The shrine was a unique structure, formed of white concrete

to look like the smoothly flowing lines of a pottery lid resting on the earth. The prototype on which it was modeled was, in fact, one of the lids for the jars containing the Dead Sea Scrolls. Some of the scrolls were housed here; others were in the Archaeological Museum in Amman, Jordan. Copies of the scrolls, the earliest manuscript of the Old Testament written in Hebrew, were in the rotunda, and they were important in demonstrating the accuracy of translations of biblical text. Other ancient texts, along with relics from Masada, were displayed in the shrine, so it was a favorite place of Beit Horon.

Horon was at the glass cases in the middle of the rotunda when Talman entered. His feet clicked on the hard surface of the floor, and Horon looked up.

"I wish you were not so hard to find, Beit," he said in Yiddish.

"I have been praying, Jacob. Everyone should do so."

"That is true, I suspect. What have you been praying for?"

"The nation of Israel. I fear she is about to be split asunder. The Palestinians will leave us small islands in what used to be ours."

"Not if we work together," Talman professed, then fell in beside the old man as he walked across the floor.

"When we talked at the Wall, you withheld from me the specter of Mar Saba."

"I could do no less. Do you feel enlightened by what you saw there?"

"Of course not! And more, I do not feel as if I can contribute, bound as I am by my word of honor. That you wrung from me, Jacob."

"I confess I was more intent on impressing Minister Tayar, Beit, than you. Are you aware of what is transpiring in the city?"

"I have seen the patrols. The news has been related to me."

"What news?"

"The fanatic Kadar, who has kidnapped the doctor, is in the city."

"I need your help, Beit, but again I must ask you to keep what I say to yourself."

"My hands may be tied."

"It is not your hands I worry about, but your tongue."

"You treat an old man shabbily, Jacob."

"You know that is not my intent."

He stopped his pacing. "Again, my word. I hope I do not regret it."

"The disease at Mar Saba? Kadar created it."

The old eyes went wide. Talman thought the reaction was to the horror of it all.

"And he is in the city," Horon said. "The search for a kidnapper is a ruse?"

"No. He holds the doctor hostage, but he also has possession of a biological agent that spreads the toxic epidermal necrolysis bacteria. At Mar Saba, he used the domestic water supply, a water tank, as the agent for dissipating the disease."

"Why do you not warn the people, Jacob?"

"Can you envision the result of such a warning?"

After a moment, Horon nodded.

"If we should determine that Kadar has treated any water supply, we will sound the alarm and bear the consequences of the ensuing panic. Currently, all major water sources are secured. Still, we hope to stop him before he acts, and yes, we are using the abduction of Dr. Masters as the cover story for our pursuit."

"Kadar is intent upon destroying Jerusalem?"

"Her people. Yes, we think so."

Horon's eyes went distant for a moment in thought, then he asked, "How long does it take for this bacteria to manifest itself?"

"I do not know, Beit. Perhaps seven or eight days."

"Then, Kadar must act today or tomorrow."

Talman did not see the connection. "Why is that?"

"Today is the first of August."

"Yes."

"And the ninth of August is the birthday of Muhammad."

Many thought that the prophet of Islam was born in 570 A.D. in Mecca, Saudi Arabia, dying in 632. Some Muslims celebrated the birthday in small ways—special feasts, the exchange of gifts, or meditation about the prophet's life. Others, who believe birthday celebrations are a Western tradition, did not observe the date.

Talman knew that Muhammad began teaching in a lawless Arabia when he was about thirty years old. He professed one God, helped the poor, developed laws, and set rules for slavery. He also banned war and violence except in self-defense, or problematic, the furtherance of Islam. The literal translation of Islam meant ''submission,'' but that got confused among the zealots carrying bombs.

Many terrorists thrived on symbolism, and he suspected Horon was correct.

''He wants Jerusalem to start dying on the Prophet's birthday?''

''That would be my observation, Jacob. It would be his gift.''

''You are probably correct, Beit. What would you do to stop this madman?''

Again, Horon pondered his answer. ''Perhaps, this is truly the will of God. Kadar assumes that Muslims will fill the void created in Jerusalem, claim the city as their capital and the place of their holy relics. But he could be in error, Jacob. For such an extreme action, there could be a reaction just as extreme.''

''Give me an example.''

''The peace plan will fall apart.''

''He would want that. Like Hamas, or you, Kadar does not support the plan.''

''And terrified and maddened Jews would raise arms and spread throughout Gaza and the West Bank, eradicating those who fostered Kadar. In the end, Israel might again be whole. This city would not be divided.''

''You would let Kadar proceed, then?''

''It is one scenario.''

''It is one that includes four hundred thousand looking like those at Mar Saba.''

Horon sighed. ''You are correct as usual, Jacob. It is horrible to contemplate.''

''You will help me?''

''What can I do?''

''Your people trust you, Beit. Without having to provide the horrific details, you can urge them to join the hunt for Kadar. You yourself have told me how important it is that we act quickly. Today.''

"There are many who will not cooperate. The Muslims—"

"May surprise you. Talk to them, Beit.''

"What we do here is to promulgate the Palestinian Authority.''

"That is the law as it now stands. Working with them may be the only chance we have to prevent a disaster like the world has never known.''

"Not since the time of Noah, or of Moses.''

"Neither was on the international news, Beit,'' Talman said, then regretted it. "I am sorry. In my day I worry about CNN.''

Horon offered a small smile. "I will see what I can do. The only thing I cannot do is provide a promise.''

Blanchard didn't know where the hell they were going.

Sitting in an airport office was not his idea of participation, though, and so they cruised through the city, looking for anything. They went past every water-pumping and treatment facility they could find; all were well defended by at least platoon-strength detachments. The patrols roving the city received an evaluation.

"Bloody hell! They're not even going inside, Colonel.''

"I can understand the problem, Dickie. People don't know they're under siege, and they might begin to wonder just what the extent of the crisis is if soldiers start looking under beds.''

"We're not going to find her this way.''

Blanchard was afraid he was right.

They stopped to gas the Hummer. They rearranged their arsenal. In addition to the Uzi no one had bothered taking away from Blanchard, Armbruster had stocked the Humvee with another Uzi, magazines, and fragmentation grenades. It didn't look to Blanchard like they were going to have a chance to use them.

They rolled down the streets and alleys of the Old City, peering in windows like three overt Peeping Toms. From time to time Armbruster stopped, and Weiss got out to talk to people on the street—Arabs, Jews, Americans, Armenians, Russians.

They did the same thing in the American Colony, then moved west into the Mea Shearim neighborhood and the Russian Quarter. Blanchard felt as if the city were closing in on him. The streets narrowed, the gray and white facades leaned over him, ready to fall down.

"Mr. Blanchard, Mercy Base."

Irsay.

Blanchard picked the mike off its clip. "Got me, Roberto."

"Sir, you've had a couple overseas calls. A Brett MacDonald and a Glenda Blanchard. Your daughter, I assume."

Oh, damn! Where's my mind?

He'd been so frantic about Melanie, he wasn't tending to business.

"I'll return them, Roberto. Did MacDonald leave a number?"

He jotted the phone number on a memo pad, then ripped it off.

"It's after one, Colonel. Want to find a cafe?"

"Let's do that, Dickie. Jillian can decide on the menu."

The one they found was a smoke-filled room full of Russian expatriates, with a Russian proprietor, and a chalkboard crammed with Cyrillic characters.

"You can interpret that, Jillian?"

"I'll use a dart, Jack."

"Fine by me."

He went in search of a phone on the street. When he found one he was relieved that it was the kind that could read the magnetic strip of his credit card. Fortunately, he carried one credit card in his ID folder. Public telephones in Israel couldn't dial internationally, so he patched through Mercy Base.

"Daddy!"

"Did I wake you?"

"I couldn't sleep, you ninny. Not after watching the news."

"I made the news, huh?"

"They had that gawdawful Marine photo of you. It's five years old, and you don't have any hair."

"Just the picture?"

"No. They talked about the terrorists. You weren't hurt, were you?"

"I'm fine, hon. And I'm sorry I didn't call earlier. I didn't think you'd hear just yet, and I'm trying to find Melanie."

"That's Dr. Masters?"

"That's her."

"It must be awful for her."

"It is. We're looking hard, Glenda."

"I . . . was it difficult, Dad? I mean . . . you had to kill—"

"Just what was necessary. Them or me, like they do in the movies. With these guys, Glenda, I don't plan to lose any sleep."

"God, I worry about you."

"I appreciate it, hon, I really do. But it's unnecessary."

"Will you find Dr. Masters?"

"Have to. She wants to talk to you about med school."

"I'd like that. Is she nice?"

"She's . . . special, Glenda. You'll like her."

They talked briefly about her summer-school classes; she told him to stay out of the line of fire; and then he called MacDonald.

"What'd you do to my girl, Jack?"

"Lost her for the moment, Brett. I intend to get her back."

"Make damned sure you do. Anything I can help with?"

"I don't know what it'd be. They've got the IDF all over the place, backing up the city cops and the Palestinian Police."

"Greg Masters, Senior, has been raising holy hell here. He's been on local TV, and the rumor mill says he's jabbing sticks at people he knows in Washington. He's calling for everyone to cut off aid to Israel and to the Palestinians since they can't protect American citizens."

"Shit! All we need is additional pressure on the Knesset and the prime minister. Masters doesn't have an inkling of what's going on."

"Melanie's been abducted, right?"

"There's more to it than that, Brett, but I can't go into it."

"Political?"

"Political, ethnic, and religious. It's a confused ball of wax."

"It always is. What are her chances, Jack?"

MacDonald didn't want the optimistic assessment. He'd heard those throughout his stint in Vietnam.

"Fifty-fifty. Unless I get to Kadar, first. Then, a hundred percent."

"I haven't even really met her, but I like her a lot, Jack. Give it your damnedest."

"No other way, Brett."

He went back to the table where Jillian had ordered them *zakuski*, a platter of hors d'oeuvres including smoked fish, marinated mushrooms, and caviar, and a vegetable soup called *shchi*. There was a big bowl of hard rolls.

"I skipped the pepper vodka in favor of iced tea," she said.

Armbruster spread caviar on a cracker. "The lady knows what she's doing, Colonel."

As in the morning, Blanchard immediately thought of Melanie's hunger, and it took some effort to get through the meal. They were in the Hummer a half hour later.

As soon as Armbruster fired the engine, Blanchard called the airport on the radio, using the frequency Armbruster had written down earlier. He got Perlmutter.

"This is Jack Blanchard, Moshe. Anything new?"

"Yes, sir, there is. Someone connected up a stolen automobile report. We're looking for a 1985 Saab four-door sedan. It is dark blue with a broken left taillight and dented rear fender. There is rust below the doors and on the front fenders." He read off the license number.

"Damned good, Moshe! We're getting there."

"I certainly hope so."

He hooked the mike back on its clip. "We've got something to look for, Dickie."

"It's still a hell of a lot of cars, Colonel. In a hell of a big city."

"Then, let's get rolling," Weiss said.

Kadar had gone outside through the front door once, for about fifteen minutes, and when he came back he seemed agitated. He locked the door, then unfastened Masters's hands and feet from the couch arms. He gave her more water, cheese, and pita, the only things that seemed to be in the house's pantry. Moving her into the bedroom, he tied her down on the bed, spread-eagled, her wrists and ankles fastened by lamp cords to the four bed legs.

She didn't know what he was thinking, and she wondered if he intended to rape her. She halfway hoped he'd try, giving her a chance to reach that knife of his.

It would be surgery he'd never forget.

But he didn't. He went into the bathroom for a long time, and when he emerged, he'd shaved the whiskers on his cheeks and neck, removed his mustache, and clipped his hair short. The image was definitely different. He was almost sleek, and Masters didn't think she'd have recognized him from his picture.

There were two large wardrobes in the bedroom, and Kadar opened one and began throwing clothing out of it. That frightened her, as if he was making space for her. She was pretty certain, from the spreading aroma, that the body of the man he had killed was in the other wardrobe.

She told herself that he wouldn't have fed her if he intended to kill her now.

He apparently found what he wanted and carried a bundle of clothing out to the living room, where she couldn't see him. She heard another voice, immediately subdued, and realized it was the television.

Stateside she had rarely watched TV except for the late news. Now she'd undergo having her wisdom teeth out again to see anything at all. She halfway understood sensory deprivation with her forced withdrawal from TV and radio. She didn't know what had happened to Blanchard; he could be dead, and the thought alone washed her in dread, which was almost too much to bear. It seemed certain, though Kadar hadn't spoken to her all day, that something was wrong. Khalid and Abu had not made an appearance, and Kadar's body language suggested he was disturbed by that.

And now, the effort to change his appearance. If she was to place any face on that at all, it was that people were looking for the two of them, and they must be getting closer. She hesitated to read too much promise in that, but damn it . . .

She needed hope.
And she saw it.
Please, Jack!

Ibrahim Kadar donned the former tenant's linen slacks, blue sport shirt, and a checkered sport coat. He found saddl soap in the kitchen, and polished his shoes, buffing them wit a dish towel. He put them on over the dead man's socks.

Outside the kitchen window, drawn up into the tiny backyard was an older Chevrolet. The insignia said "Citation." H should have checked earlier, but now knew that the keys fron the man's pants fit the door locks and the ignition of the car

He also knew that there was no theft report on the Chevrole and there could be one issued for the Saab. It seemed prude to make a change.

His foray outside had taken him two blocks to the wes where he had seen at least six army and police units. The sigl of them reinforced what he had heard and seen on the televisioi The manhunt was becoming excessive.

It thrilled him in one sense. Everyone in the Middle Ea now knew who Kadar was. Currently, they thought of him only in possession of a woman from the West. Later, the peop would associate his name with far greater achievements.

The fame had adverse aspects. He would have to be extreme careful from now on. And the first priority was to rid himse of the stolen automobile.

He looked in on the bedroom and was satisfied that t woman was securely tied. Going out the front door, he locke it carefully behind him, then walked down the street to t Saab. He got in, started it, and drove immediately to the e of the block and turned north on Meir Street. At Malchel Isra he braked to a stop, and when the way was clear, crosse the thoroughfare onto Malachi Street. He drove sedately, n wanting to attract attention.

Threading his way through the residential blocks of wh was known as the Bocharan Quarter, he worked his way to t northeast and out of the Quarter. He was afraid to turn we afraid to meet an advancing tide of searchers. In late afternoc probably around four o'clock, the day was still bright, but he thought that was in his favor. His hunters would presume that he would only go out at night.

He had an awful thought.

Kadar had left the plastic box of vials in his jacket pocket in the living room. What if the woman got loose, captured the vials, and screamed for help? Everything he lived for would be for naught.

He began to worry.

Still, he resisted the urge to hurry, and he eventually reached the Police School. Being Sunday, he did not expect to find it a beehive of activity, and he did not. For all he knew, they had turned the cadets out to assist in the search.

There were a few cars in the parking lot, and he parked between two of them. He locked the car, threw the key as far as he could, and began walking. It would be a long walk, but he felt exhilarated. The car was no longer a problem and probably would not be found parked right under their noses.

There were others walking along the street, and he joined them, felt himself blend right in. There were no crises in their immediate futures, and he imitated them.

But he must act soon. Tonight, or tomorrow at the latest, if he was to celebrate the Prophet's birthday properly.

By sundown, having accomplished nothing at all, Blanchard had directed Armbruster back to Atarot Airport.

They found the Israelis in a desultory mood. Some were wrapped in their coats, sleeping against the walls. They had been up all night and through the day. Perlmutter was one of them, and Talman wasn't there. A sergeant in the outer office was tending the map, and the line of pins running north to south was a ragged one, but it appeared as if the searchers had covered the western third of the city, as well as the Old City. Some units were now working around the Temple Mount.

"I'm going to do that," Armbruster said. "Nod off for a bit."

He walked around a desk and lowered himself to the floor. Blanchard dug for his wallet, then remembered that Kadar still had it. In his front pocket, he found a wadded bundle of shekels. He handed it to Weiss.

"Why don't you check into one of the hotels and get some sleep?"

She pushed his hand away. "I'm staying right here, Jack, where the news is. But I am going to demonstrate how well I can sleep sitting up."

He knew he should do the same, and though he was tired, his mind was wide awake. He wouldn't sleep until he knew one way or the other.

Going back to the hallway, he walked down to the next office suite, pushed open the door, and stepped inside.

Deputy Chief of Police Rahman was on a phone at the first desk, and he looked up, then waved Blanchard in.

A couple minutes later, he slammed it down.

"I have coffee so thick you must cut it with a knife, Jack."

"Just what I need."

He followed the policeman into another room where Arabic hell was being shouted over the landlines. Rahman filled two thick ceramic mugs with a liquid that did look as if it moved like a wet rope, then they went into another office that was apparently the absent manager's.

Rahman shut the door, and the noise went away.

There was a couch, and they both sat on it. Rahman pulled a package of Gauloises from his pocket.

"Do you mind?"

"I was a Marine too long to mind. Go ahead."

"I have been so busy today, I almost forgot that I smoked."

He lit his cigarette with a gold butane lighter while Blanchard tasted the coffee. It *was* thick, but sweet and full. It tasted like Turkish coffee he'd once drunk.

"Have you seen the television this afternoon?" Rahman asked.

"No. Missed my favorite soap."

A smile. "You missed my performance."

"I'm sorry. I'm sure it was good."

"My best yet. Arm in arm with General Avidar and Ben Horon, I appealed to my people to join with their neighbors—Muslim *and* Jewish—in the search for Kadar."

"Who's Beit Horon?"

"You will have to meet him. He is to Jewish faith and politics what your Jesse Helms and Patrick Buchanan are to the American right."

"Oh, yeah. I may have seen him at Mercy Base."

"He made a broad step today. He spoke on television." Rahman leaned over to the coffee table, pulled an ashtray close, and tapped off the ash of his cigarette.

"It sounds like a step in the right direction."

"If we did not have Kadar to contend with, we might all take steps in the right direction."

Blanchard took a closer look at the man, trying to see beyond the Hollywood looks. "Are you an enlightened man, Amin?"

"For my first ten years in Paris, I was a hopeless romantic. Ideals were achievable. In the next five years I became a realist."

"I hope you haven't abandoned the ideals."

"No, but I realize that if I achieve them, they are no longer ideals. Instead, I just hope to come close."

"The one you want to come closest to right away is those foreign-aid dollars."

"Exactly. They will not make perfection, and they will not change the views of those in the Islamic Resistance Movement, or even those of a few in the Palestinian Authority, but they will alleviate our shortcomings in education and public works. We can put people to work, and work builds self-esteem."

Rahman's eyes radiated his sincerity, and Blanchard decided he could look beyond the facade. He even kind of liked the guy.

"To get there, we've got to eliminate Kadar. And damned soon. I want my doctor back."

"I know. And there is a greater urgency."

"What's that?"

Rahman told him that Jacob Talman had called in with a theory raised by Beit Horon. It related to the birthdate of Muhammad.

"Shit! Tonight?"

"Either tonight or tomorrow. When I called, your Dr. Wilcox

told me symptoms of the disease would begin to appear within a week of contact with the bacteria.''

''What if Kadar figures out he can't get near the water system?''

''There are other ways,'' Wilcox said. ''The food supply one.''

Blanchard sighed and sipped from his mug. The coffee was going to keep his nerves tingling all night, and it was probably a good thing.

''What about the fringe groups?''

''Hamas will not assist us, nor will the Palestinian Front for Liberation. Part of the problem there is that I cannot reveal what I know of the bacteria. They see Kadar as simply a renegade, and the loss of an American is unimportant.''

''Speaking of losses, does that phone work?'' Blanchard asked.

''It did.''

He got up and leaned over the desk to lift the handset and punch the number in. Sam Delray answered.

''Everything under control, Sam?''

''Better. We got a load of food and that made Del Camero happy again. He hates taking the heat for poor meals when he can't control his supply.''

''I'm happy for him. What's the medical front look like?''

''They're overwhelmed at the clinic. We ran nine surgeries today.''

''And the special wards?''

Delray choked up a little. ''They're thinning out, Jack.''

''How bad?''

''We lost seven today.''

''Jesus.''

''Nothing we can do about it, either. The staff is taking it hard, and I'm afraid morale is going down the chute. If they weren't so damned busy, they'd be so depressed we'd be ordering Prozac by the carload.''

''Do what you can, Sam. You up-to-date from here?''

''Timnath's on the phone right now with Jillian, so yeah, we know nothing's happening. That's depressing. You want to send Jillian back so I can get some pills?''

''Have a shot of my scotch instead, then go to bed for a few ours. Tomorrow's a brighter day.''

''I take that as a promise,'' Delray said.

Blanchard replaced the phone and faced Rahman. ''Seven ore died.''

The chief's head sagged. ''May they go in peace and find eir salvation.''

Blanchard thought his salvation wouldn't come until he got is hands around Kadar's skinny neck.

The sun was fast disappearing.

Through the curtains of the small window in the bedroom, lasters saw the light turn reddish. Sunset coming, and no adar.

She had been struggling with her bonds for hours, she ought, but to no avail. She could feel no slack developing.

The heat had built up in the bedroom all afternoon, and the erspiration dripped into her eyes. She didn't even have the eedom of movement to wipe them against her shoulders.

With the heat had come an increasing stench from the dead ody. It attacked her nostrils, acrid and nauseating. She couldn't nagine passersby not noticing.

At one point, she had tried to dump the bed over, but she as tied exactly in the center of it, and the headboard and ootboard were made of heavy wood. She couldn't budge it.

Her frustration level was high; never before had she been stymied at anything she wanted to do. And that concept rought forth an inevitable comparison of her life with Greg. he had never truly felt constrained by him. He had some reconceived notions that she didn't agree with, but she was ertain he had only acted in their own best interest. According what he thought was right. People disagreed all the time. laybe they hadn't talked. Maybe counseling would help. laybe . . .

THUD . . . THUD!

The front door! Someone was at the front door!

Kadar?

He wouldn't knock!

Someone called out in Hebrew, and she couldn't distinguish the words.

She tried to scream; all that emerged was an elevated moan through her nose.

THUD . . . THUD!

Another loud call.

She whipped back and forth violently in the bed, trying to get it to move, to make a noise, gouging the wire deeply into her wrists and ankles.

She moaned.

Can't they smell!

And they went away.

Twenty-One

Kadar walked up Mea Shearim Road and saw the army and police teams on each side of the street ahead of him. They were stopping at each house and business, knocking on the doors, working down the street toward him.

Dodging through the traffic, he crossed to the south side of the street and entered a restaurant to order *felafel* and coffee. He did not think his face would be recognized, not from the picture of himself he had seen on television, but if spotted walking, his limp was certain to get him noticed.

The restaurant was well filled; he supposed that many of the inhabitants of Jerusalem were not actively engaged in the hunt for Kadar. Life appeared to go on.

For now.

Time dragged until two policemen appeared in the restaurant. They stood inside the doorway for a few minutes, scanning the diners. The level of conversation dropped as those eating became aware of the scrutiny. Most in the cafe were Arab, and none cared to be the subject of Jewish police. One of the policemen went to talk to the proprietor, and the other crossed the floor to peer into the bathrooms and the kitchen. They met at the front door and took another last look around the room.

Kadar smiled at them as he raised his cup to his lips and received a smile from the taller man in return.

Then they left.

So. He had passed the test.

He relaxed now and took his time finishing his meal and had a second cup of coffee. He wanted them much farther down the street before he ventured out again.

After another half hour, he paid his bill, then left. It was dark now, a condition he normally appreciated, but he thought that those on the street after dark would be subject to increased examination. Two military vehicles passed him, moving slowly, their riders intently surveying the crowds. He stopped to stare in the window of a jeweler and avoid demonstrating his walk as they drove by.

He walked to the corner, crossed the intersection, then continued for another short block. Turning to his left into a narrow street, he was able to leave the heavily trafficked street and feel closer to the shadows. He was less than two blocks from his commandeered residence.

And now he had to consider carefully.

The search had obviously passed by his house, with one of two results. The woman may have been able to attract their attention and was now free, with the police waiting in ambush. If so, they controlled the bacteria vials. Again, he chastised himself for his sin of omission.

More likely, however, they had determined that the house was unoccupied and the owner was away at work. In such case, he assumed they would note the address and send other teams back to check it later.

He made his approach cautiously, staying in the shadows and away from streetlights, until he reached the corner and could look down the street. It was difficult to tell if the house was being watched. Nine automobiles were parked at the curb along the block, but he could not remember if any of them had been there when he left. He could not tell if any were occupied either. No one appeared to be near the house, and its windows were darkened.

Retreating to the alleyway, he entered it and walked slowly toward the back of the house. Garbage cans and other litter

lled the alley, and Kadar was careful to avoid it. There was
o light here, except for tiny rectangles at the backs of houses
hat did not carry to the alley, and he was forced to move
lowly.

At last he reached the shallow yard where the Chevrolet was
arked. He stood next to a shed of some kind for twenty minutes,
tting his eyes roam with infinite slowness over every nook
nd cranny surrounding the house. The smell of garbage wafted
long the alley. He could hear voices, arguments, in some of
e closer houses, where windows had been opened to admit
e breeze.

There was no breeze, though the smell of rain was in the
r.

When he was satisfied that no one lurked in the shadows,
e skirted the car and approached the back door, which led
to the kitchen. He did not know if the key for the front door
lso fit the lock at the back, but when he tried it, it turned.

Letting himself in, he stood and listened. There was nothing
be heard.

Kadar did not want to turn on a light; in the event the police
ere watching or were to return, the house should appear to
main unoccupied. Feeling his way along the walls, he went
rough the living room to the bedroom, which was pitch black.

Advancing through the darkness, he bumped into the bed,
aned forward, and patted the mattress until he found her leg.

She moaned, and her leg twitched uncontrollably.

All was well.

Greg Masters had actually considered Blanchard's sugges-
on of offering to exchange himself for Melanie, but then
alized it wouldn't work. The terrorist wouldn't believe there
as a safe place to make the exchange. He would read it as a
ap. Blanchard should make the offer, he thought. It was
lanchard who had abandoned her. Hell, look at all the ink
lanchard was getting just by killing two worthless, know-
thing terrorists. His face was all over the television, and it
as only his picture. He had turned down all interviews.

It was revolting.

Instead, Masters had spent a couple hours figuring out wha was going on. It wasn't much different, after all, than preparin, for sensitive negotiations in contract law or a merger proposa' That was his bailiwick, his world. He knew he wasn't muc good at litigation, but he was an ace when it came to word' and clauses and provisions. He could interpret the most compli cated of proposals.

There were different factions involved in this instance—fa too many of them, in fact—and they all pursued slightly differ ent goals. Sitting in his room at the Sheraton, with the TV o in the background, he had worked with pencil and paper unt he had it right.

The news reports about Kadar and Melanie on the TV wer almost constant. He couldn't quite believe the Israelis woul put so much effort into one kidnapping. The attitude seeme quite different from what he had encountered earlier, and h assumed that was a result of his father applying pressure throug the White House and Congress. Someone from the embass was now calling every couple hours to bring him up-to-da on developments, of which there were none. The embassy, least, had figured out who he was.

After a couple hours of brainstorming, he pulled his ke points together and wrote them out on a single sheet of paper

1) Israelis—maintain the status quo; don't rock the boat, don't give into terrorism. They don't want me on TV, telling the world what's really going on.

Masters had figured out that the general named Avidar ha somehow coerced the CNN reporter into suppressing his inte view with Masters.

2) Palestinians—secretly want Kadar to succeed at ?, but don't want to give up the accord since it would cost them hard-won territory. That's why they're cooperating in the hunt for Kadar.
3) Kadar—out to make a name for himself and to scuttle the peace accord. Typical Arab hoodlum.
4) Talman—serves the Israeli cause; his goal is *not* to

free Melanie, but to first silence Kadar before . . . what?

5) Blanchard—his objective is Melanie, but Kadar got in the way of his plan to split us up. It doesn't take an Einstein to realize that there's a connection between former Marine general Brett MacDonald and former Marine Blanchard. A conspiracy there, no doubt.

6) Melanie—confused by Blanchard's attention, maybe even a little enamored of him, but she stumbled into something that makes her important to Kadar. That's why he grabbed her.

Something was the key to all of this, and Masters suspected it was Mar Saba, or rather what had occurred at the settlement near Mar Saba. That was the question mark. He wished he'd ignored the warnings to stay away and taken a look inside those tents. But when he thought about it, there were other indicators.

For example, the entire town had been evacuated. He recalled walking through it and not seeing one person who was not in uniform. All of the inhabitants were in those tents, suffering from . . . something.

Both the town and the medical camp had been isolated. No one wanted strangers coming in, or any information getting out.

But Masters had been in and out. That could be documented. His rental car was still there. Minister Tayar and the Horon guy would have to back him up.

There was some kind of announcement from the Sword of God earlier. What was it? A kind of plague?

As far as he knew, the Israelis had never responded to that beyond Avidar saying the Sword of God wouldn't recognize a plague. Avidar was slick. He'd said there was no plague; he hadn't said what was actually taking place.

Why?

Because it was true, something was true. Some dreadful disease had wiped out the population of Mar Saba. When he talked to the reporter, Masters had said something like a dozen died. Christ! It was probably thousands. At least, hundreds.

Melanie was a specialist in infectious diseases. She'd figured out what the problem was, maybe how to stop it. That's why Kadar took her! He doesn't want this plague, or disease, or whatever, stopped. Neither do the Palestinians, which is why they're hindering the search.

And the Israelis don't want the world to know that something like AIDS or Ebola is spreading through the land, probably at Kadar's instigation. The Israelis were like that, so damned security conscious that the military got away with anything it wanted. Talman will kill Kadar the first chance he gets, Melanie in the way or not.

What he needed to do was to strip away the secrecy, rip the lid off the cover-up. Once the people understood what was happening, they could take the precautionary measures that would protect them. Kadar would see his scheme falling apart. He'd probably abandon Melanie and slink his way out of the country. Damned terrorists were cowards at heart.

Masters could picture it. Melanie would be so relieved after her ordeal, she'd be ready to go home. They'd get this train back on the track, get his father off his back.

Screw Talman and Blanchard.

He called CNN first. The reporter who had interviewed him earlier said, "We understand that you're distraught, Mr. Masters, but—"

"I have vital new information."

"Yes, sir. You're at the Sheraton? If I get a chance, I'll—"

Masters hung up on him, then went down to the front desk to rent a typewriter. He wrote a quick announcement of a press conference scheduled for seven-thirty and had it faxed to CNN, ABC, NBC, CBS, BBC, CBC, Radio Kol Israel—the English language news station—and the Israel Broadcasting Authority, which ran all of the local radio and television stations. For the newspapers he listed *Ma'ariv, Ha'aretz,* the Arabic *El-Quds,* and the English-language *Jerusalem Post.*

With so many outlets addressed on his fax, almost everyone feared missing out on something important, and almost all of them did show up. The CNN reporter, aced out of an exclusive, still appeared, and the press conference, held in the lobby of the hotel, went as well as he had expected.

He played mainly on his fears for Melanie, and found that

he sincerely was afraid for her. No matter the differences they were experiencing, she didn't deserve the treatment she was getting from that Arab asshole. He really missed her.

By eight-fifteen, he broke it up, rented another car, and drove out to Atarot Airport. The skies were overcast, but it only served to trap the heat on the ground. He doubted if it would rain and actually ease the temperature. The whole damned country was like that—promises, but no fulfillment.

From the first time he'd located Blanchard at the airport, in the morning, he knew some kind of operation was taking place in that particular building. But when he pulled into the parking lot and found a slot, he was amazed at the number of vehicles parked throughout the lot, most of them bunched up near the office structure. The white WHO truck was there, but so were dozens of Israeli military Jeeps, trucks, and personnel carriers. The Arabic markings on some of them suggested Palestinian Police vehicles.

He got out of the Taurus he'd rented and leaned against the door in the dimly lit lot. There were four uniformed men standing near the glass doors to the building, so he suspected he wouldn't get inside.

But he could wait here and see what happened as soon as his press conference hit the air.

Masters felt pretty confident that something would happen. And he intended to be in the thick of it. He was going to be there for Melanie.

Talman had taken an hour out of his afternoon, after meeting with Horon, to visit Deborah Hausmann in the hospital. He was entirely too familiar with hospitals and visits to colleagues and subordinates who had ended up in them, and he detested the odors, the polish, and the waiting.

She was sitting up, more or less, with the head of the bed cranked up, and she had the television turned on.

He stood in the doorway for a moment, watching her, and when she became aware of him, she said, "Jacob!"

"Ah! Now you know my name."

"I knew it from my first visit to your agency. It is on the business cards."

He remembered that she had almost used it once, when they met the second time, outside of Jericho.

He walked in and pulled a visitor chair close to the edge of the bed. "You look marvelous. The color is back in your face."

She took his hand, making the IV tube writhe. "I am ready to go to work."

"I have learned to think like doctors, and I must say I cannot allow it."

"General Avidar has promised me a new position in intelligence analysis."

"You will not play Arabic roles?"

"No."

"Then I allow it."

She appeared a trifle saddened, he thought.

"I am good at what I do."

"I know, very good. But there comes a time—"

She interrupted him by saying, "The television news is not good."

"No. We are not much closer. And I must get back to work. I wanted to be certain they were treating you well."

"Except for the food, very well. Jacob, I am to have three weeks' recuperative leave."

"Would you like to learn the travel business?"

"I would."

"Then that is what you shall do."

He stood up, and when she refused to release his hand, leaned over the bed and kissed her lightly on the lips.

The kiss was still on his mind as he paced through the offices, listened in on phone conversations, and barked at the sergeant maintaining the map. At a folding table in one corner of the front office, Blanchard, Rahman, Armbruster, and Weiss were engaged in dispirited talk. Armbruster was playing solitaire with a deck of cards that were so worn the spots were barely visible. He was also eating cheese and crackers.

Out in the corridor, lined up and sitting against the far wall, were the members of a twenty-man commando unit headed by Lieutenant Colonel Rudi Wehner. They were in black utilities and armed to the teeth, and they were experts in hostage recovery. Talman had called in the unit over Blanchard's objections—he feared a massive and overreactive strike against Kadar that would endanger Masters, but General Avidar had concurred with the decision. Kadar would go down at any cost.

He wanted to be ready for any contingency, and with Horon's dire prediction that Kadar must act tonight or tomorrow, he had elected to not put off alerting the unit any longer.

The hallway and the offices reeked of cigarette smoke, and a pale haze circulated near the ceilings.

An excited voice in the next room captured his attention, and Talman stepped to the doorway.

"We've found the Saab."

Blanchard came out of his chair like a shot and followed Talman into the office and to the desk. The technician's face fell as he listened, then passed on the report: "It was located in the parking lot of the Police School. There is no one around it."

"Have they looked inside?"

"No, sir. It is locked."

"Tell them to break whatever they need to break, and to search it carefully."

The wait lasted twelve minutes. Talman looked at his watch three times. It was nine-thirty-five before the technician spoke.

"Nothing, sir, except that the dirt on the floor of the trunk appears to be disturbed, possibly by a heavy bag or a body. There is no blood or other evidence."

"Secure the car, and call for the forensics van."

They went back to the outer office, and Talman sat at the folding table with the others. Every unfulfilling report seemed to result in more depression.

Blanchard said, "This Kadar didn't start the Sword of God, did he? It seems to me that someone once mentioned another name."

Rahman answered, "Ibn Sapir. He claimed to have been disenchanted by the Iziddin al-Qassam, a rather violent arm of Hamas, and to have voluntarily departed. Our sources suggest otherwise, that he was ejected from the organization. The reasons are unknown, but he was something of an incompetent.

He formed the Sword of God with a son named Heusseni. Badr, Hakkar, el-Ziam . . . and Kassim joined him at that time, and Kadar came along later.''

"I wouldn't put it past Kadar to have helped both Sapir and Hakkar along to heaven with the bacteria," Blanchard said. "It gets him in line for the CEO position."

Rahman shrugged. "That is also possible. Those who deal in violence are subject to it. Why these questions, Jack?"

"I've been thinking about that note Kadar left at the garage. Go the place before Jericho, or something like that."

"Yes," Talman said. "We assumed he was directing el-Ziam and Badr to the Sword of God headquarters in Jerusalem."

"Do you know where that headquarters is?" Blanchard asked.

"Of course. It was a small shop in the Muslim Quarter. I sent investigators there, and they discovered that it is now a tailor shop. There was nothing to suggest that Kadar had been there. It is still under surveillance."

"Sapir lived there?"

"I . . . I do not know. Let me have the records examined."

Talman got up and went to the telephone to call the communications center. He passed on the request and hung up as—

"Major! Come here quickly!"

He raced through the middle office to the back space, followed by Rahman, Blanchard, and a dozen others.

A small television was on, and Gregory Masters was the focal point.

". . . Minister Tayar and a Mr. Beit Horon can testify to what we saw at the compound. Not being medically trained, I cannot comment on the specifics of the disease, but I know that it is horribly incapacitating and spreads rapidly. That, after all, is my wife's specialty—infectious disease. And I know that Mr. Kadar abducted her to prevent her interfering with his plans. She is the only one who can stop him. Certainly, the government has proven itself ineffective."

"Mr. Masters!" someone yelled. "The Palestinian Authority is working closely with the government in the hunt for Kadar. Are you saying—"

"Do you honestly think the Palestinians want to stop the eradication of Jews in Jerusalem?"

"*Allah Akbar!*" Rahman exclaimed.

"I now offer myself to Mr. Kadar in exchange for my wife," Masters went on. "I will serve as his hostage. However, I don't expect him to respond because I know that his control over Melanie is Kadar's only hope for success."

The view switched to the face of an anchorwoman, who said, "That was the essence of Mr. Masters's press conference. Calls to members of the Knesset and to the prime minister have gone unanswered or received 'no comment' responses."

Talman was amazed that Masters seemed to have new respect with the media.

"I made a hell of a mistake," Blanchard said.

"What?" Rahman asked.

"I let Kadar throw him back in the pond alive."

Kadar turned on a small lamp beside the bed and released Masters's feet, retying them together. He did the same for her wrists, then levered her upward and over his shoulder.

She grunted as his bony shoulder dug into her stomach.

He wasn't a big man, and he staggered under her weight as he lurched through the bedroom doorway, banging her shoulder into the jamb. He carried her through the darkened kitchen, pulled open an outside door, then stumbled down three steps.

She thought he was going to drop her.

The night was pitch black, and she saw that clouds obscured the stars.

Kadar lumbered down the side of a car, reached the back, and lowered her to her feet. He fumbled with a key, then opened the trunk. She dreaded the thought of another long ride in a trunk.

A small light on the trunk lid flared, and she thought Kadar was amazed to find the trunk full. Construction materials— bags of cement and concrete blocks.

He muttered in Arabic, slammed the lid, and picked her up bodily, moving back to the left side of the car, where he propped her against the fender while he unlocked doors. Pulling the rear door open, he shoved her inside.

She fought to stay on the seat, but he rolled her onto the floor where she landed on her back. Masters quickly jerked her feet inside as he closed the door, quietly but firmly. Her relief that she didn't have to be in the trunk was monumental. She didn't think she suffered from claustrophobia, but she'd never been subjected to automobile trunks before.

He must have gone back into the house because it was quiet for a few minutes, but then he was back, the car settling as he slid into the front seat. The car started, and he backed out without turning the lights on.

It bounced going down the alley, then slid to a stop.

She couldn't tell what was going on, but she heard voices yelling in several languages, the sounds muted by the closed doors and windows. By the lights that flashed inside the car, on the headliner, she thought there was a great deal of traffic.

Kadar mouthed subdued curses in Arabic as he waited for an opening.

Something was going on, and she wished she knew what it was.

By ten-thirty the methodical search of the city was a shambles. The police and army units had been turned into traffic-control officers. The radio channels were swamped with reports of accidents—cars and trucks running into each other, hitting pedestrians. Some of the injured refused treatment at the aid stations, they were so intent upon leaving the city.

For those who hadn't seen the telecast, word of mouth was enough. They didn't even know what the disease was, but they didn't want to chance facing it. The reports coming into the airport office added up to pandemonium. Even the prime minister and the spokesmen for the Palestinian Authority, who were now pleading for order and calm on every channel and every radio station, were being ignored. People weren't hanging around the TV or the radio to listen to politicians, Blanchard thought.

Reverse exodus. They were streaming out of the city at every ortal, headed for God knew where.

In the middle of the first panic, Talman got a call back from hin Bet.

He crossed to the table where Blanchard was sitting and aid, "I have Ibn Sapir's former address. It was not the Sword f God headquarters."

"Let's go."

Blanchard drove; Talman, Armbruster, Rahman, and Weiss vere with him, but he was preceded by a Jeep, with a siren nd a red light, filled with commandos. Another Jeep trailed ehind.

The route in from the airport wasn't too bad. The outgoing ines were nearly gridlocked with every form of transportation naginable, and thousands crowded the roadsides, marching ith worldly goods slung over their shoulders. Trucks were acked high with people.

When they reached the city proper, the going got tough.

People darted into the streets, attempting to crawl on top of ie Jeeps. Cars dashed out of alleys, slamming into a solid line f automobiles. Fender-benders were the norm, but no one opped to complain to offending drivers.

Despite the strobe lights and wailing siren, they crawled ong Mea Shearim. A fifteen-minute trip took nearly an hour, d at the end of it, the streets were as clogged as ever.

The siren died away as they turned into Meir Street, which as curb to curb in people. They parted like the Red Sea before ie Jeeps. Two more blocks, and another left turn. When the eep in front of him flared its brake lights, Blanchard killed ie ignition in the middle of the street and bailed out.

The commandos forced a path from the street to the door. The house was dark.

Their arrival wasn't particularly unannounced, but in all the onfusion, Kadar might not realize what was going on.

Talman pushed his way to the door and tried the handle. It as locked.

He barked an order in Hebrew, and two commandos leaped rward with a battering ram. They swung it backward once, en into the door next to the lock.

The jamb splintered, and the door sprang open.

Talman and Blanchard were the first through, Talman sprint-
ing toward the back of the house. Blanchard found a door t
the right, shoved it, and dived through.

There was a small light illuminated on a table next to th
bed, but nothing else.

The odor of dead flesh permeated the air, and Blanchard wa
sickened by the thought that they were too late for Melanie.

Colonel Wehner strode through the door, sniffed the air, an
immediately charged the first of two wardrobes. He ripped th
door open on one, revealing a haphazard pile of clothing, the
stepped to the next.

Pulled the door open.

A cloud of flies surrounded the dead man. Blood from h
sliced throat was splattered all over him.

Blanchard was struck by simultaneous feelings of relief an
guilt. Relief for Melanie, guilt for feeling relieved at the expens
of this man's death.

He went back to the living room.

Talman had turned on lights, and the place was packed wit
military people in addition to Rahman, Armbruster, and Weis

Weiss said, "Jack?"

"She's not in there, Jillian. There is a body. A male."

Talman was bent over a couple knapsacks, dumping the
contents on the floor. Assault-rifle magazines, a grenade,
block of what looked like plastic explosive, clothing, Swor
of God tracts, other paraphernalia.

"He was here," Talman said as he pawed through the mes

Wehner came back. "Someone was tied to the bed. The
are bread and cheese crumbs on it, also."

Talman stood. "There are no vials."

"There wouldn't be," Blanchard said.

He saw a pile of clothing on a living-room chair and crosse
over to examine it. Picking up a jacket, he felt the weight
the pocket, and probed for it.

"This is what Kadar was wearing when I last saw hir
Jacob. He changed in a hurry because he left behind a spa
magazine for the Beretta."

"I wish he had left something else behind," Rahman sai

Talman went into the bathroom, was back in a minute. "He as probably shaved his mustache, perhaps cut his hair. The ink is full of black hair. He is a pig. Sergeant, get on the radio nd notify headquarters of a possible change in his appearance. Ie will be clean shaven."

"Yes, sir." The sergeant ran for the street and one of the eeps.

"Flashlight, anyone?" Talman asked, and someone provided t.

Blanchard followed Talman through the kitchen and out the ›ack door.

"This door was not locked," the Israeli said.

He stood on the bottom step and played the light back and orth over a yard as devoid of grass as an ice rink. Like a rink, hough, it had tracks in it.

"Colonel Wehner," he called, "have your men search the 1ouse for automobile registration papers. Or the identity of the lead man."

Five minutes later, from papers retrieved from the dead man, hey knew they were looking for a gold Chevy Citation.

In a city that was an ocean of fleeing automobiles.

Kadar was infuriated.

He did not know what had happened, but the city had gone into a frenzy. The din from high-pitched voices and automobile horns was terrible. Thinking was difficult; driving even more so. He had managed to reach Straus and turn south, a right turn. Left turns at the corners were all but impossible. No one paid attention to traffic signals, nor to the policemen and soldiers trying to organize the flow of cars.

Someone in a pickup struck the Chevrolet in the rear, and incensed, Kadar had flung open his door and pulled the Beretta from his waistband. He was going to kill the infidel.

Only at the last second did he remember his mission, fought for control of his brain, and sagged back into the car.

Mighty and Merciful God, make me mindful of my service to You.

He put it in gear and drove for two blocks, then pulled o
the street onto the sidewalk in front of an open-air market.

The woman!

He grabbed one of the blankets on the seat beside him, shoo
it out, then leaned over the seat to spread it over her. The
were so many people rushing along the street, someone wa
certain to see her through the window.

Some thief was certain to try and take the car, also. H
gathered his materials—a spray bottle full of water, a set
bolt cutters that had been intended to open locks at water plant
and one pair from the bundle of rubber gloves secured by
rubber band. From his pocket, he took the plastic box, opene
it, and removed a vial. He put the box back in his pocket.

Sliding out of the car on the passenger side, he made su
the doors were locked, then forced his way through the crow
to the gate. The force of the current in the throng dragged hi
ten meters past the gate, and he had to work his way bac
alongside the fence. He did not pay attention to the mob flowi
past, nor they to him, as he raised the bolt cutters, fitted th
jaws to the Yale padlock, and snapped it. He shoved the bo
cutters inside his belt. Quickly, he pulled the broken lock fro
the hasp, slid the gate aside, and slipped inside. He pulled th
gate closed.

He went behind the first counter, on which were stack
melons, slipped a pair of the gloves on, then peeled the ta
and worked the rubber stopper from the vial. Twisting the te
off the spray bottle, he poured the vial into the water, th
threw the vial away and replaced the sprayer top. Rapidly, a
careful to not splash the tiniest drop on himself, he ran up a
down the aisles, spraying potatoes, cucumbers, beans, cor
lettuce. When it was empty, he threw the spray bottle awa
then peeled the gloves off and threw them under the bench

He smiled to himself as he walked back to the gate, stayi
equidistant from the counters as he went down the aisles. I
would touch nothing.

This time he slid the gate fully open, pushing another sectic
then another back, opening the market for business at nea
midnight.

Some in the rushing crowd slowed to look at him.

He yelled at the top of his lungs. "You will need food! Here! is free!"

He was nearly swamped as the horde diverted from their flight out of the city into the market. They might run, but they could not starve.

God is great! God is good!

Twenty-Two

He had tied her wrists so tightly the circulation was restricted and her hands felt numb. The prospect of damage to her hands petrified her. To never again preside in the operating room was a future Masters could not envision. She did her best to force the bonds apart, then relax her hands, hoping to stretch the plastic-coated wire.

The blanket he'd thrown over her had been suffocating, and Masters had used her feet to push herself up against the door, working her way up until the back of her head was resting against the door. Shaking her head from side to side forced the blanket to slide to her shoulders, and she could breathe again. She could also see passing streetlights, lit windows, and occasionally, a street sign through the opposite window. Not that that helped a great deal. They were apparently staying on side streets, and she didn't recognize one street name.

Kadar hadn't noticed her change in position. He was too busy.

Masters didn't know why they had stopped the first time, or where Kadar had gone, but her suspicions made her heart heavy.

She did know that something was wrong in the city. The din was unbelievable—blaring horns, racing engines, shouting

eople. Somehow, the word must have gotten out, and people
were running in terror. That was the only rationale.

When Kadar got back in the car, it took him a while to get
back on the street, and when he did, they were hit from behind.
The jolt threw her back against the seat.

Kadar didn't stop. He shouted some curse, then gunned the
engine, immediately having to brake. She began to worry that
they would be hit by some truck. From the side. It would crush
her.

About fifteen minutes later, again on some side street, Kadar
stopped the car.

She couldn't see what he was doing in the front seat, but it
took him a few minutes before he once again left the car. As
soon as the door slammed, she used her bound hands to push
her way up into a sitting position on the floor. By stretching
her neck, she could peer over the lower sash of the window.

Utter confusion.

The sidewalk was crammed with people. They walked, trot-
ed, ran, carrying bundles, boxes, and suitcases. They dragged
children after them, toted babies clasped tightly in their arms.
One man was trying to balance a large television set on his
shoulder. On the street side, she saw that cars and trucks were
bumper to bumper, their horns urging the leaders to greater
speed. Exhaust fumes hung heavy, visible under the streetlamps,
penetrating the interior of the car.

Twisting her neck and shifting her eyes to the right, she saw
Kadar. He was at the door to . . . a market. As she watched,
the door gave way, and he slipped inside.

For God's sake! He was poisoning the food!

She tried frantically to get herself turned around. The blanket
wrapped itself around her, hampering her moves. Finally she
maneuvered herself facedown on the seat, got her knees under
her, then levered herself upright. Searching the door, she found
the lock, and it took an agonizingly long time to force it, using
her chin.

The door handle was another matter. It was a recessed lever
type, and though she tried to pull it with her teeth, she couldn't
get a firm grip. After several tries, she gave up, then rolled
onto the seat to get herself turned around.

Sitting on the edge of the seat, her back to the door, she sli
backward until her hands found the door, and searched for th
lever.

No.

There!

She got two fingers wrapped around it.

Pulled.

Her fingers slipped off.

Found it again.

Tugged.

Heard the click.

Shoved on the door.

It opened a few inches, and she leaned back into it.

Tumbled outside, hit the sidewalk on her back, her arm
trapped beneath her.

Looked up at people who didn't stop and barely steppe:
over her in their flight.

Heard a shout in Arabic.

"La!"

Blanchard, Weiss, and Armbruster had been abandoned by
the Israelis. Rahman had taken off with Talman and the com
mandos. A contingent of two soldiers had been left behind tc
guard the house.

Blanchard led the way outside and dodged around cars, which
were moving like wounded water beetles, to the Humvee parkec
in the middle of the street.

Armbruster beat him to the driver's door, so Blanchard wen
around and crawled into the passenger seat.

After Weiss was in, Armbruster said, "Where to, Colonel?"

"He only had one way out of that alley, Dickie, to the east
and with this traffic, I'd bet he turned right coming out of it.''

"Gotcha."

Armbruster engaged low, and the engine growled. He moved
right up on the bumper of a black Citroën.

Blanchard grabbed the microphone. "Mercy Base, Blanchard."

"Sam, Jack," Delray's baritone came back. "What the hell's going on in the city?"

"World-class bedlam. Greg broke the news!"

"Yeah. Lars Svenson had his TV on."

"Do they know the specifics?"

"I don't think so. Just something about a disease and people dying. The army doubled up their guards here, but I don't think we'll get refugees."

"Do you still have the army guy in the admin tent monitoring the radios?"

"I do."

"If anything breaks, let me know, will you?"

"You're first on my list, Jack."

He called Perlmutter at the airport and learned only that the revised description of Kadar had been put on the air.

A sudden splatter of big lazy raindrops on the hood and windshield surprised him. It lasted about thirty seconds, just enough to create swirls in the dust.

"It doesn't rain in July," Armbruster said.

"This is August."

"Doesn't rain in August, either."

Blanchard leaned his head sideways and looked up. He couldn't see any stars, so he figured the overcast was fairly complete.

"End of the block," Armbruster said. "Now right?"

"Do it."

The Citroën was trying to turn left, and not having any success at getting across the flow of traffic. Armbruster hauled the wheel to the right, went up over the sidewalk and around the right side of the Citroën. He switched the headlights to bright, blinding everyone in his path, and laid on the horn.

He got an opening.

"Help us out here, Jillian."

"I don't know Jerusalem as well as I do Tel Aviv, Jack, but we're going south now. This street will end in a couple blocks, and we'll have to go left or right."

She was correct, and when they came to the "T" intersection, they found all the traffic moving right, the shortest distance to the city limits. Armbruster bulled his way into the flow, halted it, and . . .

"Left," Blanchard said.

"Gone."

"Okay," Weiss said, leaning up between the seats so she could see, "if we can get across the next intersection, we'll come to Strauss. That's a main street that changes names a few times, but becomes King George the Fifth."

"Let's try for it," Blanchard said. "That's one I recognize."

The eastbound direction was easier, with fewer cars, and while Armbruster blustered his way through the next intersection, Blanchard checked back with Perlmutter on the radio to ask about the water plants. Every street he looked down, he could see the blue and red strobe lights of emergency vehicles, but they weren't making any more progress than the Hummer was.

"No one's made an attempt on the plants, Mr. Blanchard."

"Thanks." He slapped the mike back on its hook.

"You think Kadar's figured out he can't reach them, Colonel?"

"I tried to plant the idea in his mind, Dickie. I may have succeeded."

"So, what does he do?" Weiss asked.

"Food, I think."

"That's terrible!" she said.

"I know. A big flour mill, a canning plant would be a good target."

On Strauss, Armbruster turned south. Making a swing to the north would have been like swimming *up* Niagara Falls.

"We're looking for possible mass food outlets?" Weiss asked.

"Only thing I can think of, Jillian."

But something else was trying to form in his mind, and he couldn't quite figure out what the shape of it was.

Greg Masters cursed as the white truck leaped into the flow of traffic on Strauss and got away from him. He was blocked by assholes who wouldn't let him in.

Since it was a rental car, he decided he didn't give a damn about sheet metal and inched forward until he ran into the left front fender of some kind of foreign car. The soft metal crunched, and both cars came to a halt. The other driver swore and yelled at him, but Masters ignored him, spun the wheel, and pulled out into the southbound traffic. He was becoming accustomed to his aggressive behavior.

The WHO truck was about a block in front of him.

He had been following the distinctive truck since it left the airport after the press conference was aired. He'd heard it on Radio Kol Israel, sitting in the Taurus. Masters had been self-congratulatory about his success in warning Jerusalem of its impending danger. It was thrilling to see thousands of people react to his words.

His intention had been to protect the city's people. Second-arily, he thought he might spook Kadar from his hiding place and be able to rescue Melanie.

Now he was starting to have second thoughts. The panic was grossly evident, and the streets were all but impassable. He hadn't thought these urbanites would be so confused about where, and how, they were going to get out of the city. Why they didn't have some neat evacuation plan, like American cities had, he didn't know.

Having followed them to the house on the narrow street, he was pretty sure Talman and Blanchard had found a hideout of Kadar's, but that the terrorist was long gone. He was less certain of how he was going to spot Kadar in this mess, so he figured his best shot was to keep Blanchard in view. Blanchard had two-way radios and was probably communicating with every-one under the sun.

Masters stabbed the brake pedal as the car ahead of him lurched to a stop. He heard several cars smacking into each other.

After several minutes nothing was moving.

He stuck his head out his open window and looked ahead. Down beyond Blanchard's truck, a number of emergency lights were flashing. So, probably a wreck. This was getting damned ridiculous.

He wished it would rain again. It was hot, and if he could

at least conjure up a downpour, he'd be happy to get out and stand in it.

He kept a wary eye on the white truck. Blanchard wasn't getting out of his sight again, not until Masters had Melanie safe in his arms.

As the two Jeeps fought their way south on Strauss, Jacob Talman spotted the open gates of the market and the swarm of people pilfering it.

"Now, we have looting," he told Colonel Wehner, who was driving.

"Food for their journeys, no doubt," the colonel said.

"Unless," Rahman said from the back of the Jeep, "Kadar has been here."

"Pull over, Colonel!"

Wehner hit the siren once to warn pedestrians as he swung out of line, bounced over the curb, and stopped on the sidewalk.

Talman swung out of his seat, stared down a man who looked like he wanted to take the Jeep, and pushed his way through the mob. They were packed tightly, many clutching prizes of cabbages and corn. The siren and the emergency lights did not faze them. They were taking what was needed.

The commandos spilling from the other Jeep began to blow whistles, and that caught some attention. At first, a few people diverted from the market, then more followed. When the remaining looters realized their numbers were dwindling, they also bolted for the open gates.

Talman did not try to stop them, but stood at the side of the gate as they fled.

Then he walked the aisles. Rahman caught up with him as they perused the almost empty counters.

Near the back, Rahman said, "There!"

Talman followed the pointing finger to a spot underneath a melon counter. The floor was littered with crushed vegetables, but he immediately saw the pair of yellow gloves. There was also a spray bottle.

"The sprayer is significant, I think," he told Rahman.

"Absolutely."

Talman had to fight a thinner stream of refugees rushing along the sidewalk to reach the radio. He dialed in the frequency and asked for Avidar.

"Yes, Jacob, I am here."

"He is targeting produce markets, General. Using a spray bottle."

"Oh, my God! It is under way then?"

"Apparently so. I have a recommendation."

"Go ahead."

"Make a general announcement to all police and military units to abandon traffic control and move to the nearest markets and food stores to protect them. Any that have been breached should be sealed off. No men should enter open stores."

"Yes. We will do that at once. If there are other stores, we may be able to pinpoint a direction for Kadar."

"Yes, sir."

"Hold on, Jacob. Beit Horon wishes to talk with you."

The old man was very worried, if he succumbed to using a radio.

"Hello, Beit."

Someone had to show him how to use the transmit button. His voice broke up a couple times before he finally said, "This is maddening. I know now of your fears."

"We are past the point of convincing people to help us find Kadar, Beit. We must now soothe this beast. I will tell you what you must do. You must tell ten of your friends that no harm will come to them if they avoid food they purchased or found after midnight today. Tell them to remain calm, to go home, to tell ten of their friends to do the same thing. If we can have everyone passing that message to another ten, we will restore order."

"And after I do that, Jacob?"

"Tell ten more. You have many friends."

"I will do this."

Talman started to replace the microphone, but Rahman took it from his hand. "That is excellent advice, Jacob. I will now call ten of my friends."

He stepped out of the way to let the Arab have the seat, and ran into Blanchard.

''Where did you come from, Jack?''

Blanchard pointed over the top of the Jeep to the Humvee stalled in traffic.

''I can walk damned near faster than drive. Kadar's been here?''

''Yes. He used a spray bottle.''

''Shit! No way we're going to track down potatoes and lettuce.''

''I know. The best we will be able to do, once the people have calmed down, is to make public announcements about symptoms and where they may go for treatment.''

''At least it's not the water supply.''

''Still, with thirteen vials, that is thirteen markets. It will translate into thousands of deaths.''

''Maybe. He must be going south?''

''We are trying to divert the police and military to guarding the stores.''

''Okay.''

Blanchard walked back into the street and climbed into the Humvee, which advanced perhaps twenty meters.

Talman wished he could put himself into the mind of the terrorist and predict what direction he might take.

Kadar had picked her up off the ground and had thrown her back in the car. Not one of the dozens rushing past them complained in the least. He then unlocked the front door, slid back in behind the wheel, and took off, fighting his way back into traffic with brazen confidence.

''If you try to escape again, I will pour one of the vials over you. Then, I will not worry about you. You will die in all good time.''

From the floor of the backseat, she whimpered.

When he made his next stop, on Narkis Street, off King George V Road, he used tape to secure the rear-door locks and latches. If he hurried, she would never have time to work the tape off. She was a strange woman; he never for once doubted that she would again attempt to escape.

He donned another pair of rubber gloves and recovered a

vial and a spray bottle. He had only three of the spray bottles left, then he would have to simply scatter droplets directly from the vials. Unless he found a store with more sprayers. He would look for them.

He got out and locked the car door. Not one of the drivers passing gave him a second glance. The torment of Jerusalem was the best disguise he could have.

This was an enclosed store, and he used the bolt cutters to snap a link in the chain holding the grillwork across the front of the store. He shoved the grilles aside, used the cutters to smash the glass in the door, then broke the shards from their seats in the rubber seal. He stepped through, pulled the stopper, and dumped the vial into the sprayer.

Here, he sprayed canned goods on the shelves, went behind the meat counter, pulled open the glass doors, and sprayed the meats. Against the back wall were hanging chickens. He sprayed them.

The produce.

The fruits.

The bread and cakes.

And when the bottle was empty, he tossed it aside and carefully peeled the gloves from his hands.

Stepping through the broken door, he came face-to-face with a soldier, who was almost as surprised at the meeting as Kadar was.

"Hey!"

Kadar whipped the gun from his belt and shot the soldier through the mouth.

"Stop!"

He spun to his right, saw the other soldier, and shot him.

The man stumbled, dropping his weapon before he even had it unslung from his shoulder, then slumped to his knees. A bright stain of blood spread over the right side of his chest.

He looked up at Kadar, a prayer in his eyes.

Kadar hoped it was the right prayer.

He aimed the semiautomatic pistol and fired once into the man's forehead.

Then he went back and got in the car. He had just started it when the car's back window erupted.

Glass showered everywhere.

He heard the staccato burst of an Uzi submachine gun.

Bullets thunked into the car.

The woman moaned loudly.

He shoved the accelerator pedal down, flying down the sidewalk. In the rearview mirror, he saw the soldier—a third one!—on his knee, attempting to change magazines.

The car fender hit a newspaper kiosk. Paper and splintered wood flew everywhere.

A trash can. It banged away, spinning, into traffic on the street. Cars tried to avoid each other, to get out of the way of the can, and they smashed into each other.

An iron fence surrounding an outdoor cafe appeared in his headlights. He swerved back to the street, knocking down the corner of the fence, banging off the side of a blue car. Then he gunned it around the corner, and he was free.

Kadar smiled.

He was feeling very good about this.

Blanchard found a city map in the glove compartment, and Weiss spread it out on the backseat next to her. The overhead light was on.

"Every bloody car looks like a gold Chevrolet," Armbruster complained.

"Here it is!" she exclaimed

Blanchard leaned over the seat to see where she pointed. The location of the second market identified as broken into was to the west of King George V and south of Agrippas Road.

"He's still moving south, Dickie, staying on the side streets now."

"You want me to get off King George?" Armbruster asked.

"No. We'll just keep muddling along. He can't be making better time than we are."

"You call this making time, Colonel?"

Blanchard could see some of the big hotels ahead. Once they made it around the curve, they would come upon an arm of Independence Park. This was almost the center of the city, and he thought the traffic was thinning a little. As cars and people

reed themselves from the outskirts of Jerusalem, freeing up
space for those behind them, the center of the city was going
to clear first. Still, evacuating 400,000 people wasn't accom-
lished in an hour or two.

There was less foot traffic, also. He wondered if the hotels
ad spilled all of their guests into the maelstrom.

"Blanchard, Perlmutter."

He grabbed the mike. "Yes, Moshe?"

"Another contact, a half block off King George on Narkis."

He didn't like the sound of Perlmutter's voice. There was
grief in it.

"Come on, Moshe!"

"Two soldiers killed. Executed, according to the witness."

"I'm sorry, Moshe. Was it Kadar?"

"The witness isn't sure because he wasn't close enough. It
was a gold American car. It got away, but not before he fired
thirty-two rounds into the back end of it."

Oh, shit! Don't be in that trunk, Mel!

"Here!" Weiss cried, and Blanchard spun around to look
at the map.

"We're four blocks away, Moshe."

"He turned right off Narkis, heading north," Perlmutter said.

"Hang a right, Dickie!"

"Going."

The ex–Special Air Services sergeant went over the curb
again, scattering six pedestrians, and straightened out on Bezalel
Street, flashing his lights at cars ahead of him and blowing the
horn.

To no real avail.

It took five minutes to reach the next corner, and Armbruster
spun his wheel to the left, right into oncoming traffic. The
approaching cars gave way to the larger vehicle and ground to
a halt as he cut through their lanes and aimed south.

"Easy, Dickie! There it is."

Ahead on the left, angled up on the sidewalk, was a gold
Citation. Other drivers appeared oblivious to it as they limped
past.

Armbruster slapped the gearshift into neutral and yanked on

the emergency brake. Blanchard reached under his seat and found the Uzi. A duplicate appeared in Armbruster's hands.

"Stay here, Jillian."

"Jack . . ."

"Stay here."

The two men opened their doors and stepped out. Cars behind were determined to make themselves heard by way of the horns.

Armbruster pushed off the hood of an approaching car and ran for the opposite sidewalk.

Blanchard ran down the center of the street. Some of the drivers noticed the gun and started swiveling their heads, wondering where the trouble was, or where it was going to come from.

He kept his eyes on the Chevy.

Didn't see any movement around, or in, it.

When he came opposite it, he raised his hand to the driver of the nearest car. The woman inside saw the gun and immediately froze. Her Volkswagen banged into the one ahead of it.

Blanchard ran around the back of the Volkswagen, holding the Uzi at port arms, and came up on the back of the Chevy. Armbruster covered him from twenty feet away on the sidewalk, backed into a recessed doorway.

He went low as he slid up to the trunk. The taillights were gone, shot out. He smelled gasoline and figured the tank had been hit. The back panel was peppered with bullet holes. The rear window was gone. He couldn't believe some soldier had opened up in what had to be a very populated area.

Unless the Israelis had ordered everyone to shoot Kadar on sight. Melanie, or no Melanie.

Working his way up the side, he peered through the glassless window.

No one in the backseat.

Edged along the rear door.

No one in the front seat.

Nothing. The engine was still running.

He signaled Armbruster, then jerked the door open, and reached inside to shut off the engine and remove the keys.

Armbruster joined him as he popped the trunk.

Bags of concrete and concrete blocks.

The near bags had bullet holes in them.

"If she was in the backseat, Colonel, those bags saved her."

"I hope so, Dickie."

Had to be, though. If she were hurt, Kadar wouldn't have taken her along.

"He's probably commandeered another car," Armbruster said.

A crowd had gathered, probably afraid to pass by the abandoned car with the two armed men. Weiss, who wasn't good at taking orders, Blanchard decided, was circulating among them, asking them what they'd seen. Sirens indicated someone official was trying to get through.

"Yeah, Dickie. I don't think he'd take her along if he was on foot. Better get on the radio and spread the bad news."

Twenty-Three

By three-thirty in the morning, Talman and Rahman had returned to the airport. General Levi Avidar was in the office waiting for them.

Perlmutter brought coffee for everyone, and they gathered around the folding table in the front office.

"The peak of the panic has dissipated," Avidar said.

"The highway between the city and the airport was much less congested," Talman agreed. "What are the conditions elsewhere, General?"

"It is estimated that over fifty thousand have arrived in Tel Aviv. They are trying to house them at athletic facilities. To the north, Ramallah is inundated, perhaps seventy thousand there. The road to Hebron is choked with disabled vehicles and the cars that cannot get around them. In all, we estimate two hundred thousand have left Jerusalem, most with no idea of where they are going. Many have simply driven off the road and set up camp in the countryside. Those on foot are gathered into similar bivouacs. General Schweiss and Chief Rahman have split their forces. Some are still guarding the markets and water plants, but sixty percent are now returned to the search for Kadar and Masters."

"Many people are already returning to their homes," Moshe erlmutter said. "I believe Horon's and Chief Rahman's inter-entions have assisted in that regard."

In their last circuit of the city, Talman had noted the changes king place. The furor was dying down, people on the streets ere much calmer. They yelled less. While not normal, traffic as manageable, and drivers spent less time leaning on their orn buttons, and more time obeying traffic signals.

He had seen men dressed in black, their *peiyot* and *streimel* rominent, walking side by side with Arabs in checkered head-ress, approaching clusters of people on the streets and the rivers of cars. They engaged everyone in earnest conversation, nd apparently, they were having some success. Whole families urned around and headed in the direction from which they had ome.

"What we are seeing on the streets," Talman said, "is very ncouraging."

Two days before, he would not have believed it possible. o, there were more Arabs he could trust. He hoped the number ncreased dramatically in the future.

"The cooperation is admirable," Rahman said. "I am proud f all our peoples."

"As am I," Avidar said. "The Authority shall hear of your ervice, Amin."

The policeman shrugged. "It is what is expected of me. I ould do no less. Also, I wish to thank you, Jacob, for the reatment of Oma Kassim."

Talman had expedited the medical examiner's procedures nd had the body returned to Gaza City. He waved away the gratitude. "We should always honor each other's rituals, Amin."

"As a perhaps interesting aside," Rahman said, "the Temple Mount is swarming with devout Muslims, and thousands of Jews have gathered at the Wailing Wall. It seems that many have turned to prayer in this crisis."

"Perhaps that is what will save us all," Avidar said, "Now, the current status?"

Perlmutter said, "The Mahane Yehuda Market in Jaffa Road has been contaminated. That occurred about an hour ago, and

it is now under quarantine. Still, many hundreds absconde
with their arms full before we could close it.''

The market was one of the largest and most colorful
Jerusalem. Talman frequently did his own shopping there, ar
he wondered if he would do so again.

"That makes four markets?" Avidar asked.

"That we know about," Perlmutter said. "As stated, mo
are now under surveillance."

"What is the projection for dispersion of the bacteria?"

"I talked to Dr. Wilcox," Talman said. "It is probably ne
calculable since, as he pointed out, one person might handle
head of lettuce, then give it to another, and yet two or thre
others will eat from it. If four thousand people entered thos
markets, the eventual contagion might reach twelve to twent
thousand. We might anticipate a final death toll of six thousanc
At Mar Saba, the number of fatalities is now sixteen.

"I have discussed the situation with health officials and wit
Magen David Adom, and they are, if not prepared, at leas
anticipating an infusion of cases. They will confer with th
medical staff from the assistance team."

Magen David Adom was the Red Star of David, the equiva
lent of the Red Cross, and managed ambulance services an
first-aid stations throughout Israel.

"And Kadar?" the general asked.

"Out of sight, but not out of mind," Talman said. "H
apparently has Dr. Masters with him still. Forty-five minute
ago, a Palestinian police patrol discovered the body of an Arme
nian woman on Heleni Hamalka, north of the Russian Cathedra
She had been shot in the head—it is probably .380 caliber an
similar to the wounds of the soldiers on Narkis Street. I assum
she was the unfortunate driver of an automobile that Kada
wanted. We are determining the car she may have had."

"Indicating that Kadar is moving around on the east side o
the city now," Rahman said.

Perlmutter added, "We have asked General Schweiss to
concentrate his search units in the area."

"Projections?"

"We assume Kadar still has nine vials," Talman said, "bu
by now, he knows that the markets and water services are

enied him. His methods of dispersal are disappearing quickly.
If he is intent on using all of the bacteria, I do not know where
he will go next."

"It is raining, off and on," Rahman said.

Talman automatically looked upward and noticed for the
first time that the ceiling was stained. He heard the airplanes
landing and taking off.

"We will alert the airports."

"If he uses Dr. Masters as the pawn in attempting to comman-
deer an aircraft?" Perlmutter asked.

"He is not to have an airplane," Avidar said. "He is to be
shot, no matter the consequences."

Once again, she was in the trunk of a car.

And despite her panic, and contrary to it, Masters was vastly
relieved to be there. It meant she was alive. In the last few
hours, the fear had slowly dissolved into numbness. She no
longer knew what she was feeling, or if it would make the
slightest bit of difference.

Though she knew there were men, and perhaps women, like
him, Masters still found it difficult to conceive of how little
regard Kadar had for life.

When the gold car had faltered to a stop—she thought the
transmission had given out, perhaps hit by a bullet, Kadar had
run it onto the curb, grabbed his bags, and leaped from the car.
He pulled the rear door open, grabbed her arm, and yanked her
out of the car. She had to hop because of her bound legs, and
only Kadar's grip kept her from falling.

He walked right up to a white sedan that was jammed in
traffic, walked around the front of it, with Masters hopping
madly to stay with him, and approached the driver's door.
Masters looked at every driver around her, imploring with her
eyes. They looked away. Marital spat, no doubt. Not their
business. Her white lab coat, her bindings, meant nothing to
people in fear of their own lives.

The woman tried to lock the door, and Kadar showed her
the gun. She released the lock, her eyes wide and white.

Kadar pulled the door open, reached around the center post,

and unlocked the back door while telling her, ''Slide acros
the seat.''

She didn't respond, and he repeated it in Hebrew.

The driver scooted across to the passenger side, and Master
was forced into the backseat. The woman looked at Master
with apparent incomprehension.

As soon as Kadar got in the car, he pulled out of the line
traffic, scraping the back end of the abandoned automobile a
he did so, pulled up on the sidewalk, and scattered pedestrian
as he raced to the next corner and turned right. He hit two
people with glancing blows from the car.

The woman said something to him in Hebrew.

He raised the gun and shot her.

The detonation echoed in the confines of the car. The doo
window behind the woman blossomed briefly with her blood
then shattered.

Masters screamed quietly against her tape gag.

Several blocks later, Kadar pulled to the side of the stree
near a gathering of trash barrels, reached across the seat t
open the door, then shoved the body out with his foot. Master
heard it hit the pavement with a terrible crump.

Then he lurched onto the street again, throwing her sideways
She fought to get herself upright. It was such a relief to b
sitting, rather than lying on a floor. Tears stung her eyes; sh
wept for the unknown woman.

The Jaffa Gate went by.

Kadar was hunched over the wheel, staring straight ahead
He didn't seem to notice the people cursing at him for hi
driving.

When they reached the next market, Kadar was in a frenzy
but he took the few seconds needed to transfer her to the trunk
not being gentle nor saying a word. This was a man, she thought
who was on the very brink of self-control. She knew he was
a fanatic, but he was taking the word to new heights.

She had been keeping count. Four stops, and she assumed
four vials. There were nine to go, and the night seemed endless.
She hoped someone was aware that he was infecting foodstuffs

ith the bacteria. Masters tried to tell herself that it was better
an water, which would have reached a hundred times more
eople, but knew that the agony that ensued would not be less.

A rat-a-tat sounded on the trunk lid above her, and it took
er a moment to realize it was rain. She prayed that there
ouldn't be a downpour, with gutters rushing full. It would be
o made-to-order for Kadar.

She wondered where Blanchard and Talman were.

It was as if they had completely forgotten about her.

She was very alone in this world, and all her weapons were
seless.

Weapons! I have never used a weapon! What is happening
 my mind?

Kadar had approached three more markets—the last one the
rab Market on David Street, but was faced with soldiers
arrounding them. He was enraged to see that Arab police were
so in attendance. His own were turning on him.

They would meet their justice before Allah. He knew this
 be true.

Praise be to God, the Compassionate. Your servant beseeches
ou! Give me guidance. How do I serve You?

The little bursts of rainfall encouraged him. It was a sign,
n affirmation of his mission. Soon, the skies would open, the
noisture would blanket the earth, and the land of his forefathers
ould blossom with grass and flowers and forests. The West
ank would be paradise, and the holy city would beckon to
ll of Islam.

As he turned off David Street and worked his way south in
ne Armenian Quarter, he could see beyond the Temple Mount
ne faint pink tinge of dawn. It was diffused by the overcast,
ut it called to him, welcoming him into Allah's favor. He
nust pray!

Near the middle of Armenian Patriarchate Street, he parked
ear St. James Cathedral, which dated from the times of the
Crusades in the 12th Century.

It was appropriate, for Kadar had mounted his own crusade.

From here, he would make his final dash to glory.

After his morning prayers. Allah's devotions must alwa: come first.

Jillian Weiss scrambled into the back of the Hummer. S had interviewed policemen and bystanders surrounding t blockaded Mahane Yehuda Market.

"A white car, four doors. That's all I could learn, and th was from two women who weren't sure. They didn't see Me nie, just a clean-shaven man getting in the car."

"That's a lot better than a phantom car, no doors, Jillian Blanchard told her.

"He seems to be sticking around the Old City," Armbrus said as he pulled away from the curb. "Hey, Colonel, we' getting low on petrol. Another twenty minutes or so, we'll ha to open up some pump by force."

"If it comes to it, we'll walk, Dickie."

Armbruster looked worn out. The thick black whiskers his cheeks matched his head. He'd tried his razor, but t battery was dead. Blanchard was certain he didn't look a better.

Fifteen minutes later, as they traveled east on David Str toward the Temple Mount, just crossing El-Munadellen, whi divided the Armenian Quarter from the Jewish Quarter, Blanc ard said, "Pull up over there, Dickie."

Armbruster found a place at the curb, which was now Cha Street. Auto traffic had dwindled substantially in the last ho and there weren't too many people hanging around this interse tion, either.

At the end of the street, though, he saw large crowds at t Temple Mount, near the Chain Gate. All the gates on the we side were for use by non-Muslims, but in the dim light of dreary morning, it looked to him like about fifty nationaliti and religious proclivities were represented in the crowd. F hoped they found solace.

He wouldn't. Not until he had Melanie back.

Blanchard had called in the information on the whi

edan, but nothing interesting or startling was coming over he radio.

He kept looking at the Temple Mount. Recalled a vague notion he had had earlier, but forgot about.

"You been in the Temple Mount, Dickie?"

"Nope."

"Jillian?"

"I've visited it a number of times, Jack."

"I went through once, but rather quickly and sometime ago. Jillian, correct me if I'm wrong, but devout Jews don't run round there, do they?"

"No. Because when the temple came down, they didn't know where the Holy of Holies was located, where only the highest priests could go, and they don't want to take the chance of being wrong."

"As I remember, there are two major structures, the El Aqsa Mosque on the south end, and the Dome of the Rock about in the middle."

"Plus a number of other minor domes, structures, and fountains," Weiss said.

"What's the fountain in front of the Dome of the Rock?"

"The El-Kas Fountain. It's used for ablutions."

"Lot of people use it?"

"I don't know. I suppose. Oh! A dispersal point."

"Wouldn't that pick mainly on Muslims, Jack?" Armbruster asked.

"I don't think Kadar cares. He's after anyone who supports the peace accord. But now, the Dome of the Rock structure encircles the top of the rock of Moriah. It's a magnificent place, lots of detail in the architecture. Inside there are several rings, and at the center, the rock stands about six feet high and is nearly sixty feet long. I remember a cave is visible. What else? There's some kind of fence around it."

"A grille," Weiss clarified. "Installed by the Crusaders."

"But the big thing, Jillian, is . . ."

"Jewish belief has it that the rock is where Abraham prepared to sacrifice Isaac. There may have once been a sacrificial altar here."

"The other big thing, Jillian."

"Oh. Muslims think this is where Muhammad ascended heaven."

"Bloody hell! You think Kadar's going to walk off heaven?"

"After treating the fountain and making a human sacrifice Hell, I don't know, Dickie. I'm grabbing at straws."

"Maybe we ought to take a hike over there," the Brit said "Let's go."

The three of them had the doors open, and Armbruster ha one foot on the ground when he yelled, "Colonel!"

Blanchard saw Armbruster pointing back down the street

He saw four cars coming toward them, a blue Volvo in th lead.

And behind it . . .

White sedan. A BMW.

"Good eyes, Dickie! Crank up this baby! If it's the rig car, take it out!"

"Damned well done," Armbruster yelled back as he leape behind the wheel.

Blanchard grabbed Weiss's arm and slammed the doors shu He pushed her across the sidewalk.

"Stay against that wall, Jillian!"

She ran to the side of the building.

The Hummer's engine fired.

The Volvo went by.

The five-in-the-morning sun was nonexistent this mornin because of the overcast, but Blanchard could still make out single driver in the white car.

Clean-shaven.

Black hair.

Bent over the wheel, eyes intent on the Temple Mount ahead

"Hit it, Dickie!" he yelled.

Armbruster came off the clutch and whipped the wheel lef

The Humvee plowed into the BMW's right front fende startling the driver, who turned left in the attempt to avoid th truck.

Armbruster stayed with him, pushing him across the stree

DARK MORNING   429

Kadar slammed into reverse, backed up thirty feet, then hit the accelerator hard as he came back, curving toward Blanchard, to get behind the Humvee.

He came up on the curb, riding it with his right wheels. The bumper slammed a trash barrel, which went sailing toward Weiss.

"Down!" Blanchard yelled at her and managed to get a hand on the can, diverting its flight into the side of the building.

Armbruster came back hard in reverse, and the back end of the Humvee clipped the rear quarter of the BMW as it shot past.

"Damnit!" Weiss shouted.

Blanchard didn't wait.

He started running as soon as he saw Kadar was going to pass the Hummer.

Kadar didn't stop the car until he had hit three people in the crowd, knocking their bodies to either side of the car. The hood and bumper smashed into a fourth person, who folded over against the hood, then slid to the ground. Men and women yelled and scattered.

He pressed the release button for the trunk and left the car in gear as he slid out the door, drawing his knife from his sheath.

The car continued to inch forward.

More people screamed; children started to wail.

Some tried to push against the hood, to back it off the man under the car.

The trunk lid was partially raised, and he threw it up, used the knife to slash at the wire around the woman's ankles, then pried her out of the trunk by her arms.

She could barely stand. Her legs were weak. He forced her ahead of him, using the butt of the knife in his left hand as a prod.

Men yelled at him.

When one of them lunged forward, Kadar pulled the semi-automatic from his pocket and aimed at him.

He fell back.

Kadar did not shoot because he could not remember ho~
many rounds were left in the magazine, and he feared he ha~
left the spare magazine in his other jacket.

"Go!" he shouted at her. "Run! Your life depends on it!

The crowd parted before them as the sea had for Moses.

Screaming and yelling, people rushed to get out of his way
Many fell, and their neighbors trampled them.

It was very gratifying to have others respond to his bidding

The Hummer outraced Blanchard to the end of the stree~
but not by much.

As he ran by it, he called out, "Ambulances! Backup!"

"I'm on it, boss!" Armbruster yelled back to him, reachin~
for the microphone.

Most on the fringe of the multitude had gone to the aid c
the people hit by Kadar. Wailing was the order of the day
friends and relatives knelt over the injured, and sobbed.

He had seen Kadar pulling Melanie from the trunk, and hi
heart had leaped. She was alive! Fresh energy rushed into th
muscles of his legs.

Blanchard yelled at people, urging them to get down, to ge
out of the way, but English was the language of maybe hal
of them; only that many went to the ground or pushed other
aside for him.

Kadar and Melanie neared the gate, a portal in the massiv~
wall of the Temple.

The gun! I left the damned gun in the Hummer!

And just as well. Too many people around.

And then he heard the rapid pace of small feet beating th~
ground behind him and Weiss's voice as she shouted warning
in Hebrew and in Arabic.

More people went to the ground.

Kadar stopped at the gate, which looked puny in the wall
and looked back at who was yelling. When he saw Blanchard
maybe thirty yards away, he raised the pistol and fired three
shots.

More screams and yells.

Blanchard felt the concussion wave as the bullets whipped
ver his head.

A piercing squeal of agony.

Someone behind him was hit.

He kept running.

Kadar fired again.

Blanchard's left leg went out from under him, and he
lammed face first into the earth.

When Greg Masters had seen the truck pull out into traffic
nd slam into the BMW, he'd thought, "Jesus! The sons of
itches can't even drive!"

He climbed out of his car, which was parked around the
:orner on El-Munadeleen Street, the first spot he'd seen open
vhen Blanchard's truck stopped on Chain Street.

In the succeeding moments, with the car and the truck jock-
ying for position on each other, then the BMW escaping past
t, he realized what was really happening.

Melanie was in that car!

He started running, crossing the intersection, bouncing off
he front of a van, hitting the sidewalk on the other side to find
3lanchard running a half block ahead of him. Some woman
vas running after him. The white truck came racing down the
:treet, passing him.

He was gasping for air by the time they reached the throng
standing around some fortress.

God, the noise!

They were yelling, screaming, crying. The guy in the white
truck was on the radio. Down to the right he saw soldiers
running his way. More cops were coming from the north. Whistles blew. Sirens in the distance.

Kadar and Blanchard created a path through the crowd. The
woman chasing Blanchard was yelling something or other, and
more people ran off to the sides, or went to the ground.

Then the shots!

Shit! The terrorist was shooting at *him!*

And Blanchard went down.

The woman went down right beside him.
And Masters didn't know what to do.
So he kept running toward the opening in the wall.
But Kadar and Melanie were no longer there.
Melanie! I love you!

Twenty-Four

The cold gray clouds above threatened rain, but that was all: just the threat and no relief. Speckles of an earlier shower dotted the paving stones of the court, and the gold dome on her left gleamed in the dreary light. A few hundred people were in the court, protected by the walls, or trapped by them, and a few of them noticed Kadar and Masters. Some pointed them out to their companions. A few began to back away.

Masters stumbled going down the two steps to the level of the fountain, and Kadar nearly lost his grip on her arm, then let go and shoved her. As she fell, Masters twisted in the air and managed to land on her left side. The blow shook her; a brief stab of pain shot through her shoulder.

She didn't want to be on the ground, and she quickly rolled onto her stomach, got her head down against the stones, and levered herself onto her knees. The fact that her ankles were free and she had use of her legs was almost a Christmas gift.

Kadar was at the fountain, a circular vat perhaps fifteen feet across, with a base of cut stone. At the center of it was a bowl-shaped structure that issued the water, and the perimeter was guarded by a high ornate fence of green-painted wrought iron. He had his hands full and seemed confused by what to do about

it for a second. Then he tucked the knife into his belt an
shifted the gun to his left hand. From his pocket he took th
black plastic box and popped the lid open.

He took a quick glance at her. "Do not move!"

She was still on her knees, and she froze in place.

Many in the nearby throng were now aware of them. Th
multiple languages of the crowd rose in confused volume a
they backed away, trying to increase the distance between ther
and what was taking place at the fountain.

Holding the box awkwardly with his gun hand, Kadar shifte
and lifted one vial out. Again his face contorted, as if he wer
perplexed by something unexpected.

She realized that he had forgotten to bring his rubber glove
He didn't know how he was going to handle it.

Masters moved her right leg and got her foot on the groun
"Let's talk, Kadar."

She whipped her head around and saw Greg standing on th
lip of the depressed fountain. He was panting heavily, tryin
to keep his voice steady. His face was peeling, and there wa
a white rectangle across his mouth.

Kadar nearly dropped the box as he spun around, fumblin
for his gun. He finally freed it and held it up toward Greg.

"So what have they got you on?" the lawyer said. "Mayb
some manslaughter charges? Let's not make it worse. Yo
release Melanie now, and they're going to take that into consid
eration."

"You are a dead man. I should have killed you before."

"Come on, guy. Hell, I'll even represent you. No charge."

"You are a fool."

Melanie was appalled. Greg had no concept of what he wa
dealing with.

"Greg! Run away, now, before—"

"I love you, Melanie. I've got to be here."

Ohhh! How could he do this!

"Look, Kadar, we can be civilized and logical about this.
I—"

Kadar fired his gun.

It clicked.

He looked stupidly at it.

And Masters rose to her feet, took one step onto her left
ot, and kicked high with the right.

Her toe mashed into his left hand. She hadn't thought she had
uch strength left, but the impact slammed his hand upward.

And the box flew free.

Rising in the air.

Rising . . . slowing . . . tumbling.

Vials and cotton spilling from it.

Over the fencing.

And into the fountain.

A dozen tiny geysers rising from the water's surface as they
it.

She didn't think any of them had broken. They could proba-
y be retrieved intact from the water.

Kadar's face suffused dark purple with his rage.

Greg came down the steps.

"Hey, Kadar—"

He fired the gun once more, and it clicked once more.

With amazing force Kadar threw the gun at Greg. It caught
m squarely on the nose, and blood gushed from his nostrils.
e stumbled backward, caught the rock step with his heels,
d abruptly sat down.

Then Kadar was upon her, his right arm wrapped around her
roat, his left hand waving the knife spastically. To her horror
e saw that he still had one vial clutched in his right hand.

Kicking her legs and yelling in Arabic, Kadar pushed and
agged her around the fountain, clambering up the steps, head-
g for the Dome of the Rock.

For a moment, Blanchard had thought that Kadar had landed
his back.

Then realized it was Weiss. Whether she was protecting him
om more fire, wrought with grief, or looking for a wound,
 wasn't certain.

He knew there was a wound. His left leg felt numb.

"Jillian!"

"Jack! You've been shot!"

"I'll live. Come on, girl!"

He rolled her off him, took one look at his pant leg and sa
the spreading bloodstain, then scrambled back to his feet. H
could stand on it, so it was probably a flesh wound. He coul
work his toes.

He started running again, a loping gait to account for th
numb leg.

Reached the gate and darted through. Weiss's foolfalls wer
close behind his own. The splendid edifice of the Dome of th
Rock was directly in front of him. He glanced quickly to th
left, then continued running to the right, heading for the ope
space of the southern courtyard. The El-Aqsa Mosque loome
at the far end of the plaza. Reaching the corner of a hug
planter, which bordered the southern entrance to the Dome an
was filled with oak, evergreens, and shrubs, he slid to a stop

Ahead he saw Kadar and Melanie at the fountain; Gre
Masters with them.

The courtyard was not packed, but there were a lot of peopl
buzzing in several languages, and many were becoming awar
of the confrontation. Still, the fountain was centered in ope
space relinquished by the mob.

And he was pretty certain Kadar was coming this way.

"Stay here," he ordered Weiss.

"I will."

"I mean it, goddamn it!"

"Jack."

He sidled along the front of the planter until he reached th
tall, wide flight of steps leading up to the south entrance. Th
predominantly blue tile work of the structure was intricatel
detailed with white, yellow, and green tiles. It was too impres
sive for this morning, he thought. Sprinkles of rain splashe
against his face.

He looked back at the fountain in time to catch Melanie'
footwork.

"Good girl!" he muttered, simultaneously fearing for her.

Kadar had turned to face the fountain, walking backwar
quickly, scraping his left foot behind him, keeping his eye o
the American. The oaf was stumbling after them, blood running

own his mouth and chin, calling out, telling him he must
please the woman.

The woman resisted, dragging her feet. She stomped on his
left foot once, and the pain made his eyes squint.

Soon now.

Up the stairs and into the Dome. He would wash his hands
in her blood after he slit her throat and offered her body as his
supreme gift.

Allah Akbar!

The grille surrounding the rock was still a challenge. But
his will was the will of a thousand men, and he would surmount
the challenge. His birth was now!

A woman behind him was yelling. Telling the soldiers in
Hebrew and Arabic not to shoot, pleading with them to spare
the woman.

He was suddenly aware of the soldiers, many of them, and
more arriving every second. There were Arab policemen, too.
They gathered to left and right, some kneeling, training their
rifles on him. The throng of people was fast dispersing as the
officers yelled at them, telling them to get out of the way.

The American, her husband, kept advancing on them.

Kadar kept backing toward the stairs, drawing his arm tight
around her throat. He felt the warmth of her body against his
own.

Soon the valleys would be green. The rivers would flow full,
and the people would eat of dates and figs and cry his name.

Soon.

For Allah, the All Merciful, the Compassionate!

Blanchard was aware that Jillian Weiss was calling to the
troops who were appearing in large numbers.

He moved across to the center of the steps and climbed up
one step.

Greg Masters appeared stupefied. His face was devoid of
expression, and he proclaimed his love of Melanie with each
step. His jaw was bright red with his blood.

Kadar backed right into Blanchard.

Jack reached over the man's shoulder and snapped as tight

a grip on the wrist of the knife hand as he could muste
Simultaneously he punched the Arab in the kidney with h
right fist, eliciting a yelp of pain. The right arm relaxed
moment, and Melanie dropped out from under his grasp.

"Run, Mel!"

She twisted herself onto her knees, and looked up at him

Blanchard put his right knee in Kadar's back and leane
backward. He wanted to snap the little bastard's spine.

But his wounded left leg gave way, and he felt himse
collapsing.

Kadar sprang backward, and the two of them crashed to tl
steps, Blanchard on his back with Kadar on top of him.

The Arab was small, but wiry and strong. He fought Blancl
ard's grasp on his left hand—his fist waving back and forth i
the air—and slammed his right elbow into Blanchard's rib
catching the one that Khalid might have cracked. Blanchar
grunted, but saw Melanie rolling away, both Greg Masters an
Jillian Weiss rushing to help her.

The soldiers and cops moved in, aiming weapons in the
direction.

Kadar squirmed to the right, and Blanchard went with hin
then Kadar abruptly went to the left, sliding off Blanchard'
torso. He twisted his arm, and Blanchard lost the knife hand

Blanchard quickly rolled to his right, falling off the step t
ground level, then spun onto his knees and regained his feet

Kadar was on his feet, also, three steps above, waving th
knife wildly. Soldiers and policemen were closing in, gatherin
in a large circle on the steps. No one moved to intervene. Thi
was a prizefight they wanted to see to its finish.

Kadar switched the knife to his right hand and somethin
else to his left.

A vial!

The son of a bitch still had a vial.

"I could just shoot the asshole, Colonel." Armbruster wa
somewhere behind him. His voice was calm and collected, a
if he had the outcome already wagered.

"He's mine, Dickie."

Blanchard could feel the blood running down his left leg
He figured he'd better move soon, before loss of blood weak

ned him, so he feinted to the right with his foot, and when adar lunged that way, went up the steps to his left.

Kadar swung to meet him, slashing out with the knife in a undhouse arc.

The stainless blade swiped at his shirtfront, and Blanchard rought his right hand down hard, getting a piece of Kadar's and, while at the same time he pistoned his right knee upward.

Kadar's wrist came down on the knee under Blanchard's rce and snapped.

The knife spun away, clattered on the steps, and Kadar reamed.

Blanchard immediately drove two left jabs into his face and lt the satisfying crunch of nose cartilage. He thought maybe e right eye socket was damaged, too. Kadar's right eye ppeared loose, as if it didn't want to track with the left.

He raised his left hand, as if he would throw the vial, and lanchard swung a hard right into the terrorist's breastbone.

The air whooshed out of him.

The vial dropped from a suddenly nerveless hand.

Hit the step.

And shattered.

Blanchard leaped backward.

It didn't splash much.

The puddle was seven or eight inches in diameter.

Bent over at the waist, gasping for air, Kadar stared down it in horror.

Blanchard took one step closer, grabbed Kadar around the ck with both of his hands, then swung his right foot and cked the terrorist's feet out from under him.

The Arab went straight down like a felled ox.

Face first in the puddle and broken glass.

Blanchard looked at all of the uniforms gathered around.

"I would suggest no one touch him. And stay away from e puddle. Also, someone better put an armed guard on the untain."

Behind him he heard Jillian translating, first in Hebrew, then Arabic.

Armbruster rushed forward and shoved Blanchard to a seat the steps, then began ripping the seam of his pant leg.

''We *know* that bloody bugger's going to die, Colonel. Let
make certain you don't.''

Blanchard searched the faces surrounding them, wanting
check on Melanie, but beyond the fringe of the crowd, I
saw that she was already walking away, arm in arm with h
husband.

Twenty-Five

On August 4 Jacob Talman installed his new clerk in his agency. The new desk took up space he didn't have to waste, but he didn't care.

The two women who had worked for him for the past three years were understandably concerned about the need for a third clerk and worried about their jobs. His explanation that Deborah Hausmann was working for free, just to learn the business, didn't go over well.

Deborah was on a three-week recuperation leave, and at the end of three weeks, Talman would make a decision about his future—and perhaps about hers. Three weeks, however, looked like eternity at the moment.

She moved stiffly about the office, but she smiled a great deal, and that made him smile, also.

"Jacob," she said, "why don't you go into your office and do your work? I am certain you are far behind, and I do not need constant looking after."

"You are correct, Deborah. I apologize for my harassment."

"Not that I do not appreciate it," she tempered.

He went into his office and spent twenty minutes staring at

a large stack of correspondence he should deal with, but d not touch, when the doorbell tinkled.

A minute later, Deborah showed the visitor into his offic

"I told him you are busy, but he insisted on talking to you

Talman stood up. "Amin, come in. Chief Rahman is an o friend, Deborah."

He liked the sound of "old friend."

Rahman appeared more presentable than the last time Talma had seen him. He wore a tropical-weight white suit, a whi shirt, and a bright yellow tie.

"You are well protected here, Jacob."

"I feel protected."

Talman stepped out to grab another chair, and both men sa Rahman began, "I really came to buy airline tickets. I a taking my family to Paris for a few days, and I have hea excellent things about your service."

Talman smiled. "We do what we can."

"I was told you went to see Kadar in his prison cell."

"It was a most unproductive visit, Amin. The man doesn speak at all. He sits on his bunk and constantly rubs his ski He will soon rub it off."

"Unless he receives a very speedy trial, he will not live lor enough to see it."

"There are those who are in no hurry."

"Yes. And his victims?"

"The hospitals and aid stations are swamped with peop who fear they may have been exposed, but it will be days y before symptoms appear. We will have to deal with it when occurs, of course, and the medical community is preparir itself."

"It is a terrible world in many respects," Rahman sai "What are those?"

The deputy chief's eyes had fallen on a stack of videotape resting on the corner of the desk.

"They are copies of an American televison show. Jac Blanchard had them expressed to me, and I am to look fc Marshal Dillon and Miss Kitty."

"Is it a joke?"

"I do not yet know."

"Tell me if it is," he said. "Have you heard?"

"Of what, Amin?"

"Our foreign aid is apparently not in jeopardy. The bankers
and governments seem to have higher hopes based on the
documentation provided regarding the cooperation between our
governments in the latest crisis."

"I would hope it is the last crisis," Talman said.

"I fear the last crisis is a long time away, Jacob, but we have
shown them we can deal with them, have we not? Together."

Talman liked the sound of that, too.

Blanchard was resting on the bunk in his tent two days later
when Melanie Masters came back. It was close to five o'clock.
She was wearing a yellow cotton dress that was obviously
new, and she was also carrying a pail of ice, two glasses, and
a bottle of Johnny Walker Black Label when she pushed through
the flap in the netting.

Blanchard sat up and swung his legs to the floor.

"Mel. I'm damned glad to see you."

She sat on the bunk next to him and handed him the glasses.
Didn't say a word while she loaded them with cubes, then
poured the scotch. Put the pail and the bottle on the floor. The
chestnut hair was freshly shampooed and swung nicely to either
side of her face.

Took her glass and held it up.

He ticked the rim of his own against it.

"I wasn't sure I'd see you again," he said. "You took off
pretty abruptly."

"You were right, Jack. I needed a vacation."

By the look of her, she was recovering nicely.

"How's the leg?"

"Lost a chunk of meat. Nothing that hasn't happened before.
Dickie and Jillian strapped it up and got me back here where
Dean Wilcox practiced his sewing and cautioned me about my
lifestyle."

"Dickie picked me up at the hotel and brought me back,"
he said. "I heard all about your exploits. I don't know that I
can ever express how much it means to me."

"Dickie exaggerates. I'm just damned sorry I couldn't g
you out of it sooner, Mel."

Blanchard wanted badly to know what was going on betwee
her and Greg.

It took courage to ask. "You spent some time with Greg?"

"We're talking. I don't know how it will turn out."

"Yeah, okay. That's good."

"I talked to the Director General, also. We're going to exten
the tour for six months at least, maybe a year."

That didn't seem to affect Blanchard. He was ready to g
back to the Rockies. The geography, not the team.

"I told him I'd stay if you would."

Masters leaned back on her straightened left arm, sipped he
scotch, and peered over the rim of the glass at him with dire
hazel eyes.

"That's what you told him, huh?" Blanchard shifted a litt
to take his weight off the bandaged thigh.

"It means I have to put up with you, Colonel, but damn
I sure want you near me."

Then she leaned forward and kissed him on the lips.

"Thank you, Jack."

What the hell was another six months or a year?

THE AUTHOR

William H. Lovejoy is the bestselling author of many novels, including SHANGHAI STAR, BACK \ SLASH, RED RAIN, CHINA DOME, and WHITE NIGHT. A Vietnam veteran, former assistant professor of English, and college president, he is the dean of planning and policy analysis and the fiscal officer for the Wyoming Community College Commission and lives in Cheyenne, Wyoming. He is working on his next novel.

BOOK YOUR PLACE ON OUR WEBSITE
AND MAKE THE
READING CONNECTION!

We've created a customized website just for our very special readers, where you can get the inside scoop on everything that's going on with Zebra, Pinnacle and Kensington books.

When you come online, you'll have the exciting opportunity to:

- View covers of upcoming books
- Read sample chapters
- Learn about our future publishing schedule (listed by publication month *and author*)
- Find out when your favorite authors will be visiting a city near you
- Search for and order backlist books from our online catalog
- Check out author bios and background information
- Send e-mail to your favorite authors
- Meet the Kensington staff online
- Join us in weekly chats with authors, readers and other guests
- Get writing guidelines
- AND MUCH MORE!

Visit our website at
http://www.pinnaclebooks.com